WITHDRAWN

MINNIE'S POTATOES

Historical, Fiction, Narrative

ISBN 978-1523753970

Book design by
Jennifer Hauschild | Hauschild-Design.com

Cover illustration by
Barbara Hranilovich | hranilovich.com

It was the autumn of 1887...

Germany was a world away from her, a comfortable world where she had felt protected by Jacob and Christina Bublitz. She longed to listen again to Boleslaw Dembinski play the pipe organ at the Parish Church. She missed singing at his salons. She missed her piano, she even missed the boring scales she played over and over for Dembinski's wife.

The old Minnie Bublitz had melted into the Michigan landscape. She had slipped away, piece by piece ... used by her husband for sex, pulled apart by her children for their ever-growing needs, the hours of her day lost to the meal schedule of the boarders. All these takeaways had made her a nonperson, a zero. Even her sleep was not her own, but that of a hungry baby wanting her breast.

She shouted to the wind. "Is this all there is?" The air current shifted. A cold rush blew the knot in her hair loose, billowing her nightdress as she shivered before the empty, starless sky. "Why should I go on being a serf? I own no land. I work only for others." Minnie sensed the answer in the numbing darkness.

She had to think clearly now that she had made her decision. Fred's jealous mind would be at peace. He would see to the children. He loved his children. He would find another woman to care for them. He wouldn't need strong drink any longer.

She took a deep breath. It was final and clear. Here she was, once the most sought-after woman in Poznan, the pollen on the flower that drew all the honeybees. This woman who could not swim had decided the hour had arrived for her to jump into the Au Sable River and drown...

Instead, she jumped into the river to save her life.

STRONGHEART

A Dog Who Was A Coward is a story about Herbie before he was a show dog.

Buy it now on Amazon!
Available in paperback and Kindle.

66 *I absolutely loved being able to see the world through a dogs eyes. I have a dog and every time I look at her now, I try to think of what her life is like and what she thinks about. The whole concept of this book was really brilliant, the fact that the author was able to blend Herbie's learning of the Potawatomi legends with him gaining courage and facing change was really interesting to me. I have recommended this book to all of my friends and even my grandparents and teachers.* 99

— Liberty Romanik, young reader

66 *We all know how lovable lions can be when cowardly. The Wizard of Oz, anyone? But author Laurice LaZebnik, a caring pet parent and accomplished writer, applies her story-telling abilities to a subject very near and dear to her big heart. And the result is the wonderful tale (not tail, but tale) of Strongheart. If this book doesn't touch you and cause you to care with increased intensity to an existing pet or propel you to acquire one as a means of enhancing your life, you should check with your local cardiologist for signs of life.* 99

— Gordon Osmond, author of *Slipping on Stardust*

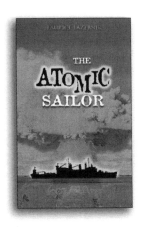

THE ATOMIC SAILOR

A story about fathers and sons, family secrets, and generations of sailors struggling with PTSD.

Buy it now on Amazon!
Available in paperback and Kindle.

66 *An ordinary-looking old man approached two women at the Big Boy restaurant in Brooklyn and renewed a proposal of marriage to one named Jenny. She declined matrimony, but invited her would-be groom to sit down and talk. And that's how Jenny's breakfast companion, Laurice LaZebnik, began listening to James McLaughlin.*

LaZebnik could not forget the stories he shared and recently published a book titled "The Atomic Sailor," which is McLaughlin's real story told through the literary device of a fictional FBI investigation. 99

—Exerpt from the Brad Flory column: The extraordinary life of the 'Atomic Sailor' of Brooklyn

66 *Your book is very ambitious; the tangled tales, the attention to detail, historical and otherwise; the realistic dialogue, and finally, the readability. I feel now as if I know these people, and as in every good novel, they continue to exist beyond the page. Congratulations! This is truly a major feat.* 99

— Faye Moskowitz, author of *A Leak in the Heart*, *Whoever Finds This: I Love You*, *The Bridge Is Love*, and *Her Face in the Mirror: Jewish Women on Mothers and Daughters*.

DEDICATION

I dedicate this book to people whose DNA I carry in my cells, Frederick Hartman (1845–1901) and Wilhelmina (Minnie) Bublitz Hartman (1855–1931). I didn't know your names when I started my research for *Minnie's Potatoes*, but I sense you are somewhere out there watching over your great-granddaughter, author of this story about your life together, leading her in the right direction.

My fact-finding began in the genealogy and history websites of the U.S. and Europe. I scrolled through ship manifests at the Ellis Island website, sifted through historical documents, maps and personal diaries of the earliest European residents of Michigan at the Bentley Historical Library in Ann Arbor, and the Jackson District Library in Jackson. I paged through documents detailing your time and place in the lumbering history of Michigan from libraries in Atlanta, Alpena, and Oscoda. I looked for traces of you and your offspring at the Archives of Michigan in Lansing. I even looked in the records of the three State of Michigan Prisons ... and found no trace of you or any of our family. My fieldwork in Michigan included traveling to ghost towns that were once lumber mills and camps where you worked. I tramped through cemeteries to locate your markers, I sourced family references in the archives of The Arenac Independent to determine the social, religious and political culture of your time. I searched court documents for minor offenses, found your signatures on deeds, mortgages, baptism, confirmation, and citizenship documents. I found your pictures from a file at the old farmhouse. I feel like I can almost reach out and touch you.

Thank you great-grandfather for having the courage to leave what was familiar in the Old Country. You had the vision to travel to an unknown land, the stamina to endure the years of back-breaking toil, and the foresight to save all you earned to bring your wife and children here. You learned to read, write, and speak another language. You absorbed the odd customs of America. You purchased and cleared land on Johnsfield Road, Lincoln Township, in Arenac County, Michigan, and gave the land to your sons ... three generations that still bear the Hartman name.

Great-grandmother Minnie, your personal pluck held our family together. You bore twelve children. You survived extreme hardship and unparalleled disappointment. A lesser woman would have jumped into the Au Sable River much sooner.

I am indebted to you both for the good life I enjoy today in America. I just wish you had left me your recipe for the moonshine.

Laurice Hartman LaZebnik

ACKNOWLEDGMENTS

I have had so much help researching and writing
Minnie's Potatoes:

Ashlee and Melissa Osmond for specific experiential
knowledge beyond that of the author.

My husband, Bob LaZebnik, for his advice and patience.

Christine Haas Mason and Shirley Haas Loper for
memories of their mother, Hattie Hartman Haas.

Gordon Osmond for his friendship and editing expertise.

Jennifer Hartman Hauschild for her graphic design,
marketing skills, and her positive support.

Lori Davis for researching early editions of the Arenac
County Independent.

Lyle and Dale Schmidt for memories of their father,
Rudy Schmidt.

Michael Hartman for memories of our neighbor,
Louie Kalo and our grandfather, Wilhelm Hartman.

Jean Lantis, Ann Green, Marti Cabbage, Lynn Eckerle,
and the Columbia Women's Writers.

Rosalee Griewohn for her research at the Jackson
County Genealogical Society.

Thank you all.

FOREWORD

This historical novel chronicles an immigrant family's struggle from the mid-nineteenth century to the days of the Great American Depression. *Minnie's Potatoes* traces the travel of a passionate woman from the sophistication of eighteenth century Europe via steerage on a steamship, to the crude, untamed wilderness of early Michigan.

The author documents her own family's struggle to survive the fires, the life-threatening accidents, the disease and the emotional crisis as a passionate beauty faces reality with two lovers who happen to be brothers.

The Hartman family survives by lumbering, farming and finally ... bootlegging. All characters and their names are real...except for one bad apple who appears to intensify the stories' conflicts. Events are real and come from newspapers' accounts, court documents, real estate transactions, family interviews and photographs.

Most of this story is true.

Note: The author changed Christine Hartman's name to Zelda Hartman in the story so Minnie's mother, Christina Bublitz would not be confused with Fred's mother, Christine Hartman.

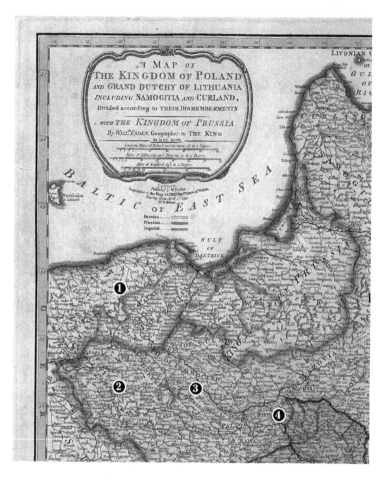

A map of the Kingdom of Poland and Grand Dutchy of Lithuania including Samogita and Curland divided according to their dismemberments with the Kingdom of Prussia by Will. Faden, Geographer to the King, HRH the Price of Wales, 1799. The borders of Poland, Russia, and Prussia (Germany) fluctuated wildly because of various wars through the centuries. This map was most likely still accurate when Minnie was born in 1855.

❶ *Bublitz in Prussian territory, where Minnie's family originated.*

❷ *Poznan in Russian territory where Minnie and Fred lived*

❸ *Louisenfelde in Russian territory where Fred and Minnie were married.*

❹ *Warsaw, at this time, was in Russian territory. Imperial Poland was just east and south shown in the darkest shaded area.*

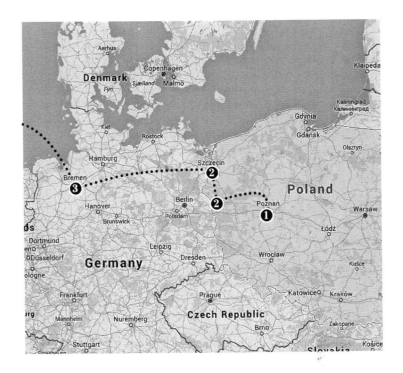

❶ *Minnie and her children begin their journey to the new world and leave Poznan via barge on the Warta River.*

❷ *The barge takes them north on the Elba River where they catch the train to the Port of Bremen in Germany.*

❸ *Minnie boards the steam and sailing ship Warra in Bremen, Germany, and after a stop in Southhampton, England, they cross the Atlantic to New York.*

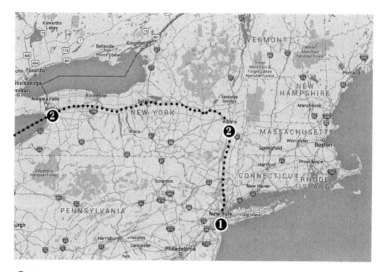

❶ *In New York, Minnie and the children get on a barge in the Hudson River, and travel north to Albany.*

❷ *From Albany they travel west on the Erie Canal to Buffalo on Lake Erie.*

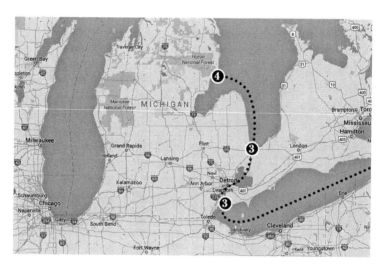

❸ *The ship travels west, the length of Lake Erie, and then north through the St. Mary's River to Lake Huron.*

❹ *Their journey ends after steaming around Michigan's thumb to Point Lookout, which is just a short distance from the village of Au Sable, where Fred meets them.*

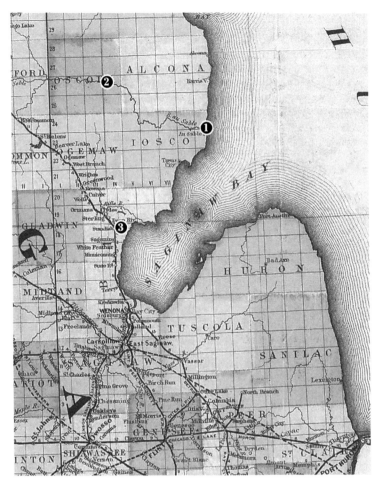

Railroad map of Michigan prepared for the U.S. Commissioner of Railroads in 1876.

❶ *Point Lookout and the village of Au Sable.*

❷ *The lumber camp in the woods of Oscoda.*

❸ *Standish, where the family farm was established.*

MINNIE'S POTATOES

PROLOGUE

Minnie can see Maestro Dembinski adjust the height of his piano seat from the platform where she waits with the other choristers. Conversation stops. They have rehearsed Brahms's new Liebeslieder Walzer … in case the oppressive Prussians show up, but will hear the maestro perform Chopin's Polonaise in A-flat major to arouse the patriotism of the predominately Polish guests. All eyes are on the renowned and multi-talented pianist and choral conductor.

His flawless rendition of what had become the Polish national anthem prompts tears from the fashionably dressed women and causes the men to stand taller. The crowd applauds and shouts out, "Bravo! Bravo!" The maestro turns to the crowd, takes a low bow, and stops. The guests are suddenly silent.

Minnie sees that today's guests at their Friends of Arts and Sciences salon are the same as they were last Sunday … except for the uniformed men who have burst into the room. The uninvited Prussian soldiers are present, they all know, to dissuade Poles from keeping alive their culture, their traditions, and even their language. A brush of Dembinski's hand demands wine for his Prussian guests. A nod from him acknowledges their presence. A formal bow excuses him and the great man returns to the performance platform.

The maestro snaps Minnie and the other singers to attention with a simple tap of his baton. He mouths the Liebeslieder Walzer to the singers, exposing his teeth in what he parades as a smile. The chorus awaits his downstroke. The baton drifts down with a gentle dip and the music begins.

"*Wundarbar! Wundarbar!*" The guests vigorously applaud the German composer's work.

It's 1870 and the usuals are all here ... the same eminent faces ... Dobrowolski, Dembinski, the same hangers-on moving around the crowded room, murmuring pleasantries to one another without meaning them, sipping wines from Poland's prestigious Zielona Gora vineyards while their eyes take inventory of who is here with whom. Grim men break into broad smiles, shake hands much too vigorously, nodding to those moving by, pretending to have conversations while they check the room for mistresses, prospective mistresses, or their wives.

Minnie can feel the heat of his stare on her cheek before she notices the tall Prussian's head moving above the crowd. As he moves, his gaze fixes on someone or something on the riser.

She rubs the side of her face. Discomfort has marked her day ... first the maestro cancelled the solo she had been practicing for weeks, and then Frau Dembinski had asked her to wear a low-cut dress that would make her Mama pale. But most of all, Minnie is annoyed with the maestro's attitude. He planted her on this platform and told her to smile and look pretty. Hadn't the great man noticed the improvement in her voice? "Smile and look pretty" ... right. Those are the same words her papa uses over and over on market days when she must stand on display to attract buyers for his vegetables.

When their glances meet, it is as if the soldier is sending her a signal. Their eyes lock. The tall, slender officer with the determined countenance stops to speak with the hostess. Frau Dembinski's eyebrows arch only for a second before she nods toward the platform and leads the man through the guests.

Minnie watches them cut through the crowd. He takes the lead, slowly sashaying his broad shoulders this way to avoid this person, carving that way around a couple deep in conversation. He pauses to excuse himself as he passes between two men gawking down a woman's plunging neckline ... and ultimately stands before Minnie with Frau Dembinski at his side. He waits as she introduces the soldier from the occupation army to her.

"Kapitän Hartman, may I present my student, Fräulein Wilhelmina Bublitz." She pauses. "Minnie, meet our honored guest, Kapitän Karl Hartman."

"*Guten tag*," he says.

His eyes leave Minnie's only for a moment as he thanks his hostess with a bow and a click of his heels. He turns back to the target of his attention. "Is this a good afternoon for you, Wilhelmina?"

As Frau Dembinski turns to leave she says, "Kapitän, call her Minnie. Everyone does."

The girl bends her knee and bows her head like Frau Dembinski taught her. She is uncertain if the soldier from the occupying army is at this salon to arrest her, to ask her to reveal the names of the revolutionaries in the room, or perhaps because he has mistaken her for someone else. She can't take her eyes off his custom-tailored uniform, the shoulders vibrantly detailed with the gold stripes of the Imperial Germany Army. The man is tall. His stare makes her uncomfortable ...woozy. Minnie reaches for the rail to steady herself. He intercepts her outstretched hand.

"*Danke*," she says, her breath abandoning her.

He raises her hand to his lips. His eyes recapture hers. She holds her breath as he turns her hand and kisses her palm.

That was Minnie's first encounter with Karl Hartman.

TOP: *Poznan Rathaus (City Hall) with clock tower, 1910.*
Photo Attribution: Bundesarchiv, ZLA 7 Bild-0001 / CC-BY-SA 3.0

BOTTOM: *Clock Tower mechanical goats do battle at noon every day.*
Photo Attribution: Radomił Binek, 2005

Chapter One
THE SEARCH

Wilhelmina Bublitz was born in the Polish Province of Poznan in the Duchy of Warsaw. It was a cloudy day, November 26, 1855, the same year floods reached Market Square and the river's overflow claimed Jacob Bublitz's wooden stall and all the vegetables his family had so carefully plucked from the rich soil behind their cottage.

Poznan, at that time, was occupied by the Imperial German Government. King Frederick Wilhelm was their puppet in power. Under Prussian rule the King ordered the floods be controlled by making his peasants fill in and redirect the Warta River, an impossible task accomplished by Polish peasants in under a year. They had no choice.

At one time Poznan had been the cultural and political capital of Poland. No more. The powerful Prussians allowed the Poles to speak their native language, but German was to be their first language. Poznan's unlucky dot on the map, located on the road between Berlin and Warsaw, was where invading armies halted briefly to conscript men and boys, drink beer, and rape women … if they had the time. A defeated Napoleon overnighted there in 1815, but shot out the next morning like a cannon ball as the Polish King's army rolled in.

Jacob Bublitz was not happy when he learned his third child was a girl, preferring an all male workforce to help him with the chores. He told his wife, Christina, that her baby girl was an omen of bad times to come, but changed his mind when perfect strangers told him that she was the most beautiful child God ever created. One of his customers told him a rich man would take her for his wife and he, Jacob Bublitz, would be set for life. They all agreed Minnie's father was lucky. Poor Jacob. He should have stuck with his gut, but he heard what he wanted to hear.

The cultural custom of presenting baby girls with pennies to save for their wedding shoes was taken to the extreme by Minnie's father. People tossed coins into her buggy during sunshine walks with her mother. Jacob saved them in a glass jar buried in the backyard garden. Passing soldiers remarked on the child's scarlet cheeks and smiling green eyes and slipped a coin into her stroller. Before she learned to walk, enough coins had been collected to start a second jar. Men stopped at her father's booth on Market Square to ask the baby's name and to touch her crimson curls. For those who proposed a future marriage match, Jacob Bublitz encouraged more coins for his consideration. He explained the coins were being saved so when the time came, he could offer a suitable man a beautiful virgin with a proper dowry.

As Minnie matured, her mother took credit for the child's good looks. She was proud she had provided the girl with vivid lips, perfect white teeth, and translucent pink skin. Minnie's father was convinced his stature in the community was hinged to her unusual beauty and her potential for marrying well. Jacob planted two pine trees in honor of Minnie's birth to be sawed down and sold when she married. Their proceeds would add to her dowry.

Jacob Bublitz and Minnie's older brothers made up a game around the supper table of finding suitable suitors for their sister. She was twelve. At one time they teased they had promised her to an elephant trainer. The two brothers offered their services to investigate the social standing of any man showing interest in their sister. They claimed they knew how to uncover a man's bad habits and how to determine his ability to make a living. This information would be available for Jacob's eyes before a suitor could be introduced to what they considered ... their shallow-thinking sister.

"It is common knowledge that a woman's brain is smaller," Minnie's oldest brother said during supper. "The brain's convolutions are somewhat less complex than a man's. We must keep Minnie from making bad decisions. Papa, we will watch over her."

Minnie's parents insisted that any suitors be sent to a physician and checked for venereal disease, tuberculosis, heart disease, cancer, goiter, arteriosclerosis, gout, and mumps ... if occurring as a boy, he could be sterile. Her father didn't want any feebleminded idiots for grandchildren, and he wanted heirs. Her mother wanted healthy grandchildren that would care for them in their old age. Obese bachelors and heavy drinkers would not make the eligible bachelor list. A hemophiliac or a man with poor blood was off the table for discussion.

One evening during supper one of Minnie's playmates arrived outside their cottage and called out her name. Jacob opened the door to a little boy who barged in and presented his daughter with flowers. Some of the fresh blooms he recognized as coming from Christina's garden.

"*Wie gehts*," he said, and made a curtsey.

"I'm fine," Minnie said. That evening she overheard her parents hatching a comprehensive plan to keep her a virgin until her marriage.

As she grew taller and her figure filled out, grown men approached her at the market and whispered strange words when Jacob wasn't listening.

One man asked, "Did God drop you out of heaven to be mine?"

Puzzled, Minnie told him she didn't know, but if he asked her father he would.

Boys found themselves unable to speak in Minnie's presence. She felt awkward when they found their voice and spewed lines from the radical poet, Heine, recently departed but widely quoted.

When Minnie ran to her mother crying her chest had tumors, Christina explained her breasts were simply budding like spring flowers. She told her daughter it was a natural occurrence for a girl her age, a girl approaching womanhood. It was a sign that her season was changing. The girl wasn't about to have anything change and tied a tea towel around her chest puffs to make them flat. That shut up the boys for a while, but the discussions between her parents changed.

"Christina, we must find a husband for Minnie before she finds one herself and is spoiled."

Minnie heard her mother describe her as being headstrong and having an iron will. "You will see, Jacob. Our Minnie is tough."

Christina Bublitz dressed her little girl in the finest that Jacob Bublitz could afford while her older brothers wore castoffs. When Minnie asked her father why she had to stand on the crate in his market booth he said, "A clever girl is always two steps ahead of everyone else. Let's say a customer is looking to buy potatoes. Every stand in the market sells potatoes. A clever girl would give the customer a reason to buy potatoes from her father's stall."

"I see. What would a clever girl say to the customer, Papa?"

"She might announce that her father's potatoes were picked early that very day, so they would be fresh and full of flavor. Minnie, you are clever. You will think of something."

On market day, Jacob's dutiful daughter stood displayed on the overturned crate like the chickens on sale across the square. She made a curtsey when she saw her father give her the look and followed his instructions.

"*Guten morgen*," she said to the customer. "My papa's potatoes will not cause leprosy like the French potatoes do."

The customer laughed. Jacob grimaced and turned so she couldn't see him take a drink from a metal flask.

"But Papa, it's true. Are you listening to me? Mama told me that's what the French thought before *Potage Parmentier.*"

"Minnie, stop," he muttered, slipping the flask into his pocket. "You're drawing a crowd."

"But Papa, I'm telling the truth." She turned to the customer. "My mama told me her father would have died in a prisoner-of-war camp if a Frenchman called Parmentier had not fed the German prisoners his potato soup."

"I said that's enough, *tochter*," Jacob said.

Minnie felt her face grow hot. She bit her lip. This was no way to treat a truthful daughter.

"Let this beautiful child speak, Herr Bublitz," a man from the crowd called.

The girl stood on the potato crate, her head lowered. She didn't understand, but was trying to reason it out. She wondered if she had revealed a family secret about her grandfather. Had he been a convict in prison and not a soldier in a prisoner-of-war camp?

Her father interrupted her wondering. "Daughter, explain yourself to this fine gentleman."

Minnie took a deep breath. "Mama told me that even though potatoes are not mentioned in the Bible, they are good vegetables, and they will help children grow to be strong. She said the French King called them poor man's bread."

The gentleman raised his eyebrows. "Go on. I'm listening."

Minnie cleared her throat. "King Frederick William threatened to cut off the noses and ears of peasants who refused to plant and eat potatoes."

"And I can see your father still has his red nose," said the gentleman.

Minnie smiled. She could tell the man was having fun with her father. The man had seen him take a drink, too. "Yes, my Papa plants potatoes. But his nose is red because he drinks potato juice from that flask. Mama makes it for him in our still and no one else gets to drink it."

"Minnie!" Jacob said.

Minnie's eyes traveled from her father to the man. "I'm sorry, sir. No one is supposed to know about the flask. My mama makes the whiskey and puts it in papa's flask. She taught me how to make it."

"Minnie?"

"Is that right. And how do you make whiskey at your house?" the man asked.

"It takes lots of potatoes. Mama and I cook the potatoes, mash them, and cool them before I add the yeast. Then we put the mash in a copper pot and seal it tight with a lid. The lid has a copper tube looping round and round from it to a big glass bottle. I'm not allowed to open the lid and peek at the mash. Mama knows when it's bubbling and has me start the fire. The whiskey comes out of the copper tub first as steam from the bubbles. Whiskey drips out the end of the tube into the bottle, but I have to wait for the first drips, catch them in a cup and throw them away. Mama says the first cup of every batch can make you blind or kill you if you drink it. We cork the bottle when it gets full and my brothers' carry it into the cellar. Then it's time to start bubbling another batch of potatoes. It's fairly simple. Anyone could do it. You could do it. But be careful. Only cook in a copper."

"Minnie!"

"I think my papa wants me to explain why the Russian people didn't eat potatoes." She glances to her father who nods his head. "It was because they thought they were unclean and unchristian. They called potatoes Devil's apples. My papa is not afraid of the Devil. He says potatoes are potatoes and apples are apples. My mama makes cider from apples and schnapps for Papa from his potatoes."

"Your papa is indeed a brave man," the gentleman winked. "I will take five pounds of potatoes every Saturday if your father promises to bring you to the market so I can learn more about his vegetables."

"Only five pounds?" Jacob says.

Minnie saw the corners of the man's lips tighten. "I'll see you next week, Herr Bublitz." He took the package of potatoes from Minnie's hands and disappeared into the market crowd.

Jacob ordered his daughter to stay by his cart to sell vegetables. "I'll be right back." But he didn't come right back and Minnie started to worry about him. When customers asked for her papa and she ran out of made-up answers, she became nervous. She stood on the crate and looked for him. As the day wound down and the young girl realized she had been abandoned, she approached a vendor who knew her father and asked for help pushing the cart home. Minnie peered beneath the swinging doors of each tavern they passed, and thanked the man when she arrived home and found her father sleeping in his armchair before the fire.

Minnie expanded her sales pitch by describing the crunch of her father's turnips, and his vine-ripened melons that were sweeter than honey. Once her spiel was up to speed, she sprinkled today's vegetables with tomorrow's news. "Papa's strawberries will be ready next Saturday and are every bit as sweet as the melons you buy here today."

Jacob Bublitz seemed to get thirsty with regularity in the late afternoons on market days. "Papa, please don't leave me here alone again. The cart is too heavy to push ... " Minnie knew how to get her father's attention. " ... and I can't always count on strange men to help me."

Boleslaw Dembinski, the famous choral conductor, was a regular customer at Jacob's booth. One Saturday Dembinski asked the little girl if she liked to sing. With her father's permission, Minnie sang a lullaby her mother had taught her. Visibly charmed, the maestro invited her to perform with one of his singing societies. He said he would see to it that she had singing and piano lessons once every week at no cost to her family if they would agree to the lessons.

Jacob was happy to agree because Dembinski was from the social stratum that included the most eligible bachelors, and this would give his daughter entry to that upper class.

Minnie was confused. Her father saw no need for her to learn to read and write, yet gave his full permission for her to learn to sing and play the piano once each week with Herr Dembinski. It didn't make sense, but at that time she would have agreed to apprentice in a slaughterhouse if she could get out of housework with her mother for one day each week.

Dembinski's wife gave Minnie a toothy grin when her brothers delivered her for her first piano lesson. She asked Minnie to turn around while she looked her over. "Em. You will join the other children in my piano class," she said. "My husband is much too busy to give you a private lesson."

The piano lessons began the next week with Frau Dembinski...endless drills up the scales and down the scales. When the teacher gave the nod that excused her piano students, Minnie exploded out the door to explore the cobbled city streets with her new friends from school. They climbed the rubble where the old city walls once stood. They followed paths along depressions which were at one time deep moats. The children held hands and snaked expeditions inside churches to view tombs of the old kings, and dashed outside into the bright tenement courtyards to pick flowers. But when the gas workers came out to ignite the street lamps, all the students hustled home.

The maestro visited Frau Dembinski's studio monthly to evaluate her students' progress. When Minnie was twelve she was invited to perform with a singing society at the Dembinski's Sunday salons.

"Don't get a big head, Minnie," her mother said. "You are just one of a dozen girls the maestro has."

"No Mama, there are ..."

"Do not interrupt your mother. You must always wait until it is your turn to speak."

"Yes Mama. I just wanted to say that Maestro Dembinski has invited some boys to join his singing society."

"Boys? Minnie, you must mind your manners with boys."

"Oh Mama, we just fool around. We play games between songs and …"

"Minnie, a gentleman may take your hand to steady you when you go up or down from the performance platform. Do these boys tip their hats when they approach you?"

"Of course not, Mama. The boys are my age. They wear caps."

"Even if a gentleman is twelve years old, he should tip his cap to a lady."

"Mama, you are so old-fashioned."

Three years later, she was on her way home from Frau Dembinski's lesson and had stopped at a shop to look at the flowers in the window.

"Would you like a blossom?" a stranger said.

"No thank you."

"It's all right. I know your parents, and they said anytime their daughter wants a flower she can have one. So … I seem to have forgotten your name."

"It's Minnie."

"Yes of course it's Minnie. I will buy you a bloom, any blossom you want from the entire *blumenladen*." He was a funny man and made Minnie laugh.

They sat together on a park bench near the Bazaar Hotel while he showed her magic tricks. He insisted he walk her home because the streets were dangerous for pretty girls like her. The two passed Minnie's older brothers without her acknowledging them. She was ashamed to be identified with them in their peasant clothes. Minnie was afraid they might tell Papa she was walking with a stranger, so she told the man she wanted to find her own way home. He insisted it wasn't safe and followed her. Minnie's brothers interceded. She never saw the man again.

The next morning while Christina was planting vegetables in their garden with her daughter she asked her if she had ever heard any of her friends talk about a disease called syphilis. Minnie shook her head and continued digging holes. "It is a malady that causes softening of the brain," Frau Bublitz said as she inserted the short-stemmed cabbage plant into the depression. She had her daughter settle some soil around the plant and stamp it firm with her bare foot. She told Minnie that women's private parts were like the closely layered leaves of the cabbage. She said, "Sometimes a germ can infect a girl's personal vegetable patch, causing a pimple or a rash similar to measles. A greenish discharge can drain from the little garden and all the hair around the patch falls out. That's when a woman's brain becomes soggy and she must be confined to an insane asylum. Men or women with syphilis are not permitted to have children."

Minnie dragged her hoe across the garden, being careful to keep the line straight for planting the carrot seeds. She asked her mother how a person could avoid the germs and the insane asylum.

Frau Bublitz smiled. "A clever person would avoid catching the germ."

"And how does a girl who is not clever catch the syphilis germ in her cabbage garden?"

"Wilhelmina, dig another row for carrots, and make it straight this time." Minnie's mother stood and stretched her back. "Syphilis can be transmitted accidentally from a kiss, a toothbrush, or even a towel."

Minnie stopped digging. "Even a kiss?"

"Remember this, daughter. Your cabbage patch is precious. Never use a public toilet … but if you must, spread paper or dried leaves over the seat. Never use a public drinking cup … but if you must, keep your lips away from the rim. Never use a public towel … like the roller towels on Market Square. They are full of nasty germs that can do worse damage than softening your brain. Never sleep in a hotel or strange bed, but if you must make sure the linen is clean and fresh. Never use another's hairbrush or comb. And most important, do not participate in any kissing games."

"But, you kiss Papa. You kiss him even when he stinks of whiskey. You kiss me. Will we all have soft brains?" Minnie finished the second ditch and planted the carrots, spacing each tiny seed three fingers from the last.

"Never kiss a friend with a sore on his lips, if the glands on his neck are swollen, or if he has a sore throat. It's best to avoid kissing strangers altogether. Save your affection for a gentleman, a proper man."

Minnie's father told her he had begun looking for a suitable husband for her. He instructed her she was not to leave the house unless accompanied by her brothers, her mother or by him. She was trapped. After talking it over with her piano school friends, she began to understand why her parents had become so protective. None of them would jeopardize the social prestige that would come to their family from the sterling marriage of a virgin to a wealthy suitor. Who would have thought a germ-free cabbage patch would be this important? Minnie wondered.

While shelling peas, Christina instructed Minnie on the duties of a wife. First and foremost she must be clean. Her nails must be trimmed. Her feet must be free of unattractive bunions, corns, or odors. And yes, a wife must wear her shoes even during the warm summer months. A proper wife must wash her feet at night before getting into bed. "Minnie, you must begin wearing shoes immediately so you do not develop ugly calluses."

While they hung wet laundry on the lines behind their cottage, Christina explained that Minnie's underwear must always be spotless and clean. She told her daughter that a wife must work to stay attractive to her husband. A proper wife must never, ever, let her husband see her in soiled underwear. "Before you are married I will take you shopping for undergarments. Men like them to be lacy, of the finest batiste and colored light pink."

There was so much to learn. Minnie's mother taught her to boil potatoes without burning them. While they picked strawberries she told her how to handle medical emergencies when she had children. She told her what to do for burns, cramps and convulsions. She said that men choose women who are clever and can be good mothers for their children over fallen women and whores.

"How can I be clever if I don't learn to read and write?"

"Don't be silly, Wilhelmina. A husband's duty is to take care of all the reading and writing that is necessary for a family. That's why men in Poland go to school and women do not. We must be clever to accomplish all we do at home." Then Christina Bublitz explained how when women marry, they become the property of their husbands.

"Mama, how can one person become the property of another? That's like serfs being owned by the landed aristocracy. Papa said the Tzar freed serfs in Russia in 1860. He says a serf is like a peasant and a peasant is like a slave, and slaves are what they have in America." Minnie's mother shifted to the next row of berries, but offered no explanation. Minnie threw her basket down, spilling the berries, and ran off to play with her friends.

The next time they peeled potatoes for supper, Christina explained how a baby was made. Minnie was horrified. "You can't mean men stick that thing from their pants that they pee with up here? Mother, that's disgusting." She had to take a long walk to get the repulsive thought of her father doing that to her mother out of her mind.

"Minnie, I'll wash, you can dry the supper dishes tonight. I want to explain to you how most men think."

What? Minnie wondered how her mother knew that.

"First, they think women are insignificant," Christina said, "and they think our brains are smaller than theirs. They think we were made only to keep their house clean, their meals cooked, and their beds warmed at night."

"Mama, you know how tiresome housework is to me. How can you want this boring, soul-killing drudgery of marriage for your own daughter? Is my sister a slave to her husband? Doesn't Caroline have any fun?"

"My dear daughter, you were born with the gift of beauty. Girls without your looks rarely find a good provider willing to marry them, procreate with them and care for their children. Most unattractive women struggle to eat. Minnie, you are a *luftmensch*, an impractical overachiever. Set this fault aside and you will find a man to marry who adores you, a man who will love your children. Learn to follow the rules of our people and you will enjoy an easy life ... all because you have been blessed with your breathtaking beauty. Mark my words. It will be so. As for Caroline, your father and I did the best we could for her. She has a husband."

Minnie bribed her brothers with the sponge cake her mother taught her to make. She asked them to walk a different route to Market Square each Saturday where she helped her father sell the exquisite produce their family grew.

When the route took them near Wilhelm's Platz, a square adjacent to the center of town, the three of them explored the Arkadia Building where German plays were performed. They fed the ducks along the River Warta. On another Saturday, they passed by the tenement houses and aristocratic residences of the mighty Dzialynski, Mielzynski and Gorka families. Minnie relayed the rich Polish history to hold their interest, stories she had memorized from her father. She promised she would make them fine puddings if they would wait while she peeked inside just one more building ... the Fara, the most exquisite baroque parish church in Poznan.

The boys grew tired of getting up early on Saturday mornings just to take their sister sightseeing. They could no longer be tempted by Minnie's bribes of warm apple strudel or sweet tomato pudding. They told her she would walk to Market Square with them or she would stay home.

Ignoring their terms, Minnie got up early and dressed in her brothers' old clothes. The twelve-year-old girl pulled a cap over her red hair, packed her own clothes in a satchel, and passed through the city without a glance. She explored the cathedral where the Golden Chapel housed the tombs of Poland's first kings, Mieczyslaw and Boleslaw the Brave. While standing there, she dreamed of becoming a princess or a queen. She spent an hour in fantasies before she had to change her clothes and time her appearance on Market Square with that of her brothers.

Minnie spent the summer submerged in the pleasures of adolescence ... swimming, competing in foot races, skipping rope, picnicking in the park ... all under the close supervision of her brothers. Her bosom had developed fully that autumn and her hips had grown round. Her brother's friends stared at her breasts and asked to touch them.

"Don't be stupid," she would say, but soon felt a certain power over the boys, especially when they stared at her chest. As the year progressed she noticed men stopped talking mid sentence when she walked by them on Market Square, leaving their friends listening to the wind. Others tracked her with their eyes as she moved in the crowd. She was uncomfortable at first, but soon grew to like all the attention she seemed to be drawing.

"May I help you with your packages?" a boy asked her while she was shopping for her mother.

"No thank you," she said in her most polite German.

"May I walk beside you?" he said.

"How old are you?" she asked.

"Sixteen."

"Sorry. I only walk with older men." She smiled politely.

Older men's heads turned toward her in a crowded room to catch her every word. "Fräulein Bublitz, will you have a cup of tea with me?"

"No thank you. I'm not allowed to speak to old men." Gentlemen trailed behind her as if caught in her invisible net. One man pestered her with questions. At last she stopped walking and asked him if he was a religious man.

"I'm a good German Lutheran," he said.

"Sir," I am a Catholic woman," Minnie lied. That stopped him in his tracks.

One man asked her to marry him. She told him she was spoken for.

Minnie tried teasing men with a wink, or a smile over a raised shoulder, completely oblivious to the consequences of her flirting. Men elbowed through crowds to stand close, to engage her in conversation, to touch her hand. Her early training in etiquette and fine manners resulted in her being modest ... a Polish national characteristic her mother insisted a proper female maintain. Minnie tried acting refined, like women in the monarchy ... like the old queen.

Minnie Bublitz had no idea what to do after attracting a man. She could converse politely about the weather, but knew nothing of politics, had never been inside a museum, and had never attended a concert other than the salons. She couldn't read or write. All she could do was play piano, sing, and sell her father's vegetables.

Jacob saw his daughter conversing with men on Market Square, scolded her, and told his wife it was time for another talk. Christina reminded her of the rules she must follow to attract, catch, and keep a man. She told her she must be polite to men, yet she warned her to be careful.

None of this set well with Minnie in 1870. Even at fifteen she was a force of her own. She enjoyed the attention of men and was amused by the power she could exert over them.

She was clever enough to know her looks were an accident of nature and would not last forever. She knew enough from her experience at piano and singing lessons that she was only moderately talented and could never be a successful musician like Herr Dembinski.

She liked singing and playing the piano, but thought the real benefit of her music might be to open doors, to introduce her to something or somewhere else. Whatever or wherever that was, she could not yet imagine. Her brothers were wrong. Her brain worked just fine. The girl had ambition and tremendous energy. She wanted more in her life than men and marriage and children. She wanted it all, and she wanted it on her own terms ... unconfined and unburdened by the social and cultural restraints of her time. That's when she realized her beauty had become her greatest liability.

Boleslaw Dembinski invited Minnie to his Sunday salons. She was to sing with a small group staged on a riser on one side of a large room in his elegant mansion. She was thrilled.

Minnie's mother chided her and announced at the supper table, "Minnie Bublitz is ahead of her time. Left to her own devices she will travel the world to sing in concerts. She will meet new people. Along the way she may discover herself and develop into an independent woman." Her mother had vision.

Her father reminded her that the times she lived in demanded something different. She must learn to adjust to fit these expectations ... marriage, motherhood, pleasing a husband, and staying close to her family.

Minnie thought a lot about what her future would bring. Impatient, she set upon making it happen on her terms. But what is it? She knew she wanted to love and be loved by someone, yet had no idea what love looked like or what she would do with it once she found it.

Minnie's girlfriends talked about being abducted by a brash, handsome man in an elegant carriage. They seemed to think love was a blissful adventure cracked by thunderstorms of extreme torture … a man and a woman thrown together by chance and torn apart by circumstance. High drama. It sounded romantic, but after the carriage ride … what came next?

She saw Frederick Hartman for the first time while walking with her brothers on Wilhelm's Strauss. Minnie's eyes were drawn to this bare-chested man. He was tall, fair, with muscular arms and curly blonde hair. He moved with purpose and grace … like a cat.

Frederick Hartman caught her gazing at him during a boxing contest after he had knocked out a man much larger and stronger. He approached her after the fight wearing his towel around his neck and still glowing with sweat. "My name is Fred Hartman," he said, "and I'm going to marry you."

Her face felt hot. She ran away without speaking to him. Growing up could no longer be put off. A real man wanted to marry her. Fred found one of her brothers at Market Square.

"Your sister is the woman I want for the mother of my children." He begged Minnie's brothers for her name and to invite him to their home to meet her father.

A year later, when Minnie was sixteen Jacob Bublitz allowed Fred Hartman to call at their home. It was summer. She wore a purple peasant gown and stood in the archway while Fred and her father talked. She heard him tell her papa he was twenty-five, had a job at the Zielona Gora vineyard and rented a summer house on land outside the city. His family was in the winery business and lived in the Wielkopolska region. He said he spoke Russian, Polish, and a guttural German.

His English sounded good to her father, who spoke none. He was a "catch" according to Christina, who whispered to Minnie from where she stood in the kitchen. Fred shook her father's hand, bowed to her mother, and winked at Minnie as he left, without saying a word.

Jacob Bublitz and Minnie's brothers must have investigated and found Fred free of alcoholism, tuberculosis, and syphilis because they told her they had approved of Fred's intention to court her. Her older sister didn't care one way or the other. Caroline always looked tired. She spent most of her time in the fields growing vegetables for her husband's booth at the market.

The next evening when he came to call, he presented her with a bouquet of fresh flowers. Minnie forced her mouth closed so she wouldn't look so surprised. She was thrilled. They were like the ones sold at the stalls in Market Square. He brought Minnie's father a bottle of wine. After an hour of polite conversation and a glass or two of Fred's wine, Herr Bublitz gave permission for Fred to take Minnie for a short walk. They strolled down Gerber Strauss, a cobbled street east of the Town Square.

He talked about his work at the vineyard. He said the winery was in the capital of the wine-making region of lower Silesia. He told her, as if sharing a secret, "The wines are not great yet; they are high in acid. I prefer mead or beer." Fred talked on and on. He had ideas … big ideas.

Fred was working with a man who had developed a grape that would grow in cooler temperatures … the northern regions of Europe. He explained to Minnie how alcohol could be made from any root that was sweet. So, it was possible to make an alcoholic liquor from grain, potatoes, beets or turnips or a wine from fruit. The taste would vary, but they could all make you drunk. He stopped and turned to Minnie, expecting a laugh. She only nodded, not understanding why becoming a drunk like Papa was some kind of joke.

"My brothers drink beer. And Papa drinks the liquor Mama makes from potatoes," she said. Fred explained alcohol didn't come from the plant itself, but from the root. By distilling these roots into wines, and then distilling the wines into brandies or spirits, a delicious alcoholic drink could be made, and sold for gold coins. She was fascinated by the alcoholic potential of a potato ... the same vegetable she knew how to grow in the garden.

The head vintner had been teaching Fred how to blend varieties of grapes for clarets or cream wines. Fred said the old wine maker followed recipes, similar to what Minnie might use if she made a sponge cake. The man had given him a book so that some day he could start his own vineyard. "My dream is to have some rolling land somewhere," Fred said, "maybe ten acres with a southern exposure. I could make the best wine. I could make a good living making wine."

One Sunday afternoon he took her to meet his family. Minnie was under careful instructions from her mother to check them for slowness in thinking or hesitation in speech. They lived in a fine townhouse. Fred told her he had a younger brother.

"Tell me about him," she said. "Is he as handsome as you are? What is he like ... as crazy as you?" Fred's voice was low when he spoke and vibrated inside Minnie's chest. When he laughed it tickled her chest and she couldn't help but smile. The man's eyes were the color of fresh peapods. He smelled of honest work. He had a directness about him that made his presence powerful.

Fred chuckled. "He is a strange sort of guy, but he's not crazy ... just does odd things ... like taking stuff that doesn't belong to him, especially things I value. And of course he never gives them back. Maybe it's just a phase," Fred smiled. "My brother has always been competitive with me, tries to beat me at arm wrestling, foot races, jumping challenges. He should know he can't win. He can't beat me at card games either, yet keeps trying. He's full of suggestions for my business ... stupid ones ... doesn't have a head for horseflesh ... no common sense ... doesn't have a clear notion of how to work either, or how to make money. I told him I could get him a job, but he doesn't want to work in the vineyard. The guy just doesn't use his head.

"Don't get me wrong," Fred said. "I love the kid. It's just that he can't be counted on. When I told him there was no future for him in the military of the occupying army, he ran right out and volunteered for a three-year term with the Germans. I think he may be stupid. He believes all the lies the Germans spread. But he is my little brother, and I will always love him and forgive him for all his faults."

Minnie saw Fred often. When he asked to kiss her, she made him lean in first so she could check his neck for swollen glands and his lips for sores that did not heal. He laughed and asked her why she wanted to know if he had a sore throat. Seeing no poisonous germs or lesions on his lips, she let him kiss her again and again. It was fun.

Fred came to call one Friday night and brought his brother, who was home on leave from the army. When the soldier entered their home she could not speak. It was the Prussian officer, the man she had met at the salon. Karl Hartman grinned, reintroducing himself to Minnie in grand style. With a flourish, he bowed and kissed her hand. The man effervesced male hormones ... he made her insides churn. She felt weak ... could not speak.

Fred watched in amusement and spoke to Minnie's father while Karl whispered to Minnie that she embodied sunshine. Minnie's heart was pounding when he told her that her eyes spoke faster than her tongue, catching the sparks from other people's eyes. He was so charming. She believed his every word. This time when she saw Karl, she saw the man she wanted to father her children. Fred's brother was twenty-two, much taller and thinner, and not nearly as successful. This soldier caused Minnie to tremble and stand up straight. In his presence the nipples on her breasts expanded and grew tender. Her words caught in her throat. She was intoxicated by Karl Hartman.

While Fred was away visiting vineyards, Karl appeared at their cottage and asked to speak to her father. Shortly after they spoke, he left without asking for her. That night Minnie overheard her parent's conversation through their bedroom wall.

"Christina, I don't have a good feeling about that soldier. I don't understand why a man would step in on his brother's sweetheart. He strikes me like one of those soldiers I used to know in the army … the kind of guy who finds them, beds them and leaves them … a Lothario."

"Did you see Minnie's face when that man walked in the door?" Christina said. "She likes him. I'll talk to her."

The next morning Minnie's mother took her aside. "Karl Hartman asked Papa's permission to court you." She could see her daughter's face blush red. "Papa doesn't like the man."

"Oh Mama, I think he's wonderful."

"But is he right for you, Minnie? Karl is a soldier."

"Someday he will be a general, maybe even a powerful figure in the German government."

"Soldiers spend long periods away from home. They have reputations for leaving bastard children in every town they march through."

"Karl is not like that, Mama."

"How do you know? Minnie, will this be a healthy relationship for you? Have you thought about what you want for the rest of your life? Does Karl fit your goals for love, family and children?"

"How can I know, Mama?" Minnie's eyelids drooped. "Unless," a corner of her lip tightened and raised slightly on one side, "unless I see more of him."

Karl knocked on the front door the following evening. Jacob gave Minnie the look, and she reluctantly retreated to her bedroom. After the soldier had gone, he opened her bedroom door and announced that he had given his permission for Karl to court her.

"Thank you, Papa," she said and threw her arms around his neck.

"Minnie, this man is no good. He only wants what his brother has."

The next evening when Karl came to call, she was eager to leave her disapproving parents and go anywhere with this man. The Polish community of the Wielkopolska region was home to the first Polish theater in Poznan. She listened as Karl read the words inscribed on its façade, "The nation unto itself." He explained how the Polish people had the right to self rule ... men and women alike. She liked that idea. Karl took her to a grand performance of Johann Strauss's "Blue Danube Waltz" ... popular at the time. During the concert he took her hand and slipped a black pearl ring on her finger. "This is for our friendship," he said and they danced on the grass.

The next evening during their walk he explained the layout of the ancient city before Poznan became a Prussian fortress. He showed her the nine additional forts being built between the nine forts that currently surrounded the city, making Poznan a major military post and headquarters for the German Fifth Army. They climbed the walls and ramparts that surrounded the city.

On another evening they walked to the Imperial Castle in the center of town. While they were gazing up at the towers, he told her she was meant to be a princess, his princess. He slipped a gold chain over her head that held a small heart-shaped locket. It fell in place between her generous breasts.

She loved it ... not so much the gold locket or the pearl ring. He was so attentive and kind to her. Whenever she spoke, he turned to listen. She felt like what a queen must feel ... well loved by her people. She wanted to be a princess or at least treated like a princess for her entire life.

The next evening, Karl showed Minnie the library donated by Edward Raczynski as a gift to the Polish people. He told her he believed every person had the right to an education. He said he would teach her to read and write. He told her he would be a famous German officer. He told her every German had the right to creative expression. He said he thought Minnie had great musical talent and would someday become a famous singer. They stopped at a shop near the library. Karl bought her the German shepherd puppy she admired. He told her she could name her whatever she wanted, so she called her Heidi.

Minnie fell in love with Karl Hartman in front of the Raczynski library holding her sweet Heidi in her arms.

Fred returned and discovered his brother had been courting his girl. Playfulness left his eyes. Minnie sensed his rage, yet Fred showed no emotion. She didn't know what to do or say, so she went to her room, closed the door and played with Heidi. When she heard the latch close on the front door, she came out with Heidi and found Fred was still there, talking to her father. Fred told her their courtship would continue. His tone was calm. He told her that he and Karl had spoken and agreed that the best man would win her. He forced a smile, but Minnie sensed he wasn't smiling at her.

Karl received orders from the Imperial German Army for military training. He would be gone a month, would return to Poznan to say farewell to his family, and then be shipped to the Russian front.

Fred said Karl warned him of an impending Prussian Army conscription campaign. Every man in Prussia between eighteen and forty-five was called to serve for three years. Karl said they were after older men, Fred's age.

Precedent had been set for compulsory military service after Napoleon's defeat. When the emperor's brother, Napoleon III, took power, he sold his conscripted subjects for cash so they could fight for England in the war with America. When Tzar Alexander II was in power, he hauled away every man under thirty to fight for him on the Russian Steppes. And now that the Prussians were in power, no man under the age of forty was safe from servitude, a term that could last fifteen to twenty-five years, a term that could be shortened only by death or dismemberment.

Minnie was afraid for Fred. For Karl, she was terrified.

Karl begged Minnie to marry him before he left for the Russian front.

"Yes," she said without hesitation.

Her future husband slipped a simple gold ring on her left hand to bind their commitment and kissed her with a passion she felt in her toes.

"Minnie," Jacob said as he finished his breakfast, "Fred Hartman is a decent fellow. This soldier, my gut tells me…"

"Minnie," Christina said, "talk to Fred. Papa's right. He is a decent man. He came to see your father when he learned of your wedding plans from Karl. He warned your father about his brother. Just talk to him. He will understand."

"No he won't." Minnie stood. "Karl loves me and I love him. Fred will forgive his brother, but he will never forgive me."

"Minnie, you are a vixen," Jacob said.

"I don't want to ever see Fred Hartman again." Minnie left the kitchen and slammed the door.

Christina and Jacob Bublitz knew any further attempts to change the mind of their headstrong daughter would be futile. Minnie's mother left the breakfast table and walked outside to talk to her daughter. She warned her that her soldier might never come back from the battlefield. She said officers were often the first targets in a battle.

When Minnie told Karl what her mother had said, he smiled and replied, "Should I die, I will die remembering my wedding afternoon with you."

All would be accomplished while Karl was on maneuvers. The soldier volunteered his medical records to Minnie's father before he left. Jacob had no occasion to post bans for a church ceremony. The wedding was less than two weeks away. Karl had suggested they wed at the train station. Minnie agreed, and the Bublitz home became controlled chaos. The bride and groom would have but a few hours together before Karl caught his train to the Russian front.

"I want Heidi to be at the wedding," Minnie told her mother. "Karl gave the puppy to me, and I want him to know she will always be part of our family."

"That dog?" Papa said when his wife told him of their daughter's latest request. "Who will watch the mutt? Heidi's bark could scare the horses. She could be trampled. No, the dog cannot be at this charade of a wedding, and that's final."

Jacob Bublitz said this rushed wedding didn't feel right to him. He never liked Karl Hartman. He asked an officer he knew about the rights of a soldier's widow. He learned that if Karl died in battle, his wife would be given a stipend to live on for the rest of her life. Still uneasy about the future of his Minnie, Jacob asked her to reconsider, said he had a bad feeling about the man, the wedding, and their future together.

Minnie listened to her heart instead of her father. She was thrilled with the idea of getting married to the handsome soldier and threw herself into the preparations. Her family accused her of being a Prussian general when she conscripted everyone to plan and execute the civil ceremony. Jacob filled out the application for the license, reluctantly printing Minnie's name next to Karl's.

Fred disappeared.

Minnie's mother began preparing her daughter for her first bedding. She explained about the physical part of love so she would be better able to cope with her first experience with sex and later with the problems that were sure to come in her marriage. She said when her husband returns from the Russian front, the first weeks of living together would be the most important for them.

"Minnie dear, if your husband does something in bed that displeases you, you must tell him from the start to prevent it from becoming a bad habit. Your first bedding could be brutal. Some men have cruel, sadistic traits and derive pleasure from inflicting pain.

"My dear, you have a hymen like all other girls your age. It is a membrane that covers your private parts that must be broken before your husband can enter you. If it hurts you, ask him to be gentle or stop. If you start to bleed, I mean bleed a lot, like a hemorrhage, he must take you to a doctor."

"Mama, I have a girlfriend who said it is normal to bleed on your first bedding."

"Minnie, listen to me. Some women have a small vaginal entrance and the passage can be narrow. We are all built differently. Ask him to go slow if he hurts you. It may take several tries to accomplish your defloration. But if he insists, ask him to use a lubricant, like olive oil. If your hymen still does not break, have Karl take you to the doctor to cut it. It is a painless operation."

"Mama, millions of women go through this. It can't be all that awful."

"Minnie, I know of a girl who died from a hemorrhage caused by the rupture of her hymen. It was on her wedding night. Just be careful. Karl should make sex pleasurable for you. You have zones on your body that if touched and caressed give rise to pleasure."

"I do? Where?"

"The lips, the breasts, your hair, your armpits and the clitoris."

"What's a clitoris?"

"You'll find out."

"How can my armpits give me pleasure? Would he tickle me and make me laugh? Mama, how often do men like to have sex?"

"For a man Karl's age, once or twice a week."

Karl's train was scheduled to arrive late in the morning on Saturday, the customary hour for German weddings. Christina Bublitz began preparing the traditional wedding soup Thursday morning. She made broth from chicken and beef bones, celery, leaks, parsley and cloves and simmered it until it became a golden yellow. On Friday morning she skimmed off the fat, strained the broth and added egg shells to make it clear. She chopped the asparagus and carrots and steamed the meatballs. She mixed up a large batch of egg noodles and hung them over a broomstick to dry. On Saturday morning Christina was up early to simmer the fresh vegetables until they were barely done. Just before her sons carried the *Hochzeitssuppe* to the train station she added boiled noodles and broke a dozen eggs into the pot so they would float on top. Minnie's mother was fussing. Her youngest daughter's wedding had to be perfect. She had been planning this celebration since the day she was born.

Minnie had selected two of the neighbor's daughters to be at her side when the train with the groom on it pulled into the station. They would be wearing fresh floral wreaths in their hair. Jacob Bublitz rented a carriage drawn by four black horses that would be waiting just outside the station to take the bride and groom to a hotel. The preacher said the purpose of the ceremony was to break one bond and seal another. He added that he must be paid in full before the ceremony could commence. Jacob told his daughter the wedding was becoming too expensive.

The bride was up at dawn that Saturday in 1871. Minnie's mother heated water and dropped in lavender blossoms for her daughter's bath. She braided flowers into her red hair that had grown to reach the girl's waist. She piled it on top of her head and pinned it with the French barrettes she had worn on her wedding day.

The Bublitz family arrived at the station early, as did the preacher and the two flower girls who played with Heidi, the puppy. Fred Hartman reappeared with his father and mother.

Minnie smiled at him. He stood tall and stoic as if to say he would accept the situation, but didn't have to like it. Fred saw this as another instance of his brother's thievery and thoughtlessness. Minnie choreographed a rehearsal of the ceremony with simple hand gestures while they all waited for the train. She made sure she looked radiant, smiled widely, and showed off her perfect white teeth.

Bride and groom in traditional dress from the late 1800s.

Poznan was connected with Berlin via Stettin (Szczecin) in 1848 by the Stargard–Poznan Railway.

Photo Attribution: The Train Station of Poznan in 1863. Artist unknown.

Chapter Two
THE SWITCH

A whistle announced the train's arrival shortly before the hiss and steam relayed it had come to a stop. Minnie was dizzy with expectation, filled with excitement. She pinched her cheeks to give them color and licked her lips to make them shine. While the fog cleared, passengers disembarked all around the expectant wedding party. When the fog dissipated, the guests grew quiet. Minnie grew anxious. The platform was empty except for them. Karl Hartman was not on the landing. The groom did not get off the train.

Minnie's breath caught sideways in her chest. She choked and a horrific howl erupted from her throat. She realized then that the gravest insult a bride could experience had befallen her. Minnie Bublitz had been abandoned at the altar. The great beauty who men from Poznan had coveted was now a discarded sixteen-year-old girl, a soured bottle of precious wine.

The bride's family had been disgraced. All the effort and expense that had been put into securing a suitable husband for her, the hope of moving up the social ladder through her marriage, all this was destroyed on that railroad platform.

"How could he do this to me?" she bellowed, shaking her fists and glaring at the assembled guests.

Fred took charge. He checked each passenger car on the train. He entered one car and emerged in the next, calling out his brother's name. He stepped onto the platform from the last car, and turned towards Minnie. Everyone's eyes were on him. He shook his head and shrugged his shoulders.

"Damn you, Karl Hartman!" Minnie's lips narrowed to a slit. She saw her mother shrink from the sound of the guests' gasps at such an unladylike outburst. She whispered to her mother through teeth welded together by rage, "I could kill him."

She whimpered and lifted her petticoats. The heels on her wedding slippers thumped hard as she strode down the raised area next to the empty train. One long plait of hair came loose from the floral tiara that was to have crowned Karl's princess. She stomped across the landing, flinging her tresses to one side. The crowd watched in silence while she kicked the air with her feet and sputtered expletives in perfect Polish. The wedding guests moaned at the spectacle as the remainder of her braided headdress came loose. When she reached Johann and Zelda Hartman, she pushed the hair from her face and set her jaw.

"How could your son embarrass me like this?" Her hands were on her hips when she told them her father had posted the wedding license for all of Poznan to see. She wiped tears from her eyes and addressed Fred.

"How could your brother be so cruel to me and insensitive to my mother, a woman who worked for three days to make that damn wedding soup?" She blew her nose on Grandmother Bublitz's lace handkerchief ... the one her mother had given her for "luck." She glared at Fred. "Who will pay my father for hiring the rig and the four black horses?" She howled, loosening the blue ribbon tied at her waist. She wanted out of that dress, off of this platform, and away from these people. She sank to her knees. "I wanted to ride in that beautiful carriage," she sobbed. "I wanted a new life somewhere far away from here."

Fred had been watching the spectacle and had a sudden inspiration. He knelt down and took Minnie's hand. "You know, you can still ride in that carriage. I will pay for the rig.

We can all eat your mother's 'damn' wedding soup. I will see that you have a new life away from here."

Still furious, Minnie dried her tear-stained cheeks with her unlucky lace handkerchief and tried to understand what Fred was suggesting.

"Minnie, will you marry me?"

Her whimpering stopped abruptly. She checked Fred's eyes for any sign of a joke, then glanced around the station to be sure Karl had not arrived. Fred's hand steadied her as she recovered from tripping on the hem of her dress and stood. "You mean you would still marry me?"

Fred nodded from where he knelt.

Minnie glanced around at her family. Her father's nose was wrinkled in disgust. He looked away. Her mother was nodding too rapidly, her eyes serious. She had worked so hard on that wedding soup. She wouldn't do it again. Her brothers shifted from one foot to another, their upper lips raised like they had somewhere to go and she was wasting their lifespan, again.

"Well, I suppose I could, I mean I guess I could marry you," Minnie said as she pushed her hair away, and sniffed. "All right, Fred. I mean, yes, I will marry you." She nodded to the preacher, wiped the tears from her cheeks on the sleeve of her wedding dress.

The stunned guests gathered around them. They pushed each other to get closer to the spectacle. They held their breaths as the vows were read and agreed upon.

A sigh of relief came from the crowd when it was over. One guest started clapping, slowly at first until he was joined by another and another until the entire crowd applauded the resolution of the crisis.

Minnie forced herself to become her bright, old merry self again. Remembering her mother's warning to avoid those with unsightly blemishes on their lips or face, she kissed some of her family and friends and avoided the others. She was suddenly hungry. And she was thirsty. Minnie drank two cups of her mother's wedding soup and strolled through the guests on the platform. Fred gave her a sip of his beer. It tasted awful. Her skin prickled like bubbles were bursting under her skin. And then she started to itch. Am I getting the hives, she wondered. Is this new irritation from the excitement, the disappointment, or the beer? The event became merry. Beer mugs clinked into one another. No actor's performance could have been better than Minnie's on that Saturday of 1871.

A shrill whistle cut through the merriment, announcing the arrival of the next train. The wedding party moved to one side of the platform to avoid the steam and departing passengers. Friends continued toasting Fred and drinking Jacob Bublitz's beer.

As the engine steam cleared, a tall Prussian soldier appeared on the platform. The man stood erect in his formal dress uniform … long, black jacket embroidered with German silver stitching, over white trousers, his black boots reaching his knees, his hard heels clicking attention.

Fred heard the sound first, and pulled Minnie to him. With his eyes, he told her to look. The officer's white gloved salute landed just below his black helmet with the Prussian gold eagle emblazoned in front and spike on top. His silver scabbard sparkled. His elbow straightened after the salute and his outstretched arm returned to his side. His heels snapped together, again.

"*Traurig bin ich spät.*" Karl's big smile disappeared as he glanced around the startled crowd. "I'm not late by much. The last train came early … missed the first … what's going on here?" Then he saw Fred's arm around Minnie's waist, tears staining her face. "Minnie? Fred?"

The groom kissed his bride's forehead and turned her toward the carriage with the four black horses. Guests closed in around them, clapped their hands together and threw blossoms as the bridal couple took their seats.

Minnie heard none of this from inside the carriage. And she didn't hear Heidi barking, the four black horses shuffling, their hoofs clomping on the cobbled street to avoid the puppy, more barks, the pitiful squeal and then silence. The flower girls raced after the carriage as it rolled off the station platform, but stopped short when they saw the puff of black fur lying motionless on the street. The four black horses continued prancing down the Gerber Strauss.

Minnie glanced back once, but didn't see Karl.

The coachman stopped at Fred's rented summer house, a tiny wood-sided cottage with a thick thatched roof. Minnie hadn't said a word or moved during the luxurious ride through town and now her legs were frozen in place. Her throat was dry and she couldn't answer Fred when he asked if she wanted to see her new home or did she want to live for the rest of her life in this carriage? She began to cry.

"What's the matter, *liebchen*? Are you afraid?"

She didn't know why she was crying. She didn't know what she was doing here with him. She knew he expected an answer, so she nodded.

"My first time inside this cottage was frightening for me, too," Fred said.

"You?" He was so tall and strong. Minnie couldn't imagine anything scaring him.

"Yes, but then I killed the Golem and my courage came back to me."

"Oh Fred, you're joking with me. I know there are no such devils as Golems."

"Minnie, I will never hurt you. I only want to love you and take care of you. Come. I want to show you where I have already planted a few grape vines. Have you ever picked grapes and eaten them right off the vine?"

"Mr. Hartman," the coachman said, "are you stopping here?"

"Yes." Fred stepped outside, paid the man and returned to the carriage door.

"My legs won't move," Minnie told him.

"Well, Frau Hartman, it looks like you need a strong man to help you." He reentered the coach, cradled Minnie in his arms and carried her from the coach to the garden. "*Libeling*, this is now your nest." He set her down on a bench. "This little cottage will keep you safe while you sleep."

The cottage didn't look so small now that she was closer.

"This is your garden," he said. "If you like you can plant potatoes or turnips or flowers."

"I can?"

"Yes, and this will be our home." He led her to the planked front door. "Are you hungry? I will make something special for you to eat. My sweet, this place is yours and mine." Following the ancient tradition, he lifted his bride and carried her through the front door while she giggled and wiggled her feet.

Minnie liked the attention Fred was giving her. He fed her cake at her new kitchen table and made her tea. He helped her out of her wedding dress and removed what flowers were still braided in her hair. Fred seemed kind. This was not going to be like the wedding night her mother had described. Fred picked her up and carried her to her new bed.

"What about my cabbage patch? Will you make it bleed?"

"Your cabbage patch?"

"Yes, Mama told me I should tell you if it hurts."

Fred checked his smile as soon as he understood. He lifted her chin so he could look into his eyes, and kissed her softly. "Did my kiss hurt?"

"No."

"How does this feel?" He kissed her neck.

"That felt good, too."

"And, how about this, my pet?"

"Oh, Fred. What are you doing?" Minnie was getting dizzy. She felt weak. "Fred, put me down."

"Tell me if you want me to stop," he said nibbling her ear and kissing her neck.

"Don't stop." He was wonderful to Minnie, understanding and kind. He promised to rush her to the hospital if her broken hymen bled too much.

They played house in that little cottage for one whole week. Minnie awoke each morning to Fred's soft kisses. He took lots of time and taught her to relax and postpone her pleasure as he kissed the inside of her thighs. And then he paused to feed her grapes. She begged him to make love to her like he had the night before. Instead, he filled the tub with hot water and washed her back. He got into the tub and pulled her onto his lap. Minnie's husband looked into her eyes and told her he wanted to give her everything she had ever dreamed of having.

Minnie could not imagine living in a world without Fred, a world without sex. She was thinking how wrong Mama had been about sex when Fred entered her cabbage patch and her head exploded. Fred carried her back to bed to regain her strength and fed her breakfast with a spoon.

During the days that week he moved furniture to where she asked and then made her lunch. He massaged her feet as they sat before the fire at night. When they made love Fred told her if she looked into his eyes she could see his soul. That's how deeply he loved her. He said she was now a woman, his woman. He prepared food for her every day that week. She didn't think of Karl at all.

Minnie thought about her mother's cautions. She must have been remembering her own wedding night … her own bad experiences, because it wasn't like hers. She was having a glorious time … having more fun than at any other stage of her life …so far. Perhaps her father was a rough lover, or a selfish lover, or even a sadistic lover. Maybe it was her mother's cabbage that bled on their marriage night. Poor Christina

Bublitz. She may never have experienced the enjoyment sex could give a girl, she corrected herself ... a woman.

"Minnie. Minnie dear, would you like to learn to pleasure me?" he whispered.

"Yes. Yes I would!"

He showed her where to touch him, where to kiss and put her mouth. He tasted of salt. He fondled her nipples while her hands brushed his tender spots. They came together after a playful morning, and spent the afternoon napping. Everything was new and so wonderful to Minnie. Fred said that she was too young to care for a child, so they would wait. They would grow together, learn to know each other. He wanted a dozen children.

If sex this great produced children, Minnie decided she wanted two or three dozen and told him so. He laughed and said he was willing to work on three dozen, but he wouldn't hold her to that number until after she had given birth to his first son. Minnie agreed to anything he wanted, as long as they could have sex again.

During Minnie's first visit to her childhood home, her mother said her cheeks were glowing. She made tea and treated her daughter like she was a guest. The recent Mrs. Hartman felt all grown up. Christina asked her what she planned to do with her days while Fred was at work.

Minnie couldn't mention how much fun she and Fred were having, or how sorry she was for all that her mother had missed. "Fred said I should enjoy my life, continue with my piano and singing lessons. He gave me money for a dressmaker. He liked the pink underwear you bought for me, Mama. Fred said we should wait a few years to start our family because I am too young."

"Fred is a wise man," Christina said. "Have you planted your garden? If you still like to eat, you should."

"I suppose I could have a garden. I'll ask Fred. He's taking me out to meet his friends this weekend. Mama, will you fix my hair?"

"Minnie, I may not always live this close. You must learn to braid your own hair."

"What are you cooking? It smells so good."

"Potato soup. What are you making Fred for his supper?"

"I suppose I must cook him some supper."

"Minnie, with marriage comes responsibility. You can no longer depend on me or Papa, or even your brothers or Caroline to do for you what you can easily do for yourself. Make a plan at the beginning of each day for what you can accomplish by its end. You must give a hundred percent of yourself in your marriage."

"If we are partners, I should give fifty percent."

"No," she said. "It doesn't work like that. You must be an asset to Fred."

An asset? Minnie wondered if her mother meant she was now something Fred owned. That couldn't be true. She could do anything she wanted. Fred told her she could.

The next few years were worry-free for Minnie. Fred showed her the vineyard where he worked. She learned to cook and packed delicious picnics for their long walks around the city. She felt proud to be on the arm of such a handsome man. Her life had changed for the better all because she had married Fred. And, being a married woman gave her so much more freedom than she had under the watchful eyes of her family.

One afternoon while Christina was helping her daughter hang laundry, she warned her that married women were not supposed to have sexual urges. Sex is something wives are expected to do, like laundry. She said husbands didn't like their wives to be aggressive.

Minnie changed the subject. The poor woman, she thought, and couldn't wait until Fred came home that night to prove her mother wrong. The couple never verbalized their sexual desires to each other ... he showed her and she followed. He taught Minnie to relax so she could have multiple orgasms. He guided her into new positions and introduced her to new potions ... like whipped cream and wild grape jelly. She complied willingly, often initiating new pleasures for him.

Minnie always watched for her husband around the hour he was to come home so she could surprise him ... sometimes with language a German whore would use, sometimes dressed in his clothes pretending she was the ice man there to screw his wife. "Since you came home early Herr Hartman," Minnie would say, "you might as well stick it to your wife, and if your cock is not too big, you can plug me as well. I'm too tired to plug you. I've been banging your wife all afternoon and I still have ice to deliver."

Fred didn't like Minnie playing a whore, didn't find the iceman charade so funny, and swept away any idea of his having sex with a man. All was forgotten and she was forgiven as they made love on the table, and with her sitting on him in his chair, and up against a wall with her legs wrapped around his waist.

When Minnie was too impatient to wait for Fred at home, she walked to the street corner and waited. When they met she told him she wanted a hug or she wouldn't be serving him supper when they got home. He gave her a peck on her cheek and started down the street without her.

"Fred, I want a proper hug." She stomped her feet and let her coat fall open to show him what she didn't have on. He rushed back, and with his arms inside her coat, hugged her properly and then carried her home to bed. They ate supper late that night.

Minnie also liked to surprise Fred when he came home from work by standing naked inside the front doorway. She would taunt him while he struggled to remove his clothes.

"Show me your manhood," she would say. "Quick. Show me your big cock!" She would tease him, "You call that a cock? That looks like a baby sausage."

"Think you can handle it, pretty lady?" Fred loved this game.

One evening when they had agreed to meet after work at a local café, Minnie arrived late, sat down and said, "Fred dear, I'm wearing nothing under my coat." She opened her lapel wide enough for him to see one bare breast.

Fred's eyes bulged. He jumped up, knocking the table over as he grabbed his wife and pulled her coat closed.

The waiter approached the overturned table. "Sir, will you be dining with us tonight?"

Fred gulped. "Not hungry. We're leaving."

The waiter, mystified, stepped aside while Fred escorted Minnie from the restaurant. Once outside, he threw her over his shoulder like a sack of potatoes and charged home, with Minnie laughing all the way.

Minnie wanted sex so often during the night Fred became exhausted. He joked that she had more stamina because she was ten years younger, and he was an old man and tired easily.

"Minnie, are you ovulating?" Fred finally asked. "That might be why you have made me your sex slave tonight. No. No, I'm not complaining. I'll show you how much I'm not complaining. Come to me Frau Nymphomaniac."

Minnie couldn't get enough of that man. When she asked for more he accused her of trying to kill him with sex and take all his money.

In her mother's day a wife's duty was to satisfy a man's sexual appetite and produce his heirs. No provision was made for the woman's pleasure. Women weren't supposed to ride bikes. Sitting astride a bicycle seat might cause an oversexed woman to have an orgasm.

Minnie thought if she had known how great sex was when she was a little girl she would have happily biked more often. After sex, Minnie always felt at peace. She was happier, and so relaxed she felt like dancing naked in a palace ballroom.

Minnie's mother told her that over the entire span of her life, sex was to be enjoyed only between her husband and her... ... no masturbation, no sex with other women, and absolutely no sex with a man other than her husband. She warned her that husbands could, and often did have multiple partners. She said Minnie must understand and accept this fact.

She warned her daughter that if a woman had sex outside of marriage, she would be considered ruined, a fallen woman, an adulteress who would at some juncture in her life meet a tragic end. She cautioned Minnie that if a woman was raped, she was still considered to be at fault and would be condemned. A husband could divorce his wife and live comfortably, but a woman who had no way of supporting herself would end up a beggar, a prostitute, or a corpse floating face down in the Warta. Divorce for women was a social taboo. "Minnie, you must remember, for men, infidelities are acceptable. The laws don't apply equally to women."

Minnie began to understand the embarrassment and fear that grew from people's sensual appetites. Fred said men talked to each another about sex, but Minnie knew women didn't get an equal education. Her girlfriends talked, but contributed little information she didn't already know. She didn't share the joys of her sex life with her old friends or with her mother because she felt guilty she was having so much fun. She could not have imagined then that sexual violence, verbal abuse, and economic deprivation were tools some men used to control women.

German laws dictated that the wife and any children became the property of the husband to do with as he pleased. He was responsible to provide for his family's care ... a roof over their heads and food on the table, but her body was owned by him.

Minnie's marriage followed these rules. Fred controlled all property, including Minnie's wedding dowry which had blossomed into something substantial over the years. Any possessions she inherited from her father legally became Fred's. Minnie's responsibility was housework and sex. She didn't like the rules, but she enjoyed sex too much to complain.

One warm July morning in 1873 while they were still in bed, Fred asked Minnie what she wanted to do for fun … take a picnic to a park by the river, or since it was so hot, go for a swim in the Warta. She told him she had never learned to swim and was afraid of drowning. Fred clapped his hands together. "That's what we will do. Today I will teach Frau Hartman how to swim."

He was pulling Minnie from bed when she told him she had a better idea. He sat beside her and listened as she explained she had been thinking it might be fun to make a baby. Fred agreed that making a baby trumped swimming in the Warta and came back to bed.

Minnie's mother knew she was pregnant before Minnie did. She saw that her daughter looked tired and gave her the job of plucking grapes from the stems. This could be done while seated as she made the grape jelly. Minnie told her mother that she had been sick every morning for the last week, stuck out her tongue for a her mother's evaluation, and asked if she would make her the tea she drank as a child for belly aches.

Christina laughed. "My sweet Minnie, you are being launched into another world, the next season of your life." She laughed again, and again.

"What's so funny?"

"You are. You are hilarious. Fred has been poking around in your cabbage patch for almost three years. I'm surprised you waited so long to become a mother."

"I'm pregnant?" Minnie stood and rubbed her stomach. "So this is what it feels like ... being tired and sick and bloated?" She told Fred that night. He was pleased and said his parents had been asking for a grandson.

The mother-to-be went into labor on April 14, 1874 at Fred's parent's tenement in the Wielkopolska region. She was nineteen, Fred twenty-nine. His mother hired a midwife to help Minnie with the birth of their first grandchild. The woman gave her Antelope-Sage Tea to ease the pain of childbirth and Wilhelm Frederick Hartman was born a healthy boy.

Jacob and Christina Hartman were delighted with their grandson, Wilhelm. The baby was a boy, and would carry on their family bloodline and name. Fred held his heir high for all to see, and told Minnie he was a lucky man. He thanked her for his son and kissed her tenderly. Karl's name or whereabouts never surfaced in conversations with Fred or his parents.

Christina Bublitz told her daughter that as long as she was nursing one baby she could not become pregnant with another, so in 1875 Fred and Minnie continued copulating. Wilhelm walked early and needed more substantial food than what Minnie could give him, so she augmented her breast milk with mashed potatoes. As a result, in 1875 she gave birth to Wilhelmina.

One day this little girl was an otherwise healthy baby with what seemed like a common fever. The next day she was fatally ill. At first Minnie couldn't believe her child had died. She kept touching her small body, trying to get her to respond. When there was no longer hope, she grew angry.

Fred folded the baby in her blanket and took her away. Minnie's mother arrived when she heard the news and heard Minnie praying, trying to make a deal with God. She was demanding her life be taken and the baby spared. Christina held her daughter to calm her. Fred could not understand the depth of her despair. His mother arrived and warned Fred not to leave her grandson alone with Minnie. "It is not uncommon for a woman experiencing postpartum depression to strike out or even kill a sibling."

Fred was afraid she might hurt herself and stayed by her bedside.

"No dear wife. You did nothing wrong. Yes Minnie, Wilhelm is a healthy little boy. He will not leave you. I will not leave you. You have nothing to feel guilty about. It was not your fault. Babies are born and babies die. It is a common occurrence that is tragic. Yes it is unfair. Yes dear, it is hard to understand the shift your stable life has taken. I know you had plans for your little girl ... expectations. You will adjust. You must. You have a son and a husband who need you."

Wilhelmina was their first girl and their second child at the time of her death. Fred convinced her it was better for a sick child to die young instead of suffering her entire life. Minnie moved on, busying herself with Wilhelm, her piano and singing lessons, her garden, and the housework, but her little girl was always there, lurking in the back of her mind, in her dreams.

Christina advised her daughter that too frequent impregnation was unhealthy for a woman and a reprehensible practice by a man. It was a sin, a great moral crime against a wife, and a crime against the other children in the family. Having a baby every year or even every two years should be prohibited. It was considered sexual slavery. So Minnie told Fred she didn't want to become pregnant again, but sex was still okay.

A movement to halt women's reproductive slavery became a popular topic during Fred and Minnie's bedtime conversations. She told him about the birth control movement and about voluntary motherhood. She quoted from the book her friends had read about family planning. "It is more moral to prevent the conception of children than to murder them after they are born by want of food, air, and clothing."

Fred decided he didn't want to be enlightened, and Minnie became pregnant again in 1878, the year of the Knowlton

Trial. Her friends gathered at her cottage to discuss current topics. While mending socks they learned Charles Knowlton was being prosecuted for publishing "Fruits of Philosophy," a volume explaining various methods of birth control. The book was pulled from bookshelves for being immoral, but the publicity from the trial only increased the sales. One of Minnie's friends bought a copy and read it to them as they stitched patches on their children's pants, sewed buttons on their shirts, and darned the holes in their socks.

Minnie surprised the women when she said she thought sexual desire was as strong in females as in males. One friend who had read some writings of a popular professor talked about Freud's belief that the whole notion of abstaining from sex was crazy. Freud said abstaining "did not help to build up energetic, independent men of action, original thinkers, or bold advocates of freedom and reform as once thought, but rather goody-goody weaklings." Minnie's friend said she thought Freud's theory also applied to women. Most of the women agreed, but one saw a flaw in Professor Freud's theory when applied to women. She called it a "lopsided law of nature."

The woman explained that a promiscuous encounter for a man could provide entertainment and relaxation for an evening. While most women enjoy the roses, the dinner and the sex, the females are the ones who carry home the results in their wombs the next day and for years after the birth. Females bear the children. They are responsible for the care of their spawn for the next twenty years.

All the women agreed that promiscuous women were at a disadvantage over their sexual partners. It wasn't fair, the women agreed, but it was what it was.

Shortly after Baby Gustav was born in 1879, Minnie fell into a serious case of postpartum depression. She was twenty-four. Christina poured what seemed to Minnie like buckets of chamomile tea down her throat to elevate her spirits followed by milkweed tea to stop her breast milk flow. Fred spent more of his off-hours at home to cheer her from her moodiness and to play with Wilhelm and Gustav. He took her out to see the new railroad station in Jezyce that took passengers all the way to Wroclaw in half a day.

Her husband finally allowed her to purchase a diaphragm made of vulcanized rubber in 1880. Soon after, Minnie became pregnant with Roelf. "I told you that diaphragm was a waste of money," he said. "You should listen to me, not your lady friends."

Baby Roelf was born hearty. Minnie's father said his howl could stir the dead beneath the old cathedral floors. Wilhelm, now six, was bored with his baby brothers. He spent a short stint kicking balls around the yard, and then a stretch in the afternoon climbing the trellis onto the roof and sliding down the thatch. Gustav was barely walking, but was curious about all things breakable. He threw toys into Roelf's crib, shook it to wake him, and then cried when the baby didn't throw them back.

Fred's parents were delighted with their third grandson. They told Minnie they were pleased Fred found a fertile woman who could bear him sons, and hoped his boys would measure up to the fine son they had produced. Fred was thrilled he now had three sons to carry on his name, and thanked Minnie for Roelf.

Minnie threw herself into women's work ... taking care of the children and becoming a homemaker and sex partner to her husband. She milked the cow and goat and churned their milk into butter and cheese. She planted and harvested potatoes and vegetables. Much of what she produced went for sale in her father's stall on Market Square. She collected goose and chicken eggs. She made sponge cakes from the eggs that didn't sell at market. This cake, her family's favorite, soon became a best seller on market day. While Minnie was kneading bread one day she found herself throwing balls of dough on the walls, the ceiling, and on the floor.

She stopped to catch her breath. The tedium of housework was driving her crazy. Her life had become like those dollops of dough stuck to the wall … all puffy and drooping. She watched the dough give way, slide down the wall, and fall to the floor. Minnie realized then that childcare and housework would be her job for life. It was her full responsibility to make a home for her husband and babes. It was what was expected of a wife, and the wife was expected to enjoy it. Minnie got up, gathered the pieces of dough from the floor and reassembled them into a loaf. She cleaned up her mess and started her next job with tears rolling down her cheeks.

The young wife preserved cucumbers from her garden in salt water, garlic, and horseradish root, and layered them inside a wooden barrel that stood outside their back door. She shredded cabbage into crocks for sauerkraut, picked up after the boys, and did the laundry. She made candles, sewed and patched clothing, and prepared fibers for weaving and knitting. Minnie decided she would be the best housekeeper, mother, and wife she could be since she would never be a princess or a queen.

Minnie should have been angry that women did not have the right to vote, own property or file suit in court at that period in Germany's history. But she was too tired to think of what was or what should be a woman's right. She crawled into bed beside Fred's warm body at the end of a long day and looked forward to a new twist in their remarkable sex life. One night he fed her chocolates during sex.

Peasants in their region revolted after major crop failures in 1877. A potato blight caused mass starvation. An insect pest that came from America on a steamship laid waste to the wine industry in much of Europe. The decade became one of social unrest. Tzar Alexander II was assassinated in 1881 and revolution swept the continent. When Chancellor Bismark and Kaiser Wilhelm took power, the German Confederation had thirty-eight separate states housing thirty-four monarchs, various duchies and grand duchies. The fiefdoms overworked and underpaid their peasant farmers. A fifth cholera pandemic wiped out entire villages in Europe. It was a dangerous age.

Leaders of failed rebellions fled for their lives, disappearing off German soil overnight. Some emerged in the Americas. Families agreed not to exchange letters because they might implicate and endanger those left behind. No forwarding addresses were given.

During and after 1880 the government of the United States sent agents to Europe to attract settlers. The lumbering industry needed workers. Companies sent free one-way tickets to strong men willing to work hard. Thus began a decade of migration of over six million Germans who landed in the United States. Most settled in the Midwest.

While all this was happening, Minnie was 'playing' house. She had Dembinski's piano moved from her parent's house to her own. She spent the greater part of her days with her boys outside planting and harvesting fresh vegetables to sell in Jacob's stall on Market Square. Fred allowed Minnie to use the extra cash she earned however she wanted. While the boys played outside in the afternoons, she could steal an hour for her music. She practiced scales, but stopped when she realized they were too much like housework. Instead she played the romantic nocturnes and sonatas Frau Dembinski taught her. Minnie's husband saw what he wanted to see. He said he was happy that she was happy, and then rolled over and went to sleep.

Fred arrived home late one night and announced they were moving to America. He was excited. They would have a new cottage near a beautiful forest surrounded by pristine lakes in a state called Michigan. A hundred one-way fares were being offered by a Michigan lumber company for men willing to work hard. And he was.

While Minnie served her husband venison stew with buttermilk dumplings, he explained to her that workers were needed in the forests near the village of Rogers City in Michigan. Fred said it would be a wonderful opportunity for the family. He said he would go first, work and save his salary until he had enough to pay the passage for her and his three boys. Minnie listened but said nothing.

She served him warm apple cake and was handing Fred his coffee when he pulled pamphlets from his pocket. One folded sheet was from an emigration agent and one was from the German American Steamship Line operating out of the port of Bremen. He told her the new steamships had become so fast that they were contracted by the English government to carry the Anglo-American mail. They crossed the Atlantic to New York in less than two weeks. Fred exhaled and said, "It's good to live in a modern world."

Fred read that the ships departed Bremerhaven on Tuesdays and Saturdays. "The new ship, the Warra, carries a full cargo, passengers and one cabin for a special passenger, or family." He winked and pulled Minnie to his lap.

"The ship makes a stop in Southampton, England to refuel and pick up the mail before crossing the Atlantic to New York harbor in America, our new world. Steamships travel at a record pace … sixteen to eighteen nautical miles per hour." Fred exhaled and said, "It's good to live in a fast world."

Minnie listened. She had heard about the Michigan wilderness and the dangerous natives who roamed the forests. She knew about the Lutheran families from Neuendettlau who had worked lumbering the Saginaw Valley since 1845 and were now farming land they owned. They had built a German community at Frankenlust with savings from logging the pine forests of Michigan.

Flattering accounts of life in this new world were published in newspapers throughout Germany. Fred sensed resistance in his wife, so he began a campaign to change her mind. He read about their new world to her after supper each night.

Emigration soon became a topic of disagreements in the Hartman household on what had become long, cold, sleepless nights. Fred argued a man had a chance in America. He could work, save his salary and buy a piece of land ... impossible if he stayed in Germany. In America his labor could build a life for him and his family, instead of working as a peasant in the dwindling vineyards of the landed old families. He argued their children would have a better life. Fred told her men from Neuendettlau, who had emigrated twenty years before, had earned enough to send for their wives and children and were now prosperous farmers. Poznan's streets were awash with talk of the Green Gold of America's Midwest pine forests.

She didn't believe a word of what he said. Minnie's best friend had already left by 1880 and was one of those settlers in Frankenlust. Minnie heard through her girlfriends that America was a wilderness, unpopulated except for savages. It was a desperate country without the civility of concerts, paved streets, or ancient buildings with columns and frescos.

Minnie knew if she was forced to leave, she could not take her piano. She would lose the magic needles of her favorite dressmaker. She would leave behind the intellectuals who had become her friends.

Rumors rained down. Indentured immigrants, who had borrowed passage fare, worked years in America to pay it back, and then worked even longer to send for their families. Some men sent money from America to wives unwilling to face the hardship of the trip. These women kept the money and remained in their villages. Their disappointed husbands were angry, but remarried in America and started second families.

There were also men who left and never sent for their families. Some immigrants ran out of money in New York where they were stuck and lived in squalor. Smart immigrants took enough money with them to pay their passage to the Midwest where they could work and buy farmland. Emigration agents saw opportunities and were doing a banner business.

Moving to America for Minnie would mean she would leave her family forever. It occurred to her that if Fred emigrated first he might find a better woman in America and abandon his family in Germany altogether.

She told Fred she wouldn't go. She told him if he loved her, he wouldn't ask her to leave her world.

Fred was dumbfounded. He said he thought she wanted a new life somewhere far from here. "That's what you said the day we were married."

She stomped her foot and repeated, "I refuse to go."

Fred stormed out the door without finishing his coffee.

Minnie's dream had been to marry into one of the cultured, old families of Poland, not spend her life in a wasteland. They argued.

Fred insisted … demanded she obey him. He shook her in frustration. He told her he was leaving for America with or without her and stormed from the cottage after slamming the door and scaring the children awake.

Minnie became afraid of what Fred might force her to do, and was no longer a willing sex partner. She grew morose, told Fred she felt trapped, that she would not go even if he sent tickets for her and the boys. She would find a way to stay … she had always found a way to get what she wanted. Minnie insisted her family stay in Poznan where her boys had been born, where her baby girl had been buried. She would stay. She said it had been a mistake to marry him. It was 1881 and Minnie was trapped. She would think of a way to keep her family together, to keep Fred here. She could be devious if she needed to be.

Fred came home from work one night smiling widely. He invited his little family to a park at the fork of the Warta and Cybina Rivers for a family outing the next day. Minnie was delighted. This was her fun-loving husband. This was the man who put his family first, the man who would never abandon her and sail off alone to another continent. She packed a picnic.

Frederick (Friederich) Hartman(n) born November of either 1844 or 1845 to Johann Hartman(n) and Christine Zerbin. Married Minnie Bublitz in 1871 in the Protestant community of Dabrowa Biskupia, at the time called Louisenfelde.

Chapter Three
THE SPLIT

When a barge docked near the park, Fred finished his coffee, stood and announced he was taking the small boat up the Warta, a larger ship up the Oder and a train across northern Germany to the Port of Bremen where he had booked passage to America. He told Minnie he would send for her and his boys as soon as he could. He kissed each on their foreheads. Minnie was so stunned she backed away and would not let him touch her.

"You must trust me, wife. I know what's best for all of us." Fred backed away.

Minnie couldn't catch her breath. His words were like a kick to her stomach. She felt that same desperate, abandoned feeling she remembered from when her father deserted her at Market Square; the frightening loss of esteem at being cast aside for something better; that sinking feeling that she was stranded with the full responsibility of her father's cart. Now she was left with the total responsibility of Fred's three sons. She glanced around the park. Was there a stranger here who would offer to help?

The boys were crying as they threw their arms around their father and begged him not to leave them. He forced one long passionate kiss on Minnie and told her she must trust him. As Fred Hartman disappeared into the crowd he was carrying nothing with him but her dowry money tucked into his boot.

Minnie's mood changed from panic to anger when she discovered Fred had taken all his savings, her dowry, plus the money she earned selling the potatoes she had grown. The man stole nine years of her profits from the vegetables, eggs and sponge cakes Papa let her sell at his stall. Tears spilled over her work-hardened hands clenched in fists in her lap. Her teeth ground from side to side. How would she live? She owed the dressmaker, the grocer, and Frau Dembinski, who had been instructed by her husband to charge for piano and singing lessons since she had married Fred. Minnie needed food for the children and a few morsels for herself.

She made some tea when she returned home and sat at her kitchen table to take inventory of her situation. She was almost twenty-four. She had three children to raise. She lived in a rented cottage but had no money to pay the rent or to buy food for her children. She made herself stop crying and drank the tea. She knew she could be resourceful. She would figure this out.

Her breasts were still firm despite the four children she had nursed. Her figure had returned after Roelf's birth. Her face was full, wrinkle-free except for the frown line that now cut between her eyes. Men still tipped their hats when they passed her on the street. How could Fred have abandoned her when so many men still found her attractive? The tears gushed out. She dried them on her apron and crawled into bed.

"I might remarry," she said out loud. No, she thought. Who would want a penniless woman with debts and three small boys? Must I become a prostitute to feed my children? Minnie feared her life was over and cried herself to sleep. Sunlight streamed through her window at the same time she heard her children stirring in their beds.

A stoic calm replaced what last night had been a disaster in Minnie's mind. Her children counted on her for breakfast. She would put them first. They relied on her for clean clothes and for all the hugs they needed to last them until bedtime.

She sat up straight. She was on her own. She could do this. Fred didn't take everything. She still had her brain. She would make a plan.

Her intention was to continue selling what she grew at her father's stand ... until the cold weather arrived. Then she could use the dozens of eggs her chickens laid to bake sponge cakes. Apples that dropped in her yard from the neighbor's tree could be used in strudel and sold with the cakes. And for a while her plan worked.

She was desperate for cash but too proud to ask for help from her parents, her brothers or anyone in Fred's family. She gathered coal that fell from rail cars each night to heat their small cottage. She took a chance and sold the rest of the black chunks of anthracite at the market. She grew frantic and stole more coal during the night from her neighbor's pile. She knew it was morally and legally wrong and could lead to her arrest. She was hoping the jails were heated as she loaded the lumps into her apron. Minnie was determined. Her children would not freeze. She thought a judge might understand as she stacked some of the chunks on the wagon she would push to the market the next day. She thought she could explain to the judge that she had no choice and felt certain he would let her go. She covered her loot with a quilt and slipped back inside and stoked up the stove before the neighbors or her children awoke.

There was no time for piano and singing lessons, for enjoying the color and texture of the cobbled streets, or watching the glow of the red tiled roofs at sunset. The young mother was too tired to remember the merriment she had once so enjoyed dashing in and out of courtyards near Market Square. She was angry at herself for what could have been had she waited for her parents to find her a decent man ... a man who would never abandon his family. She was spent from all the physical labor, so tired she fell asleep at the supper table. Wilhelm and Gustav grew wild when she had no strength to correct their misbehavior. She strapped Roelf to her back while she hoed weeds and planted seeds. Minnie missed the rejuvenating effect that sex with Fred had given her.

A letter came in the mail from New York. It was from Fred. She rushed it to her father so he could read it to her. Fred wrote that he had enjoyed the ocean voyage as he knew his family would, and had arrived in New York in good health. He had purchased three books in English at a shop on Worth Street just outside of the Castle Rock Immigration Center. He said he was determined to speak the language fluently, and wrote that Minnie should learn to read in English. He would keep the books safe for her. The titles were The Moonstone by Wilkie Collins, The Reproach of Annesley by Maxwell Ray, and Uncle Tom's Cabin by Harriet Beecher Stowe.

When her father finished reading the letter, Minnie was furious. She stomped her feet and cried, "Fred is buying luxuries with money I earned digging in the soil." She thrust her gnarled hands in her father's face. "Look! These are hands meant for the keyboard. My once long, tapered fingers are ruined, and it is all his fault."

Her father told her to stop acting like a spoiled child, returned her letter and went back to work selling his turnips.

One morning after breakfast she was removing dry laundry from where she had strung it over the coal stove to dry when she heard soft tapping on the front door. It was way too early for her mother's daily visit and she had stopped seeing friends. When she pulled the heavy door open, a soldier stood before her.

Minnie blinked, and he was still there, tall and handsome in his Prussian uniform. Kapitän Karl Hartman held his spiked helmet under one arm, leaned against the doorway, and grinned down at her. His scabbard glistened. His tall black boots sparkled in the morning light.

She was speechless, but managed somehow to pull away her babushka and shake out her red hair. The Kapitän took one of her chapped hands in his and pulled it to his lips.

He turned it slowly and with great tenderness kissed the calluses around her palm.

It was February of 1881. Fred had been gone over two months. The boys were playing outside and came running to see the soldier standing at their door. When Minnie told them he was their uncle, they climbed all over him. The second the soldier sat, Roelf crawled onto his lap to touch his mustache. They asked to wear his helmet. Wilhelm wanted to know how many soldiers he had killed with his sword, or if he used the spike on the top of his helmet to gore the enemy like a bull.

Minnie couldn't take her eyes off his handsome face. Karl seemed so natural with the children, easily enjoying all their attention, twining them around him and throwing them in the air.

She told him his brother had left them two months before. He had stolen their savings and had taken the barge to America. She told Karl she had decided to divorce Fred for desertion and start a new life in Poznan. It was a lie, but it felt like the right thing to say at the moment.

Her husband's brother gave her some gold coins so she wouldn't need to work so hard and promised to come back ... to see his nephews, and to see her. And he did. When Kapitän Hartman was off duty he spent his hours playing with the boys. He taught each of them to stand tall and march the slow goose step like proper Prussian soldiers. One night he surprised them with a puppy. Karl made them promise to feed the dog and to obey their mother like good soldiers. And Karl comforted Minnie.

"You must miss having sex," he said one evening after the children were asleep.

She nodded. If he only knew, she thought.

"Minnie, you should have been mine." He kissed her. "You know you broke my heart."

She nodded. "I made a terrible mistake, Karl."

He kissed her hard. "You could do something for me."

"What?" She had wanted to marry this man and have his children. She had wanted to have sex with this man since she was fifteen, and now he was there and they were alone. Her mind was in a whirl.

Her husband had abandoned her. She was lonely. She needed a man who could appreciate the depth of her needs and satisfy her cravings. Her children missed having a man in the house. She needed someone to pay the bills. She would do anything this man asked, if only he would stay with them.

Karl encircled her in his arms and untied her apron. As it fell to the floor, he unbuttoned her chemise. He kissed her eyelids. She couldn't move. A cold draft sent a shiver down her spine as she realized she was standing before her husband's brother ... naked. He led her to the settee.

"Lie down on your stomach," he said as he undressed, and entered her from behind. When he was spent he lay beside her, kissed her cheek, and without saying a word, went to sleep. She curled inside his arms and joined him in slumber. When she awoke, he had gone.

The next evening when Karl arrived he took her hand and pressed it to his lips. He folded her fingers around a small package. It was an opal ring. "This is for our special friendship," he said. The frown that the months of anxiety had etched into Minnie's forehead disappeared when he kissed her. She felt again like a woman desired by a man. Karl played with the children, swung them and tossed them in the air while she made supper. They squealed with pleasure. He helped her feed the boys and then helped put them to bed. She was relaxed after he comforted her that night, yet oddly unsettled.

During their sex the next night Karl placed a pillow over her face ... "so my whiskers don't scratch your beautiful skin," he said. Their love-making had turned into sex-making and had become rough. He hurt her. She cried out. He paused and told her if she wanted to experience the full extent of his ardor, to reach a passion peak of her own, it may hurt at first, but would be well worth the pain. He reached for a cigarette. He told her if he was too much for her, perhaps he had better go back to his regiment. He lit a match.

She blew it out. "Don't go." She said she would be fine. He left later that night, saying he had to get back to check on his men.

Minnie lay in her bed unable to sleep, thinking about her soldier and the pillow he put over her face. She missed looking into Karl's eyes as she had with Fred. She missed him looking into hers. She hadn't thought her lovemaking with Karl would be like this.

It occurred to her then that he might be attracted to her for something other than her beauty, perhaps he loves her … a refreshing thought, or was it? It occurred to her that he may just want the sex.

No, she thought. The man must be lonely. A man alone at his age without a wife to come home to must want a family. Karl needs her.

Minnie learned she was pregnant on April 12, 1881.

That same day a second letter arrived from America. She bundled the bag of potatoes she had dug from her garden and piled it on her wagon beside her three children and their new puppy. She tucked the letter in her apron pocket and pushed the wagon to the market where she would ask her father to read it to her.

Fred had booked passage for her and his three boys on the German American Steamship Line. The letter included travel instructions from New York to Michigan where he would be waiting. The ticket was good for one year. Ships to America left the Port of Bremen on Tuesdays and Saturdays. He wrote that they must depart Bremerhaven in April or May so they would arrive in late spring. He said when the workers come out from the woods after six months of hard labor, the celebrations could be rowdy and dangerous.

"Being without women for six months is hard on us all, but especially on me. You, my beauty, are the most desired woman of this humble lumberjack." Jacob Bublitz winked at his daughter after he read that line.

Fred wrote that he had arranged for a release from work to spend time with his family. He had reserved rooms at a boarding house near a lumber mill. He would wait for their arrival to choose the cottage his beauty wanted for her home. He closed his message saying he was eager to see them all. He sent his love, but reminded Minnie their passage cost him seventy-two dollars … three months of his hard labor. He claimed he was saving the rest of his salary to buy farmland. He said he earned twenty-six dollars a month."

"That's a good salary, Minnie," her father said.

She nodded an automatic yes, unaware at the moment how potatoes, men, and dogs would change her life forever. Jacob Bublitz refolded the letter, handed it to her, and went back to work selling vegetables.

That night Minnie screamed into her pillow until her throat was raw.

Another child? Karl's child? What would she do? Send the boys to America alone? No. They were too young. Too sweet. She would never see them again. Will Karl be pleased to be a father, to have an heir? Of course he will. He loves her. He loves the boys. But, does he want a family? Of course he does. Everyone wants a family. Does he want her? He says he loves her. He is generous … gives her jewelry. Would he agree to raise his brother's boys? He says he loves them. Could he support her with four children?

If she was wrong and Karl didn't want an heir, didn't want a family, and no longer wanted her, what would she do? What if he was sent off to fight and was killed in battle? How could she take care of four children when she could barely take care of three?

What about Fred? If she had this child, Fred would have the right to divorce her, throw her and her bastard child out on the street. How would she be treated as a divorced woman? Would Fred take Wilhelm, Gustav and baby Roelf from her if they divorced? The law said he could.

She would be breaking the social code if she had this child outside her marriage. With no children and no income, how could she survive with an infant? What should she tell Karl?

She didn't tell him anything. A sealed envelope arrived by mail. "Ma, it's from Uncle Karl. I can read it for you."

"Received orders to move regiment at once. Will return two to three months. Until then, my *liebling*."

"Ma, why is Uncle Karl calling you his sweetheart?"

Minnie had no suitable answer for that, so she offered none and continued washing their socks.

She knew her parents and brothers had been disgusted with her for refusing to go to America with Fred. They were upset she had originally agreed to marry Karl and were aghast when she settled for Fred. They had been counting on the prestige a better match would have on their family. Her father sputtered, "At least Fred is a better man than his brother." Minnie decided she could no longer delay telling her mother she was pregnant. Christina's eyes widened and targeted Minnie.

"My daughter, an adulteress?" Her voice dropped to a whisper. "You are ruined. You have ruined this family. What will your Papa say?"

"Don't be so harsh with me, Mama. I was so unhappy. Being without a man for me is like living without sunshine."

Christina mumbled with her head in her hands. "My daughter is a fallen woman."

"Mama, what can be so wrong with me enjoying the warm body of a man lying with me at night? That pleasure takes the edge off what I suffer all day ... the children's endless squabbles, the shortage of food for their meals, and the back-breaking work I must endure every day. You have no idea how hard it has been for me since Fred abandoned me. What can be better than having a strong man bring fresh meat to my table, and share his tenderness with me at day's end? He brings me flowers. I feel like a woman again, not a workhorse."

"Minnie, stop. I brought you up better than that."

"Mama, all the feelings that come from kissing ... what about them? You must have felt them with Papa. You know how these forces cause every part of a woman's body to cheer up. They make the numbness of the unending work, the tedious days go away. Sex wakes up my body, lifts my spirits, and puts me in touch with me."

Christina turned her head away.

"Mama, these are yearnings every woman has. They are natural. How could such honest feelings make me a bad person? I am good. I hurt no one. I still love Fred and my children. I work hard every day to provide for them. I would die for them. I honor you and Papa. I walk with dignity. I help others when I can. I just want to feel good, too."

"You do not honor your husband when you have sex with another man."

"This is not about Fred. It's about me. Mama, the Lutheran church teaches us that we must love all mankind. I have so much love in me, I can love Fred, I can love my three boys, and I can love Papa and my brothers. I still have enough love left inside me to love another man."

"That's not what loving mankind means, Minnie."

She told her mother that Fred had taken all their money. "I worked so hard to please him. I bore four of his children. I lost my only baby girl. I have kept my sons healthy all these years. I keep a clean home, grow a bountiful garden and feed my family the best food. Why would a man leave a good woman like me?"

"Why didn't you go with him?"

"He said he was leaving to make a better life. I've heard stories that plenty of men grow tired of their families, travel the world for adventure, and start new families over there. He will never return to us."

"Your papa told me he sent you a ticket. Minnie, your husband is a good man. How could you?"

"I told Fred I liked our life here in Poznan. I didn't want to live in a primitive country with wild men running around the forests shooting their arrows. How could Fred expect me to leave this ancient city with so much history and so much beauty? I know the streets. I love this city. And besides, you and Papa live here. I would miss never seeing you again. It is impossible to respect a man who asks a woman to give up her life. Yet, I do still love my husband."

Mama grimaced. "Minnie, you can't love two men at the same time."

"Why not? I have loved Fred for the past nine years. I will always love him. I also love another man, a wonderful man who loves me. I must trust him to take care of my children if Fred won't. I must trust Karl to marry me."

"Karl Hartman?" Christina's eyes flashed danger. "Fred's brother is the father of this infant growing inside you? Oh Minnie, what have you done?" She stood, removed a bottle of her potato vodka from the sideboard and poured herself a glass. She was quiet while she sipped her drink.

In time she said, "Minnie, without a legal separation from Fred, you can never marry Karl. Fred's brother must have known this unless he is stupid as well as cruel. You will never get a divorce because you have no cause. Papa was right about soldiers … love a woman, bed a woman, leave a woman. Can't you see that man is using you for his own pleasure? My little Minnie, I didn't raise you to be a *dummes Huhn,* a stupid chicken."

"Mama, you're wrong. Karl loves me."

Jacob Bublitz looked sad when he came home and found his wife crying. "No Christina, that is not a good idea. No, Christina, we cannot raise another child. I will not pretend the baby is mine. I am too old. This is Minnie's problem." He wouldn't speak to Minnie, but she heard him tell her mother, "Karl Hartman will be the death of our little girl."

Two months after Fred's letter and the ticket arrived, his brother reappeared at her door with a wrapped haunch of fresh venison over one shoulder and a bottle of wine under his arm.

The handsome Kapitän Hartman played with her boys while she roasted the meat with juniper berries, carrots and parsnips. She was so happy to see him. After dinner she sent her sons next door to stay the night with playmates. Karl approached her from behind and wrapped his arms around her.

"You are so beautiful, Minnie. Have you missed me?" She turned and melted into his arms. "You have stolen my heart, again. I have something for you." He kissed her and clasped a chain around her neck. She fingered the small gold cross hanging from the chain and thanked him with a kiss.

"The thought of making love to you has kept me alive these long months." He unlaced her camisole with one hand and pulled it down around her waist. He stroked her breasts. "During the last battle," he said as he kissed her ear and invaded her ear canal with his tongue, "my men's frozen bodies lay around me."

Minnie felt a sudden shiver as his hand slid into her pink bloomers.

"I told myself that if I lived through the night," he said and pinched her nipples, "I was meant to be with Minnie." Both his hands moved down. She heard the rustle of her petticoats as they fell to the floor. "I love you not only for what you are to me, but for what I am when I am with you."

Minnie had no idea what the man meant by that, but she didn't care … she yielded. His mouth covered hers as his tongue followed the line of her lips and then dipped deep down into her throat. She felt his hand untie her bloomers. "You are so beautiful," he whispered.

She felt her underwear slip down her bare legs. The force of his pelvis against her took her breath away. His hand moved inside her thigh. She felt his warm breath as his head moved down her torso. And then his tongue … "Oh, my," she said.

He straightened and she felt him fumble with his breeches, his chest holding her upright. Her back was cold against the door planks, her nipples erect. Her head was swimming as he ground his pelvis into her.

"You want me," he said, and without waiting for a reply lifted her legs and wrapped them around his naked waist. "I am much better equipped than my brother to give you a fuck you will remember."

She could not answer him. His mouth covered hers, his tongue exploring inside her cheeks, a distraction as his member slid inside her lonesome cabbage patch. She heard a moan of desire, and realized it was hers. Waves of pleasure overtook her. She used a technique for delaying pleasure Fred had taught her until she could no longer control her passion and lightning shot through her body.

"Hold on to me," Karl said.

She could feel his penis still inside as he moved her to the kitchen table. He laid her flat. She was shivering with excitement, on the brink of exploding again when he slowed to a stop.

"More. Please Karl. More."

He moved her legs up and locked her knees over his shoulders, and then plunged deeper inside her than anyone ever had before. He didn't stop when she again shuddered with pleasure.

"We lost so many men during that battle … " he said while his hips shoved his penis inside her, over and over, again and again, "and I refused to die because I needed this, I wanted you." He clutched her buttocks with both hands as a stack of dishes fell from the table, shattering, startling her.

"Karl, you're hurting me."

He pulled out, spun her over on her belly, spread her legs and entered her anus.

"Ow! Please stop."

"You love this. Don't tell me you don't." He reached around to her breasts and pinched her nipples.

"That hurts. I'm begging you. Please stop."

"Pain can only heighten a woman's pleasure. Relax and climb higher with me, *liebchen*." He plunged deeper. "I don't want you to ever forget me."

"Karl please stop. You're hurting me," Minnie looked back at Karl and saw the fire had gone out.

"I'm almost there, my pet," he said pumping harder and deeper inside her opening, unaccustomed to this novel invasion. She felt something explode within her and then suddenly the Prussian officer slumped and slid out of her. He stumbled backwards to her window seat and stretched out on the pillows her mother had given her as a wedding present, his trousers still around his ankles. Kapitän Hartman's head tipped to one side as his snoring soared and filled every corner of her cottage.

Minnie washed herself, splashed water on her face then fumbled around the darkened room until she found her clothes. She lit a lantern and swept the broken china into the dustbin. She had to stop and rest … her bottom and her cabbage patch were both stinging. She checked the towel she had used to dry herself. It was streaked with blood.

Karl Hartman wasn't the gentle teacher and playful lover that his brother had been. He was vigorous and forceful. He invaded her like she was a military objective, and wouldn't stop until his mission was completed. She wondered then if all soldiers were so self-directed. His snoring stopped.

"Come to me, Minnie," she heard him say in the dark.

"I'm looking for my chemise," she said.

"No. I want to see you naked."

She approached him with apprehension. He pulled her down into his arms and stroked her breasts. Sensing her hesitation, he hummed to her, sang a song … something about a soldier marching off to war.

"Are you content, my love?" He slid his hand between her legs and held her cabbage patch. "Am I not the greatest lover you have ever had?" He licked the tip of her nipple, and then sucked on it until she became aroused, again, and squirmed. "Am I not a better lover than my brother?" He leaned down and licked something between her legs until she shuddered with delight. "Minnie?"

She couldn't speak.

"Minnie, would you like more? Take my cock in your mouth and suck until I am hard. I promise you I will drive you to an even higher ecstasy."

"No," she said.

"Then what do you want, my sweet?"

"You hurt me, Karl. You made me bleed." Karl's sex fell short of the love-making she had experienced with her husband.

"Fred left you. I'm here. Great passion like ours must mix with great pain to attain the peak of pleasure."

"I felt the pain. You felt the pleasure."

"You will heal, *liebchen*, and you will remember the joy of this night. Can you reach my cigarettes?"

Minnie found a matchstick, and handed it to him.

"This wine," he said, pouring himself another glass, "was for our farewell dinner. My entire regiment is being sent to Russia, again."

She stifled a scream.

Karl's hand located the correspondence from America lying on a side table. "This must be from my brother." Karl held his cigarette between his teeth as he pulled up his trousers and moved to a chair by the lantern. He read the letter addressed to Minnie and turned the ticket over in his hand. He sat there, smiling widely, clearly relieved. "I'll keep the envelope so I have your address in America. I might decide to pay my brother a visit." As he reached for his uniform jacket Karl said, "He is a good man, my brother."

Minnie watched her lover stand and put on his jacket. His attention was focused on fastening the scabbard to his belt. He asked to be remembered to Fred when Minnie joined him in Michigan. Karl looked up and wished Minnie a safe voyage, clicked his heels together, bent over like a gentleman and kissed her hand. Kapitän Karl Hartman walked out the door and, she thought, out of her life.

Minnie could not walk for two days and could not speak for three.

She was not angry with Karl. What good would that do? She sat at the kitchen table thinking the soldier had been an education for her in misjudging men, so much more important to her future than learning to read or write. Her mother had been right. Karl had been using her. Her father had been right. Karl wanted what his brother had. Fred had been right when he told her his little brother stole the nice things he had without asking and never gave them back. But Fred was wrong on one count. Karl was giving her back.

Minnie took stock. She was not a good listener. She had broken her promise of fidelity to her husband. She was an adulteress. She was pregnant with a child who would be forever stigmatized as a bastard. She was the sole support and caregiver for three healthy boys and the unborn child inside her. She could no longer expect support from her parents, brothers, or older sister. She alone would take care of her needs and those of her children.

She had to be strong and decisive. She made a cup of tea and studied the patterns on the tablecloth while she weighed her alternatives.

As a woman seeking a divorce in Germany in 1881, she would have to appear before a civil law judge. Rape was not an acceptable reason for granting divorce. But if the husband was found to be cruel, the divorce would be granted. Karl had not raped her and Fred was not cruel. How could she prove to a judge that her husband had abandoned her and her children when so many men were emigrating from Germany to North America for honest work? It was widely understood they would send for their families when they could afford the ticket. And she had that steamship ticket for America.

If she could convince a judge to grant a divorce, she would be a free woman, but would be single with four children without the liberty to travel unaccompanied by a man. She would be digging an even deeper ditch for herself.

The law held that any children under seven remain with the mother if a divorce was granted and if the woman had the means to support them. She could never support four children by selling vegetables on Market Square. She would lose Wilhelm and Gustav to an orphanage until Fred could come back to Germany to claim them, if he would. The law would find that any property she brought into the marriage in the form of land, investments or dowry would remain the property of Fred Hartman. Minnie would be left homeless and with no way to support Roelf and the new baby except with her meager earnings from selling potatoes.

There must be another way ... if she could only think clearly. She could write Fred and delay their departure until after the baby was born which would be in mid-December, 1882. That would give her time to travel to Switzerland, give birth, give the child away, and collect the boys all within the one year the ticket covered. Fred would never have to know. But, where would she find that much money? Her jewelry?

No, not enough. Savings? Gone in Fred's boot. She barely had enough to feed and clothe her little burdens.

Morning sickness weakened her ability to think logically. She asked her midwife if she knew where she could get an abortion.

"Minnie, that's against the law."

"It seems to me abortions are the only way to control unwanted births," she said.

"Listen to me," the woman said. The midwife explained that abortion had been deemed immoral by the Catholic Church after the Black Death killed more than half the population of Europe from 1346 to 1353. The church outlawed contraception, abortion and infanticide in an effort to repopulate the region.

"I could be arrested." In the 1400s, witch hunts were instigated for women dispensing contraceptive herbs or performing abortions. The male population went along with it because they were led to believe witches had powers to cause a man's penis to dry up and fall off. Women found to be witches were tortured until they would admit to anything and then be put to death.

"Abortion has continued," her midwife said, "regardless of the consequences. Silphium, an herb from North Africa, priced above gold, was overused until it became extinct. Silphium was replaced by asafoetida, a similar plant with a similar result ... aborting a fetus. Queen Anne's Lace, willow, date palm or pomegranate would successfully abort a fetus if used as a tea. Pennyroyal, artemisia, rue and myrrh were also used. But the herbs didn't always work, and when not mixed precisely, they poisoned the mother.

"There is a woman I know in Poznan," the midwife said. "Before the time of quickening, this woman will use herbal remedies like Pennyroyal oil, catnip, rue, sage, savory, cypress or hellebore to abort a baby. If none of them work, she will try thyme, parsley, lavender, tansy, savin juniper, or worm fern.

Prostitutes have used this worm fern, called prostitutes' root, to end their pregnancies for centuries. Odd remedies like camel saliva or deer hair are sometimes used. Iron sulfates, chlorides, hyssop, dittany or opium are others. Madder in beer, watercress seeds, and even crushed ants are used. But the herbs most frequently used and readily available here are tansy and Pennyroyal. All of these substances are dangerous. Of last resort," she said, "a woman wanting to abort a fetus could try violent kneading and beating.

"It has happened that this woman's patients bleed out. She calls them unlucky. Minnie, if you died, who would care for Wilhelm, Gustav and Roelf?"

The midwife told her if she had the money she could travel to Switzerland, deliver the child, and leave it there for adoption. Many young girls from families with means returned home after a year in Switzerland as renewed virgins. Is that an option for you?"

"No. I don't have the money."

"In Muslim countries, if a girl or woman gets pregnant before or outside her marriage like you have, her father and brothers have the right under the law to make her watch as they bury her newborn alive. They also have the right to behead the mother since she has brought shame on the family."

"That would be murder."

"Not in some cultures," the midwife said. "It's called honor killing. If your fetus grows full term here in Germany, infanticide after birth can be used as a last resort, but under our law it would be considered murder and you would be hung."

When the children were in bed, Minnie strode to the address the midwife had given her with clashing emotions. It was on a shadowy street on the edge of the city and Minnie would much rather have wanted to be tucked safely in her own bed. She was keeping close to a building to avoid a puddle when two men stepped from a darkened doorway and blocked her.

She was done for until she heard, "Minnie?" She stopped shaking when she recognized her older brother's voice. "Come," he said, and with a brother on each side, Minnie was escorted to the cottage she shared with the babes that needed her alive. She never discovered how they learned of her plans. They promised they would not tell her parents if she agreed to join Fred in America. Trapped with no alternative, she promised, and they left her alone with her ragged thoughts.

The next few weeks were a whirlwind of activity. Minnie's mornings were spent with her head over a commode, and her afternoons testing her organizing skills. She had the boys vaccinated, folded their records and sewed them into the lining of her coat. She checked with a shipping agent for the barge schedule down the Warta and for the earliest departure date from Bremen. She had Wilhelm pen their names on the cardboard ID tags each child was to wear. She added a string that would hold the tags around their wrists. She sewed a copy of the ID tag along with Fred's address into the lining of the boys' coats. Birth certificates, vaccination records, and baggage labels were folded into the lining of her purse. She sewed all the German gold coins Karl had left for her, including the jewelry into the hem of her coat.

When Minnie told her mother she was leaving, Christina gave her a small brooch that had been her mother's, and a small family daguerreotype on a silver-plated sheet of copper. Jacob gave her smoked sausages and rye bread for the trip. He offered some traveling advice. "Do not draw attention to yourself. Cover your hair." Her older brothers told her not to smile or speak to anyone unless it was absolutely necessary, gave her a hug, and went on with their busy lives.

She sorted their belongings and gave the neighbor whose coal she had stolen all that was left. Her father promised the boys he would look after their dog. She packed their clothes, the rye bread and the sausages in four suitcases, one for each of the boys and one for her.

Minnie's parents insisted on walking the sad little group to the fork of the Warta and Cybina Rivers where the travelers stepped on the same barge that Fred had taken over a year ago. Minnie said farewell to her mother, her father, her brothers and Caroline. She knew she would never see them again.

This is the earliest picture I have of Fred, (second from right) He may have worked for a company that processed fish in Port Hope. I found this undated photograph in the family photo box on the Hartman Homestead. It is in bad shape, probably the oldest photo we have.

The North German Lloyd Steamship Line's Werra I left the Port of Bremen in Germany on October 12, 1882 on her maiden voyage. Captain Richard Bussius was at the helm.

This photo is representative of common conditions aboard immigrant ships of the era. Photo by Bryon, 1893.

Chapter Four
THE SEA

It was October, 1882. The barge drifted on the slow currents of the Warta and the Oder for a full two weeks before Minnie and her band of little boys disembarked. They took a train across northern Germany to the North Sea harbor at Bremen where Minnie learned their departure to America would be delayed. She found a small room where she could rest and the boys could roam and keep out of her hair. Her morning sickness left her too underpowered to move from the bed or leave the room until midday. She paid for the room with the black pearl ring Karl had given her ... for his friendship. The landlady complained about the boys. She said they were all mischief and audacity. Her complaints added headaches and more worry to Minnie's misery.

During the afternoons when she felt sturdy, she took the boys exploring. They threaded their way through the crowds, her boys holding hands and trailing behind her. She pointed out the welding workshops, the steam laundries, the bakeries, and the kinds of shops that would supply the essentials for their trip. A sailor told her boys the ship line employed at least a thousand men. They passed black pyramids of coal that fueled the ocean-going steamships. A seaman who had been following them told Wilhelm the German American Steamship Line used 750,000 tons of coal a year, then grinned at Minnie and asked if she would have a drink with him.

The shipping company used Dresden and Gera class steamships that also used sails to catch the wind. They hauled freight and passengers. When their large cargo holds were not completely full, they stuffed them with steerage passengers to make up for lost income.

The next Tuesday was their scheduled departure date. They boarded the steamship Warra. Instead of the cabin set aside for that "one special passenger" or family that Fred had hinted would be theirs, she learned their tickets put them in steerage. They would be crowded into one common compartment with as many as three hundred other passengers.

Minnie backed away, deciding to go home to Poznan, give up her children and face life as a prostitute. She turned to leave when a man in a ship's uniform blocked her and stood staring down at her. What did he want? Did she drop something? She felt for each of the gold looped rings dangling from her earlobes. She had not lost either one. Her boys were tugging at her skirt. They were excited at being on a real ocean-going steamship. She looked up to question the man.

He smiled, his eyes traveling from her face down to her feet and back up to her eyes. "This way, Frau," said the ship's steward in perfect German. "My name is Heinz. I hope you have a pleasant crossing."

She realized she could not escape ashore with this man blocking her. Her smile dismissed the sailor. Heinz watched her turn and step back into line.

He was mesmerized by this red-headed beauty. He would keep an eye on her and her children during the crossing. She would need his help before the trip was over. And she would not turn away from him again.

Minnie and the boys moved from one long line to another even longer line while stewards divided steerage passengers into three classes, women without male escorts, men traveling alone, and families with children. Heinz nodded toward the line the family should follow. The line would take them to the compartment for "women without male escorts." She thanked him in Polish and climbed down a staircase that was so steep it should have been called a ladder.

Each class of passenger was housed in a separate compartment in different sections of the vessel. Theirs was dark and stuffy. Long rows of gray bunk beds were crammed with bags and bundles, the only storage space allowed. An occasional foot or arm hung loose from bunks draped in towels and blankets for privacy. If these conditions were any indication of what their future in America would be, she thought perhaps it was still not too late to go ashore or better yet, throw herself overboard into the sea. When she felt the engines sputter and start, she knew it was too late, and took a deep breath … her last clean air for the next seventeen days.

Minnie thought at first it was the closeness of the vessel walls that made her head spin. Space, she decided, was a universal human need. So were air, food, sleep and privacy. All were spare on board the Warra, but at least they were provided. Beyond these minimums, passengers were looked upon as so much freight with mere transportation as their only due.

The ship furnished steerage passengers eating utensils but required each person to retain them throughout the voyage. After each meal most people raced to the one spigot of warm salt water to rinse their plates and cups.

Minnie thought her discomfort might be caused by the stench from the other passengers crowded together in an area the size of the tiny cottage she had left behind in Poznan. The iron floors were continually damp. The wood floors reeked with a foul odor. She never saw them mopped. All the flooring was swept with brooms. Occasionally the process was repeated as an excuse for a steward to appear below decks to sell extra food for his personal profit.

Her urge to vomit could have been a result of her condition. The sickness was debilitating, but not as hard on her body as the anxiety that consumed her about Fred's reaction to his brother's baby growing inside his wife. No sick cans were furnished, nor were large receptacles for waste.

The vomitings of the seasick were often permitted to remain before being removed, causing Minnie reoccurring bouts of nausea.

Ventilation was inadequate in the limited space below deck. The stench and filth made the trip almost unendurable. Lack of fresh air affected everyone's health. When her mind was clear enough to think, she was afraid for the boys. They were vulnerable to measles, cholera, and diphtheria … all diseases hibernating in the crowded conditions of steerage. She was afraid her unborn child would be affected. She had seen the results of children born in squalor … sometimes with enlarged heads, sometimes without hands or feet … pale, fragile.

The women around her berth coughed. They wheezed. She could hear them regurgitating the meager portions they were served on deck. They may have been vomiting from seasickness, but Minnie knew it was from the bad food.

She lay in her berth in a stupor. Foul gases had replaced the oxygen that should have been in the air she was breathing. The boys appeared at her side with the ship's doctor and Heinz, the steward who had helped her find their berths. The doctor examined her. He told her that passengers who made a practice of staying on the open deck felt better. Their new friend, Heinz, was behind Minnie as she climbed the steep staircase. When she stumbled, he caught her in his arms and carried her up the rest of the way. He didn't say a word as he set her on her feet, just tipped his head, made a slight bow and walked away.

"Ma, isn't Heinz a grand man?," Wilhelm said. "I was afraid for you, afraid you would fall down and hurt yourself." Minnie hugged her firstborn son to her side. "I think Heinz is a kind man. And he's strong. When I grow up I want to be just like him."

The contrast between air out-of-doors and that in the compartment was life-saving. The next day Minnie asked the boys to fetch Heinz. He grinned when he saw her sitting up and

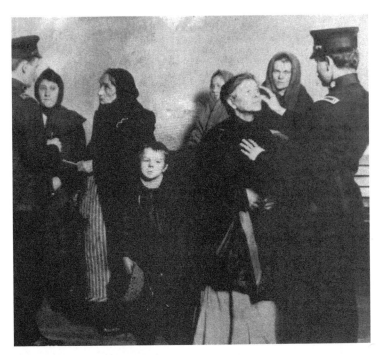

Steerage passengers aboard the Werra stood in line for meals. They stood in a line to use the single spigot of salt water authorized for their use. They stood in line to use the latrine. And when they arrived in the New World, they were herded into lines to be examined by doctors, by immigration agents and by custom officials.

Now discredited, eugenic beliefs played a role while doctors were examining immigrants for tuberculosis, cholera, trachoma and diphtheria. Procedures included the use of metal calipers to measure the circumference of immigrants' heads. Those of "superior racial stock" were often favored when entering the United States. Those who failed the caliper test were detained for mental illness and placed in the hospital's psychiatric ward. Many of these immigrants were not mentally ill. Cultural differences, the language barrier, and the immigrants' anxiety could have made them appear mentally ill.

announced the frau's coach had arrived. The boys giggled and asked if they could ride in their mother's coach. He promised to give them a ride once they were on deck. Heinz picked Roelf up and set him on his shoulders and escorted Minnie to the landing where, with great drama, he swept her into his arms. He carried the young mother all the way up the staircase with Roelf perched on his shoulders and Wilhelm and Gustav climbing at his sides. When Minnie was set down on deck, and Roelf slid from his shoulders, she was the one to bow and thank Heinz.

Minnie now found it impossible to remain below for more than a few hours each day. Her discovery was no secret on board the Warra. The open deck was always full long before daylight by those who could no longer endure the foul air below.

The crew had missed seeing the beautiful redhead from steerage standing in the food line with her sons. When Heinz asked the boys about their mother, Wilhelm told him she was too dizzy to make it up the staircase and too sick to come on deck to get fresh air. Heinz recognized this as a normal indication of seasickness. He reported Minnie's condition to the Captain, who sent the ship's doctor below to examine her. The doctor reported that Frau Hartman was both seasick and pregnant. After that, when Wilhelm appeared in the food queue the ship's cook would let him come to the head of the column of hungry passengers to get food for his mother. The cook would announce at each meal that the boys' mother was so seasick she couldn't get her own. Heinz stopped down to check her progress. Minnie was too weak to move.

The open deck available to steerage passengers was limited, and used mainly for eating. During storms the unprotected open deck could not be used at all, limiting the steerage passengers to their berths.

Minnie's boys explored the ship. Wilhelm was a handsome child. His blue eyes flashed out from curling lashes. His ivory skin was like his mother's, but his curls were blond, like Fred's, and floated like a cloud next to his pale brows. Gustav was good at following instructions but mischievous. Heinz kept him busy running errands until the boy came back with pockets of stolen trinkets. Heinz made him backtrack and return them all. Roelf had high cheekbones and the fire of passion in his eyes. He was afraid of nothing.

The crew got to know the Hartman boys and enjoyed their antics until the day that Roelf fell from the rail he was swinging on toward the foaming Atlantic. Wilhelm caught his younger brother's coattail, then his arm, all the while screaming for help in Polish. A crewman pulled Roelf to safety and scolded him in German for playing on the rail.

The crewman started in on Gustav, who had been watching, when Heinz interceded. The steward explained that the child's mother was so seasick in the hold she couldn't watch her children. Heinz comforted the frightened children and sang them a song in Polish that Roelf recognized at once. Their father had sung the same song to his sons so they would never be afraid to ask for help.

"Passing policeman found a little child. He stepped up beside him, wiped his tears and smiled. He told him kindly, now you must not cry for I will find your mama for you by and by."

Heinz started the second verse. "At the station waiting for the little boy ..." but couldn't remember the rest. The lyrics were in a book in his cabin. He told the boys he would look up the words, and when he saw them again he would sing the whole song. By that time Roelf and Gustav had stopped crying and Wilhelm was smiling again.

The boys took Heinz by his hands, and climbed down the staircase to the steerage compartment for "unaccompanied women." Minnie's sons led the steward to her iron bunk where he leaned in and took her pulse. Even though he was not a doctor he could tell a fast pulse from a normal one. He thought to distract Minnie with tales of his home in Stuttgart and assured her he would keep an eye on her rambunctious sons.

When Minnie had a good day and had help up the stairs, she sat on a bench on deck and let the salt air blow the stench from her hair. She avoided the glances of others. She wore that flat look of utter exhaustion, yet men still stopped as they approached her, and tipped their hats. When she showed no interest they continued on their way.

The ship's food was of fair quality and sufficient in quantity, yet usually spoiled by being wretchedly prepared. The disregard for providing the several food groups required by the human body made the food unsatisfying. Bread, potatoes, and meat, when not leftover from the first and second class galleys, formed a fairly substantial diet. Coffee and tea were invariably bad. Milk was supplied for small children.

When baby Roelf cried from hunger Minnie brought him to her bunk, kissed his eyes and forehead, and then surveyed him at arm's length. She beckoned the steward that was sweeping the floors to come to her berth. She showed him the cross that lay on her breast, the gold cross … the one Karl had given her. She pointed out its intricate workmanship. He agreed to trade the gold cross for bread and fresh milk for her children. Roelf gobbled his down while he sat beside Minnie. She called to Wilhelm who, with a shrug of a shoulder and a dramatic gesture of his small, grimy hand, walked to Minnie's berth, took the bread and gulped down the milk. Gustav ate his share willingly and asked for more.

Seasickness did not qualify a steerage passenger for admittance to the ship's infirmary. Since this was the most prevalent ailment among the passengers, not one thing was done for either the comfort or convenience of those suffering. Passengers ill in their berths received only such attention as the mercy and sympathy of their fellow travelers supplied.

The congestion in steerage was so intense, so injurious to all their health and morals that there was nothing on land to equal it … they thought. The crossing held an abundant opportunity to weaken the body and implant germs of disease to develop later.

Sleeping was all Minnie was good at doing, yet when a child shrieking in German for a glass of water awoke her, she spent the next few hours staring at the wood slats of the mattress above. She listened to a mother too sick to comfort her child and heard a fellow passenger murmuring to the baby boy, sharing her own cup of water, then soothing the child until he fell asleep. She sensed the mother was unable to acknowledge this kindness from another passenger because her head was over a pail. The stench was unbearable.

The berths were in two tiers, with an interval of two and a half feet of space above each. They were six feet long and two feet wide, a total of thirty cubic feet. It included all the room a steerage passenger had. No space was designated for hand baggage. The cots consisted of an iron framework containing a mattress and a pillow. The boys' berths held a life-preserver but no pillow. They were all given a blanket which was far from adequate in size and weight, even in the summer, so they slept almost fully dressed to keep warm. Minnie's mattress was stuffed with straw and covered in coarse canvas, and her pillow was filled with seaweed.

A piece of iron piping placed at a height where it would separate the mattresses was the partition between berths. The woman to her left snored and tossed in her sleep. During the day she stayed in her bed. So did Minnie. They were both too sick to maneuver up the steep staircases to the fresh sea air on deck. Through the entire voyage, seventeen days, the berths received no attention from the stewards.

Since the boys preferred sleeping together, Minnie packed their bags and bundles in a berth between her and the poor woman sleeping beside her. There were no hooks to hang clothing, so the boys tossed their jackets and wet towels on Minnie's bed. She tried her best to hang them over the end to dry, but on most days she was too weak.

When she could navigate down the rolling wood floors, the stench of ammonia from bodily fluids made her eyes water and kept her breathing shallow. The boys were swinging down the same aisle, delighted. When they hit the steel floors they discovered they could slide and made a grand game of it. Wilhelm slid down the step staircase and ran to tell her about the dead woman who was dumped overboard.

"What?" Minnie sat up in her bunk. "They buried someone at sea? Who?"

"Yes, Ma. We couldn't see who she was. We saw this crowd at the side of the ship, so we slipped to the front. The woman's body was covered by a German flag. The stretcher, the steward called it a bier, was lifted over the railing by four crewmen. The body was lowered on ropes into the sea while all the people bent over the rail to look. And then," Wilhelm said, "the ocean closed around the woman." He paused. "Ma, are you going to die before we get to America?"

That thought hadn't crossed Minnie's mind until then. Jumping overboard would solve two problems … ending her unbearable seasickness and avoiding Fred's discovery of the expanding lump in her belly.

Heinz fashioned pigs out of raw potatoes to distract and entertain the boys. He carved them wooden war boats and made them paper soldiers, which they dutifully brought down to where Minnie lay. They carried a message from Heinz. He hoped she would soon be well enough to spend the daylight hours on deck.

The only provision made for counteracting all the dirt of this kind of travel was cold salt water, with a single faucet of warm water for use by an entire washroom. It was the same faucet of warm saltwater passengers used for washing dishes. Floors of both the washrooms and the water closets were always damp and often filthy. The last day of the voyage stewards cleaned them in preparation for inspection at the port of entry. Soap and towels were not furnished. When Minnie was too sick to get out of bed to take the boys to clean themselves, they went on their own and lost the only bar of soap they had. They developed a grimy look, a badge of honor among boys on board the Werra.

Minnie's next view of the Atlantic Ocean was when Heinz carried her from her berth in steerage to the top of the ship. He sat her on the foredeck on an anchor chain storage bin so she could see America. She gazed out at the vast range of New York buildings dipping their feet in the bay. The streets of the city were in canyons, the buildings much higher and newer than those Minnie had left in Poznan. Chimneys were like feather plumes, spitting steam.

"You have survived the crossing, Frau Hartman," Heinz announced. "It gets easier from here on."

"Heinz, your kindness … how can I thank you for all you've done for my family?

Heinz smiled. "Stay aboard and come back to Germany with me."

Minnie threw her head back in laughter. "That is the best joke I've heard in seventeen days."

But Heinz was not smiling. When she saw the hurt in his eyes she took his hand in hers.

"My dear Heinz, I smell like vomit, my dress is dirty, and I haven't had a bath in a month. I am heavy with child and tired of the full responsibility for these three mischievous, undisciplined boys. I have never been at a lower point in my life. Do you know what a gift you have given me by that offer?"

"Forgive me for being so bold, Frau Hartman. You are just so beautiful. I understand in your condition you can't face another crossing now, but if you ever decide to return to Germany, you can find me through the North German Lloyd Line." He kissed her hand and returned to work with the other passengers.

The boys were dressed in their best clothes saved for their introduction to this new world, the country that would be theirs for the rest of their lives. Minnie had arrived in her new land with twenty-four dollars in German gold sewn into the hem of her coat.

Physicians came aboard and inspected the long lines of passengers. A rumor spread ... measles. A loud speaker announced, "Isolated cases of passengers infected with measles will be taken off the ship and quarantined on Hoffman Island. Families of those patients will be held in a waiting center on Staten Island. Passengers with cholera will be transported to Swinburne Island. If a significant number of passengers are found diseased, the entire ship will be quarantined and no passengers will be allowed to disembark." The rumor mill spread: A quarantined ship could float in the harbor, sometimes for weeks. Minnie ached for firm land.

The ship was disinfected. Stewards starting in steerage worked their way up to the top deck spraying everything. Minnie stood in line with her sons and other passengers and waited. She held the inspection cards they had been given upon arrival by the ship's health officer. Blank spaces were to be filled in by the ship's surgeon after he saw them. A red label on their baggage with a date seal would mean it had been disinfected, had passed inspection, and could enter America.

They stood. They waited until all the first and second class passengers had disembarked. When it was Minnie's turn, the surgeon told her to stick out her tongue, murmur "ah," and undress her arms for inspection. The surgeon checked the boys' chests and backs for red bumps. When their documents were approved and signed, Minnie followed her sons down the gangplank onto the Castle Rock Center for Immigration where Minnie stood in another seemingly endless queue.

Heinz appeared and instructed the boys to walk behind him through the crowds and carry the suitcases. He helped Minnie navigate the muddy street that she welcomed as American soil. Lines were long. It was hot. An English passenger from the Werra told her the weather was what Americans called Indian Summer.

Wilhelm, Gustav, Roelf and Minnie were among the two million immigrants pouring into the country, most through New York and Castle Rock. They were among the 'third wave' of immigrants from Europe.

When it was her turn at the front of the line, Minnie was advised that the 1875 United States Restrictive Immigration Law ruled that prostitutes and convicts could not enter the U.S. "Miss, are you a prostitute?"

Minnie didn't understand the question, but wanted to give the right answer, so she nodded.

"Are you a convict?"

Minnie nodded again. The agent was smiling now. She attempted to answer the agent's next question by explaining in German that her husband was waiting for her in the wildness of Michigan. She would travel there by train and then barge on the Erie Canal.

The agent looked at his watch. He told her the Act had been expanded in 1882. "Miss, are you a beggar or a contract laborer? Are you or have you ever been insane?"

Minnie nodded. "*Yah, yah, yah.*" Wilhelm, Roelf, and Gustav were tight against her, not wanting to be lost in the crowd.

The agent repeated his questions and soon grew frustrated. The official was waving his hand for assistance when Heinz conveniently appeared. He stepped up to the desk and told the agent he would translate for Minnie. He laughed and told Minnie what the agent said she had admitted. "The man says you told him you are a prostitute, a convict, and a beggar. He says you have come here to work under contract and that you admitted to being insane."

Minnie had a good laugh at that, her first in a month. "*Nein, nein, nein,*" she said. Heinz flattened his hand to stop her sputtering. He answered the rest of the agent's questions, their papers were stamped, and the agent waved them through the gate. Heinz walked them to the train station, gave her his address in America in case she got in trouble again, and wished the boys a safe trip.

"Are we Americans yet?" Wilhelm asked.

"No my sweet boy. We are guests in this country. When the American government sees we are obeying their rules and are good workers, then we can become citizens."

For the next two weeks they sat on the hard wooden benches of a train and then a barge, both powered by steam. They watched out the windows at what they were told was America's Midwest. They saw fields planted with corn that went on and on … so much land. Forests seemed endless … large hardwoods spaced between fields clear cut with nothing left but a sea of tree stumps … idle land. The train rambled along pastures with cattle grazing and ponds with men fishing in small boats. The boys ran up and down the aisles of the barge, crawled over and under seats, and played soldier using their fingers as guns. The family followed Fred's instructions when the little army arrived in Detroit, and took the next train north to Port Hope. There they were to catch another steamship to sail north to Au Sable, Michigan. The train was nearing the station in Port Hope when Minnie felt the first pangs of labor and cried out.

"*Wie gehts*, Ma?" Wilhelm said.

"Speak in English, my son. You are in America now. I will be okay. The baby is coming." The next pain was long and hard and Minnie grimaced. "I will be okay, but I want you to hold the steamship tickets. Wilhelm, don't lose them. If you need to go without me, have the train's engineer or the ship's captain help you. Go now. Tell the man in charge the baby is coming. Ask him to help me find a hospital or a midwife. Go quickly." Minnie shooed Wilhelm from her seat on the train. "Go!"

A steward from the train led them to a boarding house in Port Hope and found a midwife. Rosa Hartman was born on December 13, 1882. The woman gave Minnie licorice tea to speed the delivery of the placenta, but Minnie developed an infection and fever. She had little money left to pay the keeper of the boarding house or the woman who helped with the birth. Minnie offered her the gold locket Karl had given her. She gave her landlord a gold German coin for room and board until she was strong enough to move. She had a few more gold coins sewn in the hem of her dress for emergencies and to buy the bananas the boys begged her to buy. A passenger on the train had given one to each of her sons. It was their first banana and a big hit. Now they had an entire stalk of bananas between them and ate one after another until the midwife cautioned them to stop or they would get sick.

The fever finally broke and Minnie was able to travel. She gave the midwife her gold hoop earrings for her help. Wilhelm had been feeding his brothers from one of the sausages his grandfather had given Minnie for the trip. All the rye bread was gone. Wilhelm thanked the woman who owned the boarding house for her kindness … in English. Minnie was so proud.

"Ma, I thought for sure you would die that time. The midwife did too. In case you get sick again I don't want you to worry. I will take care of Gustav and Roelf. Even if Pa doesn't meet us like he said he would, I'll get a job and make sure they get enough to eat."

Minnie's eyes teared. She had raised a compassionate child a kind human being. "I love you Wilhelm."

"I love you too, Ma. Look over there. Is that our boat?"

The four of them embarked on a steamship. It was the next link of their adventure in this land that had become for them one long barge, train and steamship ride. Fred had described their home at the end of their journey as a "fine cottage in a forest surrounded by clean, blue lakes." Minnie dreamed of bathing in one of them.

Better known as Point Lookout, Arenac County (1902-1905).

Photo Attribution: Up-North Michigan Facebook page.

The big paddlewheel craft on the near side of the dock is the "State of New York" which carried freight from Detroit and passengers from Saginaw and Bay City. On the other side of the pier is the "Flora". Off the "Flora's" end is the "Josie".

Chapter Five
THE SETTLING

Wednesday evening the steamship docked at the lumbering port on Point Lookout on the shore of Lake Huron. It was a fishing and lumbering village south of Alpena, population two-hundred-sixty. Minnie wrapped the baby in her shawl and carried her in her valise. Fred met them at the dock. Her husband looked much larger and stronger than Minnie remembered. The man picked his boys up over his head and twirled each around with one arm. Minnie could see he was happy. He kissed her with his old passion. A wagon pulled by a sway-backed horse took them, their three suitcases, and the valise, along with the rest of the stalk of bananas to their new home … two rooms on the third floor of a boarding house next to a dusty sawmill.

The boys were full of stories. Wilhelm couldn't wait to tell his father about their travel adventures. He described the burial service for the dead lady and how she was lowered into the ocean. He told him about Roelf almost falling into the sea. "Papa, will you teach us how to swim?"

Wilhelm told his father how his mother had been seasick for the entire trip and could not leave her bed. He told him about their best friend, Heinz, who brought the doctor and made the ship's cook give the boys plates of special food for their mother. Fred glanced at Minnie for her reaction. She was too tired to explain.

Roelf told his father how their new friend Heinz had come down to steerage to see his mother, how he had made each of the boys toy soldiers from potatoes, how he had helped his mother walk up the stairs to the deck and carried her off the ship at the port of New York.

"Ma, will we ever see Heinz again?"

Fred's eyes questioned her again. Minnie sat on the bed, too tired to talk. She shook her head no.

The boys were full of questions. Fred told them he had a summer job and a winter job. He had worked hard as a log peeler during the summer. His winter job took him into the deep snow in the forest where the temperature lowered from twenty to thirty degrees below zero Centigrade. He and the other lumberjacks slept with their clothes on and covered themselves with horse blankets to keep warm. He worked alongside men called land lookers. Each man wore snow-shoes to walk on top the snow and through the forest to find and mark the largest trees. He said his job was to measure the logs and estimate how many board feet each tree could provide. Fred told his sons that if they learned their numbers, when they were old enough, they could work with him in the forest and help him with figures.

Minnie's husband told her he had been working sixty hours a week, all so his three sons and his beauty could join him in America. He would now save his wages and soon would buy land for a farm. The boys hung on his every word. They crawled onto his lap, his shoulders, stroked his face as he talked ... couldn't get enough of their father.

"Pa, will you teach Ma how to swim too?" Roelf said.

"Your mother will never learn to swim until she loses her fear of the water." He winked at them. "Now, my brave boys, I have a big day planned for you tomorrow. You must be tired. It is time to try out your new bed in your own room."

"*Guten abend*, Pa," Wilhelm said.

"*Guten abend*." Roelf rubbed his eyes.

"In English, Wilhelm, Roelf. Say it in English," Gustav said.

"Good night, Father," all three said in unison.

"Good night my sons." Fred kissed each of their foreheads.

When the boys were down, Fred sized her up with his eyes. He came to her, smiled and unbuttoned her dress. He let it fall to the floor. He untied her chemise and kissed her breasts. He loosened her petticoat and her pantaloons fell down. His eyes soaked up her nakedness. He stood back to look. "Turn," he ordered.

Her body trembled. Minnie shrank from Fred's touch and fell silent.

"What's wrong with you?" He rubbed his hand over the roundness that had been her hourglass figure. And then he heard a baby cry. He paused, looked down at the infant bundled in the valise "Is that a baby? Whose baby is it? That baby … it can't be ours."

Minnie lowered her eyes.

"Minnie?" he said. "Minnie, have you … have you cuckolded me?" He jerked her head around so he could see her face. "Who is the father?" Fred swore, and slapped her face hard. "Or, do you even know?"

"I am not a whore," she cried, holding her stinging face. At that moment Minnie swore she would never tell the brute who Rosa's father was.

He glared at her as he staggered backwards through the door, slamming it hard behind him.

Fred's kisses became as rare as snowflakes in summer. He worked long hours at the sawmill and barely said a word to her when he came back to the room in the boarding house for sex. His eyes were always angry, accusing. His every glance said adulteress. As soon as the weather turned warm Fred left with his crew for the forest. His last word to her was *schlampe*. He was convinced Minnie was a whore and a tramp.

Fred had abandoned her again. Minnie was alone in this wilderness, in this boarding house with three boys, a newborn and no money. She was on her own again and needed help. She left Rosa with the boys, walked to the mill, and asked for Fred's boss. She was taken to the man in a dusty second-story office.

"So you are Fred Hartman's wife." His German was flawless. He stood when Minnie entered and graciously offered her a chair. "Fred told us you were a beauty. And he was right. What can I do for you, Mrs. Hartman?" Minnie told the foreman she needed a job. She could work at the boarding house to pay for her room and board. She could cook.

The man studied her for a spell before answering. "I could use a cook, but the hours would be long and the work sometimes heavy for a woman."

Minnie assured him she could enlist the help of her sons if need be.

The foreman said the job would start Sunday morning at breakfast, that she would need to learn English, and that her children could have a separate room from hers in the boarding house. He said since most men cut timber during the winter and work the sawmill after the ice is melted, the number of boarders would range from four in winter to eighteen or twenty during the summer. "If you can cook for that many men you have the job."

She had never been so tired or felt so lonely. She shook the foreman's hand.

The cold during the winter of 1883 was extreme. The men worked outdoors building roads. Teams of draft horses pulled wagons that sprayed water on layers of pine boughs to form ice roads. After multiple layers of pine boughs the ice became thick and slippery. Horses driven by a lumberjack pulled the logs along the ice road from the forest to a river staging area. Men used the horses and oxen to pile logs on the bluffs near the river. Spring thaw split the river open and washed the logs downstream to the sawmill.

Fred had arranged with the barn boss for Wilhelm to work in the horse barn. Minnie's nine-year-old son left before dawn in a swirl of snow. The barn boss showed him how to push bedding straw from the hay mow above the stalls and fork it around the floor so it would be "nice and soft for when the animals sleep." The big man showed him how to keep the ice cracked in the water troughs so the animals could drink. Big Larry was his name. He was a big man with a small head and a mouth overfilled with teeth. His smile looked like an overstuffed suitcase squeezed shut. Minnie heard him tell her son, "Don't wait to get started, Wilhelm."

"Ma!" Wilhelm came to her in the kitchen. "Big Larry said I had to shovel horse shit onto a wagon and wheel it to a spot by the woodshed for your kitchen garden. Should I tell him you used aged horse manure on your garden in Germany? Doesn't he know fresh shit will burn the plants?" Wilhelm learned to feed and clean the draft horses and oxen. He was so short he had to stand on a wooden box to curry the animals.

"Ma, did you know that if you're going to work with animals, first you must learn to love them?"

"Who told you that?"

"Big Larry. He told me when I am working with a horse I must pay attention, I must know what to expect from the horse, and anticipate trouble. Ma, draft horses are quiet when they work. The barn boss told me they are temperamental and attention-demanding animals. He said they are just like women. I think horses are good company. When I pick up the lines and drive a team, I feel about eight feet tall. By the way, I think Big Larry likes you."

"Why do you think that?"

"He asks me what you are cooking every day. First he smiles and all those snaggled teeth stick out, and then he asks. Every day he asks." Hardly a day passed before Wilhelm came running into the kitchen. "Ma, Maggie is the name of the mare. She comes in from the field when I call her name. But Fritz, now he's the gelding. That horse will not come no matter how often I call. And then, when I go out in the pasture to get him, he grabs the bit with his teeth and pulls me in the other direction. Ma, I can't work in the horse barn."

During Fred's next stint at the mill town, he showed Wilhelm techniques for leading the huge animals in the barnyard. Big Larry watched, puffing away on his corncob pipe. Wilhelm learned quickly and was able to train a thousand-pound animal to follow the commands of a sixty-pound boy.

"Ma." Wilhelm walked into the kitchen. He was frowning. "I am in trouble with the barn boss. I was walking behind Fritz today, holding his reins like Big Larry showed me. Fritz let out gas from his tailpipe. I dropped the reins because I knew what was coming next, but it was too late. The stuff that shot out got all over my pants and shirt. It smelled mighty bad. I had to wash myself off in the horse-watering trough."

"It's natural for horses to poop, Wilhelm," Minnie said. "What kind of trouble are you in?"

"Big Larry said I should hold the reins even when Fritz farts. He said if the horse had run off, he could have broken a leg in the brush. When Big Larry and I were chasing the gelding around the pasture, he told me if I was going to work for him I had to learn to work with my head and my hands, not with my feet."

That evening Minnie overheard Fred talking to Wilhelm. "My boy, you need this job to help pay for your keep. No one will coddle you around here like your Ma did all those years while you lived in Germany."

"But Pa …"

"Boy, you must never contaminate the water trough with animal manure. Big Larry was right tipping all the water out and having you fill it with pails from the pump."

"But Pa …"

"I know that was hard work. I know how distasteful it is to follow a horse that floats a loose load. That horse must have gas, and if you're not careful, he could get the bloat. Wilhelm,

Fritz is a valuable horse, the best they have around here. Are you letting him feed on green corn stalks?"

"Pa, when I say 'whoa' and Fritz stops, he munches on whatever he can. Could he get bloat from eating alfalfa? He may have grabbed some leaves from corn growing along the fence row."

"That could be why he has tailpipe troubles. Wilhelm, the bloat could kill him. Are you trying to kill that horse?"

"No, Pa. I love Fritz. And I love Maggie, too. Someday I want a team of my own."

"I'll see that you get one, son, when you're old enough. But I think it's time for bed. Minnie? Upstairs!" Fred ordered.

One of Maggie's hooves was larger than Minnie's young son's head. She watched the oxen roll in the barnyard mud. One ox was heavier than Maggie or Fritz put together. A swish of an ox tail could knock her little son to the ground, and it did. The barn boss walked over and told Wilhelm, "Dust off and get up," and walked away. Minnie said nothing. And so went their days and weeks.

One of the 'jacks spent his day off showing Wilhelm, Gustav and Roelf how to set a trap line near the river for fresh meat. He told the boys they could sell cedar rails and ties for sixteen cents each, and get five cents each for cedar posts. All they had to do was wade into the swamp, saw them off, and haul them to the mill. Fred cautioned the boys to wait until the ground and black flies froze before attempting the swamp. That extra job kept Wilhelm and Gustav busy most of the winter when they weren't working in the barn or helping Minnie in the kitchen. Roelf was too little to stay outside all day. When he was cold, he came back to the boarding house and warmed himself by the kitchen cookstove.

Breakfasts were served way too early for Minnie's taste. Back in the old country Minnie took her coffee around ten. This early meal at the boarding house was the most trouble for her to prepare and serve on time. Not one person pampered her like she had become accustomed to in Poznan. Minnie tried making excuses for her tardiness. The men looked at her like she was crazy. They were hungry and had to go to work.

The woodsmen must have sent the foreman to see her because he let her know it was unacceptable for breakfast or any meal to be late. Excuses were intolerable. Minnie must expect nothing. He said the men didn't care when Minnie made the meals, or how much trouble Minnie had making them. They wanted their food edible, on the table when they were ready to eat, and they wanted it hot. It didn't take a second angry outburst from the men for her to learn how to work.

Minnie needed this job, so she planned her work around her usual morning fog, preparing as much as possible the night before. She kneaded sourdough starter into the flour, formed the breakfast rolls and braided sandwich bread the night before they were to be eaten. Before bedtime Minnie put them in the empty ovens to rise. Evenings when Minnie wasn't too tired, she ground whatever meat was left over from the day and stuffed it into animal casings for sausages.

The foreman told her Fred's salary was being held for him at the mill office. Like most of the men, her husband was putting away almost all he earned to buy farmland. The foreman said if she needed cash, she was to come to see him. He would pay her sons for their work, but it was for her to decide if their wages went into Fred's land account or into the boys' individual accounts. Her salary was to be traded for two sleeping rooms in the boarding house, as much food as her family needed, and a small stipend in cash for extras … like shoes and clothing and women's special needs.

By 1883 the boys had made their transition into the wilds of Michigan with great gusto. Wilhelm learned to catch fish, clean and salt them, and string them up to dry. He liked to surprise his mother with a fresh catch and have her fry them up for supper. The men were pleased when the menu changed and called Wilhelm in to the dining room to praise him.

Her oldest son learned to gut the deer the men would shoot and hang them on the pole for the meat to age. When Minnie needed meat, Wilhelm, now thirteen, would slice off a haunch for a roast, or some ribs to make stew, or flavor the *kartoffelsuppe*, his favorite potato soup.

Another lumberjack showed the boys how to tap maple trees and bring the buckets of sap to their mother for boiling down into maple syrup. They begged Minnie to use it to make cookies for them and some for the boarders. As the golden cookies came out of the oven, her children insisted they taste them first to make sure they would meet the high standards the men held for such desserts. "Minnie," the men would call her in from the kitchen before they touched them. "Have our tasters approved these sweets?" The children would hide their faces and giggle.

Gustav helped her in the kitchen and garden. She showed her second son the magic of potatoes. She cut one potato into six pieces and planted each piece in a separate hole. When Gustav dug them in the fall each small piece had produced eight or ten new potatoes. The boy pumped water from the well and carried the heavy buckets inside. He chopped firewood and stacked it in the woodshed. The boy kept the cookstove stoked from early morning until after supper.

When Minnie needed potatoes from the garden, she sang out "*kartoffelroder*," and Gustav would run outside and grab his potato fork. Minnie's potato digger would come back a few beats later with a bushel of freshly dug potatoes. He pulled the onions, red beets and carrots from the ground behind the building and packed them in fresh straw in the root cellar, but preferred digging potatoes … he said it was like digging for buried treasure.

Gustav was a proud potato peeler, and pared a bushel each afternoon for the millwrights' evening meal. When Minnie needed extra spuds for breakfast she would call out, "*kartoffelschaler*," and Gustav would be at her side. Her potato scaling child also collected eggs from the henhouse and occasionally slaughtered chickens. He carried water from the river and logs from the wood shed. After the last meal of the day, Gustav filled the woodstove in preparation for the morning meal. His reward for his good work was a *kartoffelpuffer*, a crisp potato pancake.

Her little Roelf worked beside his older brothers without complaint. Minnie longed for a normal childhood for all her children ... fishing, school and playing games with friends. Their work was their play.

The young mother was the first one to hit the cold floor in the early morning. She built a fire before running outside to the cold outhouse, and then skated back into the kitchen to thaw. The boarding house cook started water boiling for coffee while the ovens were heating. She added eggshells to the ground coffee to keep the liquid clear, as her mother had done. She set the speckled blue enamel pot on the sideboard at five o'clock to steep so when the men tromped down the staircase and served themselves, the coffee was strong.

Minnie brushed the dough-lined sheets with bacon grease, sprinkled them with coarse sugar, and when the ovens were hot enough, slipped in the breakfast rolls. Two other sheets of sandwich bread for the men's lunches went into the second oven. She tried to make it up to the men for botching her first day on the job. She added poppy seeds to the loaves ... always a treat at her home in Poznan. When the crusts were golden, Minnie tested doneness by knocking on the loaves with her bare knuckles. If they sounded hollow they were ready, and she pulled them out to cool. She filled the empty ovens with the rising sourdough for bread the men would eat for supper.

Roelf, Gustav and Wilhelm awoke to the inviting smell wafting through the boarding house ... freshly baked bread. It didn't take them long to dress and meet her in the kitchen for the cakes Minnie made special for them by frying the raw dough in lard.

Wilhelm's workday began by cracking four dozen eggs onto baking sheets greased with bacon fat. Minnie slipped the wiggly sheets into the oven and let the eggs bake until they were firm. She fried mounds of the morning meat and heaped it onto platters for the sideboard. Some days the meat was freshly slaughtered pig. Pigs were kept around the camps to eat the garbage. Sometimes the meat was squirrel that Wilhelm shot, but mostly it was venison the men brought in from the woods. Always, baby Rosa was strapped tightly to her back, chattering to all who would listen.

Gustav and Roelf's duties started when they heard the men moving around their rooms but before they came pounding down the staircase. They laid the boarders' table with clean plates, cutlery, and coffee mugs. One bowl of fresh grease for slathering on hot rolls was set at each end of the long plank table within every man's reach. After breakfast Roelf carried the dishes to the kitchen and dropped them into a washtub of boiling water. Minnie gave her sweet sons the rest of the morning off to play and enjoy being children.

When all the men had gone to work, Minnie unstrapped Rosa and put her down to crawl. She put her feet up to lessen the swelling in her legs and began to enjoy her daily mug of coffee.

"Ma, Wilhelm called me a *dummer Huhn!*" her small boy said.

"Roelf, you tell your brother you are not a stupid chicken. Tell him you are a clever pig." And the chaos for the day commenced.

Before the fire went out, Minnie fished the dishes from the hot water with a small hook, similar to the cant hooks the river men used to handle and roll the logs downstream. After the dishes drained, she stacked them on the sideboard.

When the soft early morning sunlight filled the kitchen, it was time to stage the mid-day meal. She sautéed the onions and carrots Roelf brought in from the root cellar, added whatever meat and bones were left from the last meal, and filled the pot with river water. The soup simmered until the broth was a deep golden yellow. Then she dropped in egg noodles that dried on a broomstick over the cookstove. Before the men arrived for dinner at noon, she tasted everything and added salt and fresh herbs from her kitchen garden to balance the flavors.

Dried beans came in big fabric bags. Salt pork and corned beef came in barrels. Minnie soaked the beans overnight and then baked them in large, rectangular sheet-iron pans with salt pork or corned beef. They usually baked all day, which gave the boarding house a welcoming smell.

The first man to arrive for lunch, Big Larry the barn boss, offered to move the heavy soup pot and trays of beans to the sideboard. He set them down between the bowls and soup spoons and the loaves of bread still warm from the oven. Then he found his usual seat on one of the long benches that lined the table. The men needed substantial meals to fill their stomachs before they went out to the saloons for beer.

Minnie found it odd that men at the boarding house avoided speaking to her, and when she entered the dining room conversation usually stopped and the men looked down at their plates. She could feel their eyes on her when she left the room, and sometimes paused and turned back to catch them glancing her way. In Poznan, Minnie had been the center of conversation and a magnet for men's eyes. She missed the Old Country ... missed how men treated her. She longed to see the ancient buildings and smell the gas torches lighting the cobbled streets. She missed all the people shopping on Market Square and even missed Jacob Bublitz's vegetable stall, a job she loathed at the time.

One morning Wilhelm mentioned a conversation he had overheard between two woodsmen who had lingered after supper the night before. "A log peeler called Pork Chop Charlie was speaking to a land looker the men called Cruiser. He told Cruiser he had met Fred Hartman while foraging in the forest for large trees. Fred told him to spread the word that any woodsman hanging around the mill kitchen or even looking at his wife would pay dearly. He would douse him with kerosene while he slept and throw down a kitchen match when he awoke."

Wilhelm continued. "The other man told Charlie that Pa threatened a shanty boy who drops off supplies to you each week. He said Papa found him in the forest cutting a tree with a one-man crosscut saw. He pinned the boy against the fall side of the tree with one hand and continued sawing with the other. Papa threatened to fell the tree on top of him unless he promised not to hang around the mill kitchen or talk to you. Why would he say that, Ma?"

November 9, 1917: Prohibition carried Arenac County by a two to one vote.

March 3, 1921: The sheriff of Arena County arrested a hooch manufacturer with a barrel of wheat mash in his possession.

August 4, 1921: The sheriff of Arenac County discovered a thirty-gallon still in Whitney Township and commented, "It is the largest I ever found."

Chapter Six
THE STILLS

A mill hand came to Minnie late one afternoon with an idea about making moonshine. He said he would share his secrets for distilling some mighty fine firewater with her if she would agree to be his partner. Minnie recalled the distilled potato beverage she helped her mother make in Germany and how much of it her father drank. Distilling beverage alcohol could be lucrative in a forest teeming with thirsty men, and she could use the extra cash.

"Isn't it dangerous for you to be talking to me, proposing that we be partners?" Minnie asked him.

"Who do you think sent me to you? Mr. Hartman said you knew how to distill alcohol safe to drink, that you had done it before in Poland."

The still had to be built near a clean water source, out of sight of nosy neighbors and downwind from any inhabited cabins who might complain of the smell of smoke or simmering potato mash. A constant supply of firewood and a fire tender were needed. Minnie said she knew the perfect place, but had a few requirements of her own. No lead coils or lead soldering could be used to build the stills. To protect customers from being poisoned she insisted no creosote or embalming fluid be added to the product before it was sold. The partners shook hands and Minnie became a bootlegger.

Her new partner arrived at the boarding house kitchen after supper carrying empty glass bottles and a long length of copper tubing. Minnie had cleared a space in the woodshed behind the cords of stacked firewood, a few steps from the back door of her kitchen, and a stone's throw from the Au Sable River.

He started the fire and had her watch him cook the potato mash. He told her quality hooch could be made from any vegetable, root, or grain that would ferment, a fact she already had learned on her first date with Fred. Her partner preferred starting with fermented potato mash and sugar syrup. He had several roots he added for flavoring, but said the extra work was not necessary. The men drank cough syrup they bought from the mill doctor to get drunk.

"Medicinal cough syrup?"

"That's what the men call the pure alcohol Doc sells them from the medical supply at the mill. Those 'jacks would lap up a bowl of moose piss if it would help ease their muscle pains or forget their woes. Sorry for the rough language, Mrs. Hartman."

During the first week of the new venture, Minnie stepped outside her kitchen each afternoon and threw a log on the fire to keep it going. Her partner slept in the woodshed nights the still was operational to keep the fire going. By the end of the week their first batch of beverage alcohol was ready. The two toasted each other before braving the first taste together … like true partners.

Minnie sipped the clear liquor, swirled it inside her mouth, and swilled it down as she had seen Fred do. That was her first experience drinking firewater. "Euuu. This is disgusting!"

The mill hand laughed. "The men will like it. It's too strong for ladies. Stir in a spoonful of honey and some lemon. I think you will like it better with a sweet tangy flavor."

Minnie added the honey and lemon juice. It did taste better, Minnie had to admit. She drank the entire cupful in one long swallow. "What do you call this concoction?"

"Walk into a saloon and ask the bartender to make you a 'Bee's Knees,' and this is what you will get." He poured Minnie another, but made her promise to take it up the three flights of stairs to her bedroom before she drank it.

Her partner handled sales to the men and offered her half of the profits. Minnie knew better and even imagined she heard her father talking in her ear. "I'll take half the income. I know how profits can be eaten away by expenses."

She started keeping a bottle of shine on the boarding house breakfast sidebar. The boarders called this new morning drink Minnie's Corpse Reviver.

The partners needed potatoes, bushels of potatoes. That first season, Minnie fed boarders pie crusts and noodles and saved all the potatoes for what they now lustfully referred to as Minnie's Rotgut.

Fred came back the following spring smelling of sawdust and sweat. A sullen sadness had crept over him while he was in the back woods. He barely spoke to his wife, would not touch her, would not sleep in her bed, but took the boys hunting and fishing. Minnie grew melancholy. She tried everything to reconcile with Fred but whatever she did never seemed like enough. Minnie was twenty-eight and was excluded from her own family's life. She felt like her heart was pumping wood ash, the white powder she cleaned from beneath the still each morning, a continuous stream of useless waste. "Save me," she cried out at night. "Mama? My brothers? Where are you now that I need you? Won't someone please come and take me out of these woods?"

When it was clear no one was coming to save her like they had when she was a little girl, Minnie lay awake nights counting the knots in the pine ceiling boards, looking for strategies to survive what Fred had promised her would be a better way of life. He had told her she would live in a beautiful cottage by a pristine lake next to a lush forest of hardwoods. "The lush hardwood forest" turned out to be a lumber camp outpost in a prairie of stumps in an uncivilized wilderness called Michigan. The "pristine lake" turned out to be a swift running river Minnie was terrified her toddlers would fall into. The "beautiful cottage" was nonexistent. They lived in two tiny rooms on the third floor of a sun-bleached, wood-sided, unpainted boarding house with thin walls and two dozen crude and demanding woodsmen. The "better way of life" turned out to consume all of her waking hours ... working from before daylight until after dusk seven days a week. She was tired and unhappy, and to top it off she thought she might be pregnant again.

The last words from her hostile husband after supper that night had been, "*Hinden*, you have put me in my grave while I'm still in my prime." Then he disappeared like a puff of smoke into a crowd of woodsmen on their way to the saloon.

Minnie fumed. A bitch she was not. An angry, overworked woman impregnated every other year by a man who left her by herself with the full responsibility of raising the children he sired, yes, that she was. She looked down at her once beautiful hands, red and rough from scrubbing the boarders' laundry and washing greasy pots and pans. They were puckered from all the hot water. Her fingers were scarred from oven burns and would never grace piano keys again. But what did that matter? She didn't have a piano to play. She counted up all her belongings. They amounted to nothing.

Minnie understood that her husband's vanity had been wounded, his love for her broken by her betrayal, and that he felt another man had robbed him of his wife. She refused to tell him the snake was his own beloved brother. Fred would crush his skull with a thump from one of his burly hands.

Minnie could see Fred wasn't sleeping or eating well. He was growing thin, looked tired. She overheard the men say he was drinking heavily at the saloon. Granted, his possessive jealousy was well-founded, but it was killing their marriage and killing him. She didn't know what to do, but she was determined to figure it out.

Minnie had received a letter from Karl Hartman that week. She asked the foreman's wife to read it to her. It was brief. He had been wounded in battle and was recovering in a hospital in Vienna. The letter was a last request … to see that he was buried in Poznan with his family should he not survive. Minnie used the letter to start the breakfast fire that day.

"Fred, let's go back to Poznan," Minnie said one night after her work was done for the day. She had tucked the children in their beds and Fred had climbed the stairs to hear their prayers. "We had a good life there," she closed the door and walked toward her room. "Your parents and brother must miss you. They must miss the kinder terribly, and the children miss them." She waited while he opened the bedroom door. "I want to go back to Germany. I am bone-tired, weary from taking care of the children and working in the kitchen. And yes, I'm lonely with you away for months at a time. We have enough saved for the journey back to the old country."

"I can't go," Fred said.

"What's holding you? You never worked this hard in Germany. None of us did."

"I would be embarrassed." Fred slid his suspenders from his shoulders. "Returning home would be admitting to my family and all my friends that I am a failure." He unbuttoned his shirt. "I can't. What's wrong with living here?"

"I'm tired and sad so much of the time." She sat on the bed, her hands folded in her lap.

"Wilhelmina Bublitz, you are possessed by the devil," Fred glared at her. "You must have been struck down with this madness back in Germany." He pulled his suspenders up over his shoulders. "You probably want to go back to be with your lover." He took her chin and tipped her face up. "That's it, isn't it." He pushed her face away with such force she fell back on the bed. "Keep away from me, you selfish bitch. I will never trust you again." He stomped to the door.

"Where are you going?" Minnie stood. "Where is your compassion?"

"Compassion?" Fred's eyes pelted hers. "You will see no sympathy from me." Minnie took a step back, afraid of where this tirade was going. "No, Minnie Bublitz. Instead of kindness, you will witness my lack of concern." He stepped towards her and put a hand on each of her shoulders. "You will feel my coldness until you are mad." His hands moved up around her neck. "You will be as crazy as I have become." He squeezed.

"Fred, stop!"

He released his grip, turned and fled down the stairs.

Minnie's sleeplessness was relieved only by nightmares. One sweaty dream had Fred throwing the baby he had not fathered into the river and making Minnie watch as the little one struggled and drowned. Another had Fred's foot holding her head over a stump as he wielded an axe high above his head like she was a chicken about to be decapitated ... with him laughing, hysterically. The only light flickering in her miserable world was that she knew their boys would be okay with Fred after she died. He did love his children. He would look after them, but for how long? She wondered how long a man could live who drinks as much as he does.

Minnie encouraged Fred to drink tea made from alfalfa blossoms to help with his yellowing complexion that she knew was jaundice. She offered herself for sex instead of the ladies he frequented at the saloon. He preferred her potato rotgut, and emptied the bottle of "Corpse Reviver" with each short visit to her room.

Minnie waited until her husband was sober before asking the questions that were burning inside her. "What happened to your dream to buy ten acres of rolling land for a vineyard with a southern exposure? You wanted to plant grape vines ... the ones developed to thrive in northern climates. You planned to use what you learned while working at the Zielona Gora vineyard to make great wine. Remember? Fred, where is the man you used to be?"

His answer was a rattling snore.

When Minnie entered the kitchen early the next morning, she found the pantry window open and the room freezing cold. She pulled her shawl tight and lit a lantern. A hickory broom handle had pierced a flour sack and the white powder had soaked into swill from a barrel that had been tipped over on the floor.

"*Mein Gott im Himmel.*" The shelves were bare. Fried cakes freshly baked the night before were missing ... cakes that were for the morning meal less than two hours away. Minnie panicked and stepped outside, and with the light from her lantern recognized bear tracks in the snow. The animal had made a mess moving logs from the woodpile, breaking bottles she had readied for schnapps. Surely someone upstairs had heard. She wondered why one of the brave boarders hadn't come down to investigate. Not one of them cared enough to get out of their warm beds and shoot the beast before breakfast. Mill hands, who enjoyed hunting Michigan black bear, could be as cranky as hungry sows before they filled their bellies. And they would be hungry soon and would want their food hot and plentiful when they came down the stairs.

Minnie went into action. She soaked slices of white bread in whipped eggs and fried them golden. The men stood at the kitchen door demanding their coffee. "A bear ate your breakfast. If any of you bums had shot the beast, you would have finished eating already." They stopped complaining about the wait after they tasted the fried egg-bread soaked in honey.

"Ma, the bear was hungry," Roelf said. "Don't be mad at him. He would like this fried bread. Can I take him some?"

"No!" Her answer was unusually firm. Roelf began to cry. "Come here my son." Minnie sat him on her knee and began to laugh at the mess the animal had made. "You stay away from the bear."

"That bear would eat a boy your size," a boarder said.

"Would you shoot the bear for me?" Roelf asked the man.

"Minnie, don't be so hard on us," said the boarder. "This is the only place we can complain without getting fired. Roelf, one of us will shoot that bear for you. And then we will all eat the bear."

Amelia Hartman was born in 1884, another sweet baby girl. The boys adored their sister Rosa, and were delighted to have a new baby ... especially a girl. They played in the muddy garden while Minnie worked inside the kitchen. One of the boarders had fashioned a tree swing, and that day Amelia babbled to Rosa and Roelf from the swing while Minnie's angels with dirty faces watched their baby sister.

Minnie heard a child call for her while she was kneading dough for the evening meal. She was wiping flour from her hands when Rosa came running into the kitchen.

"Ma, a big dog came in the garden and took Amelia away." She lifted Rosa into her arms, ran outside and stopped. Her heart dropped.

"Help! Someone help me." Minnie set Rosa down and ran after the wolf that had Amelia gripped between its jaws. "Help me," she gasped as she chased the predator as it entered the brush bordering the woods. Minnie followed the kidnapper, but the thick thorn bushes slowed her, caught her, stopped her. Spines ripped her skirt and tore at her ankles. She brushed them aside as they gouged her hands, leaving tears in her skin on her arms and face. Entangled in a low branch, Minnie was caught, defeated. "A wolf has taken my child," she cried and sank to her knees.

One of the boarders was in his room recovering from a mill accident when he heard Minnie's screams. He came limping from the boarding house holding his rifle. The children pointed to the woods.

"Mrs. Hartman! Where are you? Which way did the animal go?" He found her huddled deep in a thorn bush, bleeding. She managed to point in the direction she saw the beast last, and he pursued the wolf, leaving Minnie praying for him to find her baby.

"Don't come in here," she called out to her children who were crying and trying to find her. She unbuttoned and stepped from her shredded skirt and blouse. "I'll come out. Wait for me." She backtracked through the broken brush in her petticoat, leaving parts of her clothing and blood to mark the wolf's entering point.

"Where is Amelia?" Rosa said. "Ma, you're bleeding."

Minnie's body jerked when she heard the gunshot. She gathered her children to her and walked them back to the garden. She was sitting on a chair by the woodshed with her arms wrapped around her knees when the boarder returned. He was holding one of Amelia's shoes.

"I missed him, Mrs. Hartman. You better keep the young ones inside until we get some men together to track down that flesh-eating beast."

When the mill doctor found Minnie, she was curled in the same chair in a foetal position. Her eyes shone vacant. They stared into the woods to the place where the wolf had taken her baby. Her children surrounded her in the dirt beneath her, holding to her torn slip, whispering to one another.

"Don't talk to Ma."

"I'm hungry."

"Where did Amelia go?"

"Did you see that doggie?"

Minnie was trembling and refused to rise and move into the kitchen. The doc stitched up the torn skin on her arm, cleaned the blood from her face and ankles and gave her a shot of something to make her sleep right there in her chair.

When she awoke, the foreman's wife was sitting by her bedside. She fed Minnie hot soup, gave her another sedative and told her she was to stay in bed until her husband arrived. A man had been sent to find Fred. Minnie came in and out of consciousness, each time calling for her lost girls ...

Wilhelmina ... Amelia, each time pulling a pillow over her face to scream until the sedative took effect and the realities of her life were lost in sleep.

Fred came home a week later. By that time Minnie was back at work cooking, and taking care of her remaining children, but she still could not speak. She was having trouble swallowing.

He told her to buck up, that she could have another baby. She choked back her pain, ran outside and threw up behind the woodshed. He came out and found her on her knees. "Minnie, get hold of yourself." He pulled her to her feet.

She turned away. "Fred, you talk like children are a commodity, like potatoes. Amelia was a human, a little girl with a big future."

"Forget her. You will have another child."

Minnie faced her husband. "I will never forget Amelia," she shouted. "And I will never forget Wilhelmina. My children will never forget their sisters. I'll see to that."

Two weeks after Amelia was taken, another hammer dropped. An engine failed while a train was negotiating a sharp curve on a logging track. The train overturned, taking the lives of two of Minnie's boarders. Her children had grown fond of these men ... men who had treated them like their own. The children were confused and saddened by these violent deaths and were still mourning the missing Amelia. They were terror-stricken by every dog that wandered into their yard.

A few days later, Emil Miller's saw mill caught fire in Krakow, a town near Alpena, and in a matter of minutes exploded. Minnie stood barefoot in her garden, staring at the streak of red on the horizon. To her the wildfire seemed thousands of miles away. She couldn't imagine it would reach their camp in Au Sable.

By some miracle the wind changed and the fire blew out. Minnie knew the wives of the men who were killed at the mill, and prepared baskets with fresh bread and crabapple jelly. She packed each woman a mason jar of whiskey to help them over their initial shock. Her children surprised her with their kindness, each choosing handmade toys for the widows' children and voluntarily placing them in Minnie's gift baskets. The other people's misfortune had somehow diminished her own.

The foreman's wife invited the woodsman's wives for tea and to work on a quilt for the families burned out by fire. Each one of them brought scraps of sturdy cloth, or batting, or colorful thread if they had it. While they stitched the scraps together the women shared their worries, their fears and their dreams for their children.

Not long after one of those quilting sessions the foreman announced the mill would be building a log school so everyone in camp could learn to read and write English. Minnie would make sure her children would attend. She was determined that even Rosa would learn to read and write. Wilhelm, Gustav and Roelf already communicated in English without noticeable German accents. They had learned from the men at the mill. It wasn't long before those same men had the two room structure erected and roofed with cedar shake shingles. A flock of children flooded each wing on opening day and the learning began.

"Watch me print my name, Ma," Roelf said and scrawled R A L P H in the sand by the boarding house kitchen door.

"Not like that," Wilhelm said and scrawled R O E L F. "I learned how to write in the Old Country."

"I'm an American schoolboy now, and I write my name like this," the boy insisted. "Ma, the teacher showed me. Wilhelm's wrong."

"Don't fight, boys. That name belongs to Roelf'. He can print it like he wants," Minnie said, not being able to read either spelling of the child's name. She had her boys write their names on school paper, which she included in her next letter to her parents in Germany.

Minnie's children enjoyed teaching their mother new words they learned in school while they worked in their garden or the boarding house kitchen. Each of the children spent evenings memorizing lessons and learning new words under the light of kerosene lamps.

Fred discovered an empty envelope from Karl in a drawer. He screamed at Minnie. "Why is my brother writing you? Are you intending to marry him?"

"Fred, please lower your voice. You'll wake the children."

"Could it be that you are still in love with him? Is he the lover? Is he Rosa's father? Minnie! Answer me. Come here at once!"

Minnie could tell from the incomprehension on his face that he wasn't sure, couldn't believe what he had guessed was true, that Karl, his beloved little brother had cuckolded him. "Is Karl Rosa's father? Answer me!" Fred had been drinking vodka all day, the liquor she had brewed and bottled in the woodshed.

"Fred, please control your rage."

"That primitive bastard," he whispered through his teeth. He threw the mason jar at the wall, spilling the liquor and broken glass on the floor. "He was always jealous of what I had, helped himself to my belongings … the ones that were nice and useful. He never could pull his life together … flitted from one thing to another." Fred turned on Minnie. "Do you love him?" He shook her shoulders.

Minnie answered honestly. "Yes. Let go of me."

"Do you love me?"

Minnie answered honestly, again. "Yes, you know I do."

"Minnie, how can you love two men at the same time?" Fred dropped his arms to his side and paced, trying to understand the incomprehensible.

"It is possible," Minnie told him gently, "for a woman to love two men at the same time with equal tenderness. I'm not lying when I show each of you my passion. Fred, I love you for certain qualities, and I love your brother for others. I can't say I love you equally, exactly alike. And my love for one of you does not mean I don't love the other."

The lines in Fred's face softened as he listened. Minnie could see he was trying to understand. "Why did you bed my brother?"

"I thought you had left us … that you would never send for us."

"But I told you I would, and I did."

"I remember your saying it, but I didn't believe you. Fred, I was devastated when you left. I tried doing it all … taking care of the children, growing the potatoes I needed to sell at the market. I didn't have any money. Remember? You took all our money to America with you. When the weather turned cold, I even had to steal coal from my neighbor to keep the cottage warm. There were days when there was no food in the house and the boys were hungry. I couldn't ask my parents to feed them. I wouldn't ask yours. I was so lonely after you left. And then your brother showed up with food and gave me money so I wouldn't have to work so hard.

"Yes Fred, don't look so shocked. Your brother gave me money. He brought fresh meat for the table with each visit. He played with the boys. Yes, he played with your sons.

"All three boys were driving me crazy, getting into trouble with the neighbors, stealing fruit from stands at the market … terrible trouble. I tried punishing them by having them go outside to find a switch, and then bring it back in to me so I could give them a spanking. It always worked for you. For me, the boys disappeared into the brush, and turned their punishment into a hide-and-seek game. I had to look all over the neighborhood and often didn't find them until after dark. Your sons needed the presence of a strong man, and you weren't there. I didn't have the energy to correct their behavior. I tried, but I was so tired.

"I was buried by housework, by being the cook, the gardener, the vegetable dealer, the nursemaid and the peacekeeper for the children."

"Minnie, you are babbling."

"You asked. Now listen. Your brother found me when I was at a low point. He was romantic. Karl offered me love. He made me feel like a desirable woman, again."

"Does he love you?"

"I don't know. He said he did. He told me what I wanted to hear and I believed him."

"You little fool. Don't you realize all he wanted was sex?"

"I know that now," she said.

"I don't want to hear any more, Minnie. Your whoring around has broken my heart. I can never trust you again."

So, all is lost for me, she thought. "Fred, what about Rosa?"

"Rosa is and will always be my daughter. She must never know otherwise. And my brother must never know that he has any part in our family." Fred paused. "Was he a better lover than me?"

"No, Fred." Minnie knew his masculinity was fragile. "You are the most passionate lover any woman could ask for ... kind, gentle, and patient. Karl was a selfish lover, a brute."

Fred looked at Minnie with feigned tenderness. She knew that look and leaned back in bed and let him take her. He lay beside her after he was spent and stared at the ceiling.

"I want to believe you will keep Rosa's secret between us," he said, "but I can't count on you anymore, Minnie. I can't be sure what you will do next ... if you will push your dagger all the way in and finish me off, or stab me anew. I loved you once. You took my love and turned it into something ugly! I treated you kindly and you betrayed me!" Fred looked at Minnie with such anguish. She could see the man was openly wounded, vulnerable, that he thought he was a spurned lover. "What happened to you?" he shouted.

"You are my husband." Minnie lowered her voice and spoke slowly to calm him. "You are the father of my children ... most of them. You are the man I love. But I am not another horse or buggy that you own, another piece of property that no man is allowed to touch, to have a conversation with ... share a joke with, or a story. I can still be a good and faithful wife to you and enjoy the company of other men, even the pressure of another man's hand on mine, or even an occasional kiss."

Mentioning the kiss was Minnie's mistake and she knew it, but it had already escaped her lips. Fred's possessive jealousy popped. His temper blew. He screamed. "I will kill that barbarian! I will find that cursed wanderer, that rapist of other men's wives. This sordid tale of adultery will end in homicide. If I am unable to do it, someone else will. I swear it!" He threw a chair in his rage, broke the window glass, and caused so much commotion the children came running in the room to see what had happened. Minnie was afraid he would hit her in front of them. Protecting her face with her arms, she tried to warn Fred. But before she could speak, she heard Wilhelm.

"Pa! Stop!"

Fred saw his children watching from the open door.

"Don't hurt my mother," Wilhelm shouted and stepped inside.

Fred pushed past their little bodies and stormed out the door, hammered down the staircase and stomped out of the boarding house.

Rosa ran to Minnie. "Ma, why is Papa so mean?"

"Children, come to me." Minnie climbed onto the bed and they crawled in beside her. "Distrust and suspicion have poisoned your father's love for me. Remember this: jealousy is like a terrible disease. It is a mean feeling, a sign of weakness in a man, a woman or in a child. It is degrading to the person who exhibits it. You must all try to control your emotions when you fall in love. You must suppress that harmful way of thinking when trying times come into your life. And yes, those times will come into each of your lives."

Fred did not come back to their room that night. He must have continued with his drinking because the foreman sent a man looking for him the next morning when he didn't show up for work. Minnie overheard the boarders talking at breakfast. He had been in a fight and was found unconscious behind a saloon.

Barney Hartman was born on June 14, 1886. Minnie counted his fingers and toes, then looked at the perfect child and wondered. How can such a healthy boy come from the union of a vengeful drunk and a woman like me? When Fred first saw the baby a week later, his first words were, "Am I the father of this boy?"

Later that month, news around the boarding house was that a four-hundred-sixty-pound bell arrived in Rogers City on the Great Lakes steamer, The Atlantic. It had been purchased for the new St. John Church at a cost of one hundred dollars. Minnie thought that was an enormous amount of money for a bell, then learned that individuals donating from that parish were given free lots in the church's cemetery. She could understand people donating for a musical sound they would hear for eternity. Then she thought about her own death, her own eternity ... where she would be buried. Would it be where her parents, her brothers and Caroline were to be buried, or under the cathedral floor where the ancient kings of Poland rested?

She remembered the grand church of her childhood with the two goats fighting as they came from the top of the clock tower. When they locked horns, the church bells rang, announcing the new hour. She recalled hearing the uneven sounds of her heels hitting cobblestones as she walked. She missed the rattle of carts and clopping of horses' hooves along the pavement on Market Square.

The sounds were different here in Michigan. The clatter of cookware and children crying were "the music" she heard each day. The songs of drunken brawls from the saloon down the road or the boarders snoring in their rooms upstairs were the "lullabies" her children heard before they slept. Minnie lay awake listening to the few hours of dreadful silence before dawn, broken only by chirping crickets and the occasional hoot of an owl.

She had been catnapping on a cot in the corner of the kitchen. Her legs were swollen from standing and from the extra weight of baby Barney strapped to her back all day. She didn't trust her legs to climb the stairs to the third-floor bedroom, afraid she might trip and fall on the baby. Minnie wrapped him in a blanket and laid him in the kitchen sink to sleep.

On that moonless night Minnie slipped from the boarding house in her nightdress and followed the path to the river worn bare by her children's feet. She could smell a storm brewing, an earthy, moist fragrance. Thunder was growling in the distance. She stood there alone, numb to the cold, thinking of her life in the old country.

Germany was a world away from her, a comfortable world where she had felt protected by Jacob and Christina Bublitz. In that world the kindness of her brothers had saved the life of her clever girl, her Rosa, from being flushed away. She longed to listen again to Boleslaw Dembinski play the pipe organ at the Parish Church. She missed singing at his salons. She missed her piano, she even missed the boring scales she played over and over for Dembinski's wife.

The old Minnie Bublitz had melted into the Michigan landscape. She had slipped away, piece by piece ... used by her husband for sex, pulled apart by her children for their ever-growing needs, the hours of her day lost to the meal schedule of the boarders. All these takeaways had made her a nonperson, a zero. Even her sleep was not her own, but that of a hungry baby wanting her breast.

She shouted to the wind. "Is this all there is?" The air current shifted. A cold rush blew the knot in her hair loose, billowing her nightdress as she shivered before the empty, starless sky. "Why should I go on being a serf? I own no land. I work only for others." Minnie sensed the answer in the numbing darkness.

She had to think clearly now that she had made her decision. Fred's jealous mind would be at peace. He would see to the children. He loved his children. He would find another woman to care for them. He wouldn't need strong drink any longer.

She took a deep breath. It was final and clear. Here she was, once the most sought-after woman in Poznan, the pollen on the flower that drew all the honeybees. This woman who could not swim had decided the hour had arrived for her to jump into the Au Sable River and drown.

Logger's boots, called "corks," are leather nail-soled boots worn by lumberjacks for traction in the woods and especially in timber rafting. The boots are part of a lumberman's basic equipment along with his axe and crosscut saw. In the early days a logger was given a new pair of boots once a year as part of his pay.

Vast fires raged in the Midwest after clear-cut logging practices left mounds of branches and debris. Several dry summers in a row created tinderbox conditions that exploded in windstorms of fire that swept across Michigan and Wisconsin.

Photo Attribution: (wisconsintrails.com) An Artist's depiction of the scene of confusion and terror in Peshtigo on Oct. 8, 1871. The citizens raced for the river after a "huge black ball" drifted over the village and burst into a ball of flame.

Chapter Seven
THE SEARING

Instead, she jumped into the river to save her life. It was the autumn of 1887. Someone said the forest fire started with a lightning strike. Someone else said it had been ignited by a smoldering cigarette. No one could say for sure. She was startled by the blunt, thunderous roar coming her way. It was midnight before the wheel of flames rolled into the lumber camps south of Alpena. The fire had already eaten away the better part of the uncut white pine forest in northeast Michigan.

That got Minnie's attention, pulled her from the river's edge, and reversed the track she had chosen to end her life. The snarl of the fire burning the timber was like the loud growl she remembered from the engines of the steamship Werra. The sky had turned yellow with stringy red roots growing up from the horizon. Yellow sparks floated overhead like fireflies. It was all happening fast.

"Fire!" Minnie ran towards the boarding house, her nightdress flowing behind her. "Fire!" she screamed as she lunged up the steep stairs to her third-floor children's room. "Fire! Roelf! Wilhelm! Rosa! Gustav! Get up. Get dressed. Be quick. Put your shoes on." Minnie pulled a shawl over her nightdress. "Bring the blankets from your beds. Come with me. Hurry. We must get out of this building. The forest is on fire." Baby Barney was still asleep in the kitchen sink when Minnie pulled him out and lashed the little bundle to her back with her kitchen apron.

The children moved quickly. They scampered down the staircase beside the sleepy boarders Minnie had awakened and ran out into the street where buildings were already on fire. Sparks caught by the wind moved the flames to the roof of their boarding house. The sawmill was ablaze on the south road. Men were standing in long lines passing buckets of water from the river to drown the flames. The air was already hot and thick with smoke. Sparks shot across the sky like meteors.

They ran to the river and waded into the water. "Ma, you can't swim. Did you forget you can't swim?" Wilhelm asked.

When the water reached Minnie's waist and the boys' chests, they all stopped. "The river is our friend tonight," she said. "I'll be okay." Little Rosa whimpered from the cold. "Let's hold hands and make a circle." She was concerned the current would sweep them out into Lake Huron. She knew her children were frightened … they were quiet and followed her directions without arguing. "Roelf, wet your blanket and pull it over your head. Wilhelm, do the same. When it gets too hot to hold, dip it down in the water again. Do you understand, Gustav?"

"Yes Ma," Gustav said. "Are we going to die?"

"Are we going to burn up?" Roelf asked, shivering in the cold water.

"No, my little fish. We will not burn if we stay together in the river and cover our heads with blankets. Wet blankets will protect us from the heat. We are going to live. Roelf, hold on to Rosa."

"Ma, look. It's a bear swimming in the river over there," Gustav pointed.

"Look over there," Roelf pointed and nearly dropped the corner of his blanket. "Can you see the antlers? The deer are swimming from the fire just like we are."

"How big is the fire?" Wilhelm asked.

"It looks like the forest is burning," said Roelf. "Is it burning all of Papa's trees?"

"Don't worry, Roelf. Papa will be all right," Wilhelm said. "He is strong. He will come back to take care of us like he promised. Remember what he said?"

"I'm cold," Roelf sniffled.

"Come here by me." Minnie pulled the children to her. They dipped their blankets each time the steam made them too hot to hold. After a while the cold water warmed and became almost comfortable. The four of them held on to each other for another two hours until the heat from the blaze rose into the sky. The wind was still howling and carried sparks high into the heavens. It looked to Minnie like a shower of burning bugs seeking fresh tinder to ignite.

When the flames had devoured all that would burn, Minnie's family crawled out of the water and collapsed on the riverbank. Every building was gone, burned to the ground. White ashes covered what once had been a garden bench, a chicken coop, a boarding house. Her family had been spared, but now had nowhere to go.

Minnie sank to her knees in the warm earth that had once been her garden. She drew her children to her. She was thanking God for sparing those she loved most in this world when she heard a soft thump from behind where her work kitchen once stood. She turned and saw a single doorframe fall, the sparks fanning out like fireflies at a summer picnic and sensed her luck had changed.

She looked down at her shivering babes, their arms and legs entwined, touching her for warmth and protection. The woman wrapped wet blankets around her three sons' sleeping bodies. Rosa curled her arms around her mother's neck, snuggled close to baby Barney, and said, "Ma, I'm hungry."

The irony struck her as she sat on the scorched landscape. She began to laugh. They were sitting on her potato patch. She dug her heel into the earth until it struck something hot. Minnie uncovered a potato baked soft by the firestorm, rubbed the soil on her nightdress and gave it to her little angel.

"Ma, I'm hungry too," Gustav said. The children awakened one by one as she dug them each a hot potato. Minnie smiled as they were nourished by the fruit of her labor and laughed out loud as they dug their toes into the warm soil exposing even more baked potatoes.

"Ma, the chicken coop is gone," Gustav said. "What will we eat tomorrow?" Gustav finished his spud and reached for another. "What happened to my baby chicks?"

"Gus, quit complaining," Wilhelm said. "We are like Ma's potatoes. If we keep our feet on the ground we will grow strong and good like her potatoes. We will buy more baby chicks. We will find oranges in our stockings at Christmas, like we always do. We will plant another garden, and this time you will help." But Wilhelm's words were wasted on his brother who had fallen asleep.

Minnie could not sleep. She held her children close and studied the stars. Awed by the courage of those lights to come poking through the smoke after so much destruction, she felt a surge of courage. She knew she could survive tragedy no matter how often it crossed her threshold. It was dawn when she saw the man walking toward their mound of wet wool heaped beside the Au Sable.

"Minnie?" Fred shouted.

The boys stirred when they heard their father's voice, pulled away from their mother and struggled from the damp blankets. They ran to Fred's outstretched arms. He held his sons and carried all three of them to where Minnie sat huddled beneath the wet blanket, holding Rosa and Barney. He knelt beside her. With tears streaking the black ash on his face, Minnie's husband told her that he loved her. He said he had loved her from that first glance she gave him on Market Square. He said he would always love her.

The Hartman family sat on the bank of the Au Sable River near a lumbering village that was no more. They gazed in disbelief as equipment, stock and countless personal belongings lay in ashen heaps. One tall chimneystack and a scorched potbelly stove stood above the ruins as the only reminders of what had been.

The boys slept in Fred's arms as the couple watched the dawn bring in a new day. Beside them the river flowed, the river that had been the lifeblood of the logging industry and the reason for their existence in Michigan. It was the same river that almost took Minnie's life. This river spared the lives of animals and humans clever enough to submerge in it during the firestorm. Fred and Minnie sat holding each other, holding their children. The boys were still asleep when a horse and wagon appeared on the barren landscape. The Red Cross from Alpena was out looking for survivors. Minnie heard the whistling first.

The two men in the wagon whistled as the wagon drew up beside them, and whistled as they gave the family dry blankets, fresh oranges and bananas. The hungry children were so excited by the fresh fruit they asked if it was Christmas. Crates and barrels of food had been donated by a grocery store in Alpena spared from the fire. Red Cross volunteers directed the Hartmans to a clearing between trees the fire had missed near the Au Sable. Stacks of old Civil War tents had been unloaded at the site by these same two volunteers an hour before they discovered the soaked and sooted Hartmans huddled by the Au Sable. The tents were to be emergency housing for any survivors they could find. Minnie asked the Red Cross volunteer the name of the tune he was whistling.

"Oh that," he said. "It's a new song I heard at a square dance last week. It's called, "Turkey in the Straw." Hop in the wagon. We will give you a ride to your new village. I'll teach you the words on the way. You children pay attention now. Are you ready?" The children jumped in the wagon and sat next to the driver.

"'As I was goin' on down the road,'" the driver sang and nodded for Fred and Minnie to get into the wagon, "'… with a tired team and a heavy load.' Now you sing the words," he said. The children repeated the words and copied the melody perfectly. The driver sang the next verse. "'I cracked my whip and the leader sprung, I say day, day, to the wagon tongue.'" This time both Fred and Minnie joined the children singing the words. "'Turkey in the straw. Hey, hey, hey. Turkey in the straw. Ho, ho, ho. Roll 'um up and twist em up. A high tuck a haw, and hit em up a tune called turkey in the straw.' Got it?" the driver asked. "Now let's start from the beginning." By the time the tired team of horses let the Hartman family off their wagon they each knew all the words.

They all helped clear brush from the spot near the river and set up their new canvas home. Fred whistled the song while he worked. The children and Minnie sang the words over and over for the remainder of the day.

Fred turned to his wife as they sat looking out at the Au Sable. "It's a miracle I escaped the blaze and that agonizing heat at our logging camp. I may be the only one of the 'jacks still alive. Thank God you managed to flee the firestorm here. Minnie, we have all survived for a reason."

Minnie looked at her husband and wondered if this man had finally forgiven her. Will their life together be different? She knew she could survive a disaster like this fire. She didn't know if she could survive her husband.

Fred explained his crew had been working at the Meredith Camp located about five miles southwest of Metz on the north branch of the Thunder Bay River. The camp was not yet in full operation. His crew had finished their midmorning meal after having cut dry, drought-weakened timber since daybreak. A woodsman called their attention to the telltale signs of a forest fire … an orange sky on the north horizon. He rang the warning bell used only for emergencies. "Wildfire blowing in our direction!" was the call passed from one villager to the next.

House construction at that stage was flimsy. The temporary structures were built of kindling wood on heaps of sawdust and sand. If a fire came, the entire town could be lost in five minutes.

Fire was a woodsman's greatest fear. The warning bell was a call to action. The crew assembled and rallied men from the village to help fight the fire. They would start a small backfire to combat the blaze. The new fire was meant to suck in lower fires and prevent sparks from jumping to even more of the valuable timber.

Fred said he worked alongside men digging the fire break along the northern border of town while others dug on the east and west. Then they torched bushes and the low-lying undergrowth.

Village residents rushed to outrun the blaze. They knew their evacuation had to be immediate. Women and children fled their homes wearing wool blankets they soaked in water from their horse troughs. The blankets would protect their clothes from igniting from flying sparks.

The Meredith family saved themselves in the river, but their camp was destroyed. Fred told Minnie he had seen four small children crouching in the ditch beside the railroad track, seeking protection from the flames and smoke. One looked to be about six months old. Fred carried the baby and led the family toward a nearby farmhouse, but the smoke was so dense they had to lie down on the ground to breathe. The children told him their mother had gone back into their house for something. Later they found her in the field, overcome by smoke, holding what was left of an album of family pictures.

By noon the air had cleared and Fred and the children from the Meredith camp arrived at a farm. Horses were still alive in the pasture. Fred found the farm family safe in their orchard. They were covered with blankets. The mother told him she had watched for sparks and put them out on her children's blankets. Her dress was singed and full of holes. Her eyelids were burned and swollen. Her hands were covered with blisters. She told Fred her husband was working on the next farm and she feared for his life. Fred left the children with her and ran toward the funnel of smoke just over the hill.

A 'jack working with Fred's crew had been driving one of their teams toward the farm where the mill kept their horses when he saw a haystack next to their barn burst into flame. He pulled his team to a stop, released the team poles from the wagon, and removed the harnesses from the horses. He slapped the animal's flanks to set them free, and then headed toward a wooden building downwind from the burning mound of dry hay.

The structure was surrounded by a familiar fence … he had erected one behind his own cabin to keep a fox from killing his wife's chickens. The 'jack slid the door aside and looked in. The flock lay limp, bunched together in one corner of the coop, already asphyxiated by the smoke. The woodsman dashed to the next building … the sheep pen, and was releasing the already badly burned animals when he noticed the horse team running back to the only shelter they knew. He waved his arms and hollered as he tore toward the mares, intercepting the team just outside the barnyard. He closed the gate to block the animals from reentering the barn that was now in flames, turned and saw Fred Hartman running up the road.

Fred and his co-worker had their guns drawn and were about to end the suffering of the burned sheep pulled from the fire when a train crawled by, moving towards Metz. It was hauling empty wooden railcars and a dozen lumberjacks to fight the fire.

"Hartman!" shouted a 'jack and waved Fred to board. "Emergency. Fire headed for Metz." Fred jumped on the flatcar. When the train arrived at Metz, the men could see there was no stopping that fire. Almost every person in town climbed on the train that promised escape south to the river.

Instead of boarding the evacuation train, Fred ran to a recently plowed field. He had to get back to his family ... east toward Au Sable. He saw the train pull out of town and wondered if he had made the right decision.

The wind changed direction. The fire closed in around the train. The steam engine picked up speed. It was clear the engineer was attempting to break through the blaze. Fred could see mounds of what must be people huddled under blankets on the flatcars. A tree ignited and fell over the rails. The engine pushed the tree trunk to one side. A rush of hope stirred Fred's chest as the train went even faster, but the engine abruptly veered to the right and tipped. Fred realized then that heat from the fire had twisted the steel tracks. The spikes must have popped and the narrow gauge rails warped, derailing the engine. The fire was too hot, so hot the steel turned yellow.

One figure jumped from the train and ran, but the fire must have taken his breath away, burned his lungs. Fred held his breath as he watched, as if willing his breath to the man. He watched, screaming for the man to get up, to keep running, but nothing moved from the haze. The figure disappeared in the steam and the smoke.

Children leapt from the burning cars. Nothing stirred after their jump. If those still aboard the doomed flatcars screamed, Fred could not hear them. The roar of the fire was deafening. He saw the train's fireman crawl on top the water wagon and drop down inside. Even in the extreme heat, Fred said he shivered when he realized the fireman must have boiled to death.

Within minutes, the fire moved on. Piles of ash were all that remained on the railcars … railcars that minutes before had been mounds of humans huddling in hope. Fred had known these people. He had been talking to some of them less than a week ago. He had taught one of the boys to play catch. "He was the same age as you, Roelf. One of the women reminded me of you, Minnie. She worked at the saloon."

Fred told them the sky had turned the color of mustard. Buildings that had once housed the villagers had slumped into the ground. The railcars that had been their only hope of escape were now their caskets.

He said he saw an opening in the flames and another plowed field beyond. He got to his feet and ran. This was his only chance to avoid being burned alive, and what may be his last chance to see his family.

"I had to believe you were all still alive." He pulled his sons closer. He said he ran through smoke, through flames, through a field still green with alfalfa. He crawled close to the ground to get under burned timbers, to stay under the cloud of smoke hovering waist high. He ran on and on through the night, all the way to the camp … eleven miles. When he saw the bright yellow sky over Au Sable, he stopped to catch his breath and pray. Fred said he told God he was afraid. He told God that if he lost his wife and his children he no longer wanted to live. He said he asked God to save his family.

Reports came in slowly on the death toll. Red Cross workers had to wait for the ashes of Au Sable to cool before searching for survivors or the bodies of those that didn't make it to the river.

One family saw the fire threatening their home, the Red Cross worker told them. The father and son went for water. They lifted empty barrels onto a wagon and drove it to a water hole in the swamp. While they were filling the barrels, the man looked through the clearing and saw his buildings were on fire. He saw his wife run from the house with her dress on fire. He ran back to the house and rolled her on the ground until her fire was out. She lost both of her feet and her right hand, but she survived. Their son and the team were trapped in the swamp and perished.

Fred was not the only survivor from Metz. A man who escaped from the burning train told the Red Cross his story, which was later published in the Alpena paper.

"The fire was so hot ahead of us, the train did not dare run through. We started to back up, but the flames closed in on us. There was nothing to do but go ahead. The engine stopped right between two blazing piles. I got my wife and baby off. Some of the others got out, too. The cars were so hot that when they stopped, the wood flashed into flames."

The Red Cross gave out old tents, and soon a field of canvas structures stood by the river.

Fred's work took him all over northern Michigan to find stands of trees spared by the fire. He never seemed well when she saw him at week's end. He looked bloated; his eyes and skin had taken on a yellowish tint. He said he was fine, but it still looked to Minnie like jaundice.

Molly Amelia Hartman was born December 11, 1888 in Minnie's new home ... a twelve by fourteen tar paper shack the Red Cross built for them to replace the tent that had blown down in a storm. They also provided her family with food and clothes. Fred heard the insurance company went broke and could not pay claims.

The husband of Minnie's midwife had been killed when a tree fell on him two months before the firestorm. The woman had stayed with her during her long labor and painful delivery, giving her sage tea to ease the pain, and a bowl of fresh raspberries to eat after the birth.

"Fresh raspberries?" Minnie was delighted. "Where did you find berries after the fire?"

The woman said after seven pregnancies, Minnie needed to eat raspberries to strengthen and tone her uterine wall. The fire had jumped her cabin and her berry patch. She was happy to put her treasure to good use.

Fred welcomed his new baby daughter into his family, and then disappeared into the forest again.

That night the children crawled into Minnie's bed to meet their new sister and be near their mother. They surprised her by bringing gifts. Wilhelm said they were birthday presents for their mother for bringing them a new sister. Wilhelm laid fresh wildflowers on her bed. Gustav gave her a glass of cold milk. The others brought unusual stones, a piece of driftwood found near the Au Sable that looked like a duck, and a hermit crab in a glass jar. Minnie was touched by their thoughtfulness. She thanked each child for their gift and let those who wanted to sleep in her bed crawl under the covers. That night, with the warmth of her children snug around her, Minnie realized how lucky she was. These naughty, demanding, wonderful children were keeping her alive.

The widow took care of Minnie's children while she was bedridden and until she was strong. She even cooked at a makeshift boarding house that had been slapped together after the fire. Minnie gave her the two silver dollars that she still had from those sewn into the hem of her skirt. It wasn't much but it was for her four days work. The midwife had no other source of income.

Other survivors from the fire were housed in similar shacks clustered around a single campfire.

When Fred returned a week later, he told Minnie he and some of the men had trekked out to a copse of pines the fire had missed. They sawed the trunks from their roots, trimmed them into logs, and hauled them to the riverbank. They stacked them for use, rebuilding the mill and a proper boarding house for the sawmill workers.

The mill leased some of its land near the river to the foreman for a new house. The lumber company built his house, the boarding house, and the new sawmill. The foreman's wife was a kind woman and had become a friend of Minnie's. She told her she would see if her husband could provide building hardware so Minnie could have her own cabin.

When Minnie learned the woman knew how to read and write, she asked her to write letters for her to her family back in Germany. She started with letters to her parents, describing her life in the timber woods. Later she wrote her mother-in-law to tell her about her grandchildren. The letters were never answered and Minnie was never sure they received them.

When the lumber company's buildings were completed, Minnie's former boarders volunteered after work and on weekends to stack together the extra logs and insert the doors and windows provided by the foreman into a small log cabin for Minnie and her children ... and for her husband when he came out of the woods.

Fred bought the family a potbellied stove with money held for him at the mill ... a great sacrifice from savings set aside to buy land. He also purchased two baby lambs and a dozen chickens for Minnie so she could feed her children and sell eggs. She was receiving a cook's wage from the foreman now that she no longer traded her work for room and board.

One of Minnie's friends was not so lucky. Her husband had died earlier of tuberculosis, leaving her struggling and alone in a log cabin in the woods with five children. The fire had razed her home. The foreman let her little family sleep in the schoolhouse until a new cabin could be built. They had to pack their belongings and leave each morning before the pupils arrived for classes. Minnie invited the family for a daily hot meal in the boarding house dining room before they returned to the schoolhouse in the late afternoon for their sleeping shelter. The woman's oldest son went to work stripping bark off hemlock trees. He was eight. The bark was shipped into Alpena by horse and wagon and sold to the tannery for the processing of leather. It wasn't long before her family left the timberwoods and moved south.

Wilhelm turned the charred ground behind his mother's new cabin into a rich bed of lush soil before he left to work in the woods. She tied baby Molly to her back, and with Rosa, Roelf, and Gustav dropping seed potatoes into holes, her little family planted twenty hills. Ten would be to feed her family and the other ten would be for the new schnapps still her partner was erecting in her woodshed.

Barney played in the mud while Wilhelm dug a long trough into which Roelf dropped seeds for carrots, radishes, and parsnips. They planted cabbages in individual hills as Minnie had when she was a child in Poznan. This would be a cash crop. Half the ripe cabbage would be shredded to fill crocks for sauerkraut for the boarders, and the other half used to feed her family. The boarders preferred eating Minnie's smoked pig hocks and sauerkraut in the dead cold of winter over any of her other suppers.

Another long ditch was dug in the garden for onions and red and yellow beets. Still another was sliced into the ground for kitchen herbs like dill, parsley, rosemary and thyme. The last one directly behind the cabin was for medicinal herbs.

Minnie grew, gathered, and slaughtered all that her family consumed. She sold the extra chickens, eggs, and homemade butter to the mill kitchen for the boarders, the neighbors or used them for barter in Alpena. She learned to trade for the essentials her family needed at the Alpena General Store. She bought tea dust for ten cents a pound. Coffee cost her dearly and came in a four-pound pail. One orange from the store could be had for five cents. She rarely saw bananas, but when she did she bought all they had for her hardworking children.

Minnie was frugal with money. She managed to save several gold coins each week and buried them in the garden where she buried everything else. She sewed some gold coins in the hem of her skirt for emergencies. Fred could save for farmland. Minnie was saving for a ticket back to Poznan.

Log cabins like this one were built throughout Michigan to keep out the cold and keep in a lumberjack's wife and kids. Minnie lived in such a home on the Au Sable. Few if any remain.

Photo Attribution: A Man Sounding the Dinner Bell at the L.B. Curtis Lumber Camp. Midland County, Michigan.

Chapter Eight
THE SICKNESS

The winter of 1888 was brutal. An unexpected blizzard caught two families, isolating the women and children in their cabins in the woods from their men caught by the storm in lumber camps miles away. The women watched the snow accumulate and decided to combine households and supplies before the snow was so high they couldn't open a door or push out a window. After two weeks, they were out of supplies and nearly out of wood. They had cooked the last kernels of rice and given them to their crying children. The mothers were desperate.

Facing starvation, one of the mothers suggested shooting the children first, then drawing lots to see which woman would shoot the other and then herself. They talked it over and decided to wait one more day before committing the grisly act. The next morning they fired off their guns, hoping someone would hear and save them. Their weary husbands, tramping through waist high snow with provisions, heard the shots. They replied by shooting off their guns. One man had fallen into a spring and frozen his feet, but both men managed to get back to save his family.

Two children who lived near Minnie's cabin developed a barking cough after a severe cold. Their mother had trudged through deep, blowing snow to ask Minnie for help. Wilhelm was fourteen. Minnie sent him for the mill doctor, left Gustav in charge of the babies, and trudged through the snow with the worried woman.

Both her children were in a stupor and breathing heavily when they arrived. Minnie noticed swelling around their little necks and remembered the signs from back in the Old Country during an epidemic of diphtheria.

Wilhelm pounded on the woman's door an hour later, but Minnie wouldn't let him in. Wilhelm told her the doctor was drunk and wouldn't wake. Minnie told her son to go home and keep his brothers and sisters inside their cabin. She whispered that diphtheria could spread quickly and was deadly.

Minnie and the mother propped the sick children into sitting positions. The woman found sulfur in her medicine chest, which they burned the entire night. The strong smoke was the only way Minnie knew to keep the children breathing.

The woman's husband had been working in the woods for several months. She was alone and exhausted. Minnie did what she could, but both children died before daybreak. The mother was devastated and took to her bed.

Ordinary people could not survive such hardships. Minnie found she had been developing an uncanny ability to improvise and was at her best during disasters. She called on the mill foreman and asked him to send men to prepare the ground for graves. He sent four men to clear the snow and build fires on the small patches of bare earth to thaw the frozen ground. When the fires had ebbed, the men were able to dig two small graves. They carried the woman from her bed and set her down on a chair near the burial site. They said prayers, buried the children, and carried the woman to the mill's boarding house. She was grieving and couldn't be left alone.

The foreman's wife convinced her husband to have the company pay to have the distraught woman sent to her relations near Detroit. She was on the next train south, and didn't return until well after the cold weather had lifted.

On a beautiful blue-sky afternoon in the fall of 1889, Minnie was gathering huckleberries on some open land in the new-growth pine forest when she noticed a small boy wandering at the edge of the clearing. He looked too young to be out alone. When the boy saw Minnie with baby Molly strapped to her back, Barney toddling at her side and four-year-old Rosa carrying her own small bucket of berries, he ran to them.

Rosa offered him berries from her bucket, which he scarfed down at once and then put his hand out for more. He looked hungry and lost. Minnie took his hand and they walked to her cabin by the river. The boy played with Rosa and Molly while Minnie filled a plate with food. When he had finished the food, the boy walked out the door without uttering a word.

Minnie followed him into the woods and watched as he climbed a tall oak tree. The boy stood on a branch that could barely hold a crow. He held himself with one hand, shielded his eyes with the other, and seemed to be looking for something or someone. He wouldn't come down when she called.

Minnie had to get back to the kitchen to fry up some chickens for the men's evening meal, so she left the boy standing in the top of the oak tree. After supper Roelf walked her back to the oak where she had last seen the boy, but he was gone.

Minnie heard her children jabbering in their room next to hers. "I'm telling Pa." The small voice Minnie recognized was Gustav. "Look, a lot of things have gone wrong since we came to Michigan ... like all the work we do and no time to play. Ma says we have to work so we can eat. It wasn't like that in Germany."

"You don't remember Germany. You were just a baby when we left," Ralph said. "Gustav, you're always stirring the pot. Shut up."

"How was it in Germany, Gustav?" Rosa asked, ignoring her older brother.

"Oh, we got to play with other children instead of working all day. *Grobmutter* Hartman gave us sweets ... as many as we wanted."

"I like sweets," Rosa said. "Who is *Grobmutter* Hartman?"

"She is Pa's mother … our grandmother," said Ralph. "She lives in the Old Country. Gustav was too little to remember anything. He's making this up. You must have heard this from someone."

"Pa told me," Gustav said.

"Why are we living here? I want to live by grandmother Hartman," Rosa said.

"I am not making this up, Ralph. Pa told me we had to leave Poland for Michigan because of Ma. He says she's no good."

"That's not true. Pa left Poland for Michigan first, long before he sent for us. And our Ma is a good person. How can you say that about her?"

"I'll tell Pa we want to go with him to live in Poland," Gustav said. "Ma can stay here with you, Ralph. She doesn't deserve to eat sweets. She doesn't work as hard as we do. She made one of the boarders build a boiling pot in the wood shed to make whiskey. She hides out in the kitchen all day. I know she's not working. I bet she's drinking the schnapps."

"I'm telling Pa," Rosa said.

Gustav came to Minnie's bedroom. "Ma," he said. "Pa told me there are men out there in the woods, not good ones like him, but mean men that want to kidnap and hurt little children. He said they like to tie up children and leave them in the forest for the wolves. He told us to watch for men lurking around the boarding house talking to you. He told us to get their names and when he came out of the woods he would see to it that they were gone and we were safe. Is that true? Are we in danger?"

Minnie couldn't fall asleep that night. She couldn't believe her husband would try to turn her children against her, scare them into spying for him. She could no longer live with a man who hated her. That's when she asked the foreman's wife to write the words for her and address the envelope. Her letter to Karl Hartman said, "Save Minnie."

The Fourth of July celebration was held in a grove not far from Minnie's log cabin. Families of woodsmen came to join the fun and games. The 'jacks that worked within walking distance came in from the woods to compete in foot races and eat homemade ice cream. Ralph sold them moonshine from Minnie's new still. All proceeds from the hooch went to Minnie's special family fund buried in mason jars in their potato patch. Minnie intended on using this and other moonshine profits for a ticket back to Germany for her and any of her children who chose to return with her.

A friend of Minnie's opened a shack behind her cabin on weekends for square-dancing. The woman made sure plenty of free donuts and coffee were ready to feed the merrymakers. Her husband and his brother were excellent fiddlers and drew folks from miles around to dance and join in the fun.

The sound of fiddling pulled the boarders from their rooms. When her children heard the music, they followed the boarders. The music was like the Pied Piper drawing them all to the shack behind her friend's cabin. Minnie's girls joined in the dancing, often with each other. Her boys headed for the donut table. Under the spell of Fred's jealous nature, Minnie restrained herself and stood outside, tapping her toes to the beat of the music. Her friend understood her predicament and asked her inside to call the square-dancing. That evening was Minnie's first entertainment since coming to Michigan.

Fred came home in the spring. He was still drinking heavily and fell into bed each night in a stupor. He wasn't eating, was getting thinner and complained of abdominal pain. Minnie had saved enough for the steamship ticket for her and the children from New York to Bremen, but couldn't bring herself to leave a sick man. Taking his children from him might kill him. Before he left that fall for his six-month winter camp, he made sure Minnie was pregnant, again.

20,000 feet of logs near Turner Michigan. September 16, 1909

Chapter Nine
THE SAWING

Edith Amelia Hartman was born on January 10, 1890. When Fred first saw the little girl in the spring he said, "Is this baby mine?"

Minnie strapped the newborn to her back as she had with her other children and prepared meals for the mill workers. Wilhelm was sixteen and already working in the woods with his father. Ralph still helped in the kitchen, in the garden, and worked in the stable caring for the horses, a job Wilhelm had taught him. Rosa was eight and Barney was six. Both helped her in the kitchen after they finished their schoolwork.

Months went by when Minnie wouldn't see Wilhelm. Each camp housed fifty to a hundred men in five or six log buildings. There was a bunkhouse, a cook's shack where Wilhelm worked and slept, a horse barn for the teams of oxen and workhorses, a blacksmith shop, and a camp office that usually doubled as a camp store. The foreman and log peeler lived in the back of the camp office. Wilhelm's job in the camp was to cook for the men, a skill he had learned at his mother's elbow.

Cook shacks were portable so they could be moved with the woodsmen as land was lumbered out. They were makeshift buildings slapped together quickly … a cookstove surrounded by a few sleeping cots. When it was time to break camp, Wilhelm loaded the cast iron stove, the utensils and the sleeping cots aboard a wagon pulled by oxen. He drove the team to the next camp site where the 'jacks helped him erect another cook shanty.

Cold weather was brutal on the men's bodies. The 'jacks sawed down three hundred-year-old white pine trees during the dead cold of winter. Some trees were two hundred feet tall and eight feet across. Two men on a crosscut saw would work all day on one of those trees. The next day they would tramp though the deep snow to a new location mapped out by the camp boss. Work hours were from sunup to sundown, six days a week. Sunday was for rest.

A woodsman's physical labor in one day could burn up to nine thousand calories. They required four to five meals a day. The men called Wilhelm their "cookee" or their "shanty boy," and demanded only that their food be edible, hot and plentiful and ready to eat at any time, day or night. The menu for every meal was the same … beans, pork and biscuits.

When Wilhelm's camp was moved to a new location, and before he had access to a cookstove, he fried meat in an iron skillet with legs that set over an open fire. It was called a spider. He baked biscuits in the spider. He carried water from a nearby stream or river to soak beans, boil them, and serve them from the spider. Wilhelm chopped, split and stacked firewood. When his kitchen eventually grew sides and a roof, he set the spider aside. Experimenting with his menu required a larger surface. Wilhelm returned to preparing the food on the pot-bellied cookstove.

The men taught him to snare rabbits and other small animals and even net fish for a small change in their diet.

Spring thaw melted the river ice and changed the normal workday from first light until dusk. Days were filled with excitement but fraught with danger. Each logging company branded or hammered log marks onto one end of the cut trees. Trunks that had been piled high on the ice during the winter now broke through the melting surface and joined others drifting towards the mouth of the river at Lake Huron.

Each spring, Wilhelm's cook shack was dismantled and rebuilt on a barge that floated behind the log flow. The food was always within easy reach of the cold, wet, and hungry lumberjacks.

Floating fences were made to keep each company's logs together.The blunt ends of tree trunks were fastened together by a boom chain with rafting pins. Logs were strung together to encircle the company's winter production.These floating fences ensured all their winter work would be accounted for when they reached the mills at the mouth of the river.

The flow was kept moving by men called river hogs or drivers. If needed, these men would build a dam to divert the river to keep the logs moving to the mills.These agile fellows jumped from one floating log to another wearing calked boots.The spikes in the bottom of the boots kept them from slipping into the icy water while they kept the log boom flowing downstream. Log jams were prevented by the river hogs by maneuvering the boom around a bend with a pike pole to turn the logs blocking the ice jam.

A driver fell while untangling a log jam and sprung his back during that winter.Two 'jacks laid him flat on the wagon and brought him to the boarding house to heal. Minnie kept him in bed for two weeks. Edith fed him meals with a spoon … mostly potato soup.

Ralph was eleven when he commenced working on road construction.Minnie's sweet son was now driving oxen while the men built the ice roads.Tree roots had to be removed to form straight roads without turnouts for the stumps, so the 'jacks taught Ralph to handle dynamite without blowing his hands off.

Gustav kept an eye on Ralph for Minnie and helped the men set down the wood railroad tracks that carried logging trains.He was fourteen.When the area was logged out,Ralph and Gustav helped move the tracks to the new camp.

Ralph told her about the ox with bloat when he came home.The animal had refused to eat.Its belly ballooned out. The ox lay on the ground and wouldn't move. Minnie's son said he knew what to do. He used what he learned from the barn boss.

He found an ice pick in the cook shack, wiped it clean and stuck it through the swollen animal's side. He told her he remembered to stand to one side as he pulled the pick out. A hiss of steam shot into the cold air. The smell was rank. After a few minutes a trickle of the foulest fermenting stomach juices that ever passed his nose dripped from the opening in the animal. The ox, relieved of the pressure, rolled onto its side and stood up. Steaming from the prick hole stopped. Once the gas pressure was relieved, the animal shook his body, the stomach uncoiled, and the big animal went back to work."

Minnie hugged her son. "Good work, Ralph. I'll remember that and use it on the mill hands when they've had too many beans. I knew I could get a smile out of you if I tried."

Fred worked as a river hog because it paid more ... ten dollars extra a month. Accidents happened sometimes when a man lost his footing and slipped into the icy waters during the float. Some men were able to pull themselves up and out, then scramble to the cook shack, strip and warm themselves beside Wilhelm's cookstove. The shanty boy dried their wet clothes on a line fastened above the stove, fed them biscuits, beans and pork, and sent them on their way.

Accidents happened sometimes when a man fell into the river, slipped under the logs and was unable to find an opening between the floating tree trunks to climb out. If another driver didn't notice a hand clutching a log or waving for help, he was a goner. If he did see the hand but the trunks were jammed in so tight he couldn't push them apart wide enough to pull the man out, the corpse would eventually wash up downstream. The body, if found, was rolled into a blanket by a river hog, tied to a log and let float to the mouth of the river for burial.

Accidents happened sometimes when a driver slipped and hit his head on a log before slipping under. These men were always goners.

Men who fell into the freezing spring waters had a chance if they were physically powerful and healthy. That's why drivers were young men in their twenties. Their bodies were still sturdy enough to recover from a dip without catching a cold or pneumonia. Men over fifty couldn't stand the cold water like the younger men.

Fred was forty-three when he first fell in. It happened during the winter of 1888. He had been an unusually well-built and healthy man when he was younger. Then he could shake himself off, dry his clothes and go back to work. The frosty water exacted a toll on older men who lost concentration.

Three years later, in 1891, he slipped into the water again. This time he caught a cold and spent the next week warming himself in Wilhelm's floating cook shack. Fred Hartman was a hard worker, but he was getting old for this kind of work. He was forty-six.

The foreman assigned Fred a less dangerous job, which paid less. He would be marking trees to be cut based on their soundness and the number of board feet they could mill out. He would be a land-looker. Fred's legs were strong. He hiked ten to fifteen miles a day. He found his way through the thickest underbrush, moving as if it wasn't there, all so he could mark trees ahead of the loggers. When he was too far from camp to walk back at night, he would build a shelter with hemlock boughs, make a fire, and sleep over.

Minnie's husband made an unexpected appearance at her cabin after dark one evening in the autumn of 1891. He had transported an injured woodsman to a doctor in Alpena and was on his way back to work after a short stop to see his wife.

Supper chores were finished in the boarding house kitchen. The children were asleep in their room in Minnie's log cabin. She had washed her hair under the kitchen pump and was drying it next to the cookstove when a 'jack appeared at her kitchen door with a burlap bag of apples.

"I found a tree in the woods that was so loaded with fruit the branches were breaking," he said. "There should be enough here for five apple pies ... four for the boarders and one pie for me." Minnie laughed and agreed to make the pies if he would carry a heavy pot of compote she made from dried fruit to the sideboard in the boarding house dining room without spilling the breakfast treat on the path in between.

Fred saw the man enter Minnie's cabin. He jumped from his wagon, burst through her front door and stood there with clenched fists on his hips. His face was unrecognizable in full beard. His hair was shoulder-length and unwashed. Minnie didn't recognize her own husband.

But Fred Hartman recognized his wife. She had been laughing at something the lumberjack said. Her red hair was loose, falling over her shoulders, curling down to her waist. Fred's temper flashed. Minnie stared at him with an open mouth as he lunged for the 'jack and knocked him to the floor. The breakfast compote went flying. He kicked the lad in his side and then slipped on the floor and fell beside him. The boy curled into a ball to avoid the next painful kick. Fred struggled to his feet and caught the boy by his leg. He was pulling him to the front door, dragging him through the compote when Minnie screamed for help.

"Stop! Someone help me!" Minnie ran to Fred and tried to pull him off the young man he was now pummeling with his fists. He smelled of sweat and liquor and fruit compote.

"No!" Minnie shouted and stepped back. "No Fred, it's not what you think."

The bull of a man grabbed the boy by his arm, dragged him across the floor and kicked open the cabin door. Fred grasped the 'jack in both hands, lifted him over his head and tossed him out of the cabin. Minnie winced when she heard him hit the hard-packed ground. Fred closed the door with his hand and placed the locking board in the saddle. His feet pawed compote on the rug she kept by the door. And then Fred Hartman turned to his wife.

"Fred, stop!" Minnie kept her voice firm and backed away, avoiding the spilled fruit. She had heard the barn boss instruct Wilhelm what to do if a bull ox lowered his head and pawed the ground. He had told Minnie's son to back away from the irate bull and head for cover. "It's natural to want to run, son, but you're a dead man if you do," he had told him. Minnie grabbed a fry pan and stepped behind the cookstove.

Fred lunged across the room and threw his wife to the floor. The iron skillet clanged to one side. Minnie was too frightened to cry out. She didn't want her children to wake in the next room and see their father in such a state. She said nothing when Fred reached down and ripped open her blouse. He stood for a moment admiring her breasts.

Minnie was about to try reasoning with him, try pleading with him not to hurt her any more, try quieting him so he wouldn't wake the children when Fred pulled up her skirt and violated her right there on the cabin floor. Then he rested his full body on her small frame until he caught his breath.

Minnie lay quiet, afraid to move, unable to breathe. Fred pushed himself up on his elbows and stared down at her. With one hand he stroked her red hair. "You are so beautiful. You are all I think about while I'm working in the woods." And then, as if inflamed by the color, the bull of a man sat up and grabbed a clump.

The powerful woodsman jerked the woman into a sitting position by her hair. He withdrew the knife he used for gutting game, and sliced off her red mane dangerously near her scalp. "*Es enden*," was all he said. Minnie's husband stood, removed the top from the cookstove burner and stuffed in Minnie's locks. She could see her hair catch fire from where she was sprawled behind the stove. She could see red sparks float toward the ceiling. The smell revolted her. Fred carefully replaced the iron plate and walked back behind the iron stove. While standing over his wife, the crude dog peed on her."Bitch, you belong to me!" he said. And then Fred Hartman staggered backwards. When the big man reached the wall, he slid down into a lump and fell asleep.

Humiliated, Minnie clutched her torn blouse and chemise to her bare breast, slipped from her cabin and closed the door behind her. She should be used to his cruelty by now, but she wasn't and it hurt. Her mouth was too dry to cry. His words were the worst. I am the property of no man, she told herself.

Minnie was ashamed of the monster she had left snoring on her cabin floor. As she crept along the path she remembered the old Fred, the thoughtful Fred who rubbed her feet before the fire, the tender, loving Fred who had developed her passion into that of a woman. As she cleaned herself of his urine with fresh water from the pump in the boarding house kitchen, she recalled the happy years before Fred left for America. I was selfish to refuse to travel with him, she thought as she dressed in the dark pantry, covering her torn blouse with a fresh white apron. She had made a foolish decision, she knew that now. Minnie remembered her mother's words. "You make the bed you sleep in." She would live somehow with the consequences.

Drained of feelings, the former beauty from Poznan banked the cookstove fire and started breakfast for the mill hands the same way she had every morning since arriving in this wilderness.

The routine of cracking eggs, adding just enough of the egg shells to the ground coffee to make the brew rich and clear, and flipping flapjacks on the cookstove calmed her shaking hands. But not until she heard the rowdy men clomping down the staircase could Minnie breathe easily. She realized then that she was afraid to be alone with this man, this husband, this Fred Hartman. She preferred the company of twenty men who dared not speak or laugh with her.

While she watched the men swarm over platters of pancakes, sausages, fried eggs and beans, she was able to think. What can I do? Where can I go with my little flock of chickens? Where will I be safe? I must leave this man before he murders me. He may be mad enough to kill his brood, too.

And then she understood. A shiver snaked up her spine. Stomach acid coursed up her throat. Minnie Hartman had no place to go. She had no family or friends in America that would take her in with her children. Not one family member from Germany had responded to any of her letters.

The next Friday night, Fred staggered in and passed out on Minnie's bed. He awoke from his stupor at two in the morning and reached for her. "Go away, Fred." She sprang from the bed and ran toward her bedroom door. He removed his belt. "Don't touch me, Fred. Keep away from me." She felt the strap sting her back before she was thrown to the floor. "You dirty whore," he said and violated her again.

He lay beside her on the floor. "I'm so sorry, Minnie." He stroked her shoulder. "Stop crying, Minnie." He turned her over. "I can't help being a jealous guy." Fred lifted her onto the bed and sat beside her. "Tell me what I should do."

Minnie couldn't speak. She couldn't feel. She felt numb all over. Her eyes must have said it all because Fred stood and pulled up his pants. "No one will ever love you like I do." He kissed her mouth gently, leaving the earthy taste of cigarettes on her lips.

Minnie's tortured spirit sank like the hardwood logs the current dragged along the river's murky bottom. And when she was banged up and bleeding and certain nothing worse could happen, her spirit buoyed her body and mind back up to the river's surface.

The camp rumor mill ran wild with an incident that happened at a sawmill site in Grayling. A woman had been assaulted. The sheriff caught the man in Roscommon, brought him back to Grayling and hid him in a house. A mob overpowered the sheriff, seized the man, beat him unconscious, and strung the alleged rapist between two trees by the church. His body was left hanging until the next day.

When it was learned the dead man was of French extraction, the blood-letting escalated. Outraged French lumberjacks from camps nearby threatened to clean up the town. They stole rifles from their company stores and three men were killed. Minnie's boarders warned her to watch her girls and for her to stay close to home where she would be safe.

No mention was made of the woman who was violated. Women held little value in the minds of lumber men, it seemed to Minnie, yet she was warmed by her boarders' concern and warning. Unfortunately they were wrong. She knew she was far from safe in her own cabin.

Minnie considered reporting Fred to the foreman for assaulting her, but backed down when she reasoned he couldn't do much. Violence surrounded pioneers in this wilderness, men and women alike. She realized the foreman would see her complaint as a routine domestic dispute, and decided to keep quiet.

Cooking for the mill hands was a mindless and endless job. Scrubbing the tables and floors ended one meal, and setting the same tables with clean dishes started the next. Caught in the spin of her chores, Minnie didn't think about herself or how she would survive her husband's next drunken attack. She kept herself clean, wore spotless white aprons over her dress, and a bandana over her hair until it grew out. She rarely looked into a mirror.

Mrs. Fred Hartman focused on her work and the next child growing inside her. She settled arguments for a collection of children, her own and her children's chums, and when Fred appeared after a week in the backwoods, she turned her attention to his basic needs.

Chapter Ten
THE SUPPORT

The 'jacks and mill hands would not converse with her, not because of what Fred would do to them. They had seen the cuts and bruises. They had noticed her shorn red hair. They were afraid of what else Fred would do to her.

The woman was lonely. She was depressed. After the noon meal, she took a break to elevate her feet. Her swollen ankles were a constant problem during her pregnancies ... which seemed endless.

Sleep escaped her at night. Instead of counting nails in the ceiling boards, Minnie got up and lit the lantern. She sewed patches on trousers, darned socks, and trimmed a dress for Rosa with lace from an old gown she had worn in Poznan.

She took to wandering the forest for a few hours on summer afternoons while her children were attending the two-room schoolhouse the foreman had been coerced into expanding by the wives of the 'jacks. The second room was to house the teacher. Minnie looked forward to these nature walks in the wilderness she was so against experiencing when she lived in Poznan. She paid no mind to the muddied hem of her dress or dew from the grass soaking her shoes.

Black flies were a constant threat, their bites inflaming and itching for days. She brushed them away and danced through the jack pines to keep ahead of the swarm. The scent of the trees reminded her of Christmas in Poznan with the trees lit with candles. She remembered the smell of holiday fruit breads.

Christmas at her cabin in Michigan was made festive by stringing popcorn ropes and making paper chains with her children. The little ones were constantly asking how long it would be before their Christmas stockings would be filled with nuts and fruit their mother collected, so she had them remove one link from the chain each night after supper. When the last link was gone, it would be Christmas. Minnie had little to give her children for the holiday but hope ... and even that was in short supply.

She listened to bird calls in the forest and thought of entertainment for her babes for their birthdays ... an orange or banana from the general store. She followed a deer trail between the trees that led to a clearing where huckleberries grew. It was on one of these walks that she met Abukcheech, an Ottawa woman.

Black flies were circling Minnie, targeting her face, neck, and arms, when Abukcheech approached her and offered to smear her with oil. The woman smelled of fish. Minnie didn't understand until the woman mimicked a fish swimming with her hands and a black fly biting her cheek, and then rubbed oil on her own face.

So, it was fish oil she used. Minnie could see that the plague swarming around her was avoiding Abukcheech. She nodded to the woman, who then rubbed oil on Minnie's exposed skin.

The women communicated with sign language while they filled their baskets with blackberries. After a second chance meeting, Minnie invited the woman into her kitchen and gave her black tea and cake. Abukcheech stopped by a few days later and joined Minnie in mending the children's clothes.

Minnie learned Abukcheech's husband and sons were fishermen and trappers who spent much of the winter in the forest and along the rivers and shores of Lake Huron. She walked in the woods because she was lonely, too.

A week later she appeared with a tanned deer skin and showed Minnie how to make shoes. The two women became friends, picked wild cherries and crabapples together. And they laughed. Without understanding each other's language, they chuckled when squirrels stole berries from their baskets, they smiled at nests of baby birds competing for worms, and they giggled at two awkward baby bears exploring the forest alone. Abukcheech warned Minnie they may have to scramble up a tree if the sow came looking for her brood. Minnie signed to Abukcheech that she hoped she could run faster than the bear. Abukcheech responded to Minnie that she hoped she could run faster than her friend, Minnie.

Abukcheech explained her name meant little mouse and had been given during the brutal winter that she was born. She said the snow was so deep her father couldn't get out to shoot game. Her mother tunneled out to a pile of logs beside their wigwam, moved the logs and found a number of mouse nests. Under the nests, she found grain the mice had stored. The grain kept the family nourished until her father could hunt again. After that, he called Abukcheech his little mouse.

She beckoned Minnie to follow her until they arrived at a deep crevice in the earth with a stream running along the bottom. They walked beside the edge until the crack expanded and opened into a large sinkhole with vertical walls that looked to Minnie to be more than a hundred feet deep. Abukcheech attempted to explain an ancient story about the pit, but Minnie couldn't understand. The crater and surrounding landscape looked like one of Minnie's cakes that had cracked open and sank in the center.

On another walk, the native woman led Minnie to a waterfall where they spent an hour picking gooseberries and listening to the rustling of wind through the tall pines and the peaceful trickle of water splashing on bare rock. On the way back to camp, they met a bear on the trail. Abukcheech pointed to the gooseberries, her nose and then the bear. Minnie understood and poured her berries on the ground. Abukcheech did the same a few steps closer to the bear. The pair gave the bear his lunch and the right of way and found a new route home.

While the men were away, the women in the lumbering community counted on each other for help. Each of them was ready to act as a midwife when the call came. Minnie learned from Abukcheech that it was the same in her village. Mothers taught daughters who taught their daughters how to deliver babies. Women helped one another with all kinds of illness in the camps. They had to. The mill's doctor was nearly always drunk.

Women gardened to provide fresh food for their families, turning the sandy soil with spades, adding manure from the horse barns and chicken coops, watering with buckets from the river. Some women cultivated large patches of ground and planted corn. As it happened, Abukcheech was visiting in the autumn during the harvest and offered to show women who lived near the mill how her people harvest and store corn.

They made an afternoon party out of beating the cobs and picking all the kernels off. They drank mint tea and visited as they dropped the kernels into burlap bags. Abukcheech beckoned the women outside Minnie's cabin. She located sandy soil that was sure to drain, and then took a spade and dug a hole. She lined the depression with elm bark peeled from a nearby tree, set in the bags of corn, and covered them with sand.

She demonstrated to the group of women with hand signals how her people leave the corn buried, travel around the countryside, and when they come back the corn is there ready to be cooked. She drew her hands apart, indicating the corn would be good for a season or two if the bags were kept buried and dry. She explained to the group that women from her village mark trees near where the corn is buried for the benefit of those in need of food.

Abukcheech told them another story about a small boy that had been sugaring in a grove of maple trees with his family. He had wandered off and was lost. She said his father had looked for him for two days. The boy walked into camp the third day with a story no one could believe. He said he had been hungry and a small girl with yellow hair had given him berries. The girl had taken his hand and led him to her mother's wigwam where he was given food. When he was no longer hungry, he left the wigwam, climbed a tree to see the direction of his band, and walked home.

Abukcheech asked if any of the women knew this small girl and her mother. They all laughed when Minnie told them how she and Rosa had left a small boy standing on a limb at the top of the elm tree.

Rosa was six in 1888 and old enough to watch Barney, who was two. Their dog, Schnapps, guarded the youngsters while they played by themselves in the garden. Baby Molly was strapped to Minnie's back. That was the year Minnie became interested in herbal medicine.

Minnie learned from her Ottawa friend that native women usually gave birth alone. They would find a fast running brook with clear water, build a shelter with mats and branches, and supply it with food and a hunting knife. Then they waited. When it was their time, the baby dropped from the squatting mother onto a pile of soft leaves. Soon after birth, the mother would cut the cord and plunge the babe into the brook for cleansing. Abukcheech told the women that native babies thrived, and native women, seldom sick, didn't seem to suffer after childbirth.

She told them that women from her village help each other with difficult deliveries, like midwives do in the timber woods. Abukcheech said women who tired of the long wait for the birth would resort to scaring a child lingering in the womb. The midwife would tell the baby to get up quickly and run out of the womb because a grizzly bear was coming to eat both mother and child. The women laughed when Abukcheech admitted this tactic seldom worked.

The native woman also told her group of friends that a baby could be born sick or dead if the mother ate raccoon or pheasant during pregnancy. She said birthmarks were caused if expectant mothers ate speckled trout. Black walnuts eaten during a pregnancy could make a baby's nose grow wide and long. Women had no way of discerning if the superstitions had merit, yet they avoided those foods nonetheless.

One day Abukcheech untied the neckerchief Minnie was wearing and pulled it from her neck. She warned her that wearing it during a pregnancy could cause a baby to strangle. On another visit she saw Minnie lingering in a doorway. Abukcheech rushed to her side and pulled her inside the room. She said standing too long in an archway could slow an already painful delivery and weaken the mother. Minnie stopped that practice immediately.

When Minnie's labor began, Abukcheech somehow knew and came to be with her. She must have lingered too long in a doorway because the labor went on and on. The Ottawa woman made tea from wild cherry bark to speed things along. Soon after the second cup of tea, Otto Hartman was born. It was in February of 1892.

Chapter Eleven
THE SCARE

Otto was only a few weeks old when Minnie heard a team race by her cabin. The horses skidded to a stop by the stable. She heard the barn door slide open and then close with a bump. She wrapped her winter shawl around her shoulders and lifted the shotgun from the mantle. Holding a kerosene lantern, she stepped outside to investigate. It was Wilhelm.

"Wolves! Ma, get inside." Minnie's oldest son came running towards her with a shoulder of venison slung over his back. He bolted the door behind them before lowering the meat onto the table. "The men shot a bear and two bucks yesterday," he said sinking into a chair. "We had enough meat in the camp, so they sent me here with the team and a wagon load of fresh venison and bear." Minnie poured coffee and handed it to him. Wilhelm wiped his hands on his pants and took the cup, but the coffee sloshed over the lip onto the tablecloth. "Sorry, Ma."

Her son took deep breaths as Minnie slathered freshly churned butter on a slice of warm sourdough bread and handed it to his outstretched hand.

"I didn't get far down the logging road," he continued as he chewed and swallowed, "before I saw this pack of wolves trailing behind the wagon. The horses must have smelled the animals. They bolted. Ma, the team was running so fast I thought at first we could outrun them, but the wolves jumped up on the wagon.

"They dragged off an entire venison carcass. I thought I was next." Her son wiped sweat from his forehead with the back of his sleeve. "They kept coming and coming, pulling off hunks of bloody meat. I've never seen that many wolves in one place before. I was so scared, Ma. And the horses ... I couldn't let anything happen to the horses.

"I figured it was the meat they were after, so I dropped the reins and started kicking it off, throwing it off, pushing it off. That kept the predators busy for a while. Could I have some more coffee?"

He took a gulp, swallowed, and continued. "I tried to slow the horses ... I didn't want to break them, but they were too frightened and just kept tearing down that logging pike, their sweat flying back on my face. They began to slow when they saw the wolves blocking the road in front of them. I remembered hearing stories at camp about how smart wolves can be and how they move like an army. They must have cut through the woods ... unless it was another entire pack." Wilhelm blew out his breath and took a couple long deep ones.

"Ma, I thought we were goners ... me and the team. The horses balked. I couldn't get them to move forward. The other wolves were behind us. I didn't know what to do, but I knew I had to do something, so I threw the rest of the meat out and off the side of the wagon.

"The animals ignored the horses and me. They dove at the bear flesh piled beside the wagon, ripping the raw meat apart and then retreating into the brush. The horses were still bucking like broncos. I whipped the team and the wagon jerked forward. Those horses ran pell-mell the rest of the way to our stable. They are inside now, cooling down. I'll go take care of them as soon as I catch my breath. Could I have some more bread?"

Minnie slathered some bacon fat on another thick slice, fished out a plump dill pickle from the wooden barrel, and poured Wilhelm a tall glass of vodka she had made from the garden potatoes. Wrapped in her shawl, she stepped into the night, the lantern lighting her way. Her shotgun was under one arm.

The wolves were still sniffing the ground by the sliding stable door. Be calm, she told herself. The same tools she used dealing with drunks, like her husband, were tools she could use with these feral animals. She would not make quick, aggressive moves.

Minnie stayed her ground and swung the lantern from side to side, moving the light in wide arches to fool the animals into thinking she was larger than she was. The pack stirred, but did not move. They grew silent, their eyes glowing yellow as they looked into her light.

"One of you took my baby. I should kill every one of you for Amelia's sake." As much as Minnie wanted to avenge her daughter, she couldn't squeeze that trigger. "Go on now." Her tone was firm. She spoke with authority. She lowered the pitch of her voice and increased her volume. "You've caused enough trouble, here." Then she shouted, "Shoo!" As Minnie stepped to the left of the pack, she swung the light left, leaving the pack plenty of room to escape to the right. She waved the lantern in her left hand while holding the rifle snug between her upper arm and her hip. Her finger warmed the trigger.

"Go!" she bellowed. Frau Dembinski would have applauded the force of her voice. Minnie had learned to project from her diaphragm when singing at the salon for the grand ladies and gentlemen of Poznan. Her teacher would howl at her pupil's attentive audience tonight. One wolf that looked to weigh at least two hundred pounds lowered its head and tail and looked Minnie in the eye, but only for a moment. Then it turned and trotted off. The rest of the pack followed and they all disappeared into the brush.

Minnie's knees began to shake. She caught her breath, crossed to the stable, and slid the door open a crack. She congratulated herself for slimming down so quickly after Otto's birth as she squeezed inside, and yanked the big door closed behind her.

She set the rifle down with the butt on the straw and the barrel against the stable wall. Wilhelm had taught her to shoot and how to handle a rifle safely.

The team was still winded. Minnie walked the horses to the end of the stable and back before removing their harnesses. Their bellies were still heaving from the run, so she walked them again to cool down and toweled the white sweat from their coats. She pitched hay from the mow into their troughs, pumped enough water from the well to fill their buckets, and fed them grain before locking them inside the horse barn.

When she pulled open the door to the cabin, Wilhelm was asleep in his chair with his head on the table. Baby Otto was whimpering in his cradle, suffering from colic. Minnie walked the newborn to comfort him while his older brother slept off the generous glass of potato vodka he had consumed.

Common sense was held in higher esteem than book learning in the timber woods of Michigan. Camp foremen were at the top of the common sense heap. These men managed the Michigan woodsmen who produced 5.5 billion board feet of lumber in 1889. The lumber boom generated more millionaires in Michigan than the California gold rush ever produced.

Foremen watched for talent in the men and the few women they supervised and used their skills to the company's advantage. There was a native Ottawa man who ran a shingle mill. Minnie's foreman offered her a bonus as an incentive to keep down the kitchen costs. Fred had a sense of topography that enabled him to find potential railroad routes through the forest that avoided steep grades. The foreman used his skills to lay routes so logs could be moved to the rivers on mostly downhill grades.

Fred entertained his boys with stories from work when he came home on Sundays. He said a railroad crew had left a string of empty flatcars at Camp Six where he was working instead of Camp Four where they were needed. He knew the track. He had laid it out. It was almost all downhill to the other camp. So he climbed on board, released the brake, and had a wild ride coasting all the way to Camp Four. The children loved that one.

Fire was a constant threat to men working in the woods. The foreman posted a boy equipped with field glasses on a platform in a tall elm during the dry summer months. He stayed in that tree all day looking for fire. Fred told his boys he never wanted them to volunteer for that job even though the pay was good. He had seen a boy drop from the platform after falling asleep at his post. The job was too dangerous for his sons.

Abukcheech walked into Minnie's cabin on a sunny afternoon in April. Her clan was moving north and she came with a gift for Minnie. It was a package of ground wild cherry bark for her future pregnancies. She had come to say good bye.

And so went the days, the months, and the years.

It was a Friday afternoon when Wilhelm came home and announced to his mother that they should no longer consider themselves immigrants living in a foreign country. They were Americans now and should act like Americans. To answer the question before Minnie asked, he explained that people from the Old Country, like her, were old-fashioned and squirreled their savings in mason jars buried in the garden. Real Americans deposited their wages in banks that paid them interest to keep it there. "Brick banks don't burn down when forests go up in flames," Wilhelm told her.

Minnie learned that Wilhelm had been advised by some woodsmen that bankers were trusted men. These men were much smarter than wood workers were. They would lend money so farmland could be purchased and loans paid back with profits from crops at the end of each season. Wilhelm told his mother he and Ralph had pooled their savings and would be riding the Michigan Central south to Standish the next morning to open an account with a new bank. Mr.

C.L. Judd started the bank ... the first one in Arenac County. Mr. Barbour was the manager. "Ma, you live in America now. You should save your money like Americans do."

It occurred to Minnie then that this country had become Wilhelm's world. She still just lived in it ... temporarily. She saw no need to change her method of saving gold coins. She had been burying them in the garden and sewing coins in her hems since she was a little girl in Poznan. Mr. Judd and Mr. Barbour were perfect strangers to her. She advised her sons to hold off the deposit until they learned all they could about Judd and Barbour. She said she thought her sons were just as smart, if not smarter than some strangers. When it came to her savings, she trusted the good old soil more than some fancy banker's brick building. She told her sons she would continue to be old-fashioned, and that was that.

"Ma, you will be a foreigner forever." Wilhelm shook his head and walked away.

One of the boarders read the newspaper to Minnie that week. The top story in Montmorency County in 1895 was that the treasurer embezzled money and the county could not pay its bills. Road construction halted. New buildings were left half built in Alpena. Minnie wasn't a bit surprised.

Fred's paycheck was being tucked away by the foreman, a man Minnie trusted. Her husband's dream had been to own a piece of land, but that was where his dream ended. When he finally had the opportunity to buy clear-cut forest land at a bargain price, he could see no further. He had decided and wouldn't listen when Minnie argued how hard it would be to pull the stumps that stuck in the soil like ticks stick on dogs. She told him about the boarders clearing stumps from her garden after the firestorm. The foreman had paid them to do it. Those tired men worked late into the night for two weeks just to clear a small garden spot for her potatoes.

Fred had no inkling how long it would take before the topsoil could be made productive, and he didn't care ... in his mind it was already his. The tree trunks had been sawed off years before to build battleships for the Civil War and homes for America's great population expansion westward. The lumber barons had raped the forests and now tried to sell the untillable sandy soil riddled with roots to immigrants eager to own acreage. The millionaires stood to reap even further profits from men they had worked like animals to remove those trees.

Fred explained that if his family would lean into the early labor of clearing the land, he was certain they could all lay back later on and enjoy what they had built. He was determined to leave land to his sons no matter how much work they put into it.

Photo Attribution: (genealogytrails.com) Main Street Standish MI, approximately 1900. Contributed by Christine Walters.

Photo Attribution: (michiganrailroads.com) The Michigan Central Railroad depot in Standish, Michigan, built in 1889.

Chapter Twelve
STANDISH

The longer Minnie lived in Michigan, the thinner her dreams became of returning to Poznan. She had settled for second-best so often to keep her family together that she thought she had lost her spunk. Poznan had become just another impossible dream.

If she couldn't return, it was her idea to someday leave the lumber camps where they had lived and worked for the past nine years. But she wanted to move to a proper house with an indoor toilet, an upstairs and a downstairs … a house with boards for siding instead of the thick chinked walls of a log cabin. She wanted a stable behind the house for the livestock. She had saved her money … that part of her salary awarded her by the foreman for 'women's personal items,' her egg money, and later her monthly wages when she moved into her own log cabin.

Minnie Hartman ached for access to store-bought and tailor-made clothes and bonnets with velvet ribbons like she had worn in Germany. She had been sewing dresses for herself and for her girls made from the cloth bags that came filled with chicken mash. They didn't fit well and still looked like feed sacks. Her children's winter coats were sewn from woolen blankets lined with oil-soaked cotton batting. They were heavy and cumbersome, but warm. All of her family's winter boots were old, passed down, and had insoles regularly exchanged with folded newspaper. When she looked at her children they looked like the poor urchins she remembered from Poznan sorting through garbage for food.

During the summer her young ones refused to wear shoes. They worked and played in their bare feet. In the fall they wore the moccasins Abukcheech had taught Minnie to make. But when the snow was deep and their toes outgrew the toecaps, they needed proper boots.

Minnie wanted them to have access to school and friends outside the tight lumbering community. She wanted to be invited to parties, instead of being the baker for the cakewalks or the caller for the square dances. She missed museums and singing lessons. She longed for the sound of church bells ringing on Sunday morning.

On April 21, 1893 Fred bought sixty-seven acres west of Standish with $676.40 he withdrew from his land fund. Minnie learned of the purchase from Wilhelm.

The next day Minnie had a lock installed on the outside of the bedroom door in her log cabin. She paid a millwright to build a saddle on the inside so she could block the door with a plank.

Fred knocked on the door when he came back a few weeks later. "Woman, open this door."

"No."

"You can't lock me out of your bedroom. I'm your husband. Open up. Minnie?"

"No."

He banged into the door with his shoulder. "I said open up or I'll break the door down." He waited. He heard no movement from inside. He stormed the door, crashing into it with his bulk. "Ahhh," he sighed as pain shot through his shoulder.

"Are you all right?"

"I may have broken something. Can I come in?"

"No."

"Why don't you want me to come in?"

"I never want to see you again."

"Give me one reason. Just one."

"I'll give you three. First, you bought all that land with our money and didn't ask me. Second, without that money we can never travel back to Poznan. And three … oh, I forgot three."

"Will you let me in if I give you the land?"

"I don't want the land. Don't you get it, Fred?"

"Think, Minnie. I bought the land at a good price. Land values are sure to go up. When you get ready to go back to Poznan, you can sell the land and buy the ticket. Think of the land as an investment."

"Well," she hesitated, "slide the deed under the door and I'll think about it."

Of course Fred didn't have the deed with him. He folded a printed public announcement he had been carrying in his pocket and pushed it through. "Okay, now will you open the door?"

"No."

"Minnie, I did as you asked," he said.

"And I'm doing what I told you I would do. I'm thinking about it."

Owning those sixty-seven acres of American soil was a turning point in Fred Hartman's life. He had achieved what he had set out to accomplish in 1881 when he left Germany with nothing but the clothes on his back and Minnie's dowry tucked in his boot. He had become a naturalized citizen, voted as a Democrat in elections and now had the right to speak out freely as an American. He had a beautiful wife, three healthy daughters and five sons to pass his land to when he died. They would carry on his name. He had earned the right to feel the satisfaction that comes when a man has worked hard all his life. He was ready to reap the benefits of his labor. He was entitled, and he was tired.

Wilhelm reasoned with his father that buying sixty-seven raw acres of clear-cut land in Michigan wasn't like owning sixty-seven acres of prime farmland in Germany. The purchase was only the beginning. They would need farm tools, a team of horses, and farm buildings. It would take years of sweat to clear and till enough land to be able to produce the amount of grain necessary to feed a family and sell to pay taxes. They would need more cash. This was not the time to quit his job in the woods. Each of them had to keep earning a wage in the camps … at least during the week. They could clear land on weekends.

Fred acknowledged Wilhelm's earnestness and ambition, but knew the boy didn't understand him. In the Old Country, Wilhelm's elevation in status to son of a landholder would have been impossible. A German boy, born a serf, worked in a privileged family's fields his entire life. When he died, even the man's grave would be on land owned by someone else. Fred was proud of Wilhelm for shedding the restraints of the feudal system he had been born into. His oldest son was an American now … a savvy American with vision. "You are right. Wilhelm," Fred said. "I have five sons. We need more land."

Wilhelm, Gustav and Ralph had changed. They were no longer little boys who responded to the absolute authority of their father. They had been working alongside lumberjacks from all parts of the globe since they were small, had listened to their stories and had begun to tell their own. They each had their own ideas. Barney and Otto were too young to know what they wanted.

Minnie overheard their conversations after supper about someday having families of their own, building cabins for their wives and outbuildings for their animal stock. Wilhelm and Ralph wanted land of their own to farm.

Gustav, she learned, wanted nothing to do with farming and talked of owning a business and living in a fine house in town. Good luck, she thought. Her son had never enjoyed a good day of physical labor in his life, nor was he born with a brain for business.

Her boys had witnessed their father's success. They had worked alongside him and experienced the joys of honest sweat. Wilhelm told Minnie that Fred had taken him hunting when he was a little boy. He said he had him brace his rifle against his shoulder so he wouldn't be knocked backwards when it kicked. He showed him how to squeeze the trigger at the animal's heart before the animal stepped into his gun sight. But when he was teaching him how to line up the nubs along the barrel as he was following the target in the sight, he sat the rifle down and talked about how important it was for a man to keep a focus in his life.

"Pa set his mind on owning a piece of American soil," Wilhelm told his brothers years later. "We all worked hard so he could buy his land. If he can do it as an immigrant, just think what each of us can accomplish as Americans. And just like Pa, we can do it on our own terms."

In 1893, when Wilhelm was twenty, Fred sent him south from camp to look for more farmland. Most acreage west of Standish had been clear-cut some years before by Mr. Standish's lumber company. It was useless land, peppered with decaying stumps.

Wilhelm found a piece for sale north of the land Fred now owned on Johnsfield Road, a dirt and sawdust trail four miles west of the settlement of Standish. Minnie's son was also on a mission for her. He found a small house for sale on Front Street in the village. It was near a railroad depot that had been built with area farmers' fieldstones three years before.

Fred took Minnie south on the Michigan Central to approve the purchase of her new house and his farmland. What Minnie saw was a grand two-story structure with fine wood siding supplied by the Standish Manufacturing Company. The house was owned by the town's current prosecuting attorney, Mortimer D. Snow and his wife, Lizzy. The painted white structure was not grand like the houses in Poznan she once dreamed about living in, but it was an improvement over her log cabin on the Au Sable.

Wilhelm questioned his mother privately about spending all her savings on the house. He knew that money had been set aside for her return passage to Poznan. Over time he had seen a vacant stare creep in to replace the playful glint that characterized his mother's expressive eyes, a slackness take over her once room-brightening smile. He had surprised her more than once standing out there by the river in the early mornings, her eyes following the movement of pine logs as they washed by. He wondered what she was thinking ... if she was longing for someone or something back in the Old Country, or if she was considering jumping into the rapidly moving water. He knew she couldn't swim. She looked so tired and worked so hard. He could tell she wasn't happy. He had heard his father's rants ... had seen her bruises ... had witnessed her withdrawal from camp social life. "Ma, are you certain you want to spend your savings? I could ask the man at the bank to loan us the money for the house. I could pay him back over time. You keep your jar of gold coins, keep your dream of someday returning to the Old Country."

Minnie thought about it ... briefly. The facts were that her family had become Americans. Her dream was set in Europe, but her life was here with them. So that was that. She dug up $250 from her garden at the lumber mill and her son bought the house for her. Taxes were two dollars a year. This would be the Hartman residence in Standish until they cleared the first sixty-seven acres of Fred's land.

Minnie's husband continued to earn good wages in the lumber woods ... fifty dollars a month. He still deposited most of his earnings in the land fund, but increasingly used his salary for his pleasures.

"Minnie, look at us," he said leaning back on his chair and resting one foot on the edge of the kitchen table in their new Standish house. "I have earned enough money to buy land like I said I would. Had we stayed in Germany like you wanted we would still be working as landless serfs. Look at our children ... they are Americans. They speak the language and have the freedom to say what they want. They can vote when they are of age. Look at us, my beauty. You have given me eight children, five sons to carry on my name. We have been married for twenty-one years and you still excite me. Can't you see I was right in insisting you come to this land?"

"Fred, take your foot off the table."

Amil Rafrat Hartman was born after three days of labor in April, 1894. Fred held the baby up over his head. "This better be my child, or so help me, Minnie, I'll …"

"Give me your son, Fred. He must be hungry."

Wilhelm was now twenty-two and for the past eight years had been cooking for a hundred men, three meals a day, five days a week, twelve months a year in his portable cook shacks. Minnie's second son, Gustav pulled logs on bobsleds down the ice roads during the day and ran trap lines after supper to earn extra cash. Ralph, now sixteen, drove teams of horses that Wilhelm, Gustav and he had trained. Rosa, now a pretty girl of fourteen, worked in the office at the mill. Once a week she rode in the supply wagon with Wilhelm to deliver mail to the lumberjacks.

The 'jacks had become the Hartman children's friends, tutors, mentors and even playmates. Barney, now ten, took over Wilhelm and Gustav's old job in the horse barn. He was a small child, but worked well with Big Larry, the barn boss. Edith was only eight, but kept track of Molly, helped her mother in the boarding house kitchen, and assisted with the boarders' laundry. The washing was a new job for Edith, a job Minnie had originally taken on to build her savings for her trip back to Germany, a dream now abandoned.

Fred was drinking hard. His frame weakened and his shoulders stooped. He said he was tired, lost his appetite and complained of a stitching pain in his stomach. The foreman told him he had to stop drinking. Minnie begged him to quit. He wouldn't and lost his job.

Minnie was distressed, feared she would need to work even harder to support her children and her husband. "Let's go back to Poland, Fred. We both have family that can help us there."

Fred responded by insisting they move to Standish immediately. In March of 1896, he transferred the title of the sixty-seven acres of the idle tree stumps to Minnie for one dollar, "as I promised." Fred was too ill to sign the papers for the land transfer. A notary signed for him.

"You will stay in this country," Fred said. "You now own land. Besides, it is safer for our children here. I read in the newspaper today that Elizabeth, Empress of Austria, was stabbed by an anarchist. There may well be another war."

Minnie agreed to live in town on weekends while they cleared the land. When a proper farmhouse could be built, she would sell her house in town, stop working at the sawmill boarding house and move the family in with their father on the farm.

Minnie prepared baskets of food, bundled the children, and on Friday afternoons they all took the Michigan Central south from Au Sable to work the land. Minnie agreed with Wilhelm. The initial cost of the land was nothing compared to their investment in equipment or the sweat of their labor to work it. They would need more cash.

Fred bought a fine team of workhorses without consulting her. He wouldn't tell her how much he paid. He argued they would cover their cost and their keep, with the labor they would save them all. He said a well-broken team like Cobb and Dick would never get stuck in wet-weather mud and could work steep hillsides. Fred said he planned to use his fine new team to pull stumps and till the land once they cleared it. The team was stabled in the barn behind their new house in town, where he stayed during the week to care for the horses and to drink at the Summer Trail Inn.

Minnie sensed trouble was patiently waiting for her every weekend when she boarded the train south. She could smell it brewing when she stepped on Cobb's wagon that carried her family the four miles west from the station to the farm.

Fred caught them up on the news on the way to the farm. Herman Danckert had been quite sick. Work was progressing rapidly on Mike Schwab's house, and Tom West had recovered from a severe attack of la grippe. Minnie unpacked the basket of food from Au Sable for their evening meal in Lincoln Township. She always left extra for Fred to eat during the next week. She was never surprised the following weekend when her food went untouched. She never found out what he ate, she knew what and where he drank by the empty bottles he dropped.

Fred's health declined as his drinking increased. The verbal and physical abuse escalated. He spent afternoons at the Summer Trail Inn, stumbling to the house on Front Street after dark when he was hungry. Minnie couldn't watch the man destroy himself. She prepared special food for him so he would eat and not just drink, and left him sleeping off his hangovers while she and the children were out happily pulling stumps with Cobb and Dick. Minnie confronted her husband about what had become a major problem. "Fred, why do you drink so much?"

"Woman, the devil in you is too strong for me. Drink is my only escape from what was, what could have been, and what is. I once worshipped you for your beauty, your innocence … and now I hate the way you look, and detest what you have become. I have had a pain that twists and churns inside me since you arrived here from Germany with Rosa. You still belong to me. And I continue to want you, yet what you have become pushes me away. If I can't have what we once had, if I can't have your body when I want it, I will drink myself to death."

On Sunday night she and the children took the last north-bound train to go back to their work in the lumber woods. Fred stayed in Standish.

Mr. Judd's fireproof brick bank failed in 1896. Depositors received sixty cents for every dollar they had deposited and none of the promised interest. Minnie sensed the anger in Wilhelm's voice when he read her the news.

"I know how hard you worked for that money, Wilhelm, but it's not the end of the world," she said, "as long as you use what you have learned." And that was Wilhelm's first lesson in banking above ground.

Fred Hartman, Jr. was born that year. The midwife handed the boy to his father. "You have another son, Mr. Hartman," she said.

"I'm never sure," he said and handed the child to Minnie.

Fred gave up deer hunting in the fall of 1896 after almost shooting a fellow hunter. He was off his game, feeling the effects of his long-term romance with the shine.

Hardy's Music store in Standish captivated Minnie's attention like the candy store down the street captivated her children's. She had Wilhelm drop her off while he shopped for seed potatoes at the grain elevator and for sweets for his siblings.

Mr. Hardy, a genial man, took an inventory of the beautiful redhead as she admired his pianos that Saturday morning. He recognized her dress fabric as coming from farm animal's feedbags. It was clean, yet lacked fashion flair. Her hat at one time had been in style. Her leather boots were clean but well worn. "May I help you," he asked as she brushed her fingers over the ivory keys. "Would you care to try this Brazilian Rosewood grand piano?" Minnie answered with a delighted smile. The slim beauty swept her skirt aside, sat on the bench and started playing a scale to warm the muscles in her hands. Mr. Hardy's expression changed from cordial salesman to surprise when he heard her play the Bach. "Mrs. Hartman, this piano belongs in your home," he said as she finished.

Minnie was pregnant again in 1898 and had been working long hours at the boarding house in Au Sable. It was late and she was tired. She was moving a heavy pot of mashed potatoes when she caught her foot on a threshold. She slipped and fell, bouncing off the kettle with her belly. The pain was so intense she called for help. One of her boarders ran down the stairs, picked her up and carried her to the company doctor. It was no surprise when Minnie learned she was no longer pregnant. She was sad for the life that could have been, but she didn't mourn. She was too tired to mourn. She had to pull together a supper for the men that night and pack a basket for the trip south the next day.

It was the beginning of the new century and Minnie sensed a change was coming. Rosa was eighteen and glowing when she asked to talk to her privately. Minnie saw the signs and could tell her oldest daughter was in love. She had been staring out the window when she wasn't brushing her hair or sewing new clothes. Ralph told his mother that Rosa had met a fellow, a friend of his at a barn dance in Alger. The boy's name was Joseph and he was a fine lad.

"Ma," Rosa said. "Were you and Pa ever happy?"

"We were when we were first married … ages ago in Germany," Minnie said. "Your father is a good man. He has his reasons for not loving me now. Why do you ask?"

"Joseph asked me to marry him."

"I expected he would. He asked your father for your hand two weeks ago." Minnie told her they would like to meet his family before the wedding. She asked if Rosa had met them and if they seemed all right. "I mean, does insanity run in their family?"

"Ma? You are so 'Old Country.' People don't think like that anymore."

"It is important, Rosa. You don't want to produce children who have to be locked away in an insane asylum, do you?"

"No, of course not. And no, there are no crazy people in Joseph's family … like there are in our family. I hope he doesn't check on Pa."

"Does Joseph have venereal disease? Syphilis?"

"Ma, Joseph doesn't have syphilis! He doesn't have any of those nasty diseases."

"How do you know? Has a doctor checked him? Rosa, you haven't had sex with him, have you?"

"No, Ma. We have come close, but he always stops in time."

"Rosa, you must value your *Jungfraulichkeit* and protect your *Scheide*."

"You mean don't let him stick his penis up my vagina until after we are married? You can say virginity and vagina in English, Ma. They teach us those words in school. Why are you laughing?"

"Before I was married, your grandmother called my *Soldaten*, my private parts, a 'cabbage patch.'"

"Ma, Grandma Bublitz was joking with you. How old was she when she died? Why do women live so much longer then men?"

"Your grandmother was dead serious about my cabbage patch. Honey, women don't live longer than men. It just feels like we do. What is troubling you, dear girl?"

"Pa is so mean to you. Was he always like that, or did he change after you were married? Why would you marry a man like him? You could have had any man you wanted."

Minnie considered her promise to Fred, but at this critical point in Rosa's life, thought she should tell her. "Rosa, there is something you should know. Fred Hartman is not your father."

Rosa's eyes grew round and her mouth fell open.

"After Fred left Germany to work in the lumber woods, and before he saved enough to send for your three brothers and me, I had relations with another man."

"Ma? You did? Who?"

"Who he was is not important. He was a soldier. He lives on the other side of the world and may no longer be alive. You will never meet him."

"Did you love him?"

"Yes, Rosa. And I love Fred, too. You do know Fred Hartman loves you."

"Yes, of course. He's my fath ... well, he has always been good to me. He has always been a good father to all of us. It is only with you that he shows his anger. Is he angry with you because of me?"

"Fred and I come from a different era, a different culture where men think they own their wife's thoughts and their desires. He will never forgive me for having loved someone else. He feels betrayed by me and can't get past his jealousy. That's why he drinks so much. He loves me and he hates me, both at the same time. His passion is great and his temper is volatile."

"Did he know the man ... your lover? Did he try to kill him? I think Joseph would if I had a lover."

"Yes Rosa. Fred knew the man, and no, he never tried to kill him. He forgave him. But I think he wanted to kill me. He tried several times, but changed his mind at the last moment. He needed me to raise his children."

At a small outdoor ceremony in Minnie's orchard Rosa Hartman married her sweetheart, Joseph Frank Fisher. It was June 2, 1900. The guests were celebrating inside Ralph's small horse barn when the rains came. Children played in the hay loft and fell asleep when they grew tired. The guest's energy was fueled by their enormous consumption of beer and other alcoholic beverages. Fred butchered a pig and roasted it over an open fire. He also hired a fiddler. Minnie surprised them all by calling the square dancing. The party became rowdier as the relatively restrained afternoon turned into a boisterous evening of merrymaking.

"I know a dowry is considered 'Old Country,' so consider this a wedding gift." Minnie handed Rosa a mason jar filled with greenbacks. Joseph was pleased and said he would use the cash for a down payment on some farmland in Alger that he and Ralph had been eyeing. It was near his parents, Andrew and Jane Fisher's farm. He told Minnie he and Ralph planned to take out a mortgage on the farm that they would own and work jointly. Joseph hugged his bride and grinned. "He just wants to keep an eye on me ... make sure his sister is all right."

Minnie had been working at Mr. Hardy's piano store giving piano lessons. Wilhelm dutifully dropped her off, did the family's shopping, and then waited outside in the wagon until she was ready to go home. Minnie didn't earn much, but enjoyed playing the elegant piano and sharing her love of music with children. She made Wilhelm promise to keep these outings their secret.

"Ma, you look so much younger and more rested after spending these Saturday mornings at the music store. Have you changed your hairstyle? Is that a new dress? What is different about you?"

Chapter Thirteen
THE STEALING

Early one morning in October of 1900 Minnie looked out a window and saw four horses standing in the farmyard. She overheard Wilhelm ask his father about them. When Fred didn't answer she saw Wilhelm pull a harness over the white horse's nose and lead him into the stable. Two bay mare colts and one black mare colt followed the white horse inside. Wilhelm locked the gate, fed and watered the animals and came inside for breakfast.

"I won them in a card game," was all Fred would say.

The children named the white mare Whitey, and called the colts Brownie, Red, and Blackie. Wilhelm fastened the martingale straps to the end of the noseband in keep the untried horse from throwing her head. He hoisted two of his children up on her back and led their uninvited guest around the yard. The children cheered, wiggled and urged their father to make the horse go faster. Whitey wasn't distracted by the noise, the weight on her back and didn't flinch when the children shouted commands. This is a seasoned workhorse, Wilhelm thought and hooked her to the plough. She was no Cobb, but she would be an acceptable relief steed for both Cobb and Dick.

Gustav was twenty-two in 1900 and told Minnie and Fred he had decided to marry Elsie Walters, Charlie Walters' pretty daughter. They met the girl. She seemed pleasant and fun-loving. Minnie thought she might be a good influence on Gustav and perhaps be able to bring back the more playful and adventurous side of his nature. Fred gave him his blessing.

They were married on October 14, 1900, and moved to Two Harbors, Minnesota where they had a daughter, Charlotte.

The sheriff came out to the farm at the end of November asking about the four horses. They had turned up missing after a windstorm north of Standish. A white horse was running in Fred's apple orchard when Sam arrived.

"Mornin' Minnie." He tipped his hat to her and nodded to Fred. "Nothing wrong with old Cobb or Dick, is there Fred?"

"Nope."

"I see you have some new colts running around the barnyard." The sheriff clearly wasn't pushing Fred, but Minnie could see her husband's hands tighten into fists.

"My husband won them in a card game." Minnie held out a chair for the man to join them at the table.

"Minnie, that's not what Joe Nigl claims." Sheriff Sam dismissed her invitation with a brush of his hand. "Did you steal those horses, Fred?"

Fred hit the table with his fist. "You going deaf, Sam? Minnie told you right. I won them from old man Nigl in a card game, fair and square." He shifted in his seat. "Old Nigl was drunk … probably don't remember. You just ask the barkeep at the Summer Trail. If he says I'm lying, I'll give them back … none of them much good in the field anyway. I've been feeding those animals for three months. Who is paying me for their keep? You, Sheriff?"

"Fred," Minnie said keeping her voice calm, "if the man was drunk, we should return the four horses. We don't need them. He does."

"Nigl claims you led his horses away during the night of October first. He didn't say nothing about no card game. Are you a horse thief, Fred?"

Fred hit the table again with his fist, this time so hard the breakfast dishes bounced. "Sheriff, Minnie told you what happened. Good day." Her once-powerful husband stood facing the lawman with his hands on his hips, but had to grab a chair to keep his balance.

Minnie walked the sheriff to his open buggy.

"Minnie, Fred's going to jail this time," he said. "I can overlook a drunken brawl at the saloon, but rustling horses is serious business." The man looked at her long and hard, then squeezed her hand.

"Sheriff, let's just say I will see that the horses are returned to Joe Nigl. Will that clear this up?"

"Nigl says Fred has to walk them back himself and apologize. He's going to have to eat crow."

"Let me think on this," Minnie told the sheriff. "You will have an answer this week."

Wilhelm drove Minnie to the newspaper office in Standish where she asked them to print an announcement in the next paper: "ESTRAYED to (the) farm 4 miles west of Standish the evening of October 1st … one white horse and two bay mare colts and one black mare colt. Owner please call and pay expenses and get them. Fred Hartman."

The weather turned cold early that year. Wilhelm, Ralph and Gus had found winter work at the Laud Camp. The boys were ready to take the train north but were reluctant to leave the farm with Nigl's four horses still in their barn and their drunken father carrying a loaded shotgun wherever he traveled. They had no choice. They would lose their jobs if they were late. They promised Minnie they would be home for Christmas.

Fred read the newspaper the next week and was furious. He stormed out of house, hitched Cobb to the cutter, and headed for the Summer Trail Inn.

That evening Minnie saw the sheriff ride his mare up her driveway. She thought he was there for the horses and was glad Fred wasn't home to argue with the law. Sam knocked and removed his hat when Minnie opened the door.

"Evenin' Minnie," he said squeezing the brim of his hat flat against the band."Mighty fine weather we're havin'."

She thought he was acting strange. He was a polite man, but not that polite."Come in, Sam," Minnie said. "Would you like some coffee?"

Sam stood inside her kitchen door wringing his hat like it was a twist of chewing tobacco."I have some bad news for you."

She pulled out a chair and padded the seat."I just made a fresh pot. Sit with me Sam."

Minnie saw the man watching her from his chair as she moved around the kitchen. He was a good-looking man, not rugged and muscular like Fred, but smaller. What he lacked in stature he made up in integrity. She sensed she could trust this man.

"How you feelin' today, Minnie?"

This must be terrible news if Sam is being so considerate of her feelings, she thought."Sam, I'm not going to fall apart and get all weepy, no matter what you tell me. Just blurt it out. The truth won't kill me."

Sam scratched the whiskers on his chin."Fred got in a fight with Joe Nigl at the Summer Trail Inn. Both men were drinkin' there all afternoon. Joe hit Fred, sent him sailin'. Fred hit a concrete column with his head. Your husband is over at the undertakers'."

Minnie was having trouble understanding how Joe Nigl, a small man, could knock Fred Hartman hard enough to cause any damage. She held the edge of the table with her hand and looked at the floorboards. Fred had been in hundreds of fights in the timber woods. He was a strong fighter and had beaten men twice his size."Joe Nigl?" she said aloud as she shook her head from side to side. Her boys had told her he was afraid of his own shadow."How could it be that ...?"

"Minnie. Minnie, why don't you sit down over here," the sheriff said, prying her fingers from the coffeepot and easing her into a chair. He went to her sideboard, poured her a tall glass from the Log Cabin bottle he knew she kept for emergencies, and set it down on the table. "It was a fair fight. The barkeep told me Fred had been askin' for it, kept pushin' old Nigl until he finally took a swing at him."

Minnie sat there, stunned. The sheriff brought the glass to Minnie's lips and poured hard liquor down her throat until she coughed and pushed the glass away.

"I drove Joe home to sleep it off," Sam said. He pulled a chair up next to Minnie and took her hand. "Are you okay?"

"I don't think so. Could I have another drink? You have one with me, Sam."

Minnie took deep breaths while Sam poured her glass half full and filled one for him.

"I knew this day would come," she said and emptied the glass. "I can breathe now." Minnie wiped her eyes with the corner of her apron. "I thought I would welcome hearing that he was dead. I've been so angry with him for how he treated me that I prayed a tree would fall on him, that he would be swept into Lake Huron on the Au Sable ice flow. I've thought about killing him … with poison mushrooms mixed in his food or with the hunting knife he forgets to remove when he flops down in bed beside me in a drunken stupor.

"But I'm not strong enough for that. I couldn't live with myself if I took a life. I know how painful it is to bring life into this world. I couldn't take the life of another woman's child, even if it was the evil-spirited life of a drunk who has abused me for the last twenty-one years. I'm weak, Sam. A coward. I was trapped in a corner with the children by this beast. I even tried to end my life once, but that would have taken courage. I took the easy way out and did nothing. I waited for nature to take its course." Minnie took a deep breath to clear her head. "The truth is I'm sorry he had to die this way, or die at all. I wish things could have been different, but they weren't. Thank you, Sam, for coming out here to tell me."

"Don't try throwin' me out, Minnie. I won't leave you alone."

"It's all right, Sam." Minnie dried her tears. "The children should be done with their chores by now." Minnie looked at the timepiece on the chain around her neck. "Yes, they should be coming home to eat. Wilhelm, Gus and Ralph are up north. I'll send for them. Yes," Minnie said as if she were talking to herself, "when they get home, I'll send them out to walk the four horses over to Joe Nigl's with an apology from our family." She stopped talking, took a long draught on her drink, and said, "Sam, Fred is, was a good father to his children. I don't want them remembering he died in a saloon fight. Will you, I mean can you …" Minnie paused, "… could you possibly keep the cause of his death quiet? I don't want his children to remember their father as a drunken brawler."

"Of course, Minnie. As far as I know Fred accidentally tripped and fell and crushed his skull. I'll put it right. The barkeep will cooperate. Fred was a good customer. Joe Nigl won't be a problem. He's afraid you will press a murder charge against him. You could, you know."

"He's a neighbor and a good man. I wouldn't do that."

After supper that night Minnie called a family meeting. She told her children there had been an accident. Their father had fallen and hit his head on something hard. The blow had killed him. She had been calm up to that point. The distraught looks on her children's faces caused her eyes to well up in tears, again.

As Minnie lamented losing the once kind, gentle man she had married later that same evening, she experienced what felt like the soft touch of a cupped hand on her cheek. She brushed her face with her fingers. Nothing there. She sniffed and smelled Fred's sweat. She glanced around the room. When she licked her lips they tasted of Fred's kisses and the brand of cigarette he smoked. Strange. Minnie didn't believe people came back from the dead, but that kiss was definitely Fred's.

The following days were filled with thoughts of Fred. Her husband of twenty-nine years died on the floor of the Summer Trail Saloon on December 30, 1900. He was fifty-five. Minnie made arrangements to have his burial site marked with a small stone with the letters of his name carved on the granite. She ordered a larger stone with the name "Hartman" chiseled into the textured rock and had it placed near the entrance of the new private cemetery in Standish. She did her duty to the dead on January 2, 1901, and dropped a shovel of soil on top his coffin before it was lowered into the dark pit.

Minnie was quiet for a few days after Fred's death out of respect for the man and for his grieving children. Oddly enough she didn't feel abandoned or overburdened by the responsibility of caring for her ten children. She didn't even feel lonely. It hit her hard that third night after the burial. Her husband's death had been a huge relief. She felt liberated, physically lighter. Alone in her bedroom she laughed aloud and twirled in circles. As a widow she could live her life without the emotionally depressing constraints she had endured for the past twenty-nine years. Sex with Fred had become routine, or on occasion, brutal. She wouldn't miss that either, and she certainly wouldn't miss being pregnant like she had been every other year of her entire adult life. She walked outside to look at the stars and inhaled the cool night air. Fred was dead. Minnie was alive.

The week after Fred's burial Minnie had the Brazilian Rosewood grand piano from Hardy's piano shop in Standish delivered to her fine new clapboard sided house on Front Street. Mr. Hardy commented on her greenbacks, saying they smelled moldy. The two commiserated on the benefits of the gold standard ... the uncertainty of paper versus the value of solid gold coins. Minnie liked gold. No cashier complained of an odor when she paid them with coins dug from her garden.

The children quietly did their chores without arguing after their father was gone. A week later the emotional pressures of living with a demanding and dangerous drunk lifted and the children picked up their normal sibling rivalries, bickering and squabbles. Ralph became a terrible tease and chased Molly and Edith around the house making sounds like a pig at the trough. Minnie played the piano each evening for her pleasure and to cover the noise of her children. Each one of them sensed the change in climate.

The first frost was late in the fall of 1901. Wilhelm didn't go north to work in the woods until December 12. Minnie sent six quarts of baked beans with him from Lord's Bakery … they had a special, ten cents a quart. She knew he would be too tired to cook for the men Sunday night.

When the ground froze, Minnie's sons left for the timber woods. Both Ralph and Wilhelm took the train north to work on the Laud Line. When they came home for Christmas they read Minnie a letter they received from Gustav.

He was in the grocery business in a small town north of Duluth. He said the work was not for him and was happy his wife and daughter seemed to like it because he was leaving them there. Minnie was not surprised. Gustav had all the markings of a bad apple. She had had personal experience with a bad apple, a man who had spread emotional disease, a man who had contaminated each person he touched like a rotten apple does to all the other apples in the basket.

Rosa gave Minnie her first grandchild in 1902. They called the girl Cecelia. She had fine features that reminded Minnie of the child's real grandfather. She was wondering where life had taken Karl when Ralph stopped by. He had just finished putting up a fine barn and was proud. He wanted her to be the first to see it. Life was good.

Minnie's boys had been busy drawing lumber from the Standish mill since April and they were tired. Ralph invited the neighbors and his friends to a barn dance on July 17 in his new outbuilding. The day before the dance, Ralph went hunting for fresh venison and set his shotgun on a rock. The gun slid down, the hammer caught, and one barrel of the gun discharged. The blast hit him in the leg below the knee. People came from miles around for the party. The entire evening of his barn dance the social butterfly of the Hartman family slouched on a chair in the sidelines watching his girlfriends dance.

The land was finally cleared of enough stumps to farm. They were all exhausted from the heat, the physical labor and the long hours. They needed entertainment. With the help of her friends, Minnie organized an ice cream social and had the invitation printed in The Independent: "Call at the Hartman's residence on Front Street in Standish tomorrow afternoon or evening and get a dish of the delicious ice cream which will be served by the Division No 3 of the Ladies Union."

Minnie welcomed Sheriff Sam, his wife and sons. Everyone ate bowls of hand-churned ice cream. The children took turns sitting on blocks of ice. Ralph and Wilhelm hauled the big chunks from last winter's river harvest that were stored in the icehouse. They spread them out on the front lawn to cool the guests. Everyone made snowballs from the ice chipped for the hand-cranked ice cream freezer and had a snowball fight. Minnie served sponge cake to over fifty people that day. Before the guests went home Ralph asked Minnie to play a song for them on her Brazilian Rosewood grand piano. They gathered inside the Front Street parlour while she played, "The Star Spangled Banner." Guests crowded in the kitchen and jockeyed for position on the staircase just to hear her play, "The Battle Hymn of the Republic." The final song was a lullaby Minnie's mother had sung to her in Germany. The music calmed children over-excited from too many sweets and enabled their parents to walk them home without complaint.

It was mid-January of 1904 when the newly formed Lutheran congregation began getting out timber to build its new church on Johnsfield Road just down the road from the Hartman farmland. Ralph and Joseph Fischer, Rosa's husband, had been cutting, hauling and stacking elm logs in preparation for the building bee. Minnie's boys, along with most of the neighbors, helped build the church that same year. Her girls and the other wives and daughters provided hot meals at noon and picnics at sundown for the workers.

Wilhelm purchased another forty acres along Johnsfield Road a hop, skip and a jump from the new church. The seller was Mr. Judd, the owner of the 1896 failed bank that had clipped forty cents off every dollar of Wilhelm's savings. Shortly after the bank failure, almost too shortly after, Judd became the owner of the Standish Manufacturing, a business that built wood tubs and pails. But his company was strapped for cash again. Wilhelm was able to purchase Judd's land at a bargain ... to his immense delight. When Judd's second enterprise went bust, Wilhelm was not the only one in Standish to celebrate.

Wilhelm and Ralph proudly cut trees from land they owned to build a proper log cabin for their mother on land she owned. Cobb and Dick dragged the logs to the building site on the south side of Johnsfield Road. Until the stack of timber was high enough for a two-story log cabin, the family lived in town.

All the Hartmans worked clearing the land by day. When Fred Jr. or Otto grew tired looking for baby rabbits or scaring up pheasants late in the afternoon, Wilhelm would let them ride on Cobb or Dick if they promised to hold on. At dusk the boys hitched Cobb and Dick to the wagon and everyone piled in for the ride to town. Barney, now fourteen, fed and

Minnies Brazilian Rosewood grand piano.

bedded the horses while Minnie prepared meals with help from the girls. They ate supper when they could no longer see to work, and then fell into bed, dead tired. Minnie hardly thought of Fred and didn't think of Karl at all.

The Hartman family needed all the cash they could raise to buy what they couldn't grow ... sugar, a single bottom plough for Cobb and Dick, and money for doctor bills and funeral expenses. They needed cash to pay the taxes and the mortgage on the land.

Rosa and Frank Fisher gave Minnie another grandchild in 1904, a girl they called Hazel. They were barely making ends meet on their farm in Alger. No one had much money. Minnie invited family and their friends to her home on Sunday afternoon for German Chocolate cake and a sing-along to celebrate the new baby. She played songs Mr. Hardy said were sure to be big hits. She was to try them out on her family before the owner of the music store ordered sheet music for his customers in Standish. That night they liked and then learned the songs, 'The Yankee Doodle Boy,' and 'You're a Grand Old Flag.'

Minnie transferred forty acres of land in July of 1906 to Ralph. The property was subject to a mortgage with the Oxford Savings Bank. Ralph had been working at the Hardluck Camp. He was twenty-six and had been courting a number of women on weekends. Being a bit of a juggler, Ralph managed to get all the women to help him build and finish his log cabin.

Wilhelm took out a loan from the State Bank of Standish, but it wasn't enough to buy seed, feed the family and pay the taxes. He told his mother he was in a bind and asked if she would lend him some cash. Minnie had some experience surviving financial distress and was confident she could think of a way to pay back Wilhelm's loan at the bank and pay the taxes on his and Ralph's land. Failure to pay either could result in the loss of all they had struggled to build.

Everyone had a job. The older girls watched the little ones, scrubbed muddy clothes until they gleamed white, and prepared the meals ... all the while complaining they were overworked and underfed. Wilhelm worked on weekends planting, harvesting and pulling stumps.

Minnie listened to the children talk about current events over supper. After the dishes were cleared, washed and put away, Minnie played them a new song from Hardy's music store called 'O Tannenbaum.' It was in two-part harmony and was about a Christmas tree. Listening to her children as they stood around her Brazilian Rosewood grand piano humming the melody gave Minnie goose bumps. The harmony took her back to memories of Poznan and her family singing at Christmas time. She missed Mama and Papa. When her children added the German lyrics, Minnie's eyes glazed over in tears and she stopped playing so she could wipe them. Her children quickly translated the words to American English.

During the week both Wilhelm and Ralph, and now even Gustav, worked at the Loud Line, a lumber camp near Au Sable. The three boys were to work together on the farmland on weekends, but fought. Wilhelm said Gustav moved like a stubborn earthworm ... when he worked, and Gustav complained Wilhelm drove him as hard as he did Cobb, and he was no workhorse. Gustav said he was too tired from working all week and needed to rest on weekends. Ralph worked and wisely kept his mouth shut. Minnie worked on her plan.

When work at the Loud Line slowed, Ralph found a job boarding as a live-in farmhand for a neighbor during the week and helped pull stumps when he came home on weekends. Minnie worked the fields with Barney and with Amil, who was now twelve.

This backbreaking labor was wearing on them all. They were plugging along, going nowhere. If they lessened the pace they would backslide, lose income from the crops, and lose their ability to pay off what they owed. Minnie realized she had to work with her head instead of her back. She listened to the national news and worked on her plan.

Rosa and Joseph gave Minnie another grandchild in 1906, William Joseph. Shortly after Rosa was on her feet again, the little family boarded a westbound train and ended their journey in Two Harbors, Minnesota where Elsie Hartman hired them to work in her thriving grocery store. Rosa wrote Minnie every week describing the antics of the grandchildren and their cousin, Caroline. She said Elsie never mentioned Gustav.

On weekends when Wilhelm came out of the lumber woods he regaled the family with tall timber tales. The family had firsthand knowledge of how logging camps moved as one area was lumbered-out and a fresh stand of trees was found. Minnie and the girls had always lived in the sawmill boarding house or their small cabin on the Au Sable and knew little about navigating the packed sand trails of the pine forest. Edith asked her brother how he would find his way back to the camp after dark on Sunday nights.

Wilhelm said it wasn't hard. He would flag the engineer to stop the train when he saw a mile marker along the track that was near where his next camp was supposed to be. He told Edith it was not uncommon for lumberjacks to walk five miles down logging trails to a stand of trees to begin work. He would follow the men and set up the cook shack.

"But when you were alone, how did you know which way to go? Did you follow the stars? Did you ever get lost?" Edith asked.

"Just listen and don't ask so many questions," he told his sister. He said he entered the forest on the narrow road pounded flat by teams of horses pulling logs. He was familiar with the sounds in the forest at night … the howls of wolves, the rustling of leaves as a bear moved or a deer fled. He said it wasn't unusual for a lone grey wolf to follow a few steps behind him as he walked the path that led to his camp. Sometimes a second wolf trailed beside him in the ditch. He was used to the animals, but when they came too close or when there were more than a few, he would throw a lighted match in their direction to keep them at bay.

Edith loved her brother's stories. They frightened Minnie. That Sunday afternoon when Wilhelm boarded the train north to the Frederick camp near Gaylord, Minnie slipped a new box of kitchen matches in his pocket.

Minnie's dream was to build a log cabin at the farm large enough to hold everyone in her family. The boys had already cut logs from the stand of hardwoods at the back of the field, and Cobb and Dick had pulled those logs through the fields to the building site. She dreamed that her boys would continue clearing stumps and preparing the fields for crops. They would hunt and fish to supplement their diet. Minnie imagined they would all help build the cabin. The older girls would whitewash the inside walls. After the smaller children helped oil the cabin's wood floors, they would play outside and stay out of everyone's way. The girls would plant a garden and then walk back to town to sew and launder the clothes and prepare and serve evening meals. Every Hartman would attend the one-room schoolhouse and learn to read and write. The grand piano would be the first fixture to enter through the doors of the new log cabin. Minnie would teach each of her children her favorite Chopin sonatas. This would be how Minnie would spend the rest of her life … or so she dreamed.

Instead, weekends during the summer were in fact filled with the exhausting work of clearing the land and blowing stumps to loosen roots so Cobb and Dick could pull them out. When a pine root held so tight that the team could not budge it, Wilhelm would plant a stick of dynamite in just the right place, insert a blasting cap and a fuse. The entire crew knew to back away before he lit the fuse. Wilhelm's siblings helped pile the newly exposed branches and roots into long hedgerows to fence the livestock that would someday be grazing in those fields. Once cleared of stumps, Ralph hooked a single bottom plough to Cobb and Dick and turned the rich soil into plantable land. By summer's end, enough of the fields were fitted that crops of Alfalfa and winter wheat were planted.

Rosa wrote from Minnesota that they had packed their belongings on a railcar and would ride the train south and then east to upstate New York near a village called Virgil. "We bought a farm, Ma!" She said in her letter that she was looking forward to raising chickens and selling the eggs. She said she was getting chubby and her hair was now long enough to sit on. She told her mother not to worry, that she was keeping herself up. The bun was twisted neat and pinned on top her head. Rosa wrote that Gus had left Elsie. They got a divorce and Gus disappeared. "Did he come back to Michigan?" Elsie had sold the store and she and Charlotte were moving to Washington State to live with Elsie's Aunt Annie and her brother who Elsie described as a cowboy.

Minnie sold the house in town and directed the move to their yet unfinished log cabin on Wilhelm's farm. She needed cash from the sale of the house to pay large amounts due to the bank and the taxman.

During the long winter evenings the family listened as Wilhelm read in German from his father's book on wine production published in 1832. Fred had carried it with him from the Old Country. Minnie drew a plan to plant and stake vines in the spring along the east/west fence line. The location would give the vines a southern exposure. Starter roots for Concord grapes were easy to find. Minnie realized it would take years before the vines were heavy with grapes. What she preferred but couldn't locate were the varieties developed in Poland for colder climates.

The Hartman vineyard would be in front of Wilhelm's new barn and in plain view from Johnsfield Road. Home-brewing alcohol in small amounts for home consumption was legal, but limited to wine and hard cider. If anyone asked, Minnie instructed her family to say they were growing grapes for the church's communion wine.

Wilhelm bought four milk cows and a young bull from an elderly farmer near Sterling to add to his small herd. He and Ralph drove the animals the five miles to Johnsfield on foot. Wilhelm told Minnie he was gambling the price of milk would go up. He said he didn't expect to make a killing, but needed a plan to produce income on more than one path. If they had a wet year and couldn't get into the fields to harvest grain, they may have to survive on their weekly milk check.

He said the young bull would make a good breeding animal, and that he expected the beast would make enough from stud fees alone to pay for all five animals. Minnie knew they needed a bull to service the herd and keep the milk flowing after Wilhelm had to shoot his last bull for jumping the fence and scaring the neighbors.

"How is his temperament?" she said. "We don't need more trouble from cattle."

"The bull already has a tendency to be ornery. We better keep him isolated in a fenced field. Ma, the animal already has a name. He's called 'The Judge.'"

Wilhelm had them all planting potatoes as soon as the frost was out of the ground. Cobb pulled the wagon of seed potatoes and Ralph and Barney dug hollows ... hard, monotonous work. Molly and Edith cut the potatoes into chunks ... each surrounding one eye, and dropped at least one chunk into each hole to sprout. Fred Jr. followed along, filling in the depressions and mounding the soil on top. Otto spent most of his time playing with frogs in the swamp. Ralph wasn't a slacker, so Minnie was surprised when he didn't show up for work on the second day of the planting. Wilhelm investigated.

"Ma, Ralph shot himself in his foot with a .22 caliber rifle. He claims he was cleaning his gun and didn't know it was loaded." It was in the same leg as his other gunshot wound and kept him from fieldwork for a week. The next week the Independent printed, "Ralph Hartman has a new Edison phonograph." Minnie marched to his house and found him lying in bed with his leg elevated, listening to music. She asked him if he had a girlfriend who was a reporter for the newspaper? Ralph grinned.

"You will heal. Dr. Warren told me your friend, Albert Pepple, has typhoid fever. I've seen what an epidemic can do. You just stay here in bed, sonny. If I see you outside driving your truck or seeing your buddies, I'll shoot you in the other foot."

Chapter Fourteen
THE SCHEME

The Women's Temperance Movement was picking up steam that year. The newspapers were full of it. They wanted to ban alcohol from being sold or consumed to protect families, women and children from the disabling effects of its use. That gave Minnie a reason to share her plan that would solve their financial problems.

She called her family together after church on a Sunday in 1907 and announced, "I've got a proposal. If my plan works we may be able to pay off our debts, pay the taxes and have money left over. Before I tell you my plan, you must each swear to me that you will all work together and never speak of our business to anyone, for any reason, ever. If you swear I'll explain the plan's details and after that we will have cinnamon toast and coffee to celebrate."

Minnie's children glanced at one another. She could tell she piqued their curiosity and their appetites. They looked back at her and raised their right hands.

"We are going into the distilling business." Minnie listened as they chuckled in disbelief, but held her face expressionless.

"Ma, do you mean distilling whiskey, the kind Pa drank?" Barney asked. "Or are you talking about communion wine?"

"Barney, grow up. She's not talking about wine. Ma, do you mean make enough liquor so we could sell it like you did at the Au Sable camp?" Ralph asked.

When no response came from Minnie, her children took that as a yes.

"Ma, selling whiskey is against the law. Do you mean you want us to break the law?" Gustav asked.

They were good children and listened. She told them of the movement to ban alcohol that may become a law in the next few years. She explained to them how human nature tends to make people want what they cannot have. She told them people will go to extremes, will break the law to get that which is forbidden. She said liquor now selling for a nickel a glass, in a few years will sell for twenty-five times that amount.

"Ma, are you baking something?" Molly asked.

Minnie told her children the group of citizens behind the Temperance Movement think a law will stop people from drinking. They are wrong. This will be an impossible law to enforce. It goes against human nature. Congress sometimes passes laws that are flawed ... like the law that excludes Chinese people from becoming citizens. If Congress passes one banning alcohol, it will have to be reversed. It would be an unnatural law. People will drink.

Minnie told her children she would teach each of them how to distill a high-quality alcohol product that would be safe to drink and easy to sell. It would take a few years for all of them to figure out what they were doing, but they would be ready when the law was passed, and she was pretty sure it would be.

"Ma, do I smell meat cooking?"

"It's the cinnamon toast," Minnie said.

Molly knitted her brow. "Hmm."

"Wilhelm, you will grow the potatoes and corn, five acres of each. Ralph, you are in charge of building two stills. Wilhelm will show you the way they were built at the boarding house. Locate them back in the woods ... out of sight. Barney and Amil, you will build a small log cabin to hide the equipment and help the boys with the still. We will all dig potatoes, store half the crop in root cellars near the stills with the rest in our root cellar by the cabin. Edith and Molly, you will be in charge of cooking the potatoes into mash. I will show each of you how to run the still.

"Otto, now that you are twenty-two, you must hold a responsible job. You will be in charge of bottling the liquor in mason jars in the building back by the still. Amil and Barney, you will sell the liquor when it's ready. If we begin work this year, we will be in an excellent position with stocks of good liquor when the law banning alcohol is put into effect. If the law is not passed, we will be eating a lot of potatoes and drinking a lot of schnapps."

"Ma, is this a joke?" Gustav asked. "Our entire family could wind up in jail."

"Normally this would be wrong," Molly said. "But since our family is poor, and cannot pay the taxes, we have to sell liquor. Right Ma?"

"No it's not," Gustav said, looking around the room and realizing his was the only dissenting vote. He realized then that he was the only honest one in this family of liars and hypocrites. He didn't care about them. He decided as soon as he could he would leave them all behind again and move across the country.

"Sorry, Ma," Molly said. "That is definitely not cinnamon toast I smell." Minnie glanced around the kitchen. She noticed they were all nodding in agreement. She pulled the broiler pan from the oven with her oven mitt. The first two rows held slices of toast beautifully browned. The delicious display was marred only by a dead mouse at the back of the pan, broiled somewhere between medium and medium well.

As the Temperance Movement gained momentum, drinkers sought out illegal establishments to ensure a steady supply. Even nondrinkers stashed bottles ... just in case. Barney and Amil drew a circle on a map with a twenty-mile radius.

They identified existing taverns, homes being fitted to become illegal saloons, and the backroads leading to each.

Her boys became friendly with bar owners and bartenders. They provided them with sample bottles of Hartman's illegal whiskey. Canadian liquor was already being pulled across the frozen Detroit River on sleds by members of the Detroit River Gang who sold most in the metropolitan area. Barney and Amil's sample jars of moonshine received rave reviews from their customers, and soon the boys came home with pockets full of orders. The business was in position early in the bootlegging scene. The family was ready for when Prohibition passed.

Wilhelm saw the headline while he was in Standish delivering milk. "Arenac County Votes to Become Dry." He bought a paper, picked up his check from the International Milk Products Company and headed for Ralph's house.

"Ma! Ma, where are you? You won't believe our luck. It's 1910 and we are in business." He found her snapping green beans on the back porch. "Listen to this, Ma." A sly smile formed on Minnie's face as Wilhelm read the article. "'The people of Arenac County voted to become a dry county, the first in Michigan.' Can you imagine our good fortune?" Wilhelm said. "We are finally in the right place at the right time. We're on our way to easy street."

"Hold your horses, son," Minnie said and set down her bowl of beans. "Don't spend the money yet. We've got lots of work ahead of us."

"Oh, come on Ma, let's have a party." He rubbed his hands together. "Will you bake one of those sponge cakes, like the ones you used to bake back in Germany? I'll crack some ice from the icehouse and make ice cream." The Hartman family was in a position to prosper. They knew it, but held their celebration in private.

It was during the dry summer of 1911 that a powerful Nor'easter blew sparks from a heat lightning strike into what would become the fire of the decade. The blaze slashed through the pine forests being lumbered south of Oscoda and Au Gres and headed west to Arenac County. Flames leapt from treetop to treetop as sixty-mile-an-hour winds carried sparks to ignite haystacks, burn pallets of lumber at sawmills, and char all living creatures in its path.

Residents of Oscoda heard the fire alarm at three in the afternoon. The sky darkened and ash began to fall like gray snow. The Loud Cedar Yard was on fire. Residents of the two towns fled to beaches and steamship docks. The inferno was moving too fast to stop it with back burning or bucket lines. Oscoda, Au Gres and Au Sable were leveled.

Standish was next in the fire's path. Residents were already watering down their roofs when the winds shifted and extinguished the blaze. The village was spared, but the air smelled like soot for weeks after the fire.

Minnie listened as Wilhelm read a newspaper report. A twenty-two-year-old woman was moving mail from the post office and her personal belongs from her house when the fire threatened the town. She saved the mail but died of extreme fatigue a few hours later. Minnie shuddered when she learned five other people had been burned to death.

In 1911 the International Milk Products Company of Standish was buying 22,000 pounds of whole milk daily from area farmers. Record numbers of dairy products were being turned into cheese and sent south by train for sale in the Bay City, Saginaw, and Detroit.

Wilhelm's herd was producing Grade One milk with the highest cream content. He was able to build an addition to his cow barn, thanks to bootlegging profits. His herd was expanding, thanks to The Judge. Wilhelm was now growing hay, beans, and sugar beets ... with a large patch of potatoes earmarked for the family business.

Buying supplies for the stills in town was a challenge. Authorities were watching for anyone buying excessive amounts of copper tubing or sugar. Wilhelm took Gustav along to help load the seed corn while Wilhelm bought what supplies he could from George Cassidy at the grain elevator.

Gustav waited in the wagon to watch their purchases while Wilhelm explained to the hardware clerk he needed copper tubing for the milk house he was building on his farm. Wilhelm had an honest face. The clerk not only sold him all the tubing he needed, but carried it out to the wagon.

Gustav stormed all the way from the hardware store to the farm. "Didn't you learn anything in Sunday school?" He called his brother a disgusting hypocrite, a lapsed Lutheran, and a spawn of Satan for lying to the hardware clerk. "The preacher taught us all that lying would take us straight to hell. Listen, Wilhelm. I'm telling you this for your own good. Telling the truth is always the better road. It just always is, no matter what."

"Gustav, if I told that clerk what the copper tubing was for, he would tell the sheriff, and Ma would be arrested and put in prison. Our family would fall apart without Ma. Now, do you want your Ma in prison?"

"Fall apart? Ma is the one leading this legion of liars. She should be locked up."

"Gustav, do you want us to lose our land, our livelihood? We will unless one of us comes up with money, more money than I can make selling milk, and more money than Ralph and you can make in the lumber woods. I'm talking big money. And the cash needs to start flowing in our direction soon or you, your brothers and little sisters will be cinching in your belts because there will be nothing to eat. And the bank or taxman, and probably both, will be selling land we labored to clear at bargain prices.

"Like it or not, Gustav, our mother has vision. She saw Prohibition coming. She saw a solution none of the rest of us could have dreamed up. She's been having us stock sugar, firewood and copper tubing for the last three years. I didn't see her plan developing either. That's why she had us build that cabin in the ... oh, never mind where. My point is that I had to lie to the man. In this case, telling the truth would have been wrong."

"You say telling a lie is right?" Gustav raised an eyebrow. "Don't you see that telling one lie will lead to another, and another?"

"Look Gustav, Ma said if any of us wanted out, all we had to do was tell her. So, tell her ... but keep your mouth shut and protect the rest of us. Stop stirring the pot, and don't you go having a discussion about our family business with that preacher fellow or anyone else. Do you understand me?"

Gustav tucked his chin and said, "Okay, but I still don't like lying."

Henry Ford didn't like jazz ... thought it was evil. He did like square dancing and hired Benjamin Lovett to teach the art to folks in Dearborn for 26 years. Ford sponsored a dance program for the Dearborn public schools. Dancing classes spread to other schools, college and university campuses at Mr. Ford's expense. The auto tycoon sponsored a Sunday radio program that was broadcast nationwide. Over the radio Lovett would call dances that had been printed in the newspaper the previous week. Lovett maintained a "staff" of twelve to fourteen callers, all maintained by Mr. Ford's generosity. Eventually Henry Ford had a new, large dance hall constructed at Greenfield Village to contain the increasing numbers of dancers. Ford's good friend Thomas Edison began to produce 78 RPM square dance records under his Edison label. Old fashioned square dancing became the rage.

Chapter Fifteen
THE SCHWABS

That same year Wilhelm met Mary Schwab, a woman he desperately wanted for his bride. He discovered the beauty at a barn dance at her brother's farm. Wilhelm was Minnie's serious son, her rock, and he had earned his right, at thirty-six, for a chance at happiness for himself.

His physical appearance changed before Minnie's eyes. He stood straight and walked with a presence she hadn't noticed before. He was smiling broadly, swinging his arms and humming when he came inside her kitchen to tell her about Mary. He crinkled his nose and eyes and said, "Ma, I found a wonderful woman." He hugged his mother. "I want to marry her." Minnie's firstborn son had always put his family's needs before his, had been pitching his earnings into the Hartman family pot since he was eight. She had never seen him this happy.

The Schwab farm was four miles from the Hartman homestead. Wilhelm brought Mary to meet the family after church. They drank coffee and ate cinnamon toast as they always did. When Minnie said she wanted to have a talk with the woman and asked Wilhelm to check the potatoes on the back forty for potato bugs, he hinted that she had not had an easy life.

Minnie sent the children outside to play.

Mary told Minnie about her former husband, Louie Schmidt. She said the man fell from a hay wagon and landed on his head. Shortly after the accident he experienced seizures and severe aggressiveness. Doctors linked his unpredictable behavior to his head injury. Mary said her husband grew more and more violent and threatened her and the children. She said she feared for her life, and for that of their offspring. Mary said she had no recourse but to divorce the man on the grounds that he had developed a violent temperament. She explained the divorce law held that if a woman had no way of providing for a family, the children remained with their father.

So, Minnie thought, that foul old law that had plucked at me all those years ago had flown to America and was pecking at this young woman.

Mary said that since the children's father, Louie, was unable to work at the time or care for his children in a home with a safe environment, the children and Louie Schmidt were ordered by the judge to live with Louie's parents, one of the first families to have settled in Frankenlust. They were large landowners and carried considerable influence with the judge.

Mary said the decision of the court left her childless, homeless and a social outcast at twenty-eight. She fled her large family in Frankenlust and came north to live on the farm of her younger brother, Mike Schwab.

Like Minnie, Mary had experienced the death of her second child. Losing her remaining three children would have been too much for her spirit had it not been for the loving care and support of her extended family of brothers and sisters. They had seen to it that she moved on with her life, had insisted she participate at church socials and neighborhood events and became part of the Lincoln Township community.

Mary said she was allowed by the court to see her three children on weekends when Schmidt's mother would drive them north. Linda was three, Rudy was a toddler and Rich was an infant. Those weekends were heartbreakers for her … seeing her babies and then having them taken from her again. Mary found herself in an impossible situation. The court had ruled. She had to live with its decision.

Any woman who had been caught up in an intolerable situation that she was forced to endure would understand. Any mother who had been judged by a legal system written by men, with laws that favored men would understand. Minnie could understand Mary's pain.

She could also see that this lively young woman was in love with her son. Wilhelm wanted her. They both deserved a chance. Minnie gave them her blessing.

When Wilhelm brought Mary for the cinnamon toast the next Sunday, this time it was Mary who asked to speak to Minnie alone. She told Minnie her children were having difficulty adjusting to living with Schmidt's family. She said their grandmother had driven the children north to see her Saturday last. It had been a long and wonderful day for Mary and the children until the auto pulled into the driveway with the grandmother behind the wheel. Little Linda locked her arms around Mary's neck and was bawling. Rudy hung to her leg, whimpering. They both begged their mother to keep them with her, promising her anything to change her mind and not send them away. Even baby Rich cried, and he was a naturally cheerful child. Her children clearly didn't understand the court's ruling. Schmidt's mother, in a moment of compassion … or of ultimate cruelty … told Mary she could choose one of her children to keep with her in Lincoln Township.

"Minnie," Mary sobbed. "How can a mother be asked to choose one of her children over the others? I can't do it. I feel like I'm already drowning and water keeps pouring through more and more holes above me." She wiped sweat from her forehead, and dabbed the tears welling in her eyes. She told Minnie she hadn't been able to sleep. She said she was tormented. "I can't decide. I love each of them. Yet, I must decide or I will lose all three. What should I do, Minnie? How can I choose? Which one should I choose?"

Wilhelm came into the parlor and put his arm around his woman. "Mary, if the court will approve I will take all three of your children and raise them as my own." He smiled at her and kissed her forehead. "And Ma," Wilhelm said. "The plants have potato bugs crawling all over them. I asked Edith and Molly to go back and pick them off."

Two weeks later, Mary and Wilhelm sat next to each other in church. On Wilhelm's lap was Mary's middle child, her son Rudy. After church, they joined the family for cinnamon toast. All eyes were on Rudy who would not leave Mary's side.

Rudy had made the decision for his mother. The little boy was determined he would never leave her again. Little Rudy Schmidt clung to Mary's leg from when they arrived in Lincoln Township until it was time to go back to Frankenlust. Grandmother Schmidt tried to pull him away from his mother, but the child kicked the old woman, bit her hand, and screamed he hated her. She was angry but was defeated by the defiance of the child. "Mary, you keep that one," she said and loaded Linda and baby Rich into the Ford. The car backed from the driveway, leaving Mary and Rudy waving from Uncle Mike's porch. After that, whenever the boy misbehaved Mary would smile and say, "Thank God for Rudy trouble."

From time to time, Wilhelm would hear about Louie Schmidt's condition. The man stayed confined at his parent's home in Frankenlust with his children, Linda and Rich. When a violent fit overtook her son's mind, Schmidt's mother led or dragged him into the farm's corn crib that had been padded with quilts and pillows. She locked him inside to thrash around until he was calm and could no longer hurt anyone.

Life continued for Mary and her son Rudy in Lincoln Township. Rudy thrived with his mother and the loving support of Mike Schwab and Mike's wife, Martha. Grandmother Schmidt continued to drive Mary's two other children north for a bittersweet day with their mother every weekend.

It was 1910 and a busy year for the Hartmans of Johnsfield. Minnie packed her few belongings and moved her piano and her remaining four children across the road to Ralph's cabin.

Work was seasonal at the sawmills. Able men traveled around Michigan to find work. Barney was twenty-five and worked in the Prescott mill during the week and slept most of the day on weekends. He was the main distributor of Minnie's potato liquor, a job that could only be carried out after sunset.

Edith was twenty and worked during the week at a hotel in Saginaw. She took the train north each weekend to help Molly cook the potato mash for the still that Wilhelm and Barney had built. When the Saginaw job ended, she picked cucumbers from the family garden, bagged them in burlap, and sold them to the pickle factory in Pinconning.

Otto, well Otto was Otto. He was a lazy boy of eighteen with shifty eyes and strong opinions, a boy who liked to argue. He had been put in charge of keeping the wood burning under the stills during the night so the smoke would go undetected by the neighbors, and the sheriff. Minnie would sniff his clothes when he came in for breakfast. If she couldn't smell smoke, she would walk back and tend to the fire herself.

Amil was sixteen and rode along with Barney to learn the distribution route. Fred Jr. was fourteen and useless. He helped whenever he had a direct order from Minnie. Most of the time he was out looking for Otto.

Wilhelm and Mary had a private wedding ceremony with a justice of the peace on July 1, 1911. Minnie made a family dinner in honor of the nuptials and transferred the deed to the log cabin and the land south of Johnsfield Road to Wilhelm and his bride as a wedding present.

The couple happily farmed their sixty-seven acres of rich soil, land that had been meticulously cleared of stones and stumps with Wilhelm's family's sweat, land that had been a wasteland, a cemetery of tree stumps ten years before. This land was paid for with ten years of Wilhelm's father's labor. It had passed down from Fred's generation to Wilhelm's. It was Fred Hartman's dream realized.

Minnie, Wilhelm and Mary Hartman

Chapter Sixteen
THE STAR-CROSSED

Molly scorched batch after batch of potato mash at Ralph's still in his woods north of Johnsfield Road. Her heart was not into making hooch. The girl would rather have been reading, swimming in Nigl's gravel pit or spooning with a neighborhood boy by the name of Wagner.

Minnie called her in for a talk. Molly bowed her head and stuffed her hands deep in her apron pockets while Minnie explained that if the revenue agents happened to be driving by in their big black automobiles, they could identify the scorched smell of potatoes coming from the woods just as well as Minnie had up here at Ralph's cabin. "Nothing smells worse than burned potatoes, honey. It wouldn't take long for the men to track the smell to the still." Molly crossed her arms. Minnie told her it takes hours of patient simmering and stirring to make the mash properly. "You can do it, honey. Just don't be in such a hurry."

"Ma," Edith said. "When I cook the mash I time the boil. I'll show Molly how. She's just mooning over Louie Wagner." She slapped her thigh and laughed. "She won't burn the mash again. I'll see to it." She winked at Molly. "And Ma, we buried that scorched batch in the woods so the revenuers won't smell it."

Edith was a tall girl and a looker. She lifted her head and pushed her chest out when she spoke ... and her friends listened. She was a natural leader. She was being courted by Louie Ireland, the playboy son of Nelson Ireland.

Nelson Ireland was a man of character and substance. At one time he owned the Standish newspaper and the Ford dealership. Louie inherited the dealership but not his father's character. The car business showed amazing profits during Louie's years of management. Barney thought Louie was using the dealership to launder money from his bootlegging business in Lewiston.

"The still in Lewiston," Barney said, "now that's one business Louie Ireland knows how to run."

"That's not true. Louie's father has a hunting lodge in Lewiston. He drives up there to hunt," Edith said.

Her brother Gustav rolled his eyes. He told Edith to stay away from the scoundrel or she would end up drunk and pregnant.

Louie Ireland was Ralph's best friend. They hunted deer and chased women together. Edith listened to no one. Once she made up her mind that Louie Ireland was the man for her, she set her hat for him. Louie Ireland didn't have a chance.

The M & H sawmill in Lewiston caught on fire after running only one week. The fire was so fierce, the only way to stop it was to dynamite buildings in its path. When the foreman looked for volunteers, Wilhelm stepped up. He was a new hire recommended by Louie Ireland. He told the boss he knew dynamite. The boss set him up with a horse and sleigh and a box of dynamite on his lap. Wilhelm kept the caps in his vest pocket. He set the explosives and blew the buildings which stopped the fire. The boss told Wilhelm he saved the company and offered to call the newspaper to write a story. Wilhelm asked the man to keep it quiet. He said his mother would be furious with him if she found out.

The M & H mill buildings were rebuilt and equipped with new bandsaws, which upped the annual production to 25,000,000 board feet a year. Wilhelm's job was secure. But nothing was certain in the lumber woods.

Traveling in Michigan was slow ...by stagecoach in summer and snow train in winter. The locomotives were equipped with huge ploughs welded to the front. Edith took the train by herself to Gaylord to see her friends, the Carrolls, and then to Merenisios in Michigan's Upper Peninsula to visit Mrs. John Nizer whose husband worked at a mill. She explored Muskegon and Detroit. Minnie was concerned for her safety but couldn't stop her footloose daughter. She told her she must have been born with needles in her feet because she couldn't stand still.

Twenty-eight lumber camps dotted the landscape between Atlanta and Lewiston at that time. Saloons in the towns were kept busy on weekends with illegal gambling and booze. Edith had been traveling on a weekend and was waiting outside the saloon in Lewiston for a train. She told Minnie a few weeks after the incident about the shuffle she heard inside.

"A town bully got drunk. He was refused more liquor by the owner and became rowdy. Ma, I looked inside the front door to see what was going on. The drunk was shaking his fist at the barkeep, jumping and walking on the shiny wooden bar with his cork shoes. He damaged the bar. The owner watched as the barkeep hauled him down and threw him out the front door ... right in front of me. The guy got up and was staggering off the porch when it happened. The owner must have climbed the stairs to his living quarters above the bar because the next thing I knew he shot him from an upstairs window as the bully left the building."

"Did he kill him?"

"Sure did, Ma. The sheriff took him away. I heard the saloon keeper was sentenced to fifteen years. Louie told me he knew the man and he knew the judge. He said he wouldn't be surprised to see him back in Lewiston in a few years."

"Edith ..."

"Don't worry, Ma. I never go in the saloons. I'm not that kind of woman."

"And what kind of woman is that?" Minnie said.

"The scum of the Earth, Ma. Prostitutes. Whores who have three or four dirty children living in the back bedrooms."

"My dear, your old mother came close to becoming a prostitute years ago in Germany. I thought your father had abandoned me, I had no money and was pregnant with Rosa. Don't judge women for what work they do to feed their children."

Wilhelm's beloved workhorse, Dick, died of a heart attack in 1912. It was an emotional and economic disaster. These huge animals had become part of the family. They were their pets and co-workers. Wilhelm needed both Dick and Cobb to finish pulling stumps, plowing fields, and carting everyone back and forth to town.

Ralph hauled Dick's carcass away late that same night. A few months later, he came home carrying a bulky roll over his shoulder. We were delighted when he unrolled the rug. It was Dick, stretched flat and tanned a beautiful brown. Ralph spread it out on his log cabin floor. Dick had come home to his family, serving us as always ... this time keeping drafts from seeping up through the floorboards.

Early one morning that same year, two roan yearling steers appeared on Ralph's lawn, eating the flowers Minnie had planted. A knot curled round in her chest.

"Ralph, can I ride into town with you today?" She had him stop at the newspaper office where she placed the following ad:

"Estrayed – came to my premises 4 miles west and ½ mile south of Standish, June 10, two roan yearling steers. Owner can have same by proving property and paying charges. Ralph Hartman."

Barbara Nigl found Ralph milking cows when she came for the steers. Minnie could see her from the kitchen door. The girl stood watching him as he sat on the three-legged stool filling the galvanized steel pail with warm milk. She heard her call out his name. It must have startled him because he turned and nearly spilled the milk. He finished milking the cow and carried the bucket to the milk house. Barbara stood watching Ralph pour the milk into the holding tank where ground-temperature well-water circulated to keep the fresh milk cool.

Ralph was a good-looking lad, tall, blond, with good teeth and a smile that melted the knees of many a girl. Minnie saw him wink and heard him say, "You are a lovely surprise." He was a smooth talker, too.

The girl straightened her spine and brushed the hair the wind had blown in her face. "I knocked on the kitchen door but no one answered." She giggled. "I'm here for the steers." Ralph must not have recognized her as his neighbor because she said, "I'm Barbara Nigl."

Ralph's smile faded when he realized this beauty was the daughter of Joe Nigl, the man who killed his father in a bar-room brawl. He glanced over and saw Minnie standing in the open kitchen door, holding the newspaper.

"Got any proof the steers are yours?" he asked walking toward the house. "This is my Ma."

Barbara told Ralph and Minnie that the only proof she had was that their best milkers had come into season almost two years back, about the same time the Hartmans' old bull jumped the fence. "My Pa met up with your brother, Wilhelm, shortly after. They were both hunting deer back in the woods. The two of them walked over to our herd to chase that old bull out ... that mean one, the one Wilhelm eventually had to shoot. Well, that old bull chased Wilhelm and caught my father. Grazed his shoulder with a horn. The two men gave up on driving the bull out ... left him there. He must have bred most of our herd before he jumped the fence and walked home on his own a few weeks later. My Pa was afraid your Ma would make us pay a stud fee for the breeding."

"Excuse me," Minnie said and slipped back inside the kitchen to quell the teapot's crying on the cookstove.

"Did she make him pay?" Ralph asked Barbara.

"I can't rightly say. Your mother rode up in her cutter a week or so after the bull jumped the fence. She and my Pa sat on the front porch drinking coffee for more than an hour. Pa wouldn't tell us what she said, but I saw them shake hands before Pa helped her back up on the cutter."

"That's good enough for me," Ralph said. When he smiled at the girl, she blushed. He took Barbara's arm and led her from the kitchen door and had her wait while he rounded up the steers. Ralph cut a willow switch to drive them, and the young folks followed the roan yearlings home. Minnie saw them walk east on Johnsfield Road and then turn south on Lincoln Road. Ralph told Minnie later that afternoon that he would be returning to Nigl's to check fences the next day. "Barbara is making a picnic, so I won't be home for dinner."

Soon after Ralph started courting Barbara, Zelda Hartman wrote she was coming from Germany. Ralph read the letter to Minnie. Fred's mother said that since her husband died and now that her son was dead, she felt lost and rootless. She wanted to visit America to meet her grandchildren and great-grandchildren before she followed her men to the grave.

Minnie pressed her lips together and let out an exasperated sigh. She had never been fond of the woman and had her hands full dealing with her own brood. The mason jars of cash buried in the garden were almost empty. The yields of the farmland were not yet sufficient to sustain her own hard-working family, much less her mother-in-law's aging, toothless mouth. Minnie narrowed her eyes. "Son, that old heifer will require her potatoes to be mashed. I'll have to dig up my savings to feed and clothe her."

Wilhelm took the train south to Detroit to meet his grand-mother. When he returned, he reported to Minnie that Johann, Fred's father, had died of heart failure two years before. Her younger son had moved away and never wrote. Zelda Hartman liked the Standish house Minnie used to own, although it wasn't nearly as nice as her own house in Poland, she told Wilhelm. Grandmother said she was happy to live with Fred's family in the log cabin. Minnie didn't have the heart to tell her what a monster her son had become.

Minnie's mother-in-law dug right in ... teaching Edith and Molly how to stuff a German sausage, make a proper *Kuttelsuppe* from tripe, and make the blood soup called *Schwarzsauer.* The blood was drained from one of Minnie's geese and cooked in vinegar water. The woman was not well and napped often. She never mentioned her son, Karl, and Minnie never asked. Zelda died in her sleep a few months later and Minnie had her buried in the Hartman family plot next to Fred.

In 1910, while Ralph was seriously courting Barbara, Minnie and her six children moved from his log cabin to a farm she bought in Gibson Township that was four miles away. It was in Bay County near the village of Bentley and had a secluded swamp in the middle of the acreage.

Against her better judgment, Minnie put the deed in Fred Jr.'s name. Her youngest son was now the token head of her household at the age of twenty-two. The boy had grown to become a five-foot-eleven-inch child with curly blond hair, grey eyes and few brains. The handsome lad worked on Ralph's farm doing odd jobs before he was required to register for the army. Minnie prayed that if he was drafted he would never be given a gun. The boy was clumsy and had already shot his own foot once ... not an unusual practice in the Hartman household. Like his father, Fred Jr. was careless with his aim. While hunting in the woods with the Lutheran minister, Minnie's son shot the man's best hunting dog. He said it was an accident. Minnie's youngest son excelled at making excuses.

Minnie was sixty-four, still running the family business and seeing to her burgeoning brood when she settled at the new farm. Barney, Amil and Fred Jr. cleared the fields of stumps and built new stills. They set the distillery in a discreet location deep in the swamp accessible in wet weather only by an overhead route through trees. Barney came up with the idea after he saw a high-wire act at a circus in Bay City. When it was her turn to check the stills, Minnie could balance on the horizontal logs skillfully cut and prudently placed out of view by her lumberjack sons. She could move swiftly high above the mosquitoes and swamp snakes, starting from a tree behind her barn and arriving at the mound of earth that held her distilling operation. Minnie Hartman was satisfied with her new home. The boys turned earth for her vegetable garden, built her a coop for her chickens and fertilized the flowerbeds around the house with aged cow manure. Best of all, her Brazilian Rosewood grand piano looked perfect in the parlor straddling old Dick's posthumously donated hide.

Wilhelm and Mary's log cabin in Lincoln Township became the center for family meetings after church on Sundays. Wilhelm had been working in the lumber woods during the week to support his wife, little Rudy, and in 1912 Wilhelm's firstborn son, Lawrence.

Over a cup of tea, Minnie warned her daughter-in-law that men coming out of the woods were usually loaded with bedbugs. Mary set down her cup and explained to her mother-in-law that when Wilhelm came home on weekends she insisted he strip naked outside the cabin. He was to leave his clothes in the copper washtub for her to boil clean. A second washtub was waiting for him inside followed by clean clothes, a hot meal and a tumble with her in their bed. She said he never complained about the cold and they never had bedbugs. Minnie understood why Wilhelm loved this clever woman.

Laurice LaZebnik

In some communities a wedding night custom was held beneath the windows of the newlyweds. A bunch of friends of the bride and groom banged on pots and pans and set off an occasional dynamite blast to serve as a gentle spoof to the couple. The hoax was intended to disrupt for a while any sexual activities that might be under way. It would end when the groom came out and agreed to buy beer or whatever the crowd demanded. It was done "All in fun – just a shiveree, you know, and nobody got mad about it. At least not very mad."

Chapter Seventeen
THE SALVAGING

Minnie's playboy son, Ralph Hartman, proposed marriage to the daughter of the man who killed his father in 1913. Their guest list stopped at a hundred and included the entire Hartman family. The wedding was held outside at the Nigl farm. Reverend Harms from the German Lutheran Church knew both family histories and agreed to preside over the ceremony and keep the peace if necessary. Barbara's father invited the sheriff as a precautionary measure. Mr. Aherns played the wedding march. Edith and Barney Hartman, Clara Hufnagle and Joe Nigl were in the bridal party.

"Minnie, is this chair taken?"

"Sam, I was saving it for you," Minnie lied and patted the chair. "I hope you didn't come with more bad news."

"No bad news today. I am an invited guest." Sheriff Sam laughed. "Don't you approve of Ralph's choice? You look sad."

"I trust the sins of the fathers will not be passed on to the sons. Approve or disapprove, my children follow their own path."

" ...a tribute to their strong-minded mother. Are you feeling okay?"

"Just feeling old today, Sam. I was thinking of my own wedding, the strong passions, the high drama that were in the air that day. It was all so romantic. I was young, headstrong and impetuous."

"I remember the romance before my wedding too." He grinned. "Men do the strangest dance before they marry, like herons do before they mate. They dress in their finest, take women out to places they have never been before, buy things they can't afford. Promises are made they hope they can keep. I'm sure you experienced a lot of that. Do you miss romance from that time, too?" Sam asked.

"Romance?" Minnie chuckled. "I was like a field of wild prairie grass then, innocent. The church cut through the turf first. They planted in me a list of what was ethically and morally banned from my life. This directory of all things forbidden came straight from God via the preacher. My parents backed him and added to the list. I felt mowed down, raked over and stood up to dry like sheaves of wheat in spring. The file grew so large I was suspicious. It seemed to me there was all this candy out there growing and I wasn't allowed any of it. I rebelled, of course. Most children do. At the time I knew nothing about sex.

"The turning point for me came when my breasts developed. Overnight I became somebody important. Men who had treated me like a child before now became attentive, offered to buy me ice cream, walk me home. When I asked my mother she said men act like this when they are being romantic. So, romance was like a game I played. I ate their ice cream and let them carry my packages.

"I didn't catch on to the reason for the romance until after I married. Fred opened a world of physical pleasure to me. I was wiling to break all the rules on the forbidden list if only we could copulate often.

"But, everything has a cost, doesn't it Sam. Sex became my punishment. I have been either pregnant or nursing a child for twenty-four years. The full responsibility for twelve children imprisoned me. Sex became a curse. I was thinking about what I miss most about not having a man in my bed."

"You must miss the sex," Sam said.

"No. But I miss the touch of another human, the warmth of a body next to mine." Minnie turned to look down the aisle.

Flower pedals had been strewn along the bride's walkway. "What is holding up this wedding? You don't suppose the bride changed her mind, do you Sam? I hope the groom arrived."

"Here they come now," Sam said and took Minnie's hand in his as they stood. The wedding party came down the aisle. The bride's dress was cream messaline with fringe trimmings. Barbara wore a long tulle veil. She carried an arm bouquet of white asters tied with a white satin ribbon. Minnie liked the look her son was giving his bride. He was grinning and licking his lips. Minnie laughed aloud. She could hear Sam chuckle beside her.

"We were all young and foolish like that once. Have I mentioned that you are still a beautiful woman at … what … forty-eight?

"Fifty-eight? Sixty-four? What's the difference? Sam, don't be fooled by a woman's beauty or age. Beauty can be a curse. You married a good woman who also happens to be easy on the eyes. Why didn't she come with you?"

"She's taking treatments in Detroit. She stays with her family in Detroit in between appointments. She's been sick for such a long time. I've been so busy I haven't been down to see her in two weeks."

"I'm sorry she's so sick … sorry for her and sorry for you. When she comes home I'll call on her. And I'll keep her in my prayers." Minnie shifted in her seat. "The bride and groom will be spending a few days in Detroit. They leave tomorrow morning on the train. Ralph told me he plans to take Barbara dancing in a fancy nightclub. That sounds like such fun … wickedly silly fun. Wouldn't it be fun to have no responsibilities?"

"How long has it been since you had wickedly silly fun?" Sam asked.

"I don't remember." Minnie glanced toward the sky. "Ages ago when I was a girl dressed like a boy running through the streets of Poznan."

"You? Dress like a boy?"

"At the time I thought my parents were being unreasonable." Minnie snickered. "I dressed in my brother's clothes to escape the rules of my gender, to enjoy the freedom allowed only for males. Now that I'm a mother I understand they were trying to protect their unruly daughter's virginity. I still sometimes have the desire to dress in my son's clothes and visit a saloon."

"I'm glad I only have sons. What does Ralph want to do with his life?"

"He's such a ladies' man. I think he'd like to hunt and fish and fool with women his whole life. He says he plans to work the farm Fred and I gave him and live in the log cabin his old girlfriends helped him build." Minnie grinned. "That scoundrel son of mine had his girlfriends help him build his cabin. For the last few years they planted his garden and even cleaned his house. That rascal talked one girl into hoeing the milk-weeds out of his bean field. He plays women like he plays cards, discarding the losers and drawing another from the deck until he has a winning hand. I guess his bride was the card he needed. She will put an end to all his nonsense. The Nigls know how to win at cards, and how to win a fight." Minnie paused to look at Barbara Nigl. Saddened, she said, "Sam, the bride is the daughter of ..."

"... of the man who was responsible for the death of your husband."

Minnie's eyes softened when she saw Sam try a smile to soften her pain and look away when he couldn't. She wondered then if Ralph would tell his wife about the family business. She wondered if the Nigls could be trusted to keep the family secret.

"She will find out about your family business," Sam said.

"Sam, you know we are potato farmers."

"Yes, Minnie. Everyone enjoys what you produce from your potato farm. Would you like to dance?"

The happiness surrounding Ralph and Barbara's wedding celebration disappeared the next weekend in smoke. Wilhelm and Mary's log cabin, across the road from the newlyweds' cabin, burned to the ground. Wilhelm's family was unharmed, but the couple lost their shelter, last year's dried and bagged bean crop stored in the cabin, as well as all their personal belongings. The barn, outbuildings, and stock were untouched.

A disaster for one family in Lincoln Township was Sunday work for the neighbors. Folks brought teams and wagons from miles around to help carry away debris and cart back building materials. Some hauled huge logs cut from their own woodlots for the structural beams. Others hewed the logs square and yet others stacked them near the foundation excavation they had all helped dig. Wagonloads of stone arrived, handpicked from fields and fencerows throughout the German immigrant community.

Ralph was obsessed with his fear of fire. He would never forget wading into that cold Au Sable and watching the sawmill and boarding house burn red and collapse into white ash. He had seen firsthand the speed of a firestorm's devastation. He would do anything to protect his home now that he had a wife and soon a child.

When he brought home molds to form concrete building blocks, no one was surprised. He hauled in enough gravel, sand and cement with his yellow dump truck to pour building blocks for two fireproof homes. Wilhelm, Mary, Rudy, Ralph and even his bride, Barbara, began pouring the slurry. When the cement was set, they released the oblong forms from their molds and stacked the chunks of concrete for curing. After three months, they had enough building blocks to finish two fireproof homes.

Minnie made sure they ate well. She served up hardy picnics, which they ate at the building site ... fried chicken and German potato salad, sauerkraut and sausages, pork chops and fried red cabbage. She made cakes and cookies and cobblers

... always something different for the workers to look forward to eating.

They were taking a break from working on the fireproof house one Sunday afternoon when Ralph joined them for a piece of his mother's German chocolate cake. He passed Wilhelm the weekly newspaper and nodded for him to read the front page. Wilhelm's eyes grew round and bulged.

"You all better listen to this. The headline reads, 'Otto Hartman incarcerated in Ogemaw County Jail, West Branch, Michigan.' Ma, put that coffeepot down and come listen to this. Ralph get her a chair. 'Otto Hartman, twenty-two, and Arthur Lalonde sawed out some bars in the West Branch jail and made their escape on Sunday, August 31, 1914. Hartman lived west of Standish and was awaiting a trial in circuit court for allegedly stealing a bicycle and cashing another man's check. Lalonde resided in Pinconning and was alleged to have stolen harness rings and martingales from a barn. The two men's whereabouts were unknown as of press time.'"

"*Mein Gott im Himmel*," Minnie said. She staggered, and felt with her hands until she grasped Ralph's arm for support. "I think the Earth has dropped away and God has left me floating here, alone … and naked."

"Ma, sit here," Ralph said and led her to a stack of concrete blocks. "Watch your step, Ma," he said when she stumbled. "You better get those eyes checked."

Could her Otto be a thief? Minnie reasoned the newspapers don't always get the facts straight. She knew he was not a stupid boy, but he was a lazy one. She thought maybe it was that other fella, that Lalone boy who stole the bike and cashed the check, and Otto was just in the wrong place at the wrong time. That had to be it. None of this made sense. Her boy wouldn't steal a bicycle when he could use a horse and wagon from home any time. He knew he had only to ask.

"Wilhelm? What could he have been thinking? Wilhelm, where are you?" Minnie couldn't imagine a son of hers taking another man's money. Each of her children had experienced the drudgery of hard work. Each of them had labored long, exhausting days for cash of their own. Money was hard to come by these days. But would Otto steal a man's payroll check ... a whole month's labor? How could he do that? "Wilhelm?"

"I'm here Ma." Wilhelm knelt down so she could see him. "Otto was never a clever boy. Maybe you should rest inside Ralph's house on a proper chair. Here, take my arm." Wilhelm stood and led her across the road to Ralph's cabin and into a bedroom.

"Where could he be hiding?" She reached for the bottle in her apron pocket. "Find him, Wilhelm." She took a swig. "Make sure he's safe." She lay her head back on the feather pillow.

"Don't worry. I think I know where to find him." Wilhelm pulled one of Barbara's wedding quilts over her. "You get some rest."

Minnie turned this way and that all night ... couldn't get comfortable, couldn't get Otto out of her mind ... wondering where she went wrong with that child.

Wilhelm found his brother the next morning and brought him to Ralph's kitchen where the family had gathered for breakfast. Otto had been hiding in the cabin in the woods, the storage building next to their two active stills.

Minnie was furious. If the police had looked for him in that part of the woods, they would have located their family enterprise and busted their stills. "No excuses, Otto," she said. "Just tell me what happened?" She was annoyed and tired. Otto was hungry and eyed the sausages on the table. "First you talk and then you eat," she said.

Her son looked down and began to stammer a reply, but then announced he was really hungry and asked if he could have just one small sausage. The look his mother gave him started him talking again and Otto Hartman slowly told his family how he had been celebrating his glory days drinking at the West Branch saloon. He said one of his best friends dared him to steal the bicycle. The pace of Otto's story picked up as he saw their interest. He grinned. "We were having so much fun, you see, and the bike, she was a beauty, Ma. This silver bike was just leaning there against this building and no one was … well, it was so easy." Otto's eyes flashed with excitement. "So I grabbed it, jumped on, and rode away. Can I have a sausage now? Just one?"

"No."

Otto's voice grew strong and loud, like he was proud and wanted the world to hear his adventure. He pulled his skinny shoulders back so his chest would look bigger. He said he was feeling good and lucky because he hadn't been caught, and was riding his new silver bike along the board walkway in West Branch when he saw a piece of official-looking paper. He skidded to a stop and bent down and picked up a payroll check. Testing the length of his lucky streak, Otto said he parked his bike, walked into the West Branch bank and handed the check to a teller. "I just wanted to see if I could fool him." He grinned and looked around the table until he saw Ralph's frown.

"You bonehead," Ralph said.

Otto stuck his arms out with his palms forward. "The bank teller told him to sign my name on the back of the check."

"Which of course you did. You dimwit."

"Ralph, let your brother talk," Minnie said.

"The teller pushed a pile of cash through the hole in the glass window right to me, right into my hands. It was so easy."

"You always liked easy," Wilhelm said.

"So, I had all this free money. I didn't use it for myself, Ma. I used the cash to buy drinks for everyone at the saloon. I was the one who treated."

Minnie massaged her temples. "Otto. Otto."

"And the suspicious barkeep called the sheriff." Ralph's lip curled. "No one throws their own money around like that."

"So, I get this tap on my shoulder," Otto wiped his hands on his pants. "I-I-I turn and this big guy tells me to step outside. He asks me if the bike leaning against the wall beside the saloon is mine. Just then the bank teller walks up to the sheriff. He points at me. "H-H-He tells him some 'jack came in looking for his lost payroll check. He says the 'jack tells him his name and the bank teller remembers that I was the guy that signed the man's name and cashed his payroll check. That's when I got hauled off to j-j-jail."

"Forgery is a federal crime," Wilhelm said. "You are such a stupid chicken. I could wring your weasel neck. Lawmen will be here looking for a forger. They will find our stills."

Otto grinned. "No they won't." He was excited. "Me and Artie busted out. My friend Artie Lalone had a hacksaw blade stuck in his boot. That's a sign my lucky streak is still good. They won't find me and they won't find the stills."

"Artie? Do I know this boy?" Minnie said.

Otto shrugged. "He's from Pinconning. So, we took turns sawing the bars until they bent and we squeezed out." He smiled broadly.

"Son, you are in trouble." Minnie saw his mouth turn down and form a pout like it did when he was a toddler and wanted a forbidden sweet.

"Ma, I couldn't stay in that jail." He rubbed the back of his neck. "It was cold in there and the food was terrible. They won't find me here. I'm lucky. I'll hide in the swamp back by Nine Mile Road ... back by Molly's house."

Minnie grimaced. "I should throttle you, you little swamp rat," she said. Instead she had Ralph feed him and had Wilhelm hook up the buggy. She drove Cobb into town by herself to see the sheriff.

Minnie's great great great granddaughter Jennifer created the missing right side of this photo with the 2006 family. From left to right are William and Donna Hartman, Jennifer Hauschild, Michael Hartman, Janet Schmautz, Laurice LaZebnik, and Kurt Schmautz.

From the original photo taken around 1930 (clockwise) are Wilhelm (seated), Leonard, Lawrence, and Hedwig Hartman.

Chapter Eighteen
THE SHOOTING

The Standish lawman greeted her with a wide smile and offered her a chair.

"I admire your good manners, Sheriff Sam," she said and took her seat. Minnie was uneasy in the sheriff's company for the first time. She needed his help. She needed a miracle. "How are your boys? Your wife finished with her treatments?"

He leaned towards her, bracing himself on the arms of her chair. "Minnie, you get more beautiful with every season."

"Sheriff, please. I asked about your wife and children." Minnie wanted to keep the line between their friendship and business separate.

The man moved back and away. "Minnie, I may not be the handsomest man in town, but I'm the only one talking to you now, asking you for a small ..."

"Sir," Minnie said. "Your time is valuable and so is mine. I will get to the point."

Sam took his seat behind the desk.

"My son Otto is in trouble with the law. Life has not been easy for him. He was only eight when his father passed. He grew irresponsible without the strong guidance of a man. Otto is now twenty-two and has made some poor choices. My eldest son, Wilhelm, read me about the incident in West Branch from the newspaper."

"Minnie, do you know where Otto is hiding?"

"Let's say I have a hunch. And let's say I could find the cash to pay for the bicycle and reimburse the man for the check

Otto stole. Sam, you have sons about Otto's age. I know you would do anything for your family. I'm only a woman. I need some manly advice. What would you do if one of your sons made a poor choice and broke the law … besides give him a good thrashing?"

The sheriff laughed. "You sit there … so beautiful … and you always pull my heart strings." He stood and walked the floor behind his desk. "Minnie, I know how hard it must be to keep that brood of yours in line … all alone out there in Lincoln Township since Fred died." He scratched his chin whiskers. "Yes, I do have trouble with my own children. And yes, I do have one about Otto's age." He paced. "You say Otto could use some discipline?" He stopped pacing and turned to her. "Let's say if Otto enlisted in the army and was on the first train south heading to Fort Custer in Battle Creek tomorrow, I may be able to see that the bicycle gets replaced, the bank gets repaid, and the jail-breaking charge gets dropped."

"How much?"

"Let's say I would need two hundred dollars in cash and a fifth of that moonshine you don't brew back there in your woods … delivered to my home today."

"Sheriff, I can assure you my Otto will enlist in the army and be on the train tomorrow. Later today you shall have one hundred dollars and a fifth of totally legal whiskey that we distill for use by my family along with a bottle of the communion wine we make for the German Lutheran Church. You will have a delivery every month thereafter for one entire year." She stood and stretched out her hand.

The man grinned and took her hand. "Minnie Hartman, you drive a hard bargain for such a fine-looking woman. I can't refuse you." He kissed her hand. "Good day."

"But Ma, I don't want to be a soldier. They kill soldiers." Otto wiped sweat from his forehead on his sleeve.

Minnie leaned in. "Son, you will learn how to fight in war."

"I don't know how to fight." Otto fidgeted. "I don't like to fight. No. I won't go."

"I'll talk to him, Ma," Wilhelm said.

It was a sunny September morning in 1914 as the big engine appeared from the north. Steam billowed from between the wheels with a hiss. A metal-to-metal clatter and squeal came before the final, small lurch when the train stopped. A young man climbed aboard with his hands stuffed deep in his coat pockets. He was wearing a frown made by a deep crease between his brows. As the Michigan Central locomotive coughed, lurched ahead and began to pull away, Minnie's son, Otto Hartman, hung from the window and shouted a final farewell.

"Goodbye Ma. I'll be a good s-s-soldier. I'll make you proud."

Wilhelm had delivered the bushel basket to the sheriff's house the day before. It had been piled high with freshly dug red potatoes. Hidden in the bottom was a jug of holy communion wine and a mason jar full of 'Log Cabin' sipping whiskey. Wilhelm told Minnie the man's wife had accepted the basket without question, as if such gifts were a common occurrence. "Why are we giving the sheriff's family potatoes and alcohol? Ma, I could smell the money in the bottom of that basket. Are you bribing a lawman?"

Minnie shot a knowing grin at her son. "Wilhelm, how did you get your brother on that train? That boy has no grit and has never worked a full day in his life. He has taken the easy road ... never the shortest route. I don't know what will happen ..."

"Don't worry about Otto," Wilhelm winked at his mother. "We had a long talk about his fears last night. He has failed so often and let so many people down over his short life, has been in so much trouble that he's lost confidence in his abilities to fight in a war. I assured him I am frightened and feel uncomfortable in tight situations. I told him everybody does. When that happens each one of us has the same two options ... we get up and do something about it, or we die."

Wilhelm said he told Otto the other soldiers he would meet would be just like him ... all trying to hide their fear and none of them having a choice but to follow orders. Each man would do his best and fight, or face being shot in the back running away. A coward's death by firing squad would blight our family for generations.

"Otto was in tears when he said he would never disappoint or disgrace you again. I told him no man grows courage the night before fate lands him in the army, that developing courage takes time. I told him it's a lot like growing potatoes. You start with a small piece of spud. Well, a small part of him, like the eye of the potato, is packed with potential and is waiting to sprout. I told him to remember how we always added aged cow manure as we covered the spuds with soil? Well, I said his sergeants would shovel plenty of shit his way during his training to make him physically strong, to fertilize his nerves and to boost his confidence up and out until it flowers. I said while all this was happening, little round balls of courage would be growing between his knees."

Minnie laughed. "Wilhelm, you didn't tell him that."

"I told him I thought he might develop a taste for the army because the food is better than the food in jail. Don't upset yourself, Ma. Otto will make it work because he has no other choice."

A week later Minnie saw a long black car pull up her driveway and park next to her rhubarb patch. Her mouth felt dry ... like she had been chewing chicken feathers. Her thoughts whirled. This was it ... she must protect her children from going to jail ... the responsibility was all hers for the stills and for the distribution ... oh, hell, the entire bootlegging operation was her idea. As head of the family she was the one who should spend the rest of her life behind bars. She would turn herself in. She took a deep breath and opened the door. Two large men filled the frame.

"Are you Minnie Hartman?" The taller man removed his hat.

Minnie was intimidated. She swallowed the lump in her throat and said, "No. I mean y-y-yes sir, I am. And may I ask who you are?"

The men flashed silver badges. "FBI."

Minnie could breathe again. They were not from the Treasury Department investigating illegal stills.

"We are looking for Otto Hartman."

"Of course you are. Otto is my son," Minnie said. "Won't you come in. May I offer you a cup of coffee … a slice of sponge cake?" She closed the door behind the men. "I know he is in trouble and I heard he escaped from the West Branch jail. I can assure you, gentlemen, Otto Hartman is not on this farm. My son Otto is not on any property owned by my family. You are welcome to search."

Life went on in Lincoln Township with one less Hartman to stir the pot. And then Leonard Hartman was born. His first cry took place in Wilhelm and Mary's bedroom in the new fireproof, concrete-block house built by his family and neighbors from Lincoln Township.

Wilhelm's cattle were now lactating gallons of white gold that he sold to the dairy in Standish. The Judge had personally increased Wilhelm's herd twofold. The price of beets and hay had climbed. All of the family stills were producing record amounts of the finest-quality illegal potato liquor cash could buy. The fear of Prohibition prompted the price of a shot of liquor to soar even higher. These were enormously prosperous, trouble-free years … with one exception. Wilhelm was constantly fielding complaints about his bull, The Judge.

The animal had learned to jump fences and began impregnating the neighborhood's cattle. Farmers didn't complain when The Judge serviced their cows. They did complain when The Judge refused to budge from his girlfriends in their herds at milking time. The huge animal pawed the earth and threatened to gore intruders.

Ralph was settling into his own fireproof home in 1913. He had a telephone installed, one of the first in the neighborhood. His number, along with twelve others, was listed for all to see in the weekly newspaper. When Wilhelm read Ralph's name on the list, Minnie laughed. "Ralph likes all these newfangled gadgets. Why would anyone need a telephone?"

The State of Michigan funded the improvement of its roadways in 1915. Ralph had experience building ice roads with horses and dynamite. He saw an opportunity, but would have to upgrade his equipment. Minnie's third son mortgaged his farm, bought a new yellow dump truck, and went to work hauling gravel and crushed stone as Arenac County set out to improve its muddy roadways.

During the week, Ralph delivered road-building materials as township lanes were converted from sawdust and mud to crushed stone mixed with calcium chloride. While the sun was still shining on weeknights and weekends, Ralph worked his horses pulling stumps, plowing and planting his fields. When the sun set, Dolly and Romeo rested while Ralph tended the still.

All the loading and delivering of gravel and sand during the week ate away his days and the energy he needed for farming. Ralph hired his brothers Fred Jr. and Barney to work his farm, and his sisters Edith and Molly to run his still. He paid off his dump truck with the roadwork and the mortgage on his farm with profits from the family still. "I'm sittin' pretty," he told his mother.

At the meeting the next Sunday Barney reported a store and home had been raided in Three Oaks. The sheriff and his sponge-squad confiscated twenty-five gallons of shine. Ralph cautioned each of us to remember the oath of silence we had sworn. "Say nothing about the family business. If you get caught, keep your mouth shut."

Prohibition supporters, called dries, considered the 18th Amendment a victory for public morals and health. Anti-prohibitionists, known as wets, criticized the alcohol ban as an intrusion in rural, urban, and immigrant life. Wet or dry, dumping good whiskey was a national shame.

Chapter Nineteen
THE STRUGGLE

In 1916 the State of Michigan passed The Damon Act, which prohibited the sale of liquor. Barney had already established a clientele and ramped up his distribution route before the new law took effect. He was traveling the back roads after dark in his Model-T Ford every night of the week. When he didn't show up for breakfast one sunny winter morning, his big brother Ralph went out looking for him.

The sheriff's car pulled into Minnie's driveway later that afternoon. Sam asked Minnie if he could come in and sit a spell. She invited him into her kitchen, had him take a seat and poured him a shot from a bottle hidden behind her breadbox. "Won't you have one with me?" Sheriff Sam watched as she poured one for herself, stirred in a spoonful of honey and the juice of a lemon. "So Minnie, what is your favorite tipple called?"

"A lumberjack in Au Sable introduced me to this drink. It's called the 'Bee's Knees.' I don't tolerate the white lightning straight up. Why are you pleasuring me with your company today?"

"This is good hooch." The sheriff shuffled his feet. "The folks out here make a good product … flavor is consistent, and they haven't poisoned anybody like the bootleggers east of town. Do you know what their secret is?"

"Sheriff, are you planning on expanding your business to both sides of the law?"

The man shook his head. His smile disappeared. "Minnie, I have some bad news." He raised his glass and emptied it. She did the same and set her glass on the table. "Your son Barney was shot."

"Barney?" Her eyes popped open. "My Barney? Is he …"

"He's alive. It happened near Rose City. He and two of his buddies said they were deer hunting. They all had guns … sawed off shotguns. Sit down, Minnie." Sam removed a handkerchief from his pocket and slipped it into Minnie's hand.

"Where is he now?" Minnie poured herself a straight shot and took a seat.

"He's on the afternoon train to the hospital in Bay City."

"How bad, Sam?" Minnie refilled his glass, then blew her nose.

"It's bad. He was shot in the back."

"That was no hunting accident. Tell me what happened." She took another nip.

"Two witnesses said they saw a man come out of the woods with a gun. He shot your son and ran back into the woods. One of the witnesses went for help and the other followed the shooter. Barney was bleeding. The boy was lucky his buddies were afraid to move him. The bullet lodged close to his spine. Any movement could have killed him."

"*Mein Got im Himmel.* Will he be able to walk?" Minnie said, and took a gulp.

"Time will tell. Those doctors down in Bay City get a lot of practice removing bullets from fights at the Catacombs, that three-story saloon down on Water Street in Bay City." The sheriff finished his drink and stood up. "You all right, Minnie? Can you stand?" He waited while the woman got to her feet. "Need a lift somewhere?"

"Thank you, I could use a ride to Wilhelm's farm if you're headed that way."

When Wilhelm returned from the hospital in Bay City, he reported to the family that Barney had managed to tell him what happened before he was taken into surgery.

"Barney said he was meeting some barkeeps on a back road near St. Helens. The three of them were standing beside his Ford making the deal when a truck pulled up beside them. Two men got out carrying guns. Barney said he tried, but couldn't reach his shotgun from his Ford in time. He said he knew what was coming. The hijackers wanted all his liquor. They made Barney and his customers load the Hartman liquor into their truck at gunpoint.

"Barney said one of the hijackers, the shorter one, must have wanted to have some fun because he heard him ask his buddy if he wanted to see a couple of guys dance, and then the guy popped off a round at their feet. Barney said he turned to see if they were hurt, and that's when they plugged him in the back.

"He said it didn't hurt too much right away. He could hear the thugs talking. One of them ordered Barney's buyers to drive off in his Ford and not to look back. He said he heard his engine roll over and roar. He heard the transmission being speed shifted into high gear, and then he choked on the dust as his Ford spun out of there.

"When the dust cleared he said he saw the thugs standing beside the road pissing in the sand. Then they got in their truck, he heard the engine turn over and the hijackers drove off, leaving another swirl of dust."

"Ma, they just left Barney there, bleeding in the dirt. He told me he thought he was a goner. Next thing he remembered, he was laid out in a hospital bed. I told him his buyers had come back for him, loaded him into his Ford, and drove him into St. Helens.

"The doctor stopped the bleeding right there in the back of Barney's Ford. Barney said he didn't remember any of this. The doc said he was no good at removing bullets that close to the spine. He told the driver to take the guy straight to the train station and get him on the afternoon run to Bay City. Barney did remember he told the doc, in case he didn't make it, to remind his brother, Amil, and his nephew, Lawrence not to get shot near St. Helens. He asked the doc to see to it that his buyers each got a bottle from the compartment under the backseat to thank them for helping him. And he had the doc take a bottle for his trouble.

"The police are calling the incident a 'hunting accident.' Barney laughed out loud at that one, Ma, and then warned us not to dispute the police. He told me the surgeon in Bay City was planning to dig out that bullet later tonight, but they rolled Barney out to surgery before I left this afternoon."

"Why shoot my boy?" Minnie's forehead furrowed. "He was only doing his job. If they want us to stop producing, why not shoot me?" She stuck her hands into her apron pockets. "This liquor business was my idea." She rubbed her hands together, crossed her arms and paced. "Maybe we should stop."

"They don't shoot women, Ma," Wilhelm said. "Besides, Barney was doing what he loves. It isn't work for him. He's a big boy. He can deal with this."

It took most of the distillery profits that year to pay Barney's medical bills. He was grateful and said he felt lucky to be moving around, even if it was in a wheelchair. Edith monitored his recovery. It became clear to the family that their brother would never walk without crutches again. When Barney understood the inevitable, he started drinking heavily.

Amil Hartman appeared to be a patriotic man of twenty in 1914 and a hundred percent American. He enlisted in the army without telling his mother, and then when she found out, hunched his shoulders and listened to Minnie's tirade. "That, my son, was stupid and dangerous. Wars are designed by old men seeking power. Young men are nothing but targets. Do you want to die?"

"Ma, I feel safer fighting Germans on the battlefields of Europe than fighting the Purple Gang on the back roads of Michigan on weekends over jugs of illegal hooch." Amil had been working at a Gaylord camp making wagons and logging wheels when he read that Archduke Ferdinand of Austria was assassinated. He took the train south to enlist, but came back to Gaylord to collect his belongings. He was given a five-dollar gold coin by the company boss before he left for overseas so he would have emergency cash anywhere in the world. Minnie told him she thought that was a nice touch.

Ralph worked Fred and Amil's farmland along with his own, did what he could to help with the family business, but mainly delivered gravel and crushed stone for the new trunk line being built through Arenac County.

Amil was twenty-three in 1917 when he returned from the Great War in Europe. His brother Fred, then twenty-one, was one of fifty-four others who were sent from Arenac County to Fort Custer in Battle Creek that same year.

Amil's first civilian job was working on the Weidenthal farm. He was in much better health than his crippled brother, Barney. Amil's interest was not in distilling strong drink or farming. He found a job that suited his nature. He delivered glass bottles of healthy fresh milk in the early morning hours to the back porches and front steps of families in Standish ... a legal job.

Barney's paralyzed leg turned red and became infected. After a lengthy hospital stay, he was released to his sister who rented a room on Cedar Street not far from where she lived with her new husband, Louie Ireland. Barney was thirty-three, crippled and had no marriage prospects. The family business paid for his food, his drink, a radio and newspapers to read.

Amil stopped to check on Barney's condition every morning after his milk run. When his older brother confessed he felt depressed ... like a prisoner of war, Amil understood. He pulled him out of that little house on Cedar Street each night after dark and he and Barney drove the old routes to the blind pigs.

These illegal, residential drinking establishments had popped up in the most unlikely places … empty rooms over city hall, church basements, and peoples' country cabins. The brothers conducted their end of the illegal distribution business like they had before Barney's 'hunting accident,' only this time Amil took orders and hauled the bottles. He rigged the auto so his crippled brother could do the driving.

Barney, the oldest and most experienced salesman, consulted with Lawrence and Leonard on the distribution of the product. He cautioned Wilhelm's oldest boys on the limits of their territory and the possible repercussions if they crossed those boundaries. "A sixteen-year-old boy in Hamtramck was caught selling a gallon of shine. He told the cops he was selling it for his father. And that's all the information they needed. They took the boy home and found a thirty-gallon still in the basement. And now the whole family is in jail."

The boys rode the rounds with Barney and Amil to learn the route. Then Barney split the territory so both Hartman teams could supply the illegal drinking establishments with Hartman's finest fake Canadian Whiskey. The owner/bartenders continued to be loyal, and rightly so. They were purchasing an underpriced product that was twice as good as the overpriced rotgut sold by their competitors, Detroit's Purple Gang. Since most of Minnie's children were thinking and working like adults, she made a conscious effort to back away from making decisions for them. Ralph reminded them all before they left the meeting that a bootlegger was caught up in Escanaba for selling three pints and is going to prison for it. Treasury agents are saying in the paper they made 125 arrests so far this year. "Be careful out there."

They all made a point of visiting Minnie on Sunday afternoons for the platters of fried chicken, mounds of mashed potatoes and thick chicken gravy she served. She made buttermilk biscuits with honey she harvested from the honeybees hives in her orchard.

Edith walked in late pushing Barney's wheelchair. She had learned to drive the new car Louie gave her for a Christmas gift. As the family stood gaping at the vehicle from Minnie's windows, Edith whispered to her mother that his gift was not the shiny black body with running boards and black rubber wheels. His gift to her was the freedom the car gave her to come and go as she pleased.

Minnie understood that all too well. She knew her daughter loved to travel. Edith had traversed Michigan by train from Detroit to the Ironwood, and from Muskegon to Port Huron. Edith said she would use the freedom those four wheels gave her for her entertainment and her daily trips to Wells Addition and for extracting her brother from his isolation to join the Sunday family gatherings.

Minnie gasped when Edith pulled off her coat. It was December and cold and Edith wore a skirt so short Minnie could see her knees. Before she could get a word out Ralph clapped his hands together to get everyone's attention.

He stooped over and grasped one leg of their old workhorse. "Otto! Freddie! Help me spool old Dick into a roll and set him by the parlor wall. Edith and I are going to teach all of you some dance steps we learned in Detroit. Sis, that dress is the bee's knees. Ma, do you have any sheet music for hot dancin'?"

Minnie played 'Pickles Rag' and Ralph started in with some fancy footwork. His siblings were mesmerized by their brother's agile feet. Minnie glanced around. Without exception each one in her brood was keeping time to the music, tapping his toes, moving her hips. Then Ralph bent backwards throwing his arms over his head, touching the floor, swirling sideways. He grabbed his sister, twirled Edith around, threw her over his shoulder and shot her through his legs.

Minnie was shocked and stopped playing. "Is that a dance?"

"It's called the Black Bottom, Ma. Come on Wilhelm. You and Mary shake it up with us. Molly," Ralph said. "Dance with me."

Minnie played 'Alexander's Ragtime Band,' and 'Moonlight Bay' from the sheet music Mr. Hardy let her borrow. They had apple pie and the ice cream that Wilhelm and Mary had brought with them. Mary told everyone how Rudy scooped cream floating on top the milk. "Hedwig added eggs and sugar and Sally churned it until it was thick. And then Sally made the pie all by herself." Applause filled the room and then they each ate their dessert. Before it was time to go home Minnie had them learn Elsie Baker's new song, 'Silent Night.'

The year 1918 started on a low. Wilhelm read news of the flu pandemic to Minnie over coffee on Sunday mornings. It was spreading across America's northern prairies, ending the lives of the young and weak and knocking off the very old. This particular strain also attacked the healthy, wiping out entire families. Minnie had witnessed the social unrest and wars that followed the cholera and diphtheria epidemics in Europe.

News was not good for those in the German community in Lincoln Township. Americans were still being sent to Europe to fight Germans. Folks from Arenac County bent their heads to listen if they heard a German accent. The pastor at the Lutheran Church advised his congregation to go about their business. They had nothing to fear. They were no longer German citizens. They were Americans.

And then Congress passed a literacy requirement for immigrants on the path to becoming citizens. Discussions of citizenship for undocumented aliens was forefront in the newspapers, the street corners, and in the illegal drinking establishments.

Wilhelm stopped by the courthouse to reassure himself the family paperwork was in order. He panicked when he found his father's naturalization paperwork filed in 1887 incomplete.

He told his mother the courts had no record of Fred becoming a citizen. "Pa filled out the first part of his paperwork in 1887 but never completed the second step. He was supposed to appear before a judge to swear his allegiance but never did.

That makes us all undocumented aliens. We are living here as German citizens. The country is fighting a war with Germans. The government may look upon us as enemies. We could be deported back to Germany, back into a war zone."

The next Sunday after church, Minnie's family met at Wilhelm's house. Mary made coffee and cinnamon toast and sent the little ones outside to play. Wilhelm laid out the problems. "We are breaking the law on multiple levels. We are aliens living in America illegally."

"You mean we're not Americans?" Edith set her coffee cup down without drinking any. "We are in big trouble. If we are Germans, and this country is at war with Germany, that makes us enemies of the State. Oh my. Oh my, what should we do."

"Don't give up information on German troop movements, Edith, even if they torture you," Ralph said with a straight face.

"Don't tease your sister. This is serious," Minnie said.

"That's only part of the trouble," Wilhelm said. "Congress has just approved the Sixteenth Amendment to the U.S. Constitution, the Personal Income Tax Law."

"We're done for," said Molly. "Now, in addition to the land tax we already pay, each farmer must keep track of income from the sale of milk, sugar beets, navy beans, hay, corn, vegetables and wheat. We must record stud fees from The Judge. We must write down our egg and liquor sales. Then we must add them all together and pay an income tax. The government will find out about the family business and we will end up in prison."

"Molly, you have a brain. Use it. Think!" Minnie crossed her arms in disgust.

"But Ma, we make the most money from our moonshine sales," she said. "How can we pay taxes for selling something that is illegal to sell?"

"What moonshine sales?" Wilhelm said.

—Use the--

American

LANGUAGE

==Only==

By Order of the
State Council of Defense

Penalty For Violation

Chapter Twenty
THE SORROW

"That's not the end of the trouble," Ralph said, "We are living on land mortgaged to the bank that we cannot possibly pay off with the added debt of the new income tax. The bank has loaned us money based on our family's reputation as American citizens. We have lived in Arenac County as undocumented aliens since 1896."

Molly wiped her clammy palms on her apron. "Maybe Gustav was right."

"Molly, Molly," Minnie said. "These are only small roadblocks and nothing that cannot be walked around. We will work on our problems together, one at a time. All of you have brains. Use them. Think."

Wilhelm and Ralph addressed the most serious test on their own. They sought the advice of Judge Whiting in Standish. On September 7, 1918, both men signed part one of the application for citizenship called the Petition for Naturalization. The judge told them the Hartman family would be investigated.

The two men drove home in silence. They dreaded breaking this news to their mother. They found her bent over, darning socks over a glass egg.

"Boys," Minnie listened as she finished the sock, and then lifted her head. "We haven't been dealt a fair hand in this citizenship business." She stood. "Let's fold our cards for a while and think. I do have one idea." Minnie had Ralph drive her to town to see her old friend, Sheriff Sam. On the way into town she went over in her mind what she would and wouldn't tell him. This kind man might turn out to be her trump card.

"Sam, I'm here for two reasons. I came to pay my respects to the memory of your dear one. I'm so sorry your wife has passed."

"Thank you, Minnie. Come in and sit a spell. My wife appreciated your kindness each time you came to call. It has been a long illness. We have all appreciated the bushels of potatoes your sons delivered with that bottle in the bottom. I think she was tired of being sick and just gave up. Can't blame her."

"She was a good woman."

"You are looking splendid today. I'm serious, Minnie, for a woman your age, you are a looker."

"A compliment like that will buy you a cup of tea, Sam. Will you have a nip with me?" Minnie pulled two Rosenthal china cups from her handbag and set them on the table.

"Don't mind if I do." The sheriff stood and pulled the curtains closed on his office windows.

A bottle appeared from under Minnie's shawl. Sam smiled. "Can I pour that for you, pretty lady?" He filled each of their tea cups and pushed the bottle out of sight under his desk. "What are we drinking to today, Minnie? Bad news?" He raised his cup to hers.

"Citizenship," she said.

The sheriff tilted his head and furrowed his brow. "Okay, here's to citizenship." He clinked her teacup and drank his dry.

"Pour another," Minnie said, sipping her liquor slowly, ladylike. "Sheriff, my husband Fred, you remember him. My Fred was a good man."

The sheriff finished his second cup and poured a third, eyeing Minnie all the while.

"Fred could read and write, but he was not good with details." She took a sip. "You may recall that my husband, our three sons, and I emigrated from Germany. We have been living in Michigan for the last thirty-six years. Fred filed naturalization paperwork long ago but we recently learned he did not finish the process." Minnie finished her whiskey and held her cup up to be refreshed.

The sheriff obliged and poured another for himself. "Minnie, am I to understand that you and that brood out in Johnsfield are undocumented aliens?" He started to laugh, but checked himself when he saw Minnie's face.

"This is serious, Sam." Minnie crossed her legs and leaned back in her chair. She took another sip from her teacup. "My boys and I are as American as you are. Fred had been drinking heavily when he filed the papers, and I was afraid to … I mean, I didn't clarify the details of the naturalization process with him. Both Wilhelm and I assumed we had become citizens when he did, but we were wrong.

"So here I am, Sam, sitting across from an officer of the law, spilling my guts about breaking the law." Minnie took a handkerchief from her handbag and dabbed her eyes. "Sam, I don't know what to do."

"My dear Minnie. Don't get yourself in a tizzy." The sheriff got up from his chair, walked around his desk and sat down next to her. "You've lived here more than five years. You own land and have improved it. Fill out the naturalization paperwork. I have one of the forms right here in a drawer."

"Sam, I can't." She bowed her head and studied her clasped hands. "It's complicated."

The sheriff refilled their teacups. "These are pretty fancy cups, Minnie. They fit you perfectly."

She nodded and took another sip. "Wilhelm filed one of those naturalization forms. Ralph filed one too. Any undocumented alien living under their roofs will become a citizen if the head of the household becomes a citizen."

"So what is the problem?"

"I live with my son Fred Jr. He is the head of our household. I am an undocumented alien. He is already a citizen because I bore him in this country, so I can't be swept in under him."

"Well then Minnie," the sheriff said rubbing his chin, "why don't you fill out your own paperwork … apply yourself."

"Sam, I never learned to read or write. That is one of the requirements for citizenship."

"I see," Sam said and took another drink.

"There is another problem," Minnie said. "Let's just say I move in with Ralph who is the head of his household. When he becomes a citizen, I would be ordinarily swept in under him, but his record is not clean and the government may reject him. A clean record is another requirement for citizenship."

The sheriff rubbed the whiskers on his chin. "I'll look into Ralph's record for you. I know Judge Whiting likes your … your brand of 'tea' just as much as I do. I'll have a talk with him. The paperwork might take some time."

"Thank you, Sam." Minnie stood and kissed his cheek.

Gustav appeared at Minnie's door late in the afternoon of January 12, 1918 and introduced his new wife Pauline, their daughter Gustava and their three boys, Irvin, Roy, and Walter. "Ma, I registered for the draft. If they take me, I need you to help Pauline with our children. Can they stay here with you?"

"Come in. Come in. Take a chair Pauline. Children, would you like to check on the chickens?" Minnie pointed toward the coop and they ran off into the farmyard. "Gustav, what happened to your wife, Elsie Walters, and your daughter Charlotte?"

"Pauline, why don't you check on the children?" Gustav paused until she was out of earshot. "That didn't work out. Ma, Pauline always wanted to live on a farm. I've never asked for anything. You know I wasn't treated fairly and equally when Pa's estate was divided."

"That's because you left the family."

"You understand, Ma, I'm not asking for me, but for my wife and children."

"What exactly are you asking, Gustav?"

"At least some land and a roof over our heads. And a little cash wouldn't hurt, either, until we get settled."

"Settled? So let's be clear. You are asking for a loan."

"No, I want my inheritance and my share of the family business."

"The same family business you objected to on moral grounds when you left?"

"Ma, that was ages ago, you know … leaves off the trees, water over the dam."

Pauline re-entered the room and interrupted her husband. "As a newcomer to the family, I must say what Gustav is proposing seems quite reasonable."

"I'll have to think this over, Gustav," Minnie said. "And of course I will discuss it with other family members who worked alongside me to make our business profitable."

"I understand," Gustav said. "I also understand the law gives some protection to all of Pa's children, some rights that I can pursue."

"Son, may I have a moment with your lovely wife?"

Gustav nods. "Sure Ma, I'll just check on the chickens and the children."

"Pauline dear, as you say, you are a newcomer to this family. I watched Gustav's character develop over the years as he grew. I know what kind of a man he is. I had a damaging experience with a man like him years ago. If your husband does manage to get land and cash from this family, I wouldn't necessarily count on his later loyalty to you and his children."

When Gus reentered the kitchen, Pauline stood abruptly. "Gustav, we're done here," she said and headed for the door.

"Son, we'll have to talk later. I need to help Fred Jr. and Amil prepare for the storm. Did you notice how dark the sky has become? We could use all of your help. Pauline dear, here is your chance to see what living on a farm is like. The animals need to be herded inside, fed and watered. The chickens need to be locked inside their coop and the windows shut. We need to string ropes between the out-buildings so we can get to the animals in case the wind becomes overpowering and the snow drifts."

"Ma," Gustav said. "Pauline wants to get into town before the storm hits. You can reach us at the hotel."

A blizzard arrived in Arenac County from Saskatchewan in the late afternoon of January 12, 1918. While temperatures plummeted Millie's sons herded their animals inside shelters. While the sky darkened Wilhelm, Ralph, and Fred strung ropes from barns and outbuildings to cabins on their own farms. The winds came next, held steady at forty miles an hour, with gusts at sixty. The day ended at minus twenty-two degrees with twenty inches of snow created drifts of eight to twenty feet.

Minnie didn't have time or try to get in touch with Gustav and his new wife after the storm hit, and she wouldn't have reached them if she had.

Everyone in the family took his turn on the rope trudging and sometimes tunneling though the snow to feed and water the animals. When the stalls were cleaned and the straw bedding was laid, they returned along the lifeline with a load of firewood in one hand and the other firmly grasping the rope. Returning to a warm cabin smelling of fresh bread, venison stew with boiled potatoes was well worth the freezing trip. Minnie's children and grandchildren shucked corn, sorted beans, and made quilts when the weather kept them inside.

They mended socks, hung laundry on inside lines to dry and stoked the fire.

The war in Europe was aggravating the fuel shortage across the country but especially in Michigan during the blizzard of 1918. The mayor of Standish announced the town's coal supply would be gone in two days and instructed citizens to burn wood during the day and coal only at night. A municipal buzz saw was set up next to the train station for cutting timber into firewood.

Eight carloads of coal finally arrived nine days later, but by that time another storm from the northwest had socked the area with even deeper snow. A week later, thirty-three cars of coal arrived in town, but another cold snap struck February 5 keeping schools closed until the eighteenth of that month. Theaters, halls and some businesses were closed. Church services were limited to six hours a week until the train tracks could be cleared and the coal cars could replenish the town's supply.

Rail service, halted by the blizzard, stranded travelers on trains. People sought shelter anywhere they could stay warm. It was all in the newspaper, which Wilhelm read to Minnie when he finally made it through the snow to her house.

He read about a lumberjack near Manistique the sheriff arrested for burning a Soo Line railroad car filled with hemlock bark. The boxcar had been sidetracked seven miles south of Manistique with contents valued at $850. The young man said, in his defense, that he had worked in the lumber camps, had been laid off and was heading to town when the storm hit. It was one of the coldest days of the year. He was without food, shelter and was desperately cold. He weighed freezing to death with going to jail, and decided to burn several cords of wood before he set fire to the entire railcar. Someone saw the smoke from town, sent help and carried the half-frozen man to the doctor. At first the doc thought the young 'jack would lose both feet from frostbite. The man's face began to swell. When he tried to eat several of his molars dropped out and then …"

"Stop," Minnie said. "That's a terrible story. I'm cold enough already."

Wilhelm told his mother he had been concerned about his neighbor, Louie Kalo, afraid he was stranded. Yesterday he visited Louie's shack by the church, hauled the old Hungarian up behind him on the workhorse, and all three of them made it back through the drifts to the homestead and Wilhelm's four squalling children.

Minnie's son said he read newspapers to Louie during the day to pass the time. The children annoyed Louie with songs, games and antics when they weren't crying or fighting. He read to Louie about the Act of May 9 limiting the naturalization process to whites and Negros. The old Hungarian paced, stopped to look out to see if the snow had stopped, and then stepped over children and their toy horses to pace the floor again.

"Ma, he hasn't filed the citizenship papers either. I told him the government is tightening immigration laws and if he didn't act soon they might deport him." That stopped his pacing.

He said, "I no go back to Old Country."

"Does he have a police record here, or in Hungary?"

"I don't know. I told him I would get the papers for him from Judge Whiting, but Louie said, 'No judge. No good. Can't read. Can't write. I hide in woods.' And then he walked home."

Minnie snickered. "He must have stolen that hiding idea from Otto."

"Louie has been living alone in that tarpaper shack since his wife in Hungary cashed in the second set of steamship tickets he sent. He told me she refused to immigrate to Michigan with his two children. The man must have worked and saved for years for those tickets. I can't understand why any woman would not want to come here to join her husband.

Poor Louie. He has had to face the disappointment of never seeing his wife or children again. He's grown accustomed to living without a woman, and I think he came to like his empty life of peace and quiet down in his little tarpaper shack."

Wilhelm sat smoking his corncob pipe. "I wonder how my life would have been different had you made the same decision about emigrating as Louie's wife had. "I would have been conscripted by the Prussian Army and would be living the life of a soldier, or be crippled from a wound, or dead. I sure wouldn't have met Mary or enjoyed our family."

"I can understand why a woman wouldn't want to emigrate," Minnie said. "I didn't want to come to America. I was spoiled as a child ... lived in a big city with paved streets and ancient municipal buildings with clock towers. The town hall on market square had two goats that rolled out each hour. I loved to watch them lock horns and pretend to fight. I belonged to a singing club and took piano lessons. We had a good life in Poland. Fred was the one who decided to emigrate. I refused to come at first, too ... like Louie's wife. It never occurred to me to sell the ticket your father sent. Circumstances were different for me. I came because I couldn't stay in Poland any longer. There are at least two sides to every story, Wilhelm. Mrs. Kalo may have had good reasons to stay in Hungary."

Wilhelm said, "I've got one for you Ma. Ralph has been concerned about Louie Kalo living alone, so concerned that every morning this week he has stopped at Louie's and has the old man hop in his truck."

"Ralph is thoughtful and good company."

"That's true, but he also needs help making his sand and gravel deliveries."

"I can understand that. He's been busy since Arenac County's big push to add a layer of gravel to county roads. I'm sure he pays Louie for his help."

"That's where the other side to the story comes in. I've seen his yellow truck at a different illegal, residential, drinking establishment every afternoon this week. They call them Blind Pigs or Blind Tigers. I looked inside one and there was Louie sitting beside Ralph, both men dousing the day's dust down their throats."

"No. My Ralph?"

"Yes. And I was out plowing the north field around dusk and saw his yellow truck inch down Johnsfield Road. At first I thought Ralph was avoiding the deep ruts on the road. His dump truck was moving mighty slow, so slow and so careful that it reminded me of a snail, a prudent snail. I've ridden with Ralph. Some of those ruts are deep. Let one tire dip inside one and you could bend a wheel getting out. I've seen buggies flip over attempting to steer out of a rut. Add rain and the road turns to mud. Ralph might as well be driving on top the ice at Nigl's gravel pit. One inattentive swerve on a road with ruts can land Ralph's dump truck in a ditch and require two teams, plus Cobb and Dolly, to pull it out."

"Ralph was always a careful boy."

"Ralph, your son, after dropping Louie at his shack and pulling into his own muddy driveway became the prudent snail. He tiptoed into his own house feeling his way in the dark."

"Oh dear, I hope Barbara was asleep."

"I found out Barbara had been waiting. Ralph told me she lit the lantern, nearly blinding him, and then settled him slowly in a chair. She pulled his plate from the cookstove, handed him a fork, and waited while he ate. Then she drowned him in coffee until he was sober enough to walk out and add some logs to the fire under his still."

"Oh, Barbara knows about the stills? It had to happen."

The next time Wilhelm and Ralph met with Judge Whiting, they denounced the German Emperor, and on September 7,

1918, signed the Oath of Allegiance to the United States of America. They petitioned the court to become naturalized citizens.

Ralph registered for the WWI draft on September 12, 1918 at the age of thirty-eight. It was his first time to register and the third and last round of draft registrations before the armistice would be signed that ended the war in 1919.

On February 27, 1919, both Wilhelm and Ralph appeared before Judge Asa Whiting in the Circuit Court of Arenac County and took the oath of allegiance to the United States of America.

On June 18, 1919 Ralph Hartman became a naturalized citizen, and since he was head of the household where his widowed mother happened to be living, so did Wilhelmina Hartman. That same day Wilhelm Hartman became a citizen with his wife Mary and their four children. They all stopped at the Summer Trail Inn for a celebratory dinner before they drove home.

The years had brightened considerably for the Hartman family enterprise since May of 1917 when Michigan became a dry state. Business profits soared. Everyone did their job. Minnie continued to sit in the background during family meetings to watch her offspring think through their difficulties.

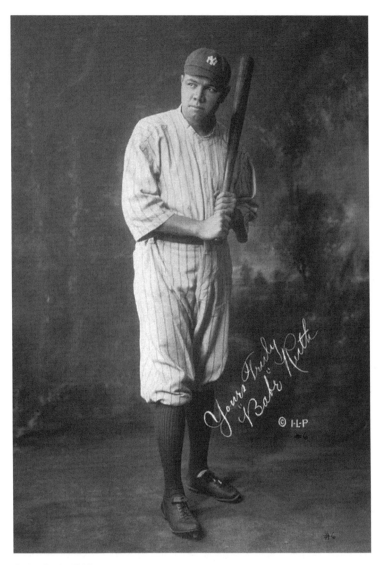

Babe Ruth, 1920.

Photo Attribution: (wikimedia.org) Creative Commons Corporation.

Chapter Twenty One
THE SOUTHPAW

An unexpected event unsettled her sons in 1919. Their main entertainment was listening to ballgames on the radio. Minnie's children had become rabid baseball fans. They knew all the teams and had memorized player's names and batting averages. They tried to copy the batting style of the great Shoeless Joe Jackson. They were partial to the Chicago White Socks and were shocked in 1919 when they learned the World Series had been fixed by the mobster, Arnold Rothstein. Disappointed in the game, they swore off baseball.

But when Babe Ruth beat the home run record in 1920, and became everyone's hero, her son's ears were back glued to the radio. The Babe's performance was legendary in Lincoln Township. It was all they talked about. He had saved baseball from the ugly scandal of 1919, and restored their love of the sport.

Babe's greatest accomplishment in the Hartman household happened when the boys learned Babe Ruth's parents were immigrants from Germany. George Herman Ruth, Jr. was just like them. The boys decided then and there that they could do anything they wanted with their lives. Only in America could this happen.

The Sunday after the "Babe's" landmark game, Barney reported rum-runners were bringing Canadian whiskey near Michigan's shores all around the Great Lakes. The Canadians were not breaking the law when they brewed the booze and drank it. They just couldn't sell it. Bootleggers in the States broke the law when they made it, sold it and drank it.

"Any tub that can float is loaded with liquor, pulled across or around the Great Lakes and anchored off shore until local rum-runners motor out to unload their stock." Barney told the family that when the Detroit River ices over, liquor is dragged across on sleds.

Amil said he heard eight cylinder Buicks were loaded with bottles in Canada and driven so fast over new ice barely four inches thick the surface would bounce on their way to Detroit.

"They must be making good money to risk losing a Buick," Wilhelm said.

"What about the risk of losing the driver?" Minnie said. "Don't any of you take a chance like that."

Barney heard a report from barkeepers in southern Michigan that a pipeline was being built under the Detroit River to provide a constant flow of Canadian liquor.

"It looks like we will be in business forever," Molly said.

Amil had been distributing Hartman's finest liquor after dark to the barkeeps in the speakeasies in Arenac County instead of milk to the children of Standish. He would deliver Barney to his tiny house in town before dawn and would make it to the farm for breakfast. He slept for a few hours, joined the family for the noonday meal, and then worked in the fields.

The Hartman stills had been pumping out a beverage made from fermented corn at thirty-six gallons a week. The potato crop failure that year caused a change in Minnie's recipe but a marked improvement in flavor.

Barney informed his siblings at the next meeting that the highest price paid for illegal alcohol came from the amber-colored Canadian brands. Wilhelm suggested the family manufacture 'Canadian brands.' "All it will take is one added step to our existing operation. We can add burnt sugar to our standard clear liquor and change the label." A vote was taken and they all agreed. Edith would burn the sugar. Molly's job was to roll the bottles on the floor to mix the sugar until it was the right shade of amber. Fred's job was to cork the bottles, screw lids on the jars, and apply the new labels identifying the brand as Canadian. Their product was now not only illegal, it was mislabeled. Barney and Amil tucked jars beneath the floorboards and behind the backseat of the Model-A Ford they could now afford to drive. They enjoyed their work.

When Congress passed the Eighteenth Amendment, the Federal government made the Hartman family. They now owned three farms, were free of all debt, and had a thriving bootlegging business.

The same year his son, Raymond, was born, Ralph surprised the family by announcing he was running in the 1920 election for Lincoln Township constable.

"Constable? Are you crazy? You can't be a lawman," Molly said. "You know too much. You could send us all to prison on your first day of work."

"Yes I could," Ralph grinned and winked at each of them.

"Ralph, you can't be on both sides of the law," Edith said.

"Why not? It's happening all over the country. If I win I could protect our operation and bust up the stills of our competition," Ralph said. "Look, I'm running for the office on the Republican ticket."

"When did you become a Republican?" Minnie asked.

"When an opportunity presented itself to become constable of Lincoln Township."

When Ralph didn't win the election, the family was relieved. He told his mother he would try again during the next election cycle. Minnie responded with a hug and a smile of approval. "I'm proud of you for using your head. This is a brilliant idea. Just be careful."

Amil had a setback when he let down his guard and began to enjoy the life of a rumrunner. He found an excuse to visit

Chicago with a load of 'Canadian Whiskey.' He sold the lot in less than two hours. Pleased with his success, he loaded his Ford and made a repeat trip the next week.

Near the edge of Chicago, Amil was ambushed by two men. They strong-armed him down on his knees beside his Ford. One gangster shoved a pistol in his mouth and threatened to pull the trigger while the other searched his car. Amil promised with the pistol still in his mouth that he would never sell liquor in their territory again. Satisfied, they let him go … but only after relieving him of what they thought was his entire load. The thug told him to consider the loss of this alcohol as a fine … like a traffic ticket for going too fast.

A shaken Amil turned his car around and headed north. He realized the men had missed the booze hidden beneath the backseat. He stopped in Bay City and sold the rest so he wouldn't arrive home empty-handed. Amil had always been a feisty child, so Minnie wasn't surprised when she found he was planning another trip south.

At the family meeting that Sunday after church Ralph read a newspaper story about a bootlegging ring that had been caught in the heart of downtown Chicago. "They were selling booze off the curb while the police looked on. It says right here agents confiscated $175,000 worth of liquor in that haul. How much of that was our's, Amil?"

"Take it easy, Ralph," Barney said. "We do have a gangster problem." He said he heard from a local barkeep that Al Capone claimed Illinois, Indiana, and Michigan as his territory. Word on the street was that the Purple Gang out of Detroit was moving their operation north. The mob is working the areas around Atlanta, Lewiston and southwest to Grass Lake. They're looking for independent bootleggers like us, smashing equipment, and hijacking stock like they did with Amil."

Barney reported trouble on a second front. Local police had located and destroyed two stills operating in Arenac County. They dumped liquor, busted barrels, and made arrests. Coppers across Michigan had been given orders to apprehend gangsters and moonshine distillers using any means at hand. They had the authority to shoot at will, killing bootleggers and gangsters without repercussions. Barney said he heard directly from a cop that police squads were not held responsible even if bystanders got in the line of fire. Judges were instructed by the Treasury Department to look the other way.

Wilhelm read Minnie the newspaper headlines: *Gangster Shootouts. Bank Robbery. Kidnapping. Policemen Shot in the Back.* This "better life" they had crossed the ocean to experience was heating up to what looked like a civil insurrection, just like she remembered from the Old Country.

"It's over," Molly said. Family emotions were at a boiling point. Some members were scared, wanted to stop, scrap the stills and go straight. Others who needed cash wanted to continue as before, only with greater caution. Amil could no longer sell outside their area. The thugs had made him a marked man. A long and arduous discussion developed until Minnie called for the vote. The count was tied. Never out of ideas, Minnie proposed they keep their production running, but discontinue their expansion program. They must stick with trusted local illegal Blind Pigs.

Ralph announced he was running for Lincoln Township constable again and assured them all he would win.

"How can you be so sure?" Edith said.

"I've got the entire population of Woodmere Cemetery voting absentee for me. I'll win."

"Ralph, I don't understand," Minnie said.

"Good. You don't need to know."

The Judge was the second order of business. Wilhelm's oldest son, Lawrence, reported the bull had chased him across the pasture and would have gored him had he not scurried up a tree at the last moment. The Judge weighed over a thousand pounds and was becoming increasingly dangerous. Wilhelm argued their prosperity was due in part to The Judge. Their herds had tripled. He advised Lawrence to stay out of the pasture and adjacent fields. "Remember, The Judge jumps fences and will chases whatever moves."

Edith told her mother that she had bumped into her brother, Otto, in Detroit. He told her he had met and married a woman from St. Claire Shores. Mamie Wognowski was her name. He said Mamie was an only child and he was working in her father's business. "True to his nature," Edith said, "the bum didn't think to bring her north to meet our family. If I hadn't run in to him we would never have known he was married. Ma, their wedding was on June 23."

A flu pandemic hit Arenac County in 1921 and killed the young and the very old. Minnie's family was spared, but most folks were left vulnerable by fear of the flu infecting them. Dread of the disease generated anxiety. The Red Scare added an element of alarm that communism was sweeping the country. Immigrants everywhere were on edge as anarchists were sought out and deported. People from the Old Country understood what living under communism could mean. Most of them, including Minnie, had lived through political unrest or war once before.

Fortunately for Minnie's family business, troubled times turned people to strong drink, and the drink of choice was moonshine.

Ralph drove his truck up Minnie's driveway early one morning in January of 1922. After coffee, he told his mother he had a phone call from Otto's wife who lived in Port Huron. Otto was dead.

"Dead? The last time I saw him was when he waved goodbye from the train headed for the army," Minnie said. "Edith ran into him in Detroit. He told her of his marriage to a Mamie Malinowski. I never met the girl. He said he had a job in her father's business. They were married such a short time. The poor girl must be devastated."

"She didn't sound too upset to me, Ma," Ralph said. "Mamie said her husband had tried his hand at her father's business, but it hadn't worked out. She gave no specifics. Mamie's father found Otto a job working for the railroad as a fireman, a dangerous traveling job, which led to his accidental death. She said Otto was rarely home and they had no children. She wanted to know what to do with his body. Her father told her there was no room for him in their family plot. I told her to send Otto's body back to us. We can bury him at Woodmere in the family plot. Is that all right?"

Otto's funeral was small and sad. Minnie had a stone carved with his name and buried him near his father. When Wilhelm checked on his status as a veteran, he learned the army had rejected him. Otto Hartman somehow had managed to live until he was thirty-two. It was a miracle.

Rudy as a boy.

Chapter Twenty Two
THE SMALLEST

Minnie's grandson, Rudy, was seventeen and took to working the Hartman homestead like Babe Ruth took to hitting home runs. The boy enjoyed the sunshine and the freedom of outdoor work. He finished cleaning the bedding straw from Cobb and Dolly's stalls and was stacking it inside the new Galloway wagon-box automatic manure spreader.

Wilhelm had bought the Galloway new in 1924 to save time moving and distributing the animal fertilizer from the barn to the fields. He paid seventy-five dollars for the machine because it eliminated the worst job on the farm … that of forking manure into the field while standing upright in it and trying not to fall. That was a rough ride, with Cobb pulling the wagon through the field ruts.

Rudy had finished loading the green box with straw from the horse barn when he heard the bell. When the dinner bell clanged, Mary's children dropped whatever they were doing and ran for the house. Mary had fed three-year-old Gilbert early and sent him outside to play while the adults and his siblings finished eating and were talking.

Rudy had stayed out all night with Lawrence and Leonard, arriving home moments before breakfast was served. Minnie's oldest grandson finished eating before the others, set his plate in the sink and walked outside to resume his work fertilizing the west field.

He hooked Cobb's harness to the spreader and climbed up onto the seat. The wagon was at the edge of the field and ready to go. He released the lock on the conveyer chain, which was driven by the right wheel. He gave Cobb the command the horse understood meant move forward ... a clicking of his tongue inside his cheek. The horse responded. The conveyer moved the manure to the rear of the wagon. Rotating spikes pulled it into the beater. But the wheels jerked, creaked, and the wagon skidded sideways, a sure sign something was caught in the spreader prongs or the beaters' spiral wheels.

"Whoa, Cobb." Rudy dropped the reins and stepped inside the wagon to break up the wedge. That was when he saw his little brother's foot. Rudy jumped from the wagon and ran to the house for help. The kitchen cleared out. Wilhelm pulled his son from the beater and tried to revive him while the others watched in horror. The sharp spikes had pierced his body. The boy was dead.

Mary wailed and dropped to her knees. Wilhelm wrapped his son's bloodied body in his work jacket and cradled him in his arms. He walked him inside and laid him on the marriage bed.

"I didn't see him, Ma." Rudy tried to comfort his mother, who was rocking with grief on the floor beside the bed. Rudy paced. "I didn't mean to kill the boy. I didn't see Gilbert sleeping there. I didn't mean it, Ma. I didn't mean it."

"It was an accident, Rudy," Hedwig offered to console her brother. "He must have been playing in the new Galloway. He must have fallen asleep."

That same night Mr. Elwell, the undertaker, came with his wagon and took Gilbert's tiny body into town. The cause of death was listed as "farm accident."

The entire Lincoln Township community mourned the toddler's untimely death. Neighbors showed up to milk and grain the Hartman's cows, slop the pigs and mash the chickens. The horse's stalls were mucked and fresh straw was laid while the family sat inside the house in silence. Food appeared on the kitchen table during the next days while the family managed their grief. The funeral packed the German

Lutheran Church just down the road from where the accident occurred. During the service, Wilhelm flagged Reverend Noack, asking leave to say a few words.

"Our son Gilbert was a tough little boy, big for his age. He wanted to help his brothers and me with our farm work. He sat on the wagon playing farmer's helper while we planted potatoes. He sat on Cobb's back playing farmer's helper while I fertilized the fields. Our little Gilbert never saw danger. He saw adventure. So that day after dinner when I gave Cobb the command to pull the Galloway spreader forward, Gilbert must have been sleeping and dreaming of his favorite horse, or of watching his Pa work when the spikes reached his pant leg and the beaters caught his little body and pulled him through. My only consolation is that Gilbert Hartman was dreaming when he died, dreaming of a heaven where even little boys could be farmers."

No one in the family corrected their father's story, least of all Rudy who was heavy with guilt. The rest of Minnie's family were so choked with emotion they could not speak.

On May 28, 1924 a paragraph appeared in the Independent thanking all for their kindness during the bereavement for their boy. It was signed, "William and Mary Hartman."

Mary sank into depression and stayed in bed. She had lost a child at birth. Two healthy children had been taken from her by the court. And now a farm accident took her three-year-old toddler. Wilhelm was overcome with grief too, but he had to think of the rest of his family. His greatest concern was losing his wife to an even deeper depression.

He invited his pregnant wife to see a moving picture show in Bay City to buoy her spirits. Mary Pickford was playing in "Rosita," a rags-to-riches story with a happy ending. Rudy drove the new seven-passenger, black Buick Wilhelm had purchased from the dealer in Standish. It had an electric start and a rumble seat built-in behind the back seat. Billy was the only one small enough to fit in the rumble seat, so he was invited to go along.

It was an outdoor cinema. They sat up high on a stack of risers. Billy wore his best shoes, his new funeral shoes for the occasion. Mary Pickford's songs were lively. He couldn't sit still and kicked off one of his new shoes. The small shoe dropped beneath the bleachers. Billy was afraid he would get in trouble if he told his father he had lost one of his funeral shoes. He had also been instructed to talk before or after the picture, but not during it, so he kept his mouth shut.

Mary Pickford's antics had lightened the mood for the family. After the show they talked about the movie as Rudy drove the forty-five miles back to Johnsfield.

Mary noticed the missing shoe when Billy stepped from the car, and questioned him. Mary Pickford's spell dissolved when Wilhelm heard his answer. Gilbert's death was still raw in everyone's mind and those shoes were purchased for his funeral. Wilhelm was suddenly furious with his son. He ripped the other shoe from Billy's foot, threw the youngster over his shoulder and carried him upstairs to bed. Then he threw the shoe into the attic.

Mary was indifferent to the lost shoe and went straight to bed. Her depression lingered. The family went into action.

Ralph called on Mary and Wilhelm on a Sunday morning. He was taking Barbara and his girls to Sand Lake for the afternoon. He asked Mary, Wilhelm and their children to join them.

"No thank you," Mary said, and went back to bed.

Minnie went to see her daughter-in-law. "I know how it feels to lose a child. I have lost four. My first sweet girl, Wilhelmina, died in her sleep after only a month. My second little girl, Amelia, was taken by a wolf. My third miscarried when I fell in the kitchen. And Otto died in a railroad accident. Mary, I remember how you grieved when your babies Linda and Rich were torn from your arms by a judge's decree. You have had more than your share of sadness in your life. Yet you have survived and thrived. Look what you do have ... a husband who loves you and six wonderful children. Baby Billy is such a free spirit. You are strong and I know you will pull yourself through the loss of Gilbert."

"Minnie," Mary said. "I'm pregnant again and I'm afraid I'm jinxed. I would rather die than have another one of my children die."

"Life is for the living, my dear. Look forward. Our families need us," Minnie said. "I will help. You have my best son. Wilhelm loves you and would clear a forest for you."

Ralph was attempting to tease his brother out of the doldrums that had overtaken him from Mary's extended mourning. He pointed at the article printed in the Independent. Wilhelm laughed for the first time in days. "You must be an important man to be mentioned in the newspaper so often." He read the article to his wife. It says here, "Ralph Hartman and Henry Reetz of Lincoln Township have the finest fields of beets in the country."

"Ralph," Mary said, "are you still seeing that woman reporter who works at the newspaper or are you paying her outright?" Ralph's chin dropped open. He looked at Mary and glanced at his mother and brother, and then burst into laughter. Minnie laughed too, and thought, this woman knows how to deal with sorrow and lift a family's spirits.

Edith arrived late one afternoon and offered to take them all to see the double feature playing at the Temple Theater in Standish: a two reel Our Gang, comedy with the main show, The Reckless Age, featuring Mary's favorite movie star, Reginald Denny.

"No thanks," was Mary's reply. "Billy's running a fever and I'm feeling tired today. Perhaps another time. Edith, I appreciate your asking."

It seemed to Mary tragedy tipped like dominos, one after another after another in rapid succession. Selma fell on a broken bottle while playing in the barn. She cut her right wrist to the bone. Rudy saw it happen and carried his bleeding sister into the house. Mary wrapped her daughter's wound in clean bandages and kept pressure on her cuff to curtail the bleeding as Rudy sped them to Standish. It took the doctor seven stitches to close the wound and a lollypop to stop Selma's tears.

Rudy told Minnie the trip to the doctor was the first time his mother had left the homestead since the movie with Mary Pickford. He described to Minnie how fast he had to drive the Buick to get his sister to the doctor before she bled out.

Minnie knew he was still carrying guilt from Gilbert's accident, and said, "You are a good man, Rudy Schmidt."

Chapter Twenty Three
THE STRESS AND THE STRATEGY

Later that same week Minnie was folding laundry when she heard someone stop a horse outside her house. She looked out her kitchen window and saw it was George Dandy's wife. The slight woman climbed from the wagon and was inspecting the back wheel when she grasped the spokes and sank to her knees, like she was in pain. After a moment she composed herself, stood and walked toward Minnie's door.

"You better come inside, Mrs. Dandy. Your wagon doesn't look like it's safe to drive. If I can locate my son, I'll ask him to take a look at it. Mrs. Dandy?"

"The wheel on the wagon is wobbling, Mrs. Hartman, and I think the baby is coming."

Minnie took the woman's outstretch arm. "Is this your first?"

The woman exhaled. "Tenth."

"How long do we have?"

"I hope it's faster than the last one."

"Let's step inside. I'll make you a cup of tea from wild cherry bark. It was a gift from Abukcheech, an old friend of mine. It will speed the baby along." Minnie took her arm. "How about resting in my bed while I make the tea?"

"EEEE, it's coming. Is this old friend a savage? Can she be trusted?"

"Right this way, my dear." Minnie stopped as the frail woman held the doorframe until the pain slackened. "Fresh sheets this morning. Come this way. You don't look pregnant. Are you full term?"

"EEEE, EEEE."

"Lay down here. That's right," Minnie said and lifted the woman's feet into her bed. "I'll just prop your legs with these pillows. Let me have a look." Minnie moved the woman's skirt and pulled off her underwear. "Abukcheech was a wonderful woman and a dear friend to me, like I hope you will be. You're dilating, Mrs. Dandy."

"EEEE. I can't have this baby. EEEE!

"Tell that to this little person trying to crawl out of you. I'll be right back." Minnie pumped her soup kettle half full of water and set it on the cookstove to heat. She pulled clean towels and a small sheet from the cupboard and hurried back into her bedroom.

"EEEE!" Mrs. Dandy screamed. "No. No. No."

"Why can't you have this baby, dear," Minnie said as she moved pillows around in the bed. She wiped perspiration from the woman's forehead.

"How can I bring another life into this world when I can't feed the ones I have. I'm so tired. EEEE. Can't you stop it?"

"Here comes the head."

The woman clasped her knees together. "No. Don't let it come out."

"Mrs. Dandy, don't do that. You'll kill the baby and kill yourself. Let it come."

"If I die will you see that my children don't starve. They are alone and cold in our farmhouse."

"I'll send for your husband. Everything will be all right." Minnie pulled the woman's legs apart. "You know the drill. Do it with me. PUSH and then puff, puff, puff and then PUSH again. Good job."

"You're a rail barrel … puff, puff, puff, PUSH …full of laughs, Mrs. Hartman. EEEE!"

"What's so funny about sending for your man?"

"He left me months ago. Said he wouldn't come back until he found work."

"I see. Well I'm here with you now. And we're going to get through this together." Minnie patted her own forehead dry.

"This baby. I can't keep this baby. I have no money. I can't pay the rent. I have no food for my children. I work in town, but the money won't stretch far enough. We don't need another ... PUSH, puff, puff, puff, PUSH."

"If you don't want the baby, I'll find a home for it." Minnie checked the baby's progress. "I see a head. It has lots of hair, dark hair like your husband's. Push, Mrs. Dandy, push."

The woman pushed and grunted until her face turned red.

"Okay. He's all out now." The baby was purple. "And it's a boy, a beautiful baby boy with ten toes and ten fingers and two squinty little eyes and one big red nose." The child was small and looked malnourished for a newborn. Minnie held the boy by his feet and gently slapped his bottom until he howled. "Here is your son," Minnie said as she wrapped him in a clean towel. "You tell me if this isn't the most beautiful baby boy in all of Bay County"

Mrs. Dandy took her son in her arms. "His nose is perfect." She counted his toes and fingers and smiled. "Thank you Mrs. Hartman."

Minnie snipped the child's umbilical cord and tied it in a knot. "We were a little busy before. Instead of tea, how about a drink of spring water?" Minnie set a cup on the bedside table and held out her arms. "I'll clean the baby while you rest. I'll give him right back to you, I promise."

Mrs. Dandy handed her son to Minnie's outstretched arms, sipped water and watched. The woman who had given birth to twelve, dipped her elbow into the water bowl until it was cool enough to bathe a baby. The boy seemed to enjoy being almost submerged again. She toweled him dry, wrapped him in a bed sheet and wedged him between pillows before she went to work cleaning his mother.

"You are so kind to help me, Mrs. Hartman."

"My husband and I worked for many years in the lumber woods. Will you roll onto your left side Mrs. Dandy? Thanks." She held the woman's belly and had her push again until the placenta appeared. "Good. We've almost done. Where was I? Oh, the lumberjacks could be out in the forest, sometimes for months. The doctor at the sawmill was useless ... always drunk. Abukcheech, the native woman who gave me the tea, told us how native mothers gave birth outside in the forest near a brook of flowing water. She showed the wives and our daughters at the camp how to use roots and tree bark from the forest to heal and relieve pain. She showed us how to store grain. We learned to survive in the wilderness from Abukcheech. Now can you roll onto your right side? That's fine." Minnie rubbed the woman's back with goose fat. She recalled the muscle strain of childbirth. "The men would come home for a week, impregnate their wives, and go back into the woods. I'm almost done, Mrs. Dandy. Try to relax. Granted, it was a lonely life out there for the men, being lumberjacks. And it would have been lonely for us too had we not had friends to help us through the rough times. So, Mrs. Dandy, your little boy is not the first child I've helped deliver. I live just down the road from you. If you need help, you can count on me. Most of the women who live around you will help if you ask."

"Can you find a home for this child? I can't keep him."

Minnie blinked and her breath caught in her throat. "I'll try if that's what you want, but for now, don't worry about anything. You have had a big day. What were you doing out riding in a wagon so close to your due date?"

"Coming home from work. I work in town."

"So, you are a modern woman. Does your husband mind you working?"

"Of course he minds, wouldn't yours? When a man can't provide for his family and it takes both his wife and son to earn enough to eat, he's likely to feel inadequate. Some men walk away from their families. It's too much for them." Mrs. Dandy's forehead folded into a washboard of lines as her eyes grew teary.

"Don't cry, dear. I'm sure your husband will come back."

Minnie heard her kitchen door squeak open. "Ma?"

"Come in here Wilhelm. I want you to meet someone."

Wilhelm stood in the bedroom doorway looking at the stranger in his mother's bed with a child in her arms. "Is that your wagon out front? You've got a bad wheel, but I can fix it."

"Wilhelm, meet Mrs. Dandy. She stopped by today just to have a baby boy," Minnie smiled.

"You must be George Dandy's wife. I'll find him, bring him to meet his son." Wilhelm said.

"He left the farm over a month ago to look for work" Minnie said. "Mrs. Dandy is expecting him back any day. Wilhelm, would you work on that wagon wheel? Mrs. Dandy won't use it tonight. She will be my guest."

"Oh no. I can't. I must get home. My children …"

"When my Ma says you're staying, ma'am, you are staying. I'll change that wheel out with an extra I've got stored back in the barn. That won't take me long. Then I'll drive your wagon down and pick up your kids. Ma, you got room and food enough for some company tonight?"

"They will all be welcome," Minnie smiled and addressed Mrs. Dandy. "I'll just walk Wilhelm to the door." When they were out of earshot Minnie whispered to Wilhelm. "Throw a couple feed bags of potatoes in her wagon. And while you're rounding up children, see what condition her food supply is in. Maybe you better take along one of those hams hanging in the smokehouse. And a couple dozen eggs. Now get going. And thanks for doing this, Wilhelm."

Mrs. Dandy rocked the baby in her arms and spoke in a monotone. "My husband was emotionally distant from me before he left. I'm not sure he's coming back. I shouldn't have insisted he go into town that last time he came home. He said applying for relief was a humiliating experience."

Minnie handed the woman a cup of tea, poured another for herself and sat beside the bed to listen.

"After that he hardly left the house. It was like he was paralyzed by the bleak chances of finding work. When I found a job in town as a domestic he became indifferent to me. He hardly spoke. I think he was embarrassed that his wife had to work as a servant. I know he hated it when our oldest son got a job at a farm that wouldn't hire him. And then he took off again. He said he wouldn't be back until he found work."

"Mrs. Dandy, let me tuck your baby here between these pillows while you drink your tea. Then try to get some sleep. The baby will want to eat soon. I've got some hot soup for you when you wake."

Minnie found her son outside changing the wagon wheel. "The woman doesn't want this baby. I'm concerned she might try to hurt it. I told her I'd find someone to take him. He's thin and looks weak, but with the proper nourishment he might make it."

Wilhelm drove Mrs. Darcy's wagon back up Minnie's driveway an hour later. All four of her children jumped down and ran into Minnie's house. "I couldn't stop them," he said. "They wanted to see their baby brother." When all were out of earshot he said, "Ma, the shelves in the cellar are empty of canned food. There are no potatoes in the basement bin and no ice or food in the icebox. I looked in the barn … no hay, no grain. I don't know how her horse is still standing." Wilhelm patted the horse's ribs that stood out on each side like stays from an umbrella. "He needs oats. He needs some of your first growth alfalfa for the nutrients. He needs a clean stall to sleep in."

"I've got a pot of venison stew simmering at the back of the cookstove and plenty of fresh bread to feed those kids. I'll have them stay the night so their mother can rest and won't worry about them, too. Thanks Wilhelm. When you get done bedding down the horse, stop back ..." Minnie turned to see what caught Wilhelm's attention.

The Dandy children were walking out of Minnie's house. They were stone-faced. Behind them was their mother carrying a bundle under one arm. "We're going home," she said. "Thank you for everything, Mrs. Hartman." She climbed in the wagon, nodded to Wilhelm and clicked her tongue for her old nag to pull them home.

Wilhelm set Minnie's venison stew on the back of her cutter along with two dozen eggs from her henhouse and then helped his mother in. They sat there as the horse pulled them along toward the village of Esty, wondering what had just happened. Minnie didn't like the look of that bundle tucked under Mrs. Dandy's arm. When they arrived at the farm they saw the family standing in their orchard. The oldest son was digging a hole with a spade. *Mein Gott im Himmel*," Minnie whispered. "She killed that baby."

"Ma, don't jump to conclusions." Wilhelm pulled the cutter up next to the house, and helped his mother down. They walked to the orchard and stood around the grave. Mrs. Dandy set the bundle inside and nodded to her oldest son to fill the hole. She nodded again for him to place the flat piece of sandstone on top.

"Children, fold your hands," their mother said. "Pray for your brother to go straight to heaven." Then she turned toward the farmhouse.

Minnie walked with her. "I'm so sorry, Mrs. Dandy. Wilhelm and I brought you supper."

"The baby stopped breathing."

"I'll get some water boiling for tea. You must be tired."

"The baby stopped breathing."

"I'm sorry that happened, Mrs. Dandy. I'll feed the children." Minnie helped her up the steps. When the children smelled the stew they crowded around the table, each holding a large spoon retrieved from a pocket. Minnie found some bowls and filled them. The children emptied them and asked for more.

Mrs. Dandy didn't eat. She went right to bed.

As Wilhelm drove Minnie home he told his mother he would shoot a buck and hang it to age in Mrs. Dandy's barn. He had unhitched her wagon and led the old horse into the barn. "I cleaned the stall and found some clean straw for bedding. I pumped her water trough full, and emptied the oats from the bottom of the bin into an old pail. There wasn't much there. Then I emptied the potatoes in the basement bin and set the ham in the ice box. Is she going to be all right, Ma?"

"I'll check in on her tomorrow. Go home, son. Mary will be wondering where you've been.

The next morning Minnie drove her cutter over to the Dandy's place. Mrs. Dandy was frying ham and scrambled eggs for her children's breakfast. She invited Minnie to join them. Minnie declined, saying she had already eaten, but would sit a spell and talk to the children.

She learned all four had been attending school in Bentley. They liked school. They could all read. The little one was just learning to write and showed Minnie her name written on the side of a paper bag. The children were dressed in remade dresses and patched denim overalls. The house had been swept clean, but the windows were cracked and curtains were in shreds.

"Who would like a ride to school in my cutter?" Minnie asked. The children all came to attention and raised their hands as if they were in school. "Mrs. Dandy, would you like to go to Bentley with us? I need to stop at Bill Baum's elevator for grain and to Mart's for supplies. Do you know Martin Wasalaski? He runs the general store and is generous with his penny candy. It's been my children's favorite store for years."

The woman smiled faintly and nodded. "I would be pleased to ride in that fine buggy," she said. Her children ran around and climbed inside the cutter.

Minnie purchased two bushels of oats and two bales of first cut Alfalfa from the elevator. She bought canned soups and a bag of penny candy for the children at Mart's. He let them each take an extra piece to eat on the ride to school.

Before Minnie left the Dandy place she walked out to the orchard to pay her respects. That's when she saw the other pieces of flat sandstone lined up between the fruit trees.

A week later Minnie pulled her cutter into Wilhelm's yard and found him whipping her grandson with a willow switch. She walked into the house and asked Mary if she could spare a cup of tea.

Mary smiled and explained that Lawrence was in trouble at the Johnsfield German school and may not graduate 8th grade. "He's such a little devil," she said and gave Minnie her tea. "The teacher saw him lifting up and peeking under a girl's skirt during *Deutsch Klasse*. He was caught a second time switching lunch pails in the cloakroom. That boy must have been hiding behind the door when God passed out the brains."

"Boys!"

"Hedwig scored a 91% on her geography and history exam. She's the smart one. The teacher wants our permission to be advanced midterm to the 8th grade. She will need to stay after school so the teacher can work with her to pass the state exams. Can you give me a lift?"

Minnie drove her daughter-in-law down the road to the one-room schoolhouse and watched her plead her son's cause as only a mother could do. The teacher was aware of the family's recent grief. She told Mary that Lawrence would be back on track to graduate eighth grade if he faced extra chores at home.

Minnie spoke up. "They need help at George Dandy's place. He and Rudy could turn the soil with old Cobb so Mrs. Dandy could plant her garden."

Mary proudly gave permission for Hedwig to continue her studies and stay late after school. In celebration, Minnie took Mary for tea at Mrs. Dandy's farm. She wanted the women to get to know each other. They shared a common bond. They had both lost children.

Minnie finished giving her piano lessons early at Hardy's Music the next Saturday morning and walked to the sheriff's office. Sam was doing paperwork, but opened the door when he saw her approach through his window.

"What a nice surprise," he said and pulled a chair out for her. "What can I do for you?"

"Sam, something happened and I don't know what to do about it, what to think. I can't give you a name, but I think a woman I know is killing her newborn babies."

The sheriff's face grew serious. "Tell me everything you know. Just leave out names and locations."

Minnie told Sam how a woman had given birth to a frail, yet healthy baby in her home. "The woman told me she didn't want the baby, that she couldn't afford to feed or care for it. I left her alone for a moment with the newborn to go outside. Shortly after she walked out of my house with the bundle tucked under her arm like it was five pounds of meat from the butcher.

She kept repeating that the baby had stopped breathing. I followed her. She had the bundle buried in the orchard next to her house and placed a flat piece of sandstone on top. Her children just stood there next to the grave, watching their mother, like they were afraid to move. They just stood there, Sam, for the longest time. All four of them were skinny with sunken eyes. They looked malnourished. They girls stood there in their made-over old dresses and the boys in patched overalls with holes in the knees."

She told Sam the woman lived alone with the four children. Her husband left them to find work. She had depended on relief and the kindness of strangers to feed her family. She had a job as a domestic with a family in town who paid cash. She owed six months back rent and said she was about to be evicted.

"Sam, that orchard has other flat pieces of sandstone in between the fruit trees. I don't know that they are graves, but they are near the hole I saw her oldest son dig for the dead child. Sam, the woman is depressed. She's tired. She's alone. She has the sole responsibility of four other lives. I'm afraid if she becomes desperate enough she could kill her older children."

"Can you prove any of this?"

"No, and I don't want anyone digging around her orchard looking for baby bones. That may put her over the edge. The woman is desperate. She looks for her husband to come home any day. I don't have a good feeling about this."

"Minnie, do you know that millions of women have been abandoned by their husbands across this country. Families have used up their life savings. Farmers can't sell what they grow because no one has the money to buy what they need. These are bad times, Minnie. People do strange things to stay alive. There isn't much I can do. I know you're upset. I've never seen you cry before."

"I know how that woman feels. Sam, I've been abandoned before ... left to fend for myself by my father, and over and over by my husband. It's a terrible feeling when your children are hungry and you have no source for food, no money to clothe them, and no help in sight. That woman is capable of anything. I know I was. "

"I almost killed myself a few years ago, Sam. A forest fire stopped me. That and my love for my children are what saved my life. I could not abandon them. There were women trapped in the winter without food that would have killed their children rather than see them starve. Sam, I am just like those women. Backed into a corner I will do anything to survive. Surely there must be something that can be done to help her. She's on relief. If she loses her home, who will take her in?"

"Has her husband been out of work long?"

"On and off for the past six or seven years. He leaves her for months at a time. I don't see much of her. She lives nearby."

"Tragedy sometimes brings people closer. Do you know the man? Do you think he would forgive her for killing their child under these severe circumstances?"

"Sam, tragedy doesn't always bring people closer; some forest fires leave only rubble. I was about to murder one of my children before I left Germany." Minnie dried her eyes. "She was the child of a former lover. My husband was not a forgiving man. He accepted the child. She was faultless. Fred was vengeful. He tried to kill me. He threatened he would drive me as crazy as he had become until I killed myself. My life with him was a nightmare.

"Sam, I don't know the woman's husband, and it's not his job to forgive her. It seems to me she needs to ask forgiveness from those dead infants because they are the ones who had their lives stolen from them. Since they are dead, the woman cannot be forgiven for what she has done. I believe the crime of murder is unforgivable. I have no idea how the husband would react, if he comes home at all. But when he does, I'm afraid of what he will do to her."

"It sounds to me like the lady needs a friend, a neighbor to stop in and see that she all right and talk to her. She wouldn't look kindly on a law enforcement officer stopping by for a chat. I'll leave this in your good hands, Minnie.

One Punch knocked on the sheriff's door and stuck his head inside. "You ready for a ride home, Ma?"

"Yes, One Punch. You're just in time. I'm ready." Minnie gathered her belongings and stood.

"I thought his name was Ralph?" Sam said.

Minnie laughed. "Les and Vic gave him the name. He's had a whole string of names: Roelf when he was born in Germany; Ralph in Au Sable when he decided he was American; and now his name is One Punch.

"The story I heard was that Ralph stopped at the Summer Trail for a beer. Les and Vic, his boys, were with him. This guy at the bar took objection to Les, the older one, and knocked him flat. Ralph reminded the man that no one hits his sons and knocked the guy cold with a single punch. Both Vic and Les were so proud of their father they gave him the name, One Punch. Ralph likes the sound of it and asks that we all call him that. You too, Sheriff Sam. Thanks for listening to me."

One Punch drove her home. "What was that all about?"

"If you have any extra milk or canned food would you drop it by the Dandy place? Their children are hungry."

Louis Wagner.

Chapter Twenty Four
THE SEPARATION

"It was 1925 and Minnie's Mollie was in love. She was a clever girl, had finished *Deutsch Klasse* at the German school and graduated eighth grade. She could read and write in English and German. Molly was seventeen and had eyes for Louis Wagner, a veteran of WWI. Minnie could see he wanted her, too.

Minnie made a wedding supper for the bride and groom after the ceremony in the church's basement. She made a point of inviting Mrs. Dandy and her children. Ralph invited all the guests to walk down the road to his barn for a fiddling contest and square dance to celebrate his sister's wedding.

Minnie called the dance, and chanted, "A right and a left around the ring, while the roosters crow and the birdies sing," while guests danced across the planked barn floor made smooth by oils from the stored straw. The fiddlers fiddled and the guests glided. "Ace of diamonds, jack of spades, meet your partner and all promenade." Mary and Wilhelm were good dancers. Some folks joined in and others tapped their feet and watched. "All join hands and circle to the south, get a little moonshine in your mouth." Most folks took a break to take a drink and catch their breath before running back to catch the next set. "All join hands and circle wide, spread right out like an old cowhide."

The sheriff stopped by to congratulate the bride and groom and enjoy the fiddling music. Minnie sent him home with a pint, but not before she got him out on the barn floor to dance a few sets with her. Folks promenaded until the sun lit the sky. The men harnessed their teams, carried their sleeping children from the haylofts, and rode home in their wagons with their wives. By then it was time for morning chores.

The widow Hartman found herself whistling the tunes and singing the square dance refrains the next morning when the sheriff pulled up next to the farmhouse in Gibson Township where she now lived with Fred Jr. and Amil. She saw him from the window and opened her kitchen door.

"You here to arrest me Sheriff, or to give me bad news?" It was 1925. Business was booming. Her family had money in the ground on three different farms. The potato crop looked promising and she was ready to start the fall harvest. "Come on in Sam. I'm betting on bad news. Let's get drunk again before you tell me." She took his hand and pulled him inside.

She saw the sheriff take out the same chair he sat in every time he came here to give her bad news, and realized after all these years they had become good friends. As Sam folded into the seat he said, "It's funny how things work out. I sit in the same chair every time I come here."

Minnie chuckled as she laid out two china teacups balanced in saucers on her kitchen table. She reached behind the breadbox and found the bottle.

"Want me to pour?" he said.

"You usually do,"

They talked about how he was managing since his wife passed, how much trouble his children were causing him. He told her he had busted up two stills that week. They talked about fast music and fast dancing and how the wedding went. Minnie had never seen the Charleston danced, so the sheriff showed her the steps right there on her kitchen floor. He whistled the tune and tapped out the tempo on her table. They laughed with their hands on their knees, and laughed with their toes kicking in the air. When the bottle was half empty, Minnie said, "You may as well tell me the bad news. I think I'm drunk enough to take it. Just let me sit down, first."

The sheriff cleared his throat. "Amil and Barney had an accident with their car."

"Are they alive?"

"Yes. Barney was driving. He's the same ... still can't walk and still uses his wheelchair. But Amil has a broken neck."

"*Mein Gott im Himmel,* will he live?"

"I don't know, Minnie. The doctors are working on him. It doesn't sound good."

Minnie sat there wringing her hands.

"Barney was driving," Sam said. "The car hit a bridge abutment."

"Barney can't drive. He's crippled." Minnie rubbed her forehead. "But Amil's a good driver. He drove a milk truck. He's a good driver, Sam. Are you sure Barney was driving?"

"He was found behind the wheel. Amil was thrown from the car."

"When did all this happen?" Minnie took another sip of her drink.

"The accident was reported around seven this morning."

"So it happened during the night. What bridge?"

"The Pine River Bridge east of Standish."

"That was no accident, Sam."

"I know," he said and poured her another.

"Was there anything suspicious near the site of the crash?'

"Nothing but some bullet holes in the side of the car ... straight line of holes spaced three inches apart ... all along one side. Neither of your boys were hit. Looks like Barney was trying to outrun whoever was chasing them."

"Purple Gang?"

"Could be. Some thugs from Detroit have been reported visiting the local speaks, they may just be small-time rod men set on terrorizing the local bootleggers that are cutting in on their action."

"How am I supposed to make a living with mobsters shooting up my boys?" Minnie's eyes were tearing. "Why don't you arrest those criminals, Sam?"

"What for? Poor marksmanship? Half of Chicago's police department is on Capone's payroll. It's hard to tell the good guys from the bad guys these days. Truth be told, they all scare me, Minnie."

"I'm scared, too."

"Why don't you retire before the mob comes looking for you. They could kill you, or worse. You don't need the money."

"We've talked about it … the family, but the boys want things … cars, new farm equipment. Wilhelm wants a milk house. They get used to having things … you know how it is, Sam. They don't want to go backward … doing without and just getting by. They are used to having a constant flow of cash. They think they need it. The tax collector needs it, too. It's hard to scale back when you've tasted the good life. My boys assure me the mob won't kill a woman."

"I'm not so sure about that. It's getting mighty hot around here, Minnie. I sure wish you would get out."

"I'll give it another year. Would you stop and tell Wilhelm about Barney and Amil? While you're there, ask him to drive me down to the hospital."

The sheriff stood. "Come here Minnie." She walked over and Sam gave her a long hug. "When are we old-timers going to start having fun?"

"You're a good man, Sam. Solid. I've always been able to count on you. Your wife was lucky to get you. My Fred was a walking stick of dynamite." She stood. "Thanks for coming all the way out here again. Wait a minute. I have something for you to hide in your trunk. Don't forget to take it out. Your boys might find it and drink the whole jar."

Amil was twenty-five when his neck was broken. The break didn't sever the spinal column. The impact from the bridge abutment broke the bones that held his skull erect. His head now leaned left, his ear riding near his left shoulder. This would be the way Amil Hartman would see the world for the remainder of his life.

Minnie's son was a survivor. He developed a way of grinning and looking up when he spoke to his mother that was unnerving ... almost like a small boy trying to look under a little girl's skirt. His activities were limited. He moved around holding the back of a chair for balance. Any sudden jerk could cause the spinal column to crack, which he knew would kill him. He learned to walk with crutches, but depended on his wheelchair.

Edith bought a little house for Amil and Barney east of Standish in Well's Addition. She was a good sister and could afford it. Both men ate well. Edith saw to it. Amil started drinking right along with Barney. Edith brought them both beer on her daily visits. What could it hurt? None of the family argued with her. None of them knew how much longer either one had to live.

Wilhelm and Mary's new baby, Esther, was almost four in 1927 when Mary had cataract surgery. The eye hemorrhaged and had to be removed. Mary recovered at her parent's farm close to the hospital. The recovery was long and further complicated by a diagnosis of cancer. Minnie stayed at Wilhelm and Mary's farmhouse to take care of the children while Wilhelm was pulled in three different directions: his ailing wife in Frankenlust, his children and the farm work, and his need to work in the lumber woods to bring cash into the household.

Hedwig, their oldest daughter, was a nurse apprentice to a doctor in Saginaw at the time. She resigned when Wilhelm's letter arrived saying Mary was sick and she was needed at home to run the house.

Hedwig didn't want to be known as a greenhorn, the daughter of an inexperienced immigrant, a setting duck for discrimination. She wanted to fit in with her American friends, so she told her brothers her name was now Hattie. "Besides," she told her father, "Uncle Roelf changed his name to One Punch years ago." The Americanization of names was being adopted by other teenagers of immigrants striving to fit in like Hattie was struggling to do. Selma followed Hattie's lead and took on the name Sally.

Hattie was given the task of feeding and watering her brothers and sisters. She was to keep the wild animals in line during the entire year Mary was recovering from what her children thought was only eye surgery. The fourteen-year-old was in complete charge of the house. She announced to her siblings they would obey her or they would be eating beans in dirty clothes every day ... out in the barn.

"Hattie," Sally whined. "Lenny took a big bite out of the last piece of sponge cake, the one I was saving. I hate him."

"Len, get over here." Hattie ordered her eleven-year-old brother. She pointed to where on the floor he was to place his feet. "Why did you eat that cake? You knew Sally was saving it."

"It was the last piece, and I wanted it," he said.

"You are a stupid boy and a selfish piece of horse manure, Lenny Hartman. Didn't you know that piece was poisoned?"

"Was not."

"Was too. The barn vermin only need a small bite. The poison causes a rat's belly to swell and ache. Next comes the cramping. And yes, eventually the rat's expanded gut explodes."

"You're just trying to scare me. If that was poisoned, Sally would be dead by now," Lenny said.

"That just shows what a lame-brained pig you are," Hattie said. "Sally didn't eat from that piece of cake. She had just finished spiking it for the rats when you walked in. Sally, you better take what's left on out to the corncrib, then get back in here. I may need help when the poison hits Lenny."

"Is there a cure, some medicine I can take to stop the poison?"

"It's called an antidote, stupid. Sally is the only one who knows how to reverse the poison. Okay, Sally, give your brother the antidote. Go ahead."

"No."

"Sally, you don't want to see Lenny suffer like a rat and have his stomach explode. You've seen rodents writhe in pain. They don't even squeak because their throats get too dry to make a sound." Hattie faked a tear, then wiped it away with her apron. "Go on now. He's your brother. Give him the antidote."

"No."

"Selma Hartman, when Pa comes home and learns Lenny died because you refused him the antidote, he will thrash you with a willow switch. Think about it. Do you want to be horse whipped plus have your brother's murder on your conscience?"

"No."

"Then give him the antidote."

"No."

"Sally," Lenny howled. "Please give me the antidote. I'm too young to die."

"No."

"Sally, give the boy what he wants," Lenny's older brother Lawrence said. Lawrence was sixteen. He had come in from the barn and had thrown his coat on a heap of other outerwear by the kitchen door. "I can't stand it when the little bastard cries. Give it to him."

"No."

"Why not?" Lawrence asked.

"I don't have the antidote."

"For God's sake, Sally. Hattie? What's going on here?"

"Lenny's going to die," the two sisters said together.

"Lenny, you stupid chicken. Dry your tears. Your sisters are foolin' with your head."

Chapter Twenty Five
THE SALUTE

Life was hard on everyone in the farmhouse without Mary's presence. The family met after church for an update on the gang wars in Detroit. Barney read and then reported on the war to disrupt illegal liquor establishments from every paper printed north of Detroit. He listened for bootleggers busted in the area and bulletins on gangster shootouts on his radio during sunlight hours. After dark he rode with sixteen-year-old Lawrence peddling moonshine on former routes to old, established customers. Barney reported on the territorial disputes gangsters in Detroit were settling with Thompson sub-machineguns. He said three men had been mowed down with one hundred and ten bullets in three seconds. Amil couldn't take the bouncing on the back roads with his broken neck and stayed home.

No one in Wilhelm's kitchen would admit they were afraid, but Minnie sensed they were. She had been using her intuition more now that her sight was failing again. Molly and Louis Wagner were operating their own stills in Gibson Township and helping her and Fred Jr. with theirs. The location was in a swamp by a stream in the woods between where Minnie lived and their farm. No revenuer or gangster would wade through that insect and snake breeding ground just to smash a still. The mosquitoes would finish them off.

Young Fred Jr. was helping Minnie with the still, but he couldn't bring himself to be responsible enough for more than hauling potatoes and firewood and keeping the fires stoked during the night. Molly was pregnant. Her morning sickness lasted most of the day. Louis was busy in the fields, so Minnie helped them with their still when she could and did most of the work on her own liquor-producing smokestack in the swamp. Moving through the treetops on the sky road was the quickest route for carrying in supplies and carrying out finished Hartman hooch. It was becoming hazardous for her. She was sixty-four and no longer spry.

Edith was waiting at Minnie's kitchen table when her mother crawled from her bed, an unusual happening in the Gibson Township farmhouse. It was a beautiful fall dawn and Edith was on her second cup of coffee. A telegram lay on the table.

Minnie saw the envelope and said, "Coffee first. Bad news can wait until the sun is up." She added fermented beverage to her cup and sat down. "Care for some, daughter?"

"Ma, …"

"Wait." Minnie took a swig from the bottle. "Okay. Let's have it."

"Gus is dead," Edith said. "This telegram is from his wife."

"Gustav? What happened?" Minnie took another gulp and waited for it to work. "Let me guess. One of his wives shot him."

"It says here he died September 25, 1925 from a complication of diseases."

"I'm sorry to hear that. Where was he living? I lost track."

"His wife, Pauline, said he died at home … 715 Solvey Avenue in Detroit. She said they had been living there for the last seven years … since moving back from Minnesota."

"The last time I saw Gus was just before that last brutal blizzard. He had his new wife with him … Pauline, yes, and some of their children … Gustavia, Roy and I forget the other little boy's name. Gustav wanted to move in here … some inheritance claim. Said he was enlisting in the army and wanted us to care for his new family … just in case. He disappeared after that. Whatever happened to his first wife, Elsie, and to little Caroline?"

"I heard Gus left Minnesota in 1905 ... left Elsie and Caroline there tending his failing grocery store," Edith said. "Elsie sold the store and moved West, settled in Ellensburg, Washington with her daughter. Last I heard she had been adopted along with Caroline by a woman called Annie Beth. Then around 1920 they moved to Kittitas, Washington. I sure hope she remarried. Gus was not much of a husband to her or father to Caroline."

"Gus wasn't much of a brother to me or a son to you."

"His temperament was a lot like his Uncle Karl, your father's brother. You never met him."

When Wilhelm left for work in the north woods, Rudy took charge of his stepfather's farm. Minnie could see him from Ralph's kitchen window when she visited her son. He would be standing by the fencerow, spilling the beans with Otto Kitzman or with Charlie Dankard while old Cobb swished his tail to kept the flies from biting his rump. He told Minnie a guy could expand his knowledge of farming best by jawing with the neighbors. He explained to Minnie over coffee one morning that a farmer's production increased in a field if it was free of standing water. He had watched Kitzman harvest his corn from tiled fields that drained excess water. His field was next to the Hartman field that was so muddy Cobb refused to plod through. Rudy said a few days of sunshine were generally all the time a farmer had to get his crops planted in the spring or harvested in the fall. A tiled field, he learned, could mean the difference between a bumper crop in a year other farmers' harvests rotted in the fields ... a bumper crop that could bring top dollar at the grain elevator.

Minnie wasn't surprised when Rudy got a side job in 1928 from Bill Laeder of Harbor Beach. He dug trenches and laid drainage tile with Laeder's tiling machine east of town for Gilbert Bordeau, Israel Chantiny, Dominick Miller and Gilbert

Trombley. Then he moved the equipment to Lincoln Township and laid the four-inch tiles four rods apart in Jacob Yarger and Ralph Hartman's low, flat fields that were heavy with clay soil and didn't drain well. The farmers paid Bill Laeder $33 to $35 an acre for digging the trench and laying the tile.

Rudy believed in this farming innovation with such passion that he had no trouble selling Laeder's service. He compared the cost per acre of laying the tile with that of one year's production of a bushel of beans per acre and six bushel of oats per acre, or two to three hundred bushels of corn per acre. Bill Laeder was a hard worker from Harbor Beach, but he couldn't keep up with work orders from clients ranging from Lake Huron to Lake Michigan. Laeder made Rudy an offer. He sold him one of his tiling machines along with the territories of Arenac and Bay Counties.

When Wilhelm came out of the woods, he was delighted his stepson, Rudy Schmidt, had developed his passion for farming into a business of his own. When Mary came home from Frankenlust and heard about Rudy, she told her son she was proud of him for undertaking a venture that would advance farming for everyone. Minnie was pleased Rudy wouldn't need help from the family. He would eventually be one less mouth to feed, body to clothe.

Ralph was kept busy delivering gravel and sand for Arenac County roads. He admitted to Minnie that he was tired of driving truck all day and working the stills at night. He said his three daughters were beginning to ask questions about the smoke coming from the woods. He said they were too young to put to work, Barbara couldn't help ... she was pregnant again. Ralph wanted out of the bootlegging business and announced his decision at the family meeting on Sunday.

Minnie was still having trouble with her eyesight, but not her influence as head of the family. Rudy and Ralph's departure from the distilling workload was felt by everyone. The decision was made to further reduce the output volume, shrink the territory even more, and limit their product to trusted local customers. Lawrence would continue making his drops on weekends when he and Wilhelm came home from the timber woods. Molly would help Fred and Minnie with their still near Bentley for one more season, and then she wanted to wind it down as well. They were all affected by what they read in the papers.

"This should make everyone's workload manageable," Minnie said. As she clapped her hands together, signaling the meeting was over, she wondered whether her family was getting soft. All of them had become dependent on the easy cash she distributed at the end of each month. None of them worried about the property taxes, the bank loans or putting away enough to run their farms for the lean years. Minnie's family had become comfortable, maybe too comfortable, she thought.

Fred Jr. drove Minnie into town to see the sheriff the next day. She told Sam her family was spooked by the gang wars down south. They read reports of police violence in Detroit. They were afraid the Purple Gang would be shaking down her boys before they made deliveries to their longtime customers. She was becoming increasingly alarmed by the local police. They had become more violent than the hoodlums. She asked Sam for his personal protection.

Sam laughed. "I've looked the other way. I've kept my men out of Lincoln Township. I've done this for you, Minnie. Listen to me, my dear. It is a dangerous mistake to question the Prohibition Bureau's unwritten rules and the violence used to enforce them. Part of the bloodshed down south is because of people like you, the law-busting brewers, distillers and distributors. Rooting out bootleggers has become the top priority of the Treasury Department. Local officials, like me, have been given the nod to do whatever we need to stop folks like you from making and selling booze, including blowtorching your stills, upending your vats, and hacking open the barrels of perfectly good shine. We even have the green light to bust skulls. Police all over the country have been assured we will not be held accountable for any injuries suffered by law-breakers. This is a dangerous time, dear Minnie. It would be a good time for you to become a serious potato farmer. I can't keep you safe any longer."

Behind Minnie's decision to cut back on the business was Barney's report. "The Purple Gang issued machineguns to all their men ... like the one they sprayed at me."

Chapter Twenty Six
THE SURGERY

Minnie still did what she could to help at Wilhelm's house while Mary was away again getting treatment for the cancer. Wilhelm barely spoke to his family when he was home. Minnie thought it was because he missed his wife. When he returned with news from the hospital, it was not good. Mary's cancer had spread to her liver.

Minnie brought over food, listened to her grandchildren's gripes and settled arguments. She walked to the woods to check the stills, checked the underground potato storage bins for rot and made sure the stocks of mason jars were sufficient. She helped fold laundry but could no longer mend the boys' breeches because of her own poor eyesight.

Mary Schwab Schmidt Hartman was forty-six and had produced ten children from two marriages. She came home from the hospital in Bay City in late August of 1929. Part of her head was wrapped in white bandages. The children were frightened when they saw their mother and full of questions: "Where were you for so long? Why are you wearing a bandage? Can I touch you? Why did they take out your eye? Can you still wink? Does it hurt when you smile? Why don't you smile? Are you going to die?"

The girls helped Mary from bed to the kitchen table when she felt up to it. Mary supervised her daughters while they canned tomatoes from the garden, peaches, plums and apples from trees in the orchard, and shredded cabbage for making sauerkraut in twenty-gallon crocks. Mary had them wait to make applesauce after the first frost when the fruit was sweetest. They pulled beets from semi-frozen ground and pickled them.

William and Esther picked flowers from their mother's garden. They laid them on her bed for a surprise when she awoke.

Minnie was there to help the girls pack a wooden barrel with layers of cucumbers, salt, garlic and fresh dill weed to make the dill pickles served at every meal. Minnie had Lawrence and Leonard carry the heavy barrel to their cool basement to ferment.

Minnie was there to change Mary's bandages and see to her personal needs. When her bed sheets were fresh from the clothesline, Minnie helped her daughter-in-law back into bed where she was spending more and more time.

Hattie and Sally were relieved of being totally responsible for patrolling and maintaining the "cease fire" between Leonard, Billy and Esther. Their mother's presence stopped the sibling's squabbles for a time. All of them were now burdened with her constant care. One was stationed by her bed any time Minnie couldn't be there. The house grew quiet.

Wilhelm came home from the sawmill to be with his wife. He knew these would be his last days with her. He sat by her bed most of the time, holding her hand. Minnie stayed with Mary in the mornings while Wilhelm was out doing chores. They had long talks about the children and Wilhelm's future. She wanted him to remarry. "He works so hard, Minnie. He is the best man I have ever known. I want him to have a long and happy life."

Pain weakened Mary's stamina. Her body was already frail from the sickness. "I want to say goodbye to each of my children, separately," she whispered to Wilhelm. Her bed was in the room usually used for storing bags of dried beans and corn being held for sale until the price was right. Wilhelm sent word and the children gathered.

When Mary saw Hattie enter the room, she motioned her to her side, asked if she loved this Charlie Haas, and gave her blessing for their marriage pending approval by her father. "You have been a wonderful daughter to me. These last years have been tough. Know that I appreciate every pail of water you carried to fill that laundry tub, every hour you stood boiling the clothes to get them clean, all the stretching and lugging you did hanging wet laundry outside to dry in all kinds of weather. You never complained. Hattie, you have the biggest heart, the most compassion of all my children. I hear from Lenny that you and Sally are some mighty fine cooks. He says you won't let anyone outside until they have cleaned their plate. I'm proud of you, and I thank you for all you are doing for me." Mary took a sip of the water Hattie was holding for her. "Hattie, I don't have much to give you. I want you to have my clothes … any that fit you. And my pretty shoes, too. Dearest, your father gave me this ring before we were married. I want you to have it … something to take into your marriage … from your old mother … so you will remember her. Is Rudy here? I would like to …"

"I'm right here, Ma." Rudy moved through his stepsisters and brothers and stood beside his mother's bed. "I brought you some flowers."

"They are so beautiful. Thank you. Give me your hand, son."

"Yes Ma." Tears rolled down his cheeks as Rudy laid the flowers on the blanket and took her small hand in both of his.

A calmness overtook Mary's smile as she looked up at him. "When you were a little boy and the judge took you and Linda and Rich from me, I was at the lowest point in my life. But you hung on to my leg, hung on to me. My little Rudy, you wouldn't leave me, even when your grandmother tried to pull you away. Your love was stronger than the judge's order. You saved me, and I thank you for that. Find a good woman, my strong son. Be kind to her, and take care of your family. You are a good man. You will make a fine husband."

Sally was in tears when she approached Mary's bed."Nothing good ever happens to me, Ma. I don't have a boyfriend. I don't have good hair. I'm not pretty. And any day now I won't even have a mother."

"Do you think I'm pretty?" Mary asked, controlling her laughter.

"Of course. I think you are beautiful. Everyone in the family says so."

"And everyone in the family tells me that out of all my children, you look the most like me. What do you think of that?"

Sally grinned and her eyes lit up.

"You are the best looker in the entire family," Mary said. "I want you to have my hair ribbons and combs for your lovely brown hair. And you can have all my fine bonnets. And Sally, I want you to have this," she said as she removed her wedding ring. "Keep it safe. Your father gave it to me when we were married. You will have lots of gentlemen calling on you when you are old enough. Wear my ring after you are married, my beauty. Whenever you feel sad, rub the ring and I'll be with you."

Mary told Lenny to help his father keep the farm. "You are my clever boy. Don't let him sell it, and don't let the bank or taxman take it from him. You have a good mind, Sonny. Use it." She smiled and took his hand. "That Arlene Nigl girl seems like a good person. Is she your girlfriend?"

Next came her oldest son. "Lawrence, you are such a handsome boy. Be careful, honey. I know you like to have fun with the girls, but you drive too fast and take too many risks. Stop the shenanigans. Get a job. Find a nice girl. And stop smoking or you'll lose all your hair. I love you, son."

"Billy, come here by me."

"Are you dying, Ma?"

"Yes, Billy. It is my turn to die. It's all right. Don't cry. See, I'm not crying. I want to talk to you. You will be eight later this month. Your Pa has a shotgun for you. Will you remember never to point it at anybody … not even if your brothers tease you and make you angry? Will you promise me to push it under the fence, barrel first, before you crawl under, and take the shell out before you clean it? And Billy, don't kill any animal or bird you don't need for food. Will you remember all that for me? And will you promise to take care of your Pa?"

"I promise. Will you be here for my birthday, Ma?"

"Mommy," Esther called out as she ran across the room. Wilhelm helped boost the five-year-old onto the side of her mother's bed.

"You are such a happy child," Mary said and stroked her baby's blonde hair. "Do you know how many people love you?" Esther held up five fingers. "No honey. That's how old you are. Now tell me how many people love you." Esther clapped her hands together and spread them wide. "Good girl. Will you always help your big sisters?" Mary's face clouded. She moaned.

Esther was still nodding when she was taken off her mother's bed. Pain was eroding Mary's respite of calm and clear thinking. She needed morphine.

Wilhelm could not bear to watch his wife suffer. They had loved each other and worked beside one another for eighteen years.

"Lenny, run across the road to Ralph's and call the doctor. Tell him your mother needs another shot."

It wasn't long before the doctor's Model-T bumped down Johnsfield Road and pulled up the driveway. Mary's family was around her bed when the doctor arrived. She was moaning and struggling for breath. Wilhelm held her hand while death rattled her chest.

"She doesn't have long, Mr. Hartman," the doctor said as he rolled his stethoscope and stuffed it back into his pocket. "All I can do is keep her comfortable."

"Stop her pain," Wilhelm whispered, tears running down his cheeks. The doctor pulled a syringe from his black bag, and filled it with morphine.

"Is that shot going to be enough?" Wilhelm asked.

The doctor looked into Wilhelm's eyes, paused, and said, "It can be. Yes. It will be." He gave Mary the morphine. Without saying another word, he replaced the syringe in his bag and left the house. They could all hear his car's engine roll over and start. The whirr of the motor moving away on the gravel road had barely ebbed into silence when Mary exhaled her last breath.

This woman who had given life to ten left the inner world of her loving family on November 24, 1929. It had been nearly a month since Black Tuesday, and the stock market crash of October 28 had changed the outside world.

Wilhelm was a widower at fifty-five. The day after Mary's death he drove his black Buick up Minnie's driveway and switched it off. He just sat there in the car, staring at the steering wheel.

"Wilhelm?" Minnie pulled open her front door and made her way to his car. "Wilhelm?" Minnie saw a shotgun resting across the backseat. "Wilhelm!" He looked up. "Come into the house." He nodded, but didn't move. "I want to show you something," she said. Her dutiful son opened the car door and came around the front fender. He took her arm and walked her into her kitchen.

"Can you see any better today, Ma?"

Her son's compassion caused Minnie to tear up. The love of his life had been taken from him and he was concerned about her hazy vision.

Her son sat while she poured him coffee, cut a thick slice of sponge cake, and pushed the plate toward him. Her firstborn, her rock, was as gray as the faded fruit and bleached leaves on the printed oilcloth under his cake. He seemed listless, like all his joy had drained from his perennially cheerful soul. Wilhelm was a single father with seven children. He was also low on cash after paying Mary's medical and funeral bills. He took up a fork and cut a small chunk from the cake … then pushed it around on his plate and stared at the tablecloth.

"Ma, your right eye is almost completely white, and now your left eye is turning. As soon as Mary's funeral is over, I'm taking you back to Detroit to that eye doctor."

Minnie nodded agreement, relieved he was planning on something after Mary's death. "You going hunting today?"

"Oh," he looked toward the door. "You saw the shotgun." A faint smile crossed his lips. He had read her mind. "No Ma, I wouldn't do that. I've got the gun down because that damn red fox broke in the chicken coop yesterday while I was, while we were all sitting with Mary. Killed four of her best laying hens before Rudy heard the racket … took their heads off and left their bodies flopping around the hen house. I know where to find him, and I'm going to blow him to bits."

She knew her son. She could tell by the hesitation of his step, his expressionless face, his lifeless gray eyes that once were a laughing blue … this man's emotions were being held in check, bound by a fraying silken thread. "Wilhelm, you must feel like your life is over, but it isn't. A door has been closed. Another will open."

The last filament unwound and he crumpled into Minnie's arms. "Ma, I don't want to live without her."

Minnie felt his pain as if it were her own. Of all her children this one talked to her, kept her in his life, made her feel needed and valuable. This one would grieve for her when she died.

"Listen to what a wise son of mine told his brother Otto when he was afraid to go off to war. My son said, 'You have two choices. You can get up and do something or you can die.' Do you remember when you said that, Wilhelm? Mary trusted you to love her, to give her children, and now she's counting on you to care for those children. You can't let her down. Wilhelm, open the next door and move on."

Wilhelm composed himself and took a long draught of his coffee. "Could I put some of your whiskey in here?" He blew his nose, and poured from the jar Minnie produced from behind the breadbox. "I know you're right, Ma." He blew his nose again and stuffed his red handkerchief in his pants pocket. "Rudy told me today he's moving in with Uncle Mike and Aunt Martha," Wilhelm said. "Ma, he's only nineteen. I'll miss him. He's a smart boy and a good worker. I know he will be all right with Uncle Mike, and he will be one less mouth for me to worry about feeding. With Mary gone so long, we have no stock of canned food to keep us through the winter. I'd rather go without food myself than lose one more person from my family." He took a long drink from his coffee cup and wiped his nose. "I'll take Lawrence back with me up north. He's sixteen. I'll find him work. At least the men are fed well in the camps."

"How will you pay Mary's medical bills?"

"All the money we had in the world was buried in Mary's flower garden. I thought after the bank failure of '96 our money would always be safe in the ground. I never dreamed her medical bills would be so high. And then there were funeral expenses. I had to dig up all we had."

Wilhelm pulled a newspaper from his pocket and read to Minnie. Governor Fred Green had pushed passage of a law in 1929 giving Michigan judges the right to impose the toughest penalties in the country for bootleggers. ... four years in jail and two-thousand-dollar fines for the first offense. "Ma, we're all scared. Governor Green is like a wrathful God and he's coming after us."

"Wilhelm, you're right. All of you are right. Our business is becoming much too dangerous for the family. Maybe it's time to get out."

"Ma, I need to keep working in the woods to bring in cash. The taxes are coming due and my boys need cars and new clothes and the girls … the girls … I don't know what to do with the girls. All my children want to get out of this damn bootlegging business." Wilhelm broke down sobbing. "But we can't. We need the money now more than ever."

Minnie left her son at the table to drain the desperation from his system. She made another pot of coffee, cut thick slices of sourdough bread and slathered them with freshly churned butter. "Eat something, Wilhelm. Everything looks better on a full stomach."

"Ma, I think you could survive anything." He laughed and took the plate of bread. "You could stop a war with your bread."

"I've had my moments of despair. Wilhelm, I've been thinking. Edith is a good sister to you. Louie and Edith can't have children of their own. She may be willing to help you raise yours."

Minnie handed Wilhelm a bottle of liquor "Pour some of this in your coffee. It's a new recipe. I cooked potato mash with juniper roots before fermentation. The juniper gives it a bite. Or would you prefer the smoother corn whiskey?" When Minnie couldn't elicit a response from him, she said, "I'll give you both," and poured two glasses and set them before her favorite son. "What about Hattie? She still eyeing that fellow, that … that Charlie Haas?" She filled his cup with coffee.

"Em." Wilhelm coughed and cleared his voice. "She's only fifteen … too young to get serious, but yes, she sees the lad at church and I don't know when else. I was never much good at keeping track of children. Mary did all the …"

"I was sixteen when I married your father," Minnie said to redirect the conversation. "You may be right about her age. I'll talk to her."

"I realize she's maturing and will soon be a woman. She will want to strike out on her own. Now that Mary is gone, I need Hattie to hold our home together. She doesn't know how much I depend on her. I sense the girl would like to run.

I just don't want her to marry the wrong man out of desperation."

"You mean like her grandmother did?"

"You did that?"

"Yes, and it didn't work out well. What are Hattie's plans?"

"She has always wanted to be a nurse." Wilhelm said, still thinking about what Minnie said..

"What's wrong with nursing? I think it's wonderful she wants to help people."

"The people she needs to help are here. Besides, I have no money for school for a girl. She knows enough to get by. She must find work to bring cash into the family. I can't do it alone. I need her to cook and do laundry and keep Sally, Len, Billy and Esther from killing each other."

"That's a lot to heap on the shoulders of a girl of fifteen. You could break her back. Think about this. I heard some girls about Hattie's age are boarding over in Huron County, working for a company that makes millstones for grinding grain. The pay is okay and includes board. Would you think about it, Wilhelm? Talk to her about it? Working over in the thumb would get her far away from that Haas boy … until she's old enough to get married. And she could send home part of her salary."

Wilhelm wasn't sure that part of Michigan was far enough away. "I'll think on it, but who will take care of the other children while I'm in the lumber woods? I can't leave them alone to bide by themselves."

"Your Mary was sick for so long, and she knew she was dying. Did you two have a chance to talk about your children's futures?"

"She knew her passing would be hardest on the baby. Esther's only five. Mary found a woman from town, a childless couple who were looking to adopt. She told me when the time came I should consider sending Esther to town to live with them. If I did that, I'd know she would have enough to eat and would go to school."

"Would you let them adopt her?"

"I haven't discussed any of this with the children. I'm not sure they fully understand the position our family is in now that their mother and our cash are gone."

"What about little Billy? He's eight now, isn't he?"

"Billy is a lot like you, Ma. He won't let anyone mess with him. Last week he went hunting on the back forty with Lawrence and Leonard. He said they were teasing him and that's why he shot at them. Lucky for his older brothers he's a bad shot or they would be on the wrong side of the grass. I reminded him he promised his mother he wouldn't do that. Billy is Billy. He will be okay, if I can only keep him in school."

"Why isn't he in school? He's eight years old."

"He quit. Sally sits close to him in school and saw what happened. She told me he was writing letters with his left hand when the teacher hit his fingers with her ruler. She said the devil lived inside his left hand and was making him write with it. She told Billy every time he wrote with his left hand she would have to hit the devil again and again until it let go of him. Billy stood up and said, "No you won't. I quit." And then he walked out the door. I saw him later at home. He said he wasn't going back. He said he was done with school."

"So that leaves Len, Sally and Billy alone on the farm while you're away working in the woods. Sally is thirteen. Can she cook?"

"She burns everything."

"I'll drop by during the week and help her make supper. Is Len responsible enough to care for the animals? You were working already at his age."

"I'll see to it that he does," Wilhelm said. "Ralph's boys from across the road will help him with chores. Ralph is away most of the time driving his dump truck. He has good boys. Vic and Les are smart and good with animals."

"So that leaves Billy. We've got to get him back in school and keep him there while you're gone, keep him out of trouble with that nasty teacher. He can help you at the farm during warm weather when there is no work in the camp. I'll see what I can do ... talk to the teacher."

"Thank you, Ma. Can we talk about Mary's casket? Is there room in the Hartman plot at Woodmere for her grave?"

"Let's see ... I buried your Pa in front of the Hartman headstone. I want a spot dug up beside him when I go. Your grandmother is there too. And so are Otto and Amelia."

"I had almost forgotten about Amelia. A wolf got her. Is that right?"

"Yes, I've been having nightmares about her for years. We never found her remains, so I buried her shoe. No, Wilhelm. That family plot is full. I'll buy another and put in a new Hartman headstone. The stonemason will carve out a nice one for Mary and I'll have them make room for you for when it's your time."

"Ma, will you have the guy carve Gilbert's and my names on the stone too? Mary never got over his death and I want to lay by them both."

"Done. Now let's talk about the funeral."

"That's all set. Reverend Myers from Sterling will say a few words. He has been performing funerals and weddings at the church until they can hire a new pastor. Ralph and Barbara's girls across the road offered to call the relatives. Mary had a large family near Bay City. The Schwab family was one of the earliest pioneers in that area. There should be a crowd.

"The Ladies Aide president called at the house this morning," Wilhelm told his mother. "She brought a casserole and told me the women would make a supper after the service. She's a friend of Edith's. Mary joined that ladies circle in 1911 as a new bride and has put out spreads for baptisms, confirmations, and funerals all these years. They wanted to do something nice for her."

Wilhelm sighed and took his head in his hands. His shoulders heaved forward and shook. Minnie got up from the table and hugged her son. This boy had been her rock from the day he was born. It hurt her heart to see him so low. "My dear son, if you need cash, I can dig some up for you."

Wilhelm left Minnie's kitchen with a firm plan for each of his seven children, with two hundred dollars in his pants pocket, and with eighteen years of memories of the love of his life weighing down his heart.

The Buick needed new tires. Rudy was driving it to town and offered to drop Minnie and Billy at the sheriff's. Sam welcomed them inside and had them each take a seat.

"Sheriff, no doubt you have seen the report from Billy's teacher." Minnie winked at Sam.

The man stifled a smile, and nodded that he had. "What do you have to say for yourself, young man?"

"I quit school. That's it. I just quit."

"How old are you son?"

"I'm eight years old. I know how to shoot and clean a squirrel for supper. I know how to catch and gut a fish. I've learned enough. Besides, I don't need that ornery old woman cracking my knuckles with her ruler. I ain't going back to school, sheriff. I'm done." Billy sat on his chair with his feet dangling above the floor and his arms crossed over his chest.

"I see. Well, Mrs. Hartman, I'm afraid I have no choice. I'll have to lock the boy up."

Minnie slumped low, as if she couldn't look the sheriff in the eye. "Please sir, don't lock Billy up with those bank robbers and horse thieves."

"I am an officer of the law, Mrs. Hartman," the sheriff said and stood. "If you are asking me to overlook your grandson's violation, you would be breaking the law and I will have to lock you up, too. Come this way, both of you." He brushed his hand towards a door at the rear of his office.

Billy wiped the sweat from his forehead with the back of his hand. He looked from Minnie's stony face to the sheriff's and back again to see if they were pulling a fast one on him. Then he followed his grandmother through the door.

The sheriff unlocked a cell with a key from a ring looped on his belt. "Ladies first," he said, ushering Minnie into the first cell and closing the door. "I've got Al Capone coming in here later today."

"Al Capone?" Billy had overheard stories of the gangster's exploits.

"Mrs. Hartman, I'm afraid you will need to share your cell with Capone. The police in Chicago are taking him on the lam, looking for an out-of-the-way jail to hide the killer until his trial, and I'm short on room this week. Billy, you will bunk in the cell where we put the men who murder children." The sheriff scratched his chin whiskers and started moving toward another cell.

"Sheriff, wait," Minnie said. "Billy is just a little boy and has never slept away from home before. Couldn't he stay in here with me … and Al Capone?"

"Wait a minute, Sheriff," Billy said. "If I went to school I wouldn't be breaking the law and you wouldn't need to arrest me or Grandma and we wouldn't need to stay in this awful place. Is that right, sir?"

"It's too late, Billy." The sheriff winked at Minnie. "You've already broken the law. You said you quit school, and now both of you will have to stay here with me."

"Sheriff," Minnie said. "What if Billy went back to his lessons, learned to write with his right hand, and didn't miss a day of school until he graduated eighth grade, would you be able to reduce his sentence?"

"Grandma, I would need hunting season off."

The sheriff opened a thick book from a shelf in the jail. He ran his finger down the margins on one page, and then stopped to look at the boy. "It's a good thing I can read. I just found a law here that says in a case like yours I could put you on probation. Do you know what probation is, son?"

"No sir."

"You need to know that. You better learn to read those big words. It means the law would be keeping an eye on you, and if you missed school again, you would be hauled off to jail. There is no provision in this law book for second offenders." He patted the thick volume. "Quit school again and you will be bunking in here for life."

"I'll try out that school again," Billy said.

"Well, in that case I see no reason to hold you, but I will have to hold your grandmother." He winked at Minnie. "She tried to convince a police officer to break the law."

"Oh no, Sheriff. Don't do that." The boy was sweating profusely. "She's a good grandmother. I'm pretty sure she was just trying to keep my record clean. Let's just say I stay in school until eighth grade, and learn to read and write English and German with my right hand. Would that make a difference in her jail time?"

"You already agreed to that. I'd be foolish to let her walk for nothing."

"Okay." Billy saw Minnie looking out at him from behind the bars of her cell. "Okay, I'll throw in church on Sunday."

The sheriff opened the door to Minnie's cell without cracking a smile and extended his hand to the boy. "Billy, when a man shakes another man's hand it means he will keep his word." They shook.

"Sheriff," the boy said. "You better call me Bill."

"Okay, Bill." Minnie saw the sheriff turn his head so the boy wouldn't see him smile. "I will be watching you." He ushered them to his office door. "Bill, you wait outside, I want a word with your grandma."

Sam closed the door. "US Marshalls raided and padlocked seventeen roadhouses and saloons in Milwaukee. Twenty-one were arrested."

"Why are you telling me this, Sam?"

"It would kill me to have to lock you up, Minnie. Now go on. Buy your grandson an ice cream. He's had a stressful day."

"Thanks for everything, Sam. I'm being careful." Minnie joined Bill and Rudy waiting in the Buick.

"That was a close call," Minnie said to Bill. "Rudy, do we have time to stop at Greanya's Ice Cream Parlor?"

I found this photo at the Hartman homestead and remember visiting here with my mother. I think it was Aunt Martha and Uncle Mike Schwab's farmhouse. No one from this generation remembers. If I'm right, Aunt Martha had a pantry off the kitchen where she kept a large cookie jar and bottles of homemade wine. When we visited we sat around her kitchen table and talked. I remember her saying to my mother, "Just a small glass, honey. It's good for your blood."

Chapter Twenty Seven
THE SIDESWIPE

Rudy had moved from the homestead on Johnsfield Road to Mike Schwab's farm to help with his uncle's fieldwork. As it happened, Uncle Mike's neighbor, the widow Demerall, was done with farming and wanted to sell her land to pay her debts before moving down state to her house in Detroit. While Rudy was working for her, she got to like the nineteen-year-old and offered him the opportunity to buy her farm at a fair price. It was harvest time. Rudy borrowed money from the Federal Land Bank, bought the farm, and harvested his first cash crop.

And then the stock market crashed. Wilhelm read the news to Minnie. "Six hundred and fifty banks closed. On Wall Street, people who lost everything were jumping out of the windows of skyscrapers to kill themselves." Wilhelm added that Arenac County window jumpers at most suffered a broken or sprained ankle. "There are no buildings over three stories here." Minnie's son was learning the secret of taking the sting out of bad news ... laughter. He was fifty-five and had no paying job. The sawmills closed and became ghost towns overnight. Her son had no way of feeding his family and had little to laugh about, yet he continued to joke.

Minnie had experienced fear of the unknown when she boarded the Werra all those years ago in Bremerhaven. Her children had experienced a much softer life in America ... their paths had been set and firm ... until now. Uncertainty about their future bred fear for all who lived in Lincoln Township.

George Dandy, Minnie's neighbor from Esty finally came home to his family after months of searching for work. Shortly after he arrived home he killed himself. The Arenac County Independent reported that George had gone outdoors to their orchard and sat down next to an apple tree. He took off a shoe and, after placing the muzzle of the gun at his chin, pulled the trigger with his big toe. It blew the top of his head clean off. The paper stated the man had been a father of ten. When he died he left a wife and four surviving children.

The Independent did an update on the tragedy several months after George Dandy's death. "Mrs. George Dandy has left her farm in Esty and has moved to Pinconning with her four children. The widow of the late George Dandy is expecting her eleventh child and has asked for donations of furniture for their new home and clothing for her children. She can be contacted at the Pinconning cheese factory where she works."

Wilhelm had given his blessing for Sally to marry Freeman Rigg. The couple took a house in town beside a creek. Freeman delivered fuel oil that people now used for heating their homes. Wilhelm moved in with them during the week so he could catch a ride into Bay City, where he now worked at the Wellman Foundry. On weekends he worked the fields and stills at the farm. Minnie was concerned. He was thin and working too much. Her son was still filled with grief ... working to forget.

Sally had supper waiting for Freeman and her father every evening. One night Freeman came home on time, but Wilhelm didn't. They waited a while, then she phoned the man who was her Pa's ride.

"That old logger?" the man said. "Last time I saw old Willie he was loaded and heading into the Catacombs. You should worry."

Sally called One Punch, who told his niece he was familiar with the Catacombs. He set out in his dump truck for Bay City. The heavy yellow truck rolled back into Sally and Freeman's driveway around three in the morning and the two brothers emerged.

"Get him out of these wet clothes and into bed," Ralph told Sally. "He'll be all right in the morning ... just needs sleep. His ride will be by at the same time to pick him up for work. Keep this between us, okay Sal?"

Edith and her husband, Louie, drove Minnie to Saginaw to see an eye doctor. On the way, Edith asked Louie about the Catacombs in Bay City.

"I haven't been there since we were married," Louie Ireland said.

"What is it, Louie? A cave?"

"It's a blind pig in Bay City, isn't it Louie?" Minnie said.

Louie chuckled. "A three-story blind pig, and one of forty saloons right in the heart of Bay City. Polly Dickens runs it." Louie whistled through his teeth. "That Polly is a looker ... pretty, fresh, pure looking, like a child. She's a one-legged, part-time hooker. She makes sure everyone has a good time and spends all their wages. Up on the third floor she runs a dance hall called 'The Den.' The orgies up there peak around midnight. Fights are as common there as raspberries in August. If a guy gets too unruly, Polly gives the nod and her henchmen drag the drunk over and stand him up on a trap door. Polly always says goodnight before she pulls the latch and the drunk drops down into the Saginaw River. That sobers most guys up. Why did you ask?"

"Is it near the Wellman Foundry?" Minnie said.

"Not far. Isn't that where your brother works, Edith?" Louie said. "Well, here we are at the hospital. I'll drop you and Mother Hartman at the front door. I'll wait for you in the car."

Minnie's doctor told her a cataract had formed in her other eye. He said she had two choices, surgery or blindness. Minnie could have the cataract removed surgically, a dangerous operation with a mortality rate second only to pulmonary emboli, "which we call heart attack." If Minnie did nothing, she would be blind in that eye within a year.

The surgeon explained the procedure, assuring both of them that numbing the eye would eliminate pain for the patient. He explained to remove the opaque lens he would make an incision halfway around the cornea.

"How will you keep her eye steady while you slice it?" Edith asked.

"That's easy. I hold it with my thumb. It's critical the lens remains intact as I remove it so that no pieces drop down inside the eyeball. The second method I use is to hit the surface of the eye with a small mallet to break the cataract into pieces. Then I use a tiny suction cup to remove the shards. Mrs. Hartman, when you have this operation, you must keep immobilized with sandbags around your head while the wounds heal. That could take several weeks."

Edith thanked the doctor and they left the hospital. When they reached the car where Louie was waiting, Edith said, "Well Ma, what do you think?"

Recalling the complications Mary had after her cataract surgery, she said, "I would rather have my leg chopped off with a dull axe. Besides, we don't have the money now."

Edith insisted she and Louie would pay, and in May of 1925 Edith and Louie drove her to the General Hospital in Bay City for the operation. After her two-week hospital stay, Minnie recovered for a few days at Edith's before returning to her home on the farm.

Sam appeared at Minnie's door a month later. "Will you take a ride with me, Minnie?" The sheriff held the passenger door of the police car open for her. "I need your help." He drove her to the Hartman family homestead. "Do you know where we can find your son, Wilhelm?"

"It's milking time, Sam. What's going on?" The two old-timers walked to the barn and found Wilhelm inside finishing his last heifer.

"Ma? Sheriff?" Wilhelm stopped short. He was holding a pail of fresh milk in each hand.

"Finish up, Wilhelm. We want to talk to you." Wilhelm walked to his milk house and poured the white liquid into the cooling tank.

"Let's go on up to the house. Sam wants to talk to us both," Minnie told her son.

They sat in the kitchen drinking coffee when the sheriff spilled the bad news. "It's Lawrence this time. There's been an accident."

"Is he alive?" Minnie held her breath.

"What happened, Sheriff?" Wilhelm stood.

"He's barely alive. He was run off a back road up north. His car was full of broken bottles and smelled like a tavern. He must have been trying to outrun the hoodlums. The tire tracks indicated he was sideswiped, pushed off the road. His car hit a tree head on. Lawrence was thrown though the windshield. His face is cut up bad. Cut his nose right off. They just left him there. He almost bled out before a car came by, picked him up and hauled him to a doctor. He's on his way now to the hospital in Bay City."

Wilhelm walked outside. We could both hear him heave.

"Minnie, I warned you it would get rough. Get out now before they find you. Please. The mob will stop at nothing to run out the small-time bootleggers."

Wilhelm came back into the kitchen. He washed his face with cold water from the pump. "I'm driving down to Bay City. Sheriff, will you take my mother home?"

Minnie stared at the ceiling most of the night. It was early when Wilhelm's Buick pulled up her driveway. She opened the kitchen door to her eldest son's comforting smile.

"He will be alright. No broken bones. No injured organs. The doctors stitched his face back together. They sewed his nose on, and expect it to take. They had to give him a lot of blood. Lawrence told me the last thing he remembered was someone standing over him talking. He even remembered what they said ... something like ... you can tell your boss this was a warning to stay out of our territory. Lawrence said he asked him who he was. The man said, "Mrs. Hartman will know.""

The Summer Trail Inn is the beer garden where Fred, his sons, grandsons and great grandsons did their drinking.

Chapter Twenty Eight
THE SWINDLE

A few days later, Minnie was adding the potatoes she had just peeled to a pot of stew on the cookstove when she heard her kitchen door rattle. She wiped her hands on a tea towel, turned the kettle to a simmer and investigated. Something other than the wind was banging her farmhouse door.

The sun blinded her as she pulled the door open. All she could make out was a tall figure and the red end of a smoldering cigarette. She blinked and saw it was a man with white hair dressed in a suit with a tie. A small dog sat at his ankle, scratching an ear. The man leaned against her doorframe and exhaled a plume of white smoke. She felt his stare move from her face down to her feet and up again.

"I read your letters," he said through a trimmed mustache.

She squinted. "Karl? Karl Hartman?" Even with the sun blinding her vision, she recognized the man.

"You are more beautiful than I could have imagined."

She had to hold on to the wall. "What letters ... where did you ... how did ... what are you doing here?"

His dog let out a low growl.

"You wrote you were wounded," Minnie said. " I thought you were dead."

"Sorry to disappoint. I came to find you ... and to see America."

Her lungs were barely producing enough air for a whisper. "Your brother is dead."

The dog's growl elevated in pitch and he walked inside.

"I know, my dear Minnie. I'm here because I have a thirst … and you smell so good … like fresh spring water."

Minnie Hartman was speechless, standing there with her back against the wall, looking up at the one love of her life. That longing feeling had awakened something deep inside her … after all those years. She was surprised she could still feel, she had been numb for so long. She was delighted to see him again.

"May I come in?" Karl pushed past her. "This is Horst. Don't look so worried, Minnie. He's well trained. In fact, he's my guard dog." The dog appeared to her to be more interested in scratching than guarding. Horst sniffed the floor under her kitchen table.

Once inside, Karl pulled her to him. His kiss was hard on her mouth; heavy with a tongue thrusting passion she could feel all the way down to her feet. She submitted willingly … still starved for the taste of him. But it wasn't that same passionate kiss she remembered from almost thirty years ago that knocked her sideways. It was a sturdy kiss, and she liked it. The man tasted of strong Turkish cigarettes. His hands flattened and moved over her hips, a movement that had always been agreeable to Minnie.

"Yours is the mouth I should never have kissed," she managed to say before sitting down without offering him a chair. "I never thought I would see you again." The dog continued to explore her kitchen and brushed against her leg.

Karl walked around the room, looking at the sideboard stacked neatly with Rosenthal porcelain from Bavaria. He picked up a plate, turned it over and clicked his tongue. "You are doing well, Minnie. How big is your farm?"

Despite the rudeness of his question, Minnie answered. "My family farms two-hundred acres … Wilhelm and One Punch each have eighty and I have forty here with Fred and Amil."

Karl's eyebrows arched. "It appears the most beautiful girl in all of Poznan has managed to produce sons with brains. My brother was always clever ... and an opportunist. I never forgave him for snatching you away from me."

"Karl, there is something you should ..." Horst's growl interrupted Minnie, grew louder, almost as a reminder of her promise to Fred.

"Forget it, Minnie." Karl sat in the chair next to her, slapped his leg and Horst moved to his feet. He told Minnie all about himself without her even asking ... about retiring from the Imperial German Army as a colonel shortly after they smashed the Russians at Tannenberg. "Their weapons were so advanced that a single gun could mow down an entire battalion of foot shoulders ... rat-a-tat-tat."

With a small amount of prodding, Karl revealed the Prussian tactical secret of *Kesselschhlacht*. He said the Imperial Army was large ... 80,000 soldiers at one time. "The men were divided into multiple armies with operations moving in concentric circles. The first army to engage the enemy would pin them down. The next circle of men would attack from the flank. Their slogan was 'March divided. Fight united.'"

"How could an officer control so many soldiers moving in separate circles at the same time?" Minnie asked.

Karl smiled. "*Auftragstaktik*."

"Karl, I've been in Michigan so long, I'm afraid my German is ..."

"The theory of *Auftragstaktik* is that when a commander issues an order, it is short and kept general. The job of subordinate officers is to pursue the objective in any way that works for him and his men. Officers think on their feet."

Minnie poured Karl coffee and sliced him a piece of cherry pie, attempting to understand *Auftragstaktik*. This military theory sounded similar to the way she ran her family business. Her soldiers were her children. Each Sunday morning after church, coffee, and cinnamon toast, she was the general announcing the target number of gallons of whiskey they needed to produce and sell each week … keeping it short and general. Their territory had started small, encircling their farms, expanding to nearby townships and counties by concentric circles. It was up to each of her "soldiers" to figure out what they needed to do, and do it. She laughed to herself. So this was the grand strategy used by officers of the Imperial German Army. It seemed to her a bootlegger from Michigan was equipped with enough common sense to lead a German army.

Karl told Minnie her American cherry pie tasted almost as good as the cherry strudel his mother made in Germany. "I see you have learned to cook, too." Karl smiled. "I'm teasing. I still love you."

Karl and Horst were staying at the Sherman House, a hotel in Standish. He was planning to leave in two weeks to drive west to Hollywood, California. After a few hours of bragging and preening, the man said he had been driving since morning and needed to walk Horst. And then in the false politeness of a German officer, Karl said, "Would you permit me to visit you again?"

Minnie was giddy. Karl had awakened feelings in her again, a seventy-two-year-old woman. It crossed her mind that she might ask him to stay.

Wilhelm stopped by later that afternoon and read Minnie last weeks article from the Bay City Times about Franklin Roosevelt's Federal Works Administration. The program had been started in 1931 to help out-of-work men. Wilhelm said he took Lawrence to town and the two men enrolled in the Civilian Conservation Core. They would be gone a week. Minnie didn't mention her visitor.

The next day the two men took the train north to work on a project called the Lumberman's Monument. Their crew built roads and walking paths through the forest, installed stair steps on trails up the steep slopes so tourists could view the bronze sculpture of working lumbermen that had been commissioned by an out-of-work sculptor. The figures could have represented Fred Hartman and his sons and grandsons who had cut trees from the once pristine forests of Michigan.

On Sunday they came home with stories for eager ears. They told of men who had once been starving and were now men who worked for the CCC to build roadside rest areas, parks and scenic overlooks that outlined the state. They earned room, board and $30 a month working for the program which fed them, adding meat to their bare bones. Twenty-five dollars was deducted from each man's paycheck and sent home to his family so they wouldn't starve. Minnie told them she would make sure the fifty-dollar-a-month check from Wilhelm and Lawrence would be spread equally among her children and grandchildren left on the farms. If she had extra money or food, she would take it to Pinconning for the widow of George Dandy.

Wilhelm and Lawrence explained that the CCC workers were planting millions of seedlings on thousands of acres of barren land to repair damage done earlier by lumbering.

Wilhelm reported that Hattie had found work at Millstone City, in Huron County on the tip of Michigan's thumb. She worked in a factory that made tools to grind grain. She earned board, a room she shared with other girls her age, and a small salary that she sent home. Minnie smiled when she heard the news.

Minnie's children and grandchildren rode the train home from work on weekends to meet up with their friends for sleigh rides, skating parties and square dances. They also helped with the stills. Folks were poor, hungry and depressed, and drank record amounts of illegal liquor. Business was not great. The territory had shrunk. It was still good enough to keep the stills simmering and food on their tables.

A few weeks later, Karl and Horst returned to her farm. The dog chased her chickens and geese until Karl ordered him inside the house. He regaled Minnie with stories about the years he had lived in Morocco. They laughed. Karl still told a good story … full of drama. He said he returned to Germany in 1905 to settle his parents' estate. He knew his mother had died in Michigan and said he had been to the cemetery to see her grave.

"Joseph and Mama took Fred's death hard," Karl said. "Fred was their favorite … their hope for a better future." He smiled. "Fred got all the breaks … a beautiful wife, and a new life in a country filled with opportunities. Tell me, Minnie. Have you found any streets paved with gold bricks?"

"You could always make me laugh, Karl." Minnie poured more coffee in his cup. "Did you ever marry?"

"No." He added sugar, clinking the china cup with the spoon as he stirred. "I probably produced a few bastards here and there. A soldier's life has no room for a wife and a family." He smiled.

Minnie didn't. She turned to the sideboard to regain her composure … and to cover her disgust. So, it appeared that Kapitän Hartman's forced deployment to the Russian front had been a ruse. This man had never intended to marry her. This insight into her former lover's character was like a fog lifting inside her head. All the mistakes she had made over her entire life were now lined up like fence posts reaching as far back along the field as the woods where they kept the stills. How could she have been such a stupid chicken?

She wondered then how many other women this soldier had impregnated and left … for the Polish front, or for Morocco or for some other remote imagined location. How many children like Rosa had been marked fatherless for life by this soldier's disappearance?

"Karl, have you ever fallen in love?"

"Of course. I was in love with you."

"After me."

"There's an old army saying. If you can't be with the woman you love, you love the woman you're with. I fell in love with every woman I was with, hundreds of them. How about you?"

"Never fell in love with any women. As for men … only two."

Minnie busied herself at the cookstove stirring the stew so she wouldn't have to look at this man, the unfortunate choice she had made for a lover. Her brothers had been right when they told Papa she had a soft brain. She was angry at herself for having believed Karl, trusted Karl, at having held Karl's memory so close to her heart all these years. She was humiliated at ever having loved this empty man. Her face felt hot. And yet, she was still drawn to him. She wanted desperately to be held in his arms. What is wrong with …

Minnie heard the kitchen door creak open behind her. Karl's dog barked and the corners of his lips drew back, exposing a full mouth of menacing teeth.

"Take it easy, pooch. I'm not here to hurt anybody," Wilhelm said and allowed the hound to sniff his hand before he ruffled the top of the mutt's head. The sound of her son's gait as he strode across wood planks was a relief to Minnie. "Excuse me, Ma," he said and lowered a bulky burlap bag to the floor. "I didn't recognize the Ford parked outside." He stood by the table and nodded to the floor. "These are the new potatoes you wanted. When I came home, the girls had them all dug for you." When no introduction came from Minnie, Wilhelm squinted at the man sitting in his mother's kitchen chair. "I know you from somewhere."

"You better remember me," Karl said, standing and shaking Wilhelm's hand. "I'm your Uncle Karl. The little boy I remember from Germany had the same blond, curly hair as yours. And your eyes are green, just like Fred's were."

Minnie poured her son a cup of tea. "Can you sit a spell?" she asked him. "You must be tired from the trip."

Sensing tension in his mother's kitchen, Wilhelm took a chair. "You are my father's brother? I remember your parents. They lived in a fine house. Your mother came to live with us before she died."

"This is my dog, Horst." Karl nudged the animal with his foot.

"Does he always scratch his ears that much? They look raw."

"I found a tick on him, threw the tick out and kept the dog. He's more trouble than he's worth. Maybe I should have kept the tick and got rid of the dog." Karl laughed.

"Ma, do you remember what herb the native's used to stop bleeding, heal wounds and infections?"

"Of course I do. Yarrow. And I have some growing in my flower garden."

"I think I can help your dog, Uncle Karl. I'll make a poultice from the yarrow for the ear. You will have to keep it wrapped." Wilhelm left the table and came back a short time later with the yellow blooms in a bowl.

"Crush them with a spoon," Minnie told Wilhelm. "I'll add some honey to make it sticky." She turned to Karl. "Honey is great for healing wounds. You must have used it on wounded soldiers."

"You were a soldier, Uncle Karl?" Wilhelm smeared the mixture on the dog's open sore and wrapped it with the clean cloth Minnie handed him. Without waiting for an answer, he gave Karl instructions for cleaning the wound. "I need to go so you can enjoy each other's company. Ma. I'm driving into town tomorrow. I'll stop by if you want a ride. I'd like to talk to you about Lawrence. He's okay and will be home soon. I want to talk to you about the business."

Minnie smiled as Karl's Ford pulled up her driveway the next afternoon. She was pouring coffee for him when she heard a second car. She recognized the sound of the black Buick. Wilhelm looked stiff when he entered her kitchen.

"Coffee?" she asked her son.

"Sure, Ma. I'll have some." He turned to Karl. "I do remember you. You were the soldier who spent time with us after Pa left for America. What brings you to Michigan?"

"Karl is on his way to California," Minnie said.

"Some time ago, Fred wrote and asked me to send you some roots from the cold climate grapes developed in the vineyard where he worked. I have them here. I've come to settle your grandparent's estate," Karl said. "You must be in charge here now that your father is gone." Karl handed the package to Wilhelm.

"No, Uncle Karl. Ma runs our business." Wilhelm set the package on the table and pushed it toward Minnie. "I remember you in your uniform." He accepted the cup of coffee his mother offered and joined them at the table with his own reminiscences about life in the Old Country.

Karl was in his element talking about himself in the Great War. He had fought in eastern France during the Franco-Prussian War. "Our soldiers successfully secured the rich coal mining region of Alsace and Lorraine for the Fatherland." He told them he had been at the battle of Verdun in 1916 and for a short time he and his men fought in Somme where "our brigade was chewed up and spit out." Then came the eastern front where Karl fought the Russians.

"My brother Amil fought in the Great War, perhaps against you," Wilhelm said.

"I doubt that," Karl said. "The Americans never fought on the eastern front. Minnie, open the package," he ordered.

Minnie untied the string and pulled away the brown paper. "Oh Wilhelm, look. These must be the roots that will produce grapes that flourish in cold climates. Is that right, Karl? How thoughtful of you to bring them. They're from the vineyard near where we were born ... near Poznan. It was your father's dream to start a vineyard."

"I remember," Wilhelm said. "I'll plant them along the fence row behind the outhouse. Thanks, Uncle Karl. Would you like to go fishing with me tomorrow? I'd like to show you Lake Huron. It's one of the Great Lakes that surround us here in Michigan."

The next day Minnie was feeling dizzy, had a slight fever and an ache in her ear when her daughter, Edith, stopped by with a dozen glazed donuts from the Standish Bakery. Over hot tea laced with Old Log Cabin, Minnie asked Edith if she had met her Uncle Karl from Germany?

Edith put her donut down. "Ma, didn't anyone tell you about the drowning?"

Wilhelm was distraught when he arrived later that afternoon. He told Minnie a child had drowned while swimming out to join Karl in his fishing boat at White's Beach. Wilhelm said he had stopped to talk to someone about business when Karl insisted he take his boat out onto Saginaw Bay by himself.

"I kept an eye on him to make sure he would be all right out there. After all, he's not a young man," he told his mother. "Karl had been talking to the little boy on the beach while he was waiting for me to launch my boat. After Karl was out in the channel, the boy waded into waist deep water and moved toward the boat. The child disappeared under the water.

"A woman screamed from shore and pointed to where the boy had gone under. 'Someone save my little boy!'" Wilhelm said he figured the boy had stepped into the drop-off near the boat channel. He said he saw the child thrashing around not far from Karl's boat. And then he disappeared again.

"This woman screamed at Karl to save her son and ran out into the water. A crowd gathered on shore to watch while

Uncle Karl sat in the boat, smoking, and watching the boy struggle." Wilhelm stopped. "Ma? Ma, you don't look so good."

"I'm all right. Just tired … haven't been able to sleep. Where is Karl now?"

"I dropped him off at his hotel and haven't seen him since. Was he here?"

"We have some business. If you see him, tell him I want to see him?"

"There was nothing I could do," Karl said when Minnie asked him about the drowning. "I don't care to discuss it further. The kid shouldn't have been out there." He took a long drag on his cigarette, and said, "Minnie, can you find it in your heart to make a place for me here? You are all the family I have left. I could be useful in your business."

"We are potato farmers, Karl. It's hard, menial work, and not what a retired military officer would find appealing." Minnie wondered if he knew about the stills.

The next day Karl drove out to take her into Standish to sign papers regarding Fred's inheritance. The bank president came out to greet her warmly like he always did, but stopped when he saw Karl.

"Are you Fred Hartman's brother from Germany? I heard about the boy drowning yesterday. What happened out there, Mr. Hartman? How was it that you didn't try to save the kid?"

"Can't swim," Karl said.

The banker grimaced. "Minnie, are you feeling okay?" He pulled over a chair, insisted Minnie sit in it and motioned to one of his employees. "Bring Mrs. Hartman a glass of water."

"I'm a little dizzy. I'll be okay. Thanks."

"One of the tellers will take care of your business," the bank president said, turned and disappeared inside his office.

The next weekend when Wilhelm returned from his work with the CCC Camp, he stopped by Minnie's after supper.

He said he had been thinking about his uncle all week. He asked her when Karl would be leaving Standish.

"Ma, from where I stood on shore, it looked like Uncle Karl could have done something to save that boy … thrown a rope or an oar. He could have taken his lifejacket off and thrown it out to the kid. Ma, he just sat there and watched him struggle. I jumped in, but when I got out to the boat, the boy had disappeared. The water was murky. A couple of guys swam out to help him, but by the time they found the boy and pulled him out … well, he had been under too long."

"Wilhelm, he didn't kill that boy. It was an accident," Minnie said and wondered why she was defending the scoundrel.

"When is he leaving?"

Karl came for Sunday night supper with his dog Horst. The dog was no longer wearing the bandage and was scratching a new spot raw. Minnie had invited Wilhelm to join them before he had to leave for the north woods. Still tall with a straight spine, Karl leaned back in his seat after supper, balancing on the chair's two back legs. "The best men always win," he said lighting a cigarette and smiling at her. "Wilhelm, did you know your mother was once the most desirable woman in Poznan. Did you know that, Wilhelm … that your mother was always such a beauty?"

Minnie blushed and caught herself, annoyed at allowing Karl to appeal to the soft spot in her brain, again. Her emotions were such a mess. Wilhelm frowned. Karl could not be stopped. "And now she runs a profitable, but illegal business selling … did you say potatoes? Don't look so surprised. I took a walk yesterday, followed a path that led to Mollie back in your woods. I caught her boiling what smelled to me like potatoes. She was cooking the mash over an open fire like my soldiers did on the Russian front. They made vodka. And you, my beautiful Minnie, are distilling alcohol. You must know it is illegal to brew and sell whiskey in this country. Have you turned my brother's children into gangsters?"

"Uncle Karl …"

"Wilhelm, wait," he ordered Minnie's son in a tone starched with authority. "Minnie, I am now the elder of this family," he smiled, "and I rather like the idea of living in Michigan."

"Uncle Karl …"

Karl flattened his hand in front of Wilhelm's face. "I saw newsreels when I lived in Morocco about gangsters in New York, Chicago, and Detroit, but I never dreamed my beauty Minnie would have her own gangsters in Standish. Fred would not have approved," he said shaking his head. Then abruptly he smiled, like he had made a great joke. "Where do you hide your machine guns? I could show you how to use them. I do have experience in leading …"

"Karl stop!" Minnie said.

Wilhelm grimaced. "Why you sonofabitch …"

"Minnie," Karl said. "What means sonofabitch?"

"You," Wilhelm stood and pointed at Karl. "It was you who impregnated my mother while my father was working like a peasant in the timber woods. You are Rosa's father."

"Wilhelm, no …"

But Wilhelm would not stop. The family picture and Karl's place in it was now clear to Minnie's firstborn son. "You poisoned my father's mind with jealousy, turned him into a bar-brawling drunk who beat my mother. Karl Hartman, you killed my father. You killed your own brother."

Karl pulled himself back to the table. "I don't understand." His voice rose. He jumped to his feet. "Minnie? Is this true?" He stared at her. "Do I have a daughter?" He had his answer when he saw Minnie's expression. "Does she look like me? Can I see her?"

"You bastard!" Wilhelm said coming to his feet.

Minnie held on to the table and stood to calm both men. "Rosa is your daughter."

"Ma, don't let him ruin my sister's life, too," Wilhelm warned.

Karl stroked his mustache."I have a daughter and her name is Rosa. So I have a child." He smiled. "This is the happiest day of my life. Does she look like me?"

"My sister is a good woman," Wilhelm said, "a kind mother and a hard worker. Fred Hartman was her father … as far as she knew. You leave her alone."

"Rosa is a mother? Where does she live?" Karl said. "I'll visit her. Do her children … my grandchildren look like me? Did Fred know about us?"

Minnie paused before she spoke. "Fred knew she wasn't his, yet he provided for her, loved her like he loved his own. Karl, you cannot upset your daughter's life. You are not now and never were part of our family. You cannot live in Standish. You would not be accepted here. Remember the reaction the bank president had when he met you?"

"Minnie?" Karl stood. "I did not kill that boy."

"I know that, but you didn't try to save him, either. You have been branded a coward by this community."

"And, you are responsible for the death of my father," Wilhelm said. "If you had kept your dick in your pants, my father would still be alive and my mother wouldn't have led such a miserable life. Uncle Karl, just take the boat … my fishing boat. Row it out on Saginaw Bay and end it there."

Wilhelm stood at the open door waiting while Karl pulled on his overcoat. "No man ever loved you like I did," he told Minnie.

"Thank God," she said.

"Minnie, you know we had something. I will not let you break my heart again." His eyes moved from her to Wilhelm and back. "Say it." When no response came from Minnie, Karl said, "Okay, but before I go, I have one last request. I want to meet my daughter. Give me her address."

"No."

"Minnie, do this one thing for me."

When she refused to speak, Karl turned to Wilhelm. "When you were a little boy I gave you a puppy. Do you remember? I will leave Michigan soon, but my dog can no longer travel with me. He is too old. Take him." Karl pointed at Horst and ordered him to stay.

Wilhelm's eyes turned as hard as stones. He wanted to refuse, but saw his mother nod. She wanted the damn dog.

The man strode by his pet, who was whimpering under the kitchen table. Karl hastened past Wilhelm on his way out the kitchen door. The man Minnie once loved didn't even stop to glance at her before he left.

And that's the last time she saw Karl Hartman.

A week later, Floyd Weaver, the revenuer, was walking on the road by Minnie's farmhouse when Horst rushed out and seized him by the leg. The dog had him below the knee, setting four of his teeth into the calf of Weaver's leg. He screamed for help. Minnie called Horst off and tied him to a tree. She helped the man into her house, cleaned and treated the wound with honey and a clean bandage and sent the man on his way.

Weaver went to the sheriff and demanded the dog be shot.

Minnie would hear none of it. She told the sheriff that Weaver was nosing around private property and the dog was earning his keep protecting her farm and his mistress.

Weaver took legal steps and went to Judge O'Keefe. The judge listened to the taxman's story and ordered the dangerous animal be destroyed.

The sheriff drove out to Minnie's farm. He was reaching for his shotgun when he heard Minnie behind him.

"Sam, hold it right there. You can put that gun down. No one is shooting Horst. He did nothing wrong."

"Come on, Minnie. I have a court order. And, Horst is such an ugly dog. Let me put him down."

"No."

The sheriff took a long look at the lovely lady, got back in his car and drove away.

A week later Karl showed up on Wilhelm's farm.

"What do you want?" Wilhelm asked as he opened the door. "I thought we had seen the last of you."

"I am the oldest male in this family ... by tradition, an elder statesman. It is my responsibility to do what I can to help my brother's family."

"I see, and what exactly can you contribute to us at this point, Uncle Karl?"

"I will marry your mother ... when she's ready."

"And she knows of this plan?"

Karl shrugged. "Wilhelm, you are not potato farmers. You are bootleggers. I know this business. You need me. I'm willing to teach you what I know to improve your operation. Your company could double its production and triple its profits within the first two years with me at the helm."

"I thought you were a soldier."

"My expertise in growing and distilling fine wines and liquors comes from my experience working at the Zielona Gora vineyards in Poznan before I joined the Prussian army. Your father and I worked side-by-side in those vineyards."

"How much will this cost us?"

"Give me Rosa's address and a share of the profits, and I will make your business a success."

"Our family business is doing fine without your help."

"Wilhelm, I'm trying to make this easy for you, but you insist on making it difficult for me. Let me put it in a way you will understand. If you don't give me Rosa's address and part of the business, I will report your operation to the police or the mob or both. Do you understand? Now, I'd like to see your stills."

Wilhelm paused before answering. "You give me no choice, Uncle Karl. Come this way," Wilhelm grabbed his wool coat. "We will be outside for a while, do you have a coat in your car?"

"No. Do you have an extra?"

Wilhelm looked at the coats hanging from hooks in the entryway and made a decision. "This one should fit you," he said and handed Karl his bright red hunting jacket.

The two walked through the yard. Wilhelm opened the gate, closing it securely behind him. They started down the lane that led to the woods. Wilhelm stopped. "You go on ahead," he told Karl. "I forgot my rifle. We may see some game to shoot for supper. Just follow that lane to the small stand of trees on the right. Do you see the hardwoods?"

"I know the way. That's the same path I took early this morning," Karl said.

"Right," said Wilhelm. "So you have seen where Molly cooks the mash. Take a look inside the log cabin at our distilling operation. I think you will find our system quite sophisticated."

Karl followed the lane which ran parallel to Kitzman's cow pasture. His long legs had carried him halfway to the turnoff when he noticed a large animal running alongside the fence inside Kitzman's field. It appeared to be a rather large bull with horns poking out from each side of his skull.

Wilhelm didn't go to the house for the gun. He backtracked to the edge of the field to watch.

The soldier increased his pace. Minnie had warned him they had a bull.

The bull increased his pace. The fence ran between them.

Karl Hartman was nearing the end of the field when he noticed the bull swing out, pick up speed and charge toward the fence. He recalled Minnie telling him the name of the bull. Karl stopped short and held his breath as the thousand-pound animal cocked his front legs and sprang forward. The Judge shot up with his front legs tucked under his massive torso and was over the fence, running flat out before the surprised Prussian Officer could take another breath.

This was the man who emasculated my father, Wilhelm thought. This man had stolen his mother's affections. He watched from where he stood.

The Judge landed in the tall grass, blocking Karl from the end of the field. The experienced military man turned and took off running toward the gate where Wilhelm stood. The Judge picked up speed, circled around in front of Karl, stopped and pawed the earth, out-maneuvering the man who understood the tactical secret of *Kesselschhlacht*.

Karl froze in place. The bully and the bull were in the same field facing one another. The Judge swayed from side to side and stomped the earth. Clods of sod flew up and out from under the beast as his hooves churned the soil.

Wilhelm watched Karl look toward the open field on his left. He looked for the lane and fence beyond on his right. He had nowhere to run, nowhere to hide. This was the man who sat in a boat and did nothing as a little boy drowned, he thought.

Wilhelm saw the bull paw the earth and lower his head. Here comes The Judge, he thought.

Karl took a few steps backward. The Judge took a few steps forward. Karl spun toward the lane and ran toward Kitzman's fence. He saw Wilhelm. "Help! Shoot him!" he screamed as he waved his hands so he could be seen.

Wilhelm watched Karl run toward the fence and thought. This is the man who is blackmailing us to get our bootlegging business. I can't shoot The Judge. He's worth something. He's the highest-producing bull in Arenac County.

Wilhelm saw his uncle turn and run up the lane toward where he stood watching. Karl's long legs extended to cover more ground, pulling his tall body forward and increasing his speed. His elbows bent in tandem with his knees. His head swiveled with every few steps, checking behind for the bull. He saw The Judge gaining on him and almost tripped.

Wilhelm thought about shouting to Karl to remove the red jacket. Instead, he watched. They were both moving straight for him at high speed. Karl was waving at Wilhelm again when The Judge lowered his head and scooped him up between his horns like a spatula scoops up fried eggs from a skillet.

The bull tossed Karl over his back and then slowed his run to a walk. Wilhelm thought it was over. But then, something stirred in the grass. He saw his uncle struggle to his feet and stumble forward, the red hunting jacket spurring the bull to action, signaling the big fellow to follow.

Wilhelm watched while his prized stud started his run slowly, and then like a huge locomotive he picked up speed. In no time at all, he caught up to the cuckolder. With a side thrust of his head, he impaled Karl Hartman's thigh. The Judge threw his head back. The man who had impregnated his own brother's wife now struggled to dislodge the spike from his leg.

The Judge gave Karl more of a chance than Karl had given his brother. The bull lowered his head and Karl slid from the skewer. "Stay down. Don't run," Wilhelm should have shouted. He saw his red hunting jacket emerge from the tall grass, move a short distance, and disappear again.

The Judge jerked his head toward the fence, his mass of neck muscles rippling with anticipation. He shifted his head toward the woods, his ears alert for the sound of his prey on the move. He kneaded the ground with his front hooves and swayed. Wilhelm understood that movement. He knew how bad a bull's eyes could be. The Judge had lost sight of the man who had caused so much pain and suffering.

Minnie's firstborn son waited. He wanted to shout to the bull, "He's over here! Over here!" But he didn't. Had this violator of civilized behavior stayed down, he would have had a chance. Wilhelm had no desire to warn him, to help the bastard. Instead, he watched.

The animal's movement caught Wilhelm's attention before he noticed his hunting jacket emerge from the grass. The Judge had lowered his head, his verdict clear. The beast shifted his weight before he accelerated forward and gored Karl in the gut. He lifted Karl's writhing carcass over his head, and running at top speed toward the far end of the field, he dispatched the limp body into the dirt. Wilhelm watched the stationary animal maul the inert mound with his hoof, and then turn and wander over to Kitzman's fence. He leapt over easily and disappeared into the neighbor's herd.

Wilhelm watched. He saw no movement at the end of the field ... until the first gray wolf slid under the fence.

There he was. So it was a wolf that had been killing his chickens. Wilhelm thought about shooting the feral beast. Instead, he watched as the wolf trotted over to where The Judge had deposited Karl Hartman. He saw the animal nose around, tug at something on the ground, and then drag it into the woods. It looked like a piece of the red hunting jacket Wilhelm had loaned to Karl.

A second wolf appeared. And then a third raced out of the underbrush. Wilhelm watched the feeding frenzy. A fourth wolf slid under the fence and pulled something edible from the red mound in the grass. And Wilhelm watched.

The Judge.

The man at the photo shop identified the oversized negatives found in the Hartman Homestead as the size used in the 1920's and 30's. The photos he printed must have been taken the same day because the women were wearing the same dresses. I could identify my grandmother, a young Mary Hartman, and my grandfather, a grinning, curly-headed young Wilhelm Hartman with his arms around both women. I concluded the second woman, as well as the one in the above photo, was my great grandmother, Minnie. She would have been in her late 60's or early 70's here. This woman gave birth to twelve children. She was a handsome woman even in her advanced years.

Chapter Twenty Nine
THE SHERIFF

Sam arrived at Minnie's farm midmorning, dressed in a suit and tie.

"Minnie," he said before she could greet him, "I want you to come to Detroit with me on the afternoon train."

"Sheriff? You can't be here to arrest me dressed like that."

"I'm here to take you dancing."

"Dancing? I haven't gone dancing in years. Dancing."

"I mean dancing at a proper nightclub after a dinner in a nice restaurant in Detroit. And tomorrow afternoon I will take you to the Fisher Theater for a show. We can catch the evening train back and I'll have you home before midnight tomorrow. Say yes, Minnie."

Minnie was overwhelmed. "Sam, I'll need an hour to pull myself together."

"I'll wait."

They boarded the three o'clock train arriving at Detroit's Addison Hotel, where Sam booked them both into a sixth-floor room that made Minnie dizzy when she looked down from the window. They had dinner at the hotel and then went dancing at the Graystone, Detroit's version of Chicago's Aragon Ballroom.

Sam was beaming when Don Redman, the leader of the McKinney Cotton Pickers, came to their table, and introduced himself. He asked Sam about the beautiful lady in his company, and then asked Minnie if she liked jazz. She told him she didn't know.

Sam said, "She may not know much about jazz, but she sure can sing."

During the next set, Redman took out his saxophone, winked at Minnie, and with the band played a rendition of "Ain't Nobody's Business But My Own." The crowd loved it. When the applause subsided, Redman walked down to their table, took Minnie's hand, and led her to the bandstand.

Sam watched Minnie on the raisers. She looked relaxed, he thought, like she must have been back in the salons she had told him about in Poznan.

"What would you like to sing?" Redman asked.

"Do you know 'Amazing Grace?'"

"Of course I do. And, she's a great gal." Redman winked. "Of course the band knows it. You start and we will follow." He nodded to his band.

Minnie turned toward the crowd and singled out Sam smiling up at her from their table. She stood tall with her shoulders back and took a deep breath. Her diaphragm expanded like Frau Dembinski had taught her.

"Amazing grace ..." and Redman came in on his sax. "How sweet the sound." And the clarinet chimed in, playing harmony with Minnie. "That saved a wretch like me." A soulful trombone soared into the mix. The percussionist brushed his drum skin for a soft rhythm and bridge to the next stanza. Minnie responded to the beat, and sang the next line with soul. "I once was lost, but now am found." Sam was suddenly on stage with her, his arm wrapped around her waist. They sang the last line together. "Was blind but now I see."

At the end of the song, Minnie and Sam left the stage. The applause was enthusiastic. Don Redman joined them at their table. "You are a fine singer, Minnie. I can tell you've had training. Sam, you surprised me, too."

"Don and I grew up together," Sam told Minnie. "He has family up north."

They danced until two in the morning, limped back to the Addison, and fell into bed. Sam took off Minnie's shoes and rubbed her feet.

"Ah Sam, that feels so good." Sam made allowances for her breasts not being as perky as perhaps they once were, and she understood what time had done to his body. Their previous sexual experience with their spouses led them both to a new and totally satisfying sexual union.

The next morning, there was a knock on the door. Sam opened it to a breakfast cart being rolled in. The waiter unfolded a white tablecloth, covered the table between their beds, and placed the silver covered dishes on each side. He poured them each a cup of steaming hot coffee and then tastefully backed from the room.

Minnie was awestruck by the Aztec-themed architecture of the Fisher Theater that afternoon. It reminded her of the grand buildings in Poznan. They saw "My American Cousin," a play starring Abby Fisher, a former slave from South Carolina, the same play Abraham Lincoln was watching when he was assassinated.

After the play, they had time to catch dinner before the late train north to Standish. "Didn't we have a great time, Minnie?"

"This was the most fun I've had in a long, long time. Thank you, Sam."

"I'm concerned about your eyes, Minnie. I wish you could have seen the actors more clearly."

Horst.

Chapter Thirty
THE SLIDE

Minnie finally relented and let Edith take her to Detroit for the second cataract surgery. She did it for Sam.

She endured the doctor's cutting and hammering on her eyeball. She allowed orderlies to strap her into bed to hold her body immobile. She waited while they wedged her head between sandbags. After that first day she would have thrown those sandbags at the nurses if her hands had been free. She had never been this nonproductive, this inactive or this bored ... ever.

After eight days the bandages were removed and she was being sprung from her prison. She saw Edith's blue eyes first, and then a bouquet of the most brightly colored flowers God ever produced. She wondered where her thoughtful daughter had found blooms in Michigan in January. As Louie Ireland drove them back to the farm, she saw fence posts and trees and buildings. She saw her hands clearly for the first time in ages. It was a miracle, and she was feeling wonderful until one of the things she saw was a rash that had developed on her leg.

Minnie noticed it first when she returned home and bent down to pet Horst, the tired old dog his master had left under her kitchen table. Wilhelm had been ready to shoot the orphaned animal because it had been Karl's. He refused to mention her brother-in-law by name, refer to his sudden departure from Standish, or comment on the likelihood of his ever returning. Minnie's soft heart intervened and stopped her son, allowing that the dog was harmless without its master, except when he chased her geese.

The rash continued to spread until it covered both her legs. It looked like a swarm of mosquitoes had bitten her, yet the red spots didn't sting or itch. She mentioned it to Edith, who insisted she see a doctor in Bay City.

The doctor examining Minnie did find what looked like a tick bite behind her knee. The rash had spread to her stomach. He gave Edith a look that said this was serious. Minnie had been experiencing symptoms for over three weeks, had lost weight, and had developed a sensitivity to light. The doctor advised Edith to take her mother to a proper hospital for treatment by a specialist.

Wilhelm insisted he be the one to take his mother by train to Detroit. At Harper Hospital her blood was drawn, sent to a lab, and Minnie was given a bed. Later that day the doctor reported to Minnie and Wilhelm that the diagnosis had several names, all of which were serious. He said Boutonneuse Fever is sometimes referred to as Rickettiosis, but the most common name for what your mother has is Rocky Mountain Spotted Fever. "I am sorry to say there is no known cure."

"No cure for a simple rash?" Wilhelm had cured cattle of the bloat, had drained puss from Cobb's infected hoof and applied poultices to draw out the bad blood. Wilhelm could not believe what the doctor was saying.

"Mr. Hartman. This is no simple rash. The rash is a symptom of a deadly disease taking over her body."

"How did I catch it?" Minnie asked. "I have been in Arenac County for the past thirty years. I have not been outside Michigan since 1882. I have never been anywhere near the Rocky Mountains."

"The fever is carried by dog ticks," the doctor said.

"So the ticks jump from the dogs onto humans, bite them and transfer the disease. Do dogs die from Rocky Mountain Spotted Fever?" Wilhelm asked the doctor.

"It's a painful, but sure death for both people and their pets," the doctor said. "Dogs linger longer than humans."

"*Mein Gott im Himmel,*" Minnie whispered.

Wilhelm turned to her and said, "A final gift from Karl Hartman."

Minnie was in the hospital for the next twenty days. Wilhelm sat with her on days when Edith, Molly or One Punch couldn't come. They reminisced about her days in Germany, about her marriage in Louisenfelde. One afternoon when Minnie and Wilhelm were alone, he asked her about when their family lived in Germany.

"Why did Uncle Karl stay in Germany and you and Pa come to Michigan?"

Minnie told Wilhelm the sobering history of her involvement with her husband's brother. "Fate saved me from marrying that man ... fate in the form of a missed train."

"What?"

"I was scheduled to marry Karl Hartman at the station," she told her son for the first time. "He didn't come in on the train. Your father stepped in and saved the day. An hour after we were married, Karl's train came in. Fred was a much better man for me, but I didn't know it at the time I married him."

"Karl Hartman was a scoundrel with bad habits. He didn't deserve you, Ma, and he didn't deserve to live," Wilhelm said.

"Don't you mean he doesn't deserve to live?"

Wilhelm said nothing.

"I was young and naïve when I met Karl Hartman," Minnie told Wilhelm. "Don't be judgmental, Sonny. When you're older you may understand that the chains of habit developed when a person is young are often too weak to be noticed ... especially by a girl with no experience. In later years, those same habits become too strong to break. Wilhelm, the next time you see Karl, would you tell him ..."

"Ma, there won't be a next time."

"What do you mean?"

"While looking for the still which Karl was intending to blackmail us with, he wandered into The Judge's territory."

"Oh no."

"Oh yes. When last I saw him, his body was leaking like a sieve. The ground was as red as my red hunting jacket, and must have attracted the wolves that took care of what The Judge left behind.

Only Minnie's illness prevented her from dancing on the sheets.

"Minnie?" the sheriff said and opened her hospital door.

"Is that you, Sam? Come in here. Have a seat … right here, by me." She patted the bed and held out her hand. "Sorry I can't offer you something to drink. You here to lock me up?" Minnie held both wrists out toward the lawman as she chuckled, then let them drop on her lap. "Sam, I'm feeling so lazy … been doing nothing but laying in this bed all day long. Can't say I deserve it. Haven't done a stitch of work in days."

Sam squeezed her hand. "It's okay to take a little rest, Minnie. You're sick."

"I'm dying, Sam." Minnie took a deep breath. "But, that's not important. What is important is that you are in Detroit. Are you here to arrest those hoodlums flooding the state with illegal liquor, or did you come south to see me?" Minnie's lively chatter melted when she saw tears forming in Sam's eyes. She squeezed his hand. "Sheriff Sam, somehow you always make me feel better."

"I'm going to miss driving out to …"

" … to give me bad news. Sam, you always made the bad news easier."

"Your whiskey helped."

"I sure could use a drink today. I'd like to duck out of here and ..."

" ... go dancing with me?"

"Yes." Minnie giggled.

"Minnie," the sheriff cleared his throat, "some folks stopped by looking for Karl Hartman."

"You won't find Karl. He's gone for good."

"Ted Kitzman said he's having trouble with ..."

" ... The Judge. He always has trouble with Wilhelm's bull. He never complains when his cows freshen each spring. The man wouldn't be happy if you hung him with a new rope."

"Kitzman said he saw the bull jump the fence and go after something or someone running in Wilhelm's field. If a dangerous bull kills a man, the law says the bull must be put down."

"That beast is a valuable breeding bull." Minnie's gaze turned toward the hospital window and the open field beyond. "It was time for that other animal to be judged."

"You're not the first one to tell me that." Sam squeezed her hand. "Shall we say the man left Standish for parts unknown and won't be coming back?"

"You are a good man, Sam ... a good man with an understanding heart."

"Minnie, I'm thinking about retiring, but I don't know what I'd do with my time."

Minnie laughed. "Sam, if you want a lucrative part-time job, stop out and talk to Wilhelm. He might be able to set you up ."

"To be a bootlegger? No Minnie, I'm too old, too tired for that."

"Keep moving, Sam. Don't let any weeds grow up between your toes. Go have some fun. You have paid your dues ... been a good husband, a decent father, but you were not a thorough revenue agent. Why didn't you ever bust up my stills? Couldn't find them, could you?"

Sam crossed his arms over his chest and laughed. "Not one of my officers wanted to stop your operation in Lincoln Township. They all liked working with Constable Ralph and knew he was steering them away from raiding the stills out there in his area. Minnie, you always had a classy operation ... never gave us trouble ... supplied quality liquor at a fair price. Everyone knew where your stills were. They could smell the mash cooking after dark and the smoke settling in the woods from when you put out the fires before sunup. Any of your neighbors could have turned you in, but they didn't because they liked your family and respected you."

"Sam, if I had known I had that much protection, I would have taken up robbing banks."

They both laughed. "Minnie, the doctor said I couldn't stay too long. I want to tell you how much our friendship has meant to me. You are and have always been a fine person ... a real lady. When I first met you, I fell for your good looks. And after I got to know you, my feelings toward you deepened into respect. Goodbye, my friend, my princess." Sam kissed her and left her room, closing the door behind him.

The doctor advised Wilhelm it was time to gather the family to say their goodbyes. One Punch had tears in his eyes when he approached his mother's bed. She told him, "Sonny, I buried some cash in a jar under the water barrel behind the barn. It is your reward for always being such a good son to me."

"But Ma, you've given me too much. You brought me to America. You gave me land I can leave to my sons or my daughters."

"Let's face it, Ralph. I can't use that musty old money where I'm going." She winked at her still-handsome son. "We've been through a lot together, haven't we?" She chuckled. "Thank you for being so loyal. Take care of your children and be good to Barbara."

Then Rosa Fisher came in. She had traveled all the way from New York State. Minnie was so happy to see her that she held out both hands to her ... an enormous effort in her condition. She was tiring. "Rosa, I want you to know your father came looking for you ... your blood father. He wanted to meet you, but disappeared before I could get you together. Honey, I buried a mason jar of cash for you on the north side of the crabapple tree in Wilhelm's orchard. It's not much, but I wanted to leave you something."

Edith pushed Barney's wheelchair inside his mother's hospital room.

"Ma," Barney howled.

"It's all right, Barney. It's my time. I'm ready. I buried some cash for you behind your house in Wells Addition. It's under that old peach tree. That tree needs trimming and some fertilizer. Will you do that for me?"

Barney nodded and Molly walked in next. "Ma, it's me, Molly."

"Molly dear, you came. Is the baby still keeping you up? Did you try alfalfa tea for his colic? Good. He's feeling better then? Good girl. I buried some cash in a mason jar for the children. It's behind your outhouse to the left of the Concord grape vines."

Edith walked over to Minnie's bed and said, "Hi Ma. It's me, Edith."

"Oh Edith, my beautiful daughter. You have a good soul. Promise me you will continue to look after Barney and Amil. Our family must take care of them both for the rest of their lives. After all, they were disabled while working for all of us. I put away a hefty amount of cash for you to use for them. It's in mason jars on a shelf in my pantry between the peach and grape preserves. I know it's silly, but I drew a picture of you on the jars. I called them 'Edith-berry Jam.' Dear girl, I want you to have all my Rosenthal china."

"Amil, come in here," Minnie said. "I can see you out there. Will you promise to take care of Barney for me? Don't let him drink too much. Edith promised to keep an eye on both of you. Don't give her a bad time. I remember your fondness for peaches. Tell Edith there are a dozen jars of peach preserves in my pantry. I want you to have them all. You are a good man."

Fred Jr. entered and sat on the side of his mother's bed. "Ma, it's me."

"Sonny, you are my youngest living child and bear the name of your father. You can follow in his footsteps or you can strive for something better. Don't let the army's refusal of you lower your confidence in what you can do with your life. You and Amil have the farm on Nine Mile Road. He can't work it now that he's in that wheelchair. You must work it or you will lose it. Land is important, Fred. Land is the only thing in this life that is permanent."

"Edith dear, I almost forgot. I want you ... to take my Brazilian Rosewood ... grand piano. Leave it to someone ... in the family who enjoys music."

Wilhelm was the last to say goodbye to his mother. Death rattled her rib cage. Her skin was turning gray. Her breath came in shallow gasps. Minnie's oldest son leaned in so he could hear her final words.

"I want you ... to feed Horst ... a good-sized helping ... of fried eggs and bacon," she whispered. "He liked to steal it ... from my plate ... when I wasn't ... looking." She coughed but caught her breath after a time. "I didn't mind feeding the little thief. Horst has been ... good company for me. And then ..." She paused. Wilhelm thought she had fallen asleep, or worse.

"Yes Ma? Ma?"

"Then I want you ..." she continued, slowing ... "to walk him back ... into the woods. I want you ... to shoot Horst ... burn his body ... and bury his ashes. Do you understand?"

"Yes, Ma. But am I shooting Horst so he doesn't suffer from the disease like you have? Or am I killing him to prevent the spread of this dreadful disease? Or Ma, do you want me to kill the dog because he is a reminder of Karl, because he was once loved by Karl Hartman?" Wilhelm watched his mother's lips curve up at the corners. He listened for her to take another breath and give him an answer, but all was silent. He waited another moment and then brushed her eyelids closed. "*Aufwiedersehen,* Fräu Hartman."

EPILOGUE

Wilhelm stood on the barren soil of his mother's grave holding the hand of his youngest daughter.

"Where should we plant the flowers?" They walked around the family headstone and then stood by the grave marker. "Is this Grandma's stone? Why does it say 'Mother?' Didn't Grandma have a name?"

"What do you remember about your grandmother, Esther?" He dropped her hand and picked up the spade. "Her name was Minnie."

Wilhelm turned the topsoil with a spade. "Rake it flat. We can plant the grass after you plant the flowers." The air was damp with dew and the scent of freshly turned loam. He smiled remembering how his mother loved flowers and would have enjoyed being here with them instead of under the roots. A flock of starlings settled in a tree above them. When the child didn't answer he stopped and asked her if she remembered the day her grandmother was buried.

"Yes, Pa. I remember. It was cold. Everyone was sad. Can I plant the geraniums here?" Esther pointed and looked up at her father. "Do you think grandma is in heaven now, or is she still in the cold ground like my dog?"

"You still miss that dog? You were so little then. I'm surprised you remember." Wilhelm raked out the hardened clots of earth and mounded the soil so the water would drain away.

"I remember everything. My dog was old. He had trouble walking. He couldn't see. Grandma told me he ran out of days to live. Is she buried here because she was old and had trouble walking? Or did she run out of time, too?"

"Esther, what do you remember about your grandmother?"

"Not much. She did need a lot of help. I had to help her plant potatoes and carrots and onions. I helped her make biscuits. I broke the eggs and stirred the batter when she made pancakes. I licked the spoon so she didn't need to wash it. She called me her car-tuffle."

"*Kartoffel,* she called you her potato. That's German."

"Why did she talk German?"

"Because she was born in a country that became Germany. It's far away from here. I was born there too." Wilhelm lifted a bale of straw from the trunk of his Buick and placed it next to the grave. "We traveled across the ocean on a ship."

The starlings stirred on the tree beside the gravesite. Both of them winced when they heard the whoosh and looked up to see the birds take flight. They watched as the flock flowed this way on one collective whim, and darted that way on another. The swarm settled in a tree in the new section of Woodmere Cemetery. There were hundreds of them.

"Grandma taught me how to play her piano, and the words to some of her songs." Esther dropped the geranium in the hole and settled dirt around it with her hands. "There." She stood up. "What's next?" Wilhelm handed her the burlap bag and showed her how to sow grass seed. "I helped grandma feed her chickens. And I gathered eggs from under her hens. Pa, when I helped Grandma plant her garden, we put straw over the seeds so the birds wouldn't eat them."

"Your grandmother taught me that too. Let's spread this straw nice and thick." Wilhelm cut the binder twine on the bale with his jack knife.

When the loud flapping of the starlings became a whisper Esther said, "Pa, I'm hungry."

"Me too. Let's go home. You set the table while I feed the animals."

Esther took her father's hand. As the two walked toward the Buick, she said, "Pa, will you tell me what it was like for you and grandma on that ship? Did the ship have a name?"

"Werra. They called it the Werra."

"Did you see whales? Was the captain a girl or a boy? What did you eat? Why did you leave? Where were the ..."

"Get in the car first and I'll answer all your questions." He glanced back at Minnie's stone and thought, there is no love that is as pure, unconditional and strong as a mother's love, or as helpful to a father as a grandmother's love. Ma, thank you for loving us.

Wilhelm F Hartman's naturalization papers. The document lists wife Mary (age 35) and children Lawrence (Curly, 7), Hedwig (Hattie, 6), Leonard (Len, 2), and Selma (Sally, 1) living at Standish #2. The Hartman family was awarded citizenship on June 18, 1919.

Wilhelm F. Hartman, oldest son of Frederick and Wilhelmina (Minnie) Hartman, next to his field companion, Cobb.

HARTMAN FAMILY TREE

Martin Bublitz 1783-1838
M Anna Dorthea Freitag 1793-1867

|

Johann Hartman
M Christine Zerben (Zelda)

Jacob Bublitz B.1818
M Christine Luedtke

|

|

Frederick Hartman   M 1871   **Wilhelmine (Minnie) Bublitz**
1844 Prussia-1900 USA   1855-Poland-1931 USA

1. Wilhelm Frederick Hartman
1874 Poland-1957 Standish, MI

M2 Mary Schwab (Schmidt) 1883-1929 ——— **M1 Louis Schmidt** 1881-1932
(Mary Schwab's first marriage)

    1. Lawrence (Curly) Hartman 1912-2002
    M Elizabeth Krueger 1921-1995

    2. Hedwig (Hattie) Hartman Haas 1913- 2006
    M Charles Haas 1901-1986

    3. Leonard (Len) J. Hartman 1916-2001
    M Arlene F Nigl 1919-2012

    4. Selma (Sally) Hartman Rigg 1918-1999
    M Freeman Rigg 1914-1982

    5. Gilbert Frederick Hartman 1920-1924

    6. William (Bill) Andres Hartman 1921-2014
    M Donna Eileen Worden 1924-2014

        1. Michael Allan Hartman 1943
        M Donna Jean Lutat 1942-2006

            1. Jennifer Hartman Hauschild 1965
            (Graphic Designer: Minnie's Potatoes)
            M David Hauschild 1960

            2. Janet Hartman Schmautz
            M Kurt Schmautz

        2. Laurice R Hartman LaZebnik 1944
        (Author: Minnie's Potatoes)
        M Robert LaZebnik

    7. Esther L. Hartman Shannon 1924-2013
    M Patrick Dennis Shannon 1924-1998

    1. Lorina W. Schmidt 1905-1905

    2. Linda Schmidt 1906-1978
    M1 John Berglund 1915-1964.
    M2 Chester McDonald 1909-1980

    3. Rudolph G. Schmidt 1907-1988
    M Alma Caroline Haas 1908-1982

    4. Rich Schmidt 1908-1973
    M Esther Reinhardt 1912